THE SMOKY HILL STRIKES

It was apparently raining yet to the west, because he could hear a low rushing murmur in that direction. Funny, though, no thunder and lightning. Now the sound was growing louder. Something was wrong. He took the blanket down from over his head to see and hear better, and peered into the darkness upstream. He had nearly figured it out when there came a flash of lightning from the receding storm, a sort of last hurrah. For the space of a heartbeat or two, the entire area was dimly lit by the flicker of the lightning. It was all of two steam-engines before the answering crash of thunder boomed, but Gabriel wasn't counting. He'd had only a glimpse of the rushing wall of water cascading down the stream bed, bursting over the banks to fill the waterway to the hills on both sides, and rushing down to camp.

"Get up!" he yelled at the top of his lungs. "Flood!"

≈ RIVERS WEST: BOOK 2 ≈

The
Smoky Hill

Don Coldsmith

BANTAM BOOKS
NEW YORK · TORONTO · LONDON · SYDNEY · AUCKLAND

To my wife, Edna, who always understands, and
without whom none of it could have happened
at all.

THE SMOKY HILL
A Bantam Book / June 1989

DOMAIN and the portrayal of a boxed "d" are trademarks of
Bantam Books, a division of Bantam Doubleday Dell Publishing
Group, Inc.

ISBN 0-553-28012-0

Published simultaneously in the United States and Canada

Bantam Books are published by Bantam Books, a division of Bantam Doubleday
Dell Publishing Group, Inc. Its trademark, consisting of the words "Bantam Books"
and the portrayal of a rooster, is Registered in U.S. Patent and Trademark Office and
in other countries. Marca Registrada. Bantam Books, 666 Fifth Avenue, New York,
New York 10103.

PRINTED IN THE UNITED STATES OF AMERICA

RAD   10 9 8 7 6 5 4 3

≈ INTRODUCTION ≈

At the time of the Westward Expansion, it was found that three rivers crossed the Kansas–Nebraska Territory, flowing from west to east. The rivers run roughly parallel, and each played an important part in the expansion movement, as each provided a landmark for a westward trail.

The southernmost of these rivers is the Arkansas, arising at the eastern slopes of the Rockies and traversing some six hundred miles of what are now Colorado, Kansas, and Oklahoma. The Kansas portion was the basis for an ancient Indian trail that became an international trade route, the Santa Fe Trail.

The northern river, the Platte, crosses the flat lands of Nebraska, just north of the Kansas border. Its trail to the West became the Oregon Trail, the major immigrant trail to the coastal states.

Between these two rivers lies a third. Not as long as the others, or as large, this river, too, flows west to east across the present state of Kansas. For its last hundred miles, it is the Kansas, or Kaw River, until it empties into the Missouri. *All three* of the westward trails enter the Great Plains at or near this point.

For most of its length, however, this third river is called the Smoky Hill, joining with the Republican near Fort Riley to become the Kansas River. The trail that followed this stream was the Smoky Hill Trail, the route to Denver and the gold fields in the gold rush of 1859. Because of the greed and avarice, violence, bloodshed, and the dangers of nature's extremes, it became known also as the Trail of Death.

With the exception of the actual historical figures who appear in this narrative, all characters are purely fictional. The Booth family is a composite, participating in events similar to historical events that actually happened. These fictional characters are intended to depict the spirit of those who opened the valley of the Smoky Hill to settlement. This is their story.

U.S. Interstate 70 now follows the Smoky Hill for much of its length. The climate was, and is, harsh and demanding. To those who do not understand and are unable to yield to its cruel demands, the region is overwhelming, uninhabitable. They feel the kinship of those who perished on the Trail of Death. But for those who love and understand the country, it is richly rewarding.

It is not the spirit of the region that makes it the Trail of Death or the promise of the future. It is the response of the people who encounter it.

≈ PART I ≈

Gabe squatted on his heels and perused the heavy structure that stood in the flat beside the river. Massive in design, it reminded him of a picture he had seen once. It had been a picture in a book, a drawing of a castle. In front of the castle had been ladies with funny-looking dunce caps on their heads, and some knights on horses carrying long lances. He wasn't sure what it was all about, and why the women had to wear dunce caps. Or, for that matter, why the horses all seemed to be work horses. As far as he could remember, there hadn't been a good saddle horse in the bunch.

But what had really intrigued him as a boy was the castle. There was a moat and a drawbridge, and turrets and towers, and a walkway around the top of the wall. There were men standing on the walkway, holding weapons. He had thought a lot about that picture since. With a setup like that, and enough supplies and water, a few stout men could hold off an army.

Now he had to admit, Bent's Fort wasn't exactly a castle, but it looked like one. The yellow adobe of the walls, several feet thick at the ground, rose impressively to the towers and the catwalk around the top. Part of the wall, not protected by the catwalk, had been planted with cactus along its top. They were in bloom now, reds and pinks and bright yellow. *Real pretty*, Gabe thought, *but a good idea, too. Anybody trying to go over the wall would find it tough going.*

His eyes drifted to the main gate. That would have been
the drawbridge of his castle. The gate at Bent's was built of
thick planks of wood, reinforced with iron fittings. It could
be burned, he supposed, if it came to it. But it would be
tough—tough on the one who had to light the fire, because
the gate was directly under the catwalk. Men above could
shoot down on any attackers.

One thing intrigued him, the massive beam that supported the arch over the gate. It was a single tree trunk,
one of the huge cottonwoods that grew up and down the
Arkansas. It must be ten, twelve paces long, and nearly as
thick as the height of a man. The log was embedded in the
yellow adobe and plastered snugly at each supporting end.
He wondered how they'd gotten it up there. It would have
taken a lot of mules or oxen just to drag it from the river, let
alone hoist it into place. Probably ropes and pulleys, he
figured, after the walls were at the top of the door opening.

Well, no matter. He knocked the dottle from his pipe and
reached to refill it. Damn, no tobacco! He'd forgotten. It
was so pleasant to sit or lie around in the summer sun, it
made a man forget such things as buying more tobacco.
There had been a time when he'd doubted if he'd ever be
warm again, when they were starving out last winter in the
Sierras' snows. He didn't hold it against Captain Fremont.
None of the men did. They'd had to eat some things that
would gag a maggot, and it had been a close call, but they'd
come through. The men would follow the captain through
hell if he said so. Especially if he could get Kit Carson to
guide them again, like before. Kit and Tom Fitzpatrick and
Joe Walker had brought them out.

He stood and stretched and sauntered down toward the
post to get his tobacco. The sun was warm on the back of his
buckskin shirt. But what a day! The sky was clear and blue,
and the south breeze fresh and clean. This was a proper way
to live.

He wondered sometimes if his brother James, back in
Illinois, ever thought about it. His brother was a little

older, a lot more set in his ways. James had a wife and three, no, four youngsters. Scratched dirt for a living and seemed to like it. That was all right, Gabe figured, for them that couldn't help it, but it wasn't for him. He had to see what was over the next hill. Maybe that's what had attracted him to John Fremont. The captain had the same sort of a gift.

He looked across the flat toward the Arkansas. There in front of the Bent brothers' trading post, called Bent's Fort almost since it was started, was a flat area maybe half a mile in diameter. It was circled by an oxbow of the river, and the level ground and lush grass made it a favorite camping ground for those who came to trade, both red and white. There were at least 150 lodges, Gabe guessed, in the near meadow and scattered along the stream. He could identify an encampment of Cheyennes, and some lodges that might be Comanche beyond. A group of Kiowa lodges were separated from the Cheyennes by a small band of Arapahoes, whose red-dyed tassels on their smoke-poles plainly spoke their identity.

Two days, it would be July 4th, Gabe recalled. Independence Day, 1844. There were enough Americans here, they'd likely have a celebration, he figured, with speeches and all. More important, a shooting match, and then everybody'd get a little drunk and disorderly and see if they could find a woman. Some of the girls looked pretty good, after a winter in the mountains, and some of Fremont's party had already paired off. Gabe had his eye on a lanky Cheyenne who had smiled at him yesterday.

He didn't see her. He walked on down to the gate and into the adobe-walled courtyard, where there was a little more hustle and bustle than in the Indian camp. He circled past a half-unloaded wagon, around the frame of the big hide-press, and started toward the store.

"Booth!" someone called.

Gabe turned, identified the speaker, Captain John Fremont.

"Yes, sir?"

He altered his course to move over toward where Fremont stood in a doorway.

"Gabe," the captain began, "are you busy?"

"No, sir. Just goin' to the store."

"Go ahead, Gabe. But then, start to pass the word. Meeting tonight in front of my tent, at dark."

"All right, Captain. Are we movin' out?"

Fremont smiled. "Not yet. We'll stay for Independence Day. Just spread the word."

"Yes, sir."

The breeze across the high prairie was growing a little chill as darkness fell and the party assembled. Gabe sauntered in and squatted next to Shaughnessy. He looked around the loose circle at the men he'd spent nearly a year with. All were burned brown by the sun and wind, except for a couple. Dodson, of course, wasn't going to change color, much. A good man, though, for a nigger. Gabe wondered some why Jake Dodson had wanted to come. He wasn't hired on in St. Louis, like most of the men. He'd come all the way from Washington to follow the captain. Some kind of a dream in that woolly head.

Preuss was another that the sun wasn't going to change much. His blond German skin never did anything but burn redder. There was a man really hard to figure out. He was the captain's mapmaker, always busy scribbling notes when he wasn't taking compass readings or studying plant specimens. He always seemed uncomfortably out of place, with his thick spectacles and clothes that would look more at home in town. Besides his scribbling at his job, Karl Preuss was always working on a continued letter or diary for his wife—that was written in German. At least, that's what Zindle said. Gabe wouldn't know. He couldn't read English *or* German.

The joke among the men was that Preuss wrote his private journal in German so Fremont wouldn't know how it maligned him. It was no secret that the German often disagreed with the captain's decisions. He said so, to Fremont's face. Even stranger, maybe, was that the captain tolerated it. In turn, there was none in the party more loyal than Preuss.

The German had few friends among the men, with his gloomy attitude and strange ways. Probably the only one close enough to call friend was young Raffie Proue, squatted there beside him. Preuss had never quite forgiven any of the others for killing his mule back in the Sierras. Well, Gabe could understand that. He'd have been put out, himself, if they'd wanted to eat his old Rabbit. But Rabbit hadn't been as fat as the German's mule.

And Karl's reaction to the time Godey killed the little dog that had followed them, up in the Klamath country. That had turned into a sort of donnybrook. Godey had the captain's permission, it turned out. He'd fixed the dog Indian-style, singeing off the hair over the fire and then scrubbing it with snow. Looked like they'd need the meat, but some of the others turned up with a load of mule meat about the time Godey was cutting up the dog. Preuss had hardly spoken to him since.

Gabe looked on around the circle. Not as many as they'd started with. They'd only lost one man, it was true. Even that wasn't in the really tough times in the mountains. It had been in a highly improbable ambush in Ute country on the way back. And not even by Utes, but by Diggers.

A couple of the men had left the expedition, with permission, at Captain Sutter's place, Sacramento. They'd wanted to stay there and settle, and Sutter was encouraging that, seemed like. For that matter, Captain Fremont was, too. Then poor Badeau had accidentally shot himself crossing the Sevier.

The scouts sat a little aside, as if they were a bit different. Part of the reason the party had survived the mountains, Gabe knew, was that they had the best scouts in the country. Kit Carson, quiet and shy, short and not very impressive. Not in looks, anyhow. He and Fremont seemed exact opposites; yet they were close friends, from the time of the expedition in '42. Carson had come up from Taos to join them last summer after they got to Colorado and had brought Godey with him.

Tom Fitzpatrick, next to Kit, there, had been with them since St. Louis. One of the old fur trappers, Fitz was said to know the West like the palm of his hand. That was an unusual hand to know, too—crippled from an accident with a rifle. Gabe had never heard the details, but old Fitz had taken a rifle ball through the wrist part. As a result, he was known to the Indians as Broken Hand. While they were at Sutter's, one of the settlers had asked Fitz about the hand. The old mountain man had stopped the stupid questioner cold with two terse words: "Got keerless."

Fitz also had the distinction of having guided the first wagon train to travel clear across the continent to Oregon, two years before.

Next to him sat Joe Walker. What Fitz was to the northern route, Joe was to the southern trail. He'd laid out, a couple of years ago, what folks were already calling the California Trail. Walker wasn't properly a part of the expedition. He'd just joined them in California, out of interest in the mapping job, and traveled back to Bent's with them. Gabe had been fascinated to watch the three of them—Fitz, Walker, and Carson—as they traveled the way back. *A man could learn a right smart*, Gabe figured, *just followin' those three*.

Fremont was counting now, half to himself. ". . . Twenty-four, twenty-five, twenty-six. Yes, all here."

He paused and cleared his throat, and the murmur of conversation withered and died.

"Well, men, are you getting rested up?"

There were nods and muttering of assent.

"Very good. Now, I want to tell you about the rest of the trip."

There were a few intense but very brief murmurs.

"We'll stay here a couple more days, through Independence Day."

A brief cheer quieted as Fremont held up his hand.

"But the next morning at dawn, we move out. Carson and Walker will remain here at Bent's. Fitz goes with us. There will be twenty-six of us, and we'll map one of the rivers of Kansas Territory on the way home."

"This one? The Arkansas?"

"No, it's been mapped, mostly. The Santa Fe Trail follows it."

There were nods, but expectant silence reigned.

"Same with the Platte and the trail to Oregon. I'm talking about the Kansas River."

There was a puzzled mutter.

"But that's where we started, at the mouth of the Kansas."

"True. But that was the *other* end. I want to find the headwaters and follow it east to the Missouri at Westport, where we started."

"How will we know we've got the right stream, Cap'n?"

There was a chuckle around the circle for a moment, but it quickly quieted.

"Mr. Bent tells me it's almost due north of here. We'll start northeast when we leave the Arkansas and strike the Kansas in a few days. It's the only stream of any size. Oh, yes, it's not called the Kansas until farther east. Out here it's the Smoky Hill."

≈ 2 ≈

*On the 5th day of July we resumed our journey
down the Arkansas, and encamped about twenty
miles below the fort.*

Fremont's report, 1844

Gabriel had a vicious hangover. Several of the others
suffered, too, from self-inflicted headaches and rotten
stomachs. Gabe could not have vouched for them; but for
himself, he thought he had never been so sick. His stomach
churned with the swaying motion of the mule, and with
each wave of churning, he vowed never again to touch
whiskey. It was a false vow and he knew it, but it seemed
like a good idea at the time.

Once he stopped and vomited beside the trail, vomited
on an empty stomach, nothing but mucus and green bile.
He had vomited all else long ago. Why in God's name, he
wondered, would a man do something like this to himself?
He had wondered that before, as he had tried to shake off
the ravages of a night's revelry.

This, of course, had been a day *and* a night, in celebration of Independence Day. There had been a ceremony and
speeches, of which Captain Fremont's had been the best.
Lord, how that man could get folks excited with his dream
of the United States stretching across the mountains to the
western sea.

"He shore talks good," Shaughnessy muttered in Gabe's
ear as they applauded and whooped and hollered when the
captain sat down.

10

"Yep. He means to do it, too," Gabriel said.

"Do what?"

"Hell, you know, Ike. Map the damn thing so settlers kin come. What'd you think we're doin'?"

They slapped each other's backs and laughed uproariously. Everything was beginning to be funny as the fiery trade whiskey started to make itself felt. Gabe almost forgot the vague feeling he'd had a time or two that maybe he didn't *want* settlers runnin' all over the damn country and spoilin' it.

There were games and races and shooting contests and more shooting, just in the air, to celebrate the patriotism of the day. Gabriel won a tomahawk throw and collected a little tobacco and a knife from his bets. Then he promptly lost it all in bets on a shooting match. The whiskey was by this time making the target unsteady.

He was urged to bet again but had nothing left except his rifle. Even in his fuzzy-thinking condition, he could remember some things: survival depended on his rifle, his knife, and his mule. His tomahawk might be handy, too. Very versatile. But he *could* do without it. The other items were necessities. He could wager his clothes before his rifle. Actually, the rifle and mule were part of the agreement when he signed on with Fremont. Each man was to furnish his weapon and his transportation.

The gun was a big-bore .58 caliber made by the Hawken brothers in St. Louis. The ball, as big as his thumb, dwarfed the .30 caliber projectiles of the long-barreled rifles made for the Kentucky frontier. Some of the men in Fremont's party favored the longer barrel as more accurate and compromised on a .40 caliber size. There were many arguments around the campfires. For Gabriel Booth, however, the answer was plain. No matter how accurate, a smaller bullet was simply unsafe in the face of a charging grizzly. The "real-bear," as the Indians said, the bear with the white-tipped fur, the bear-that-walks-like-a-man. This creature, "Old Ephraim," the mountain men sometimes

called it, was one to be reckoned with. It was a far cry from
the black bear of the eastern woodlands. Yes, when the
real-bear was around, Gabe wanted a big enough chunk of
lead to stop it in its tracks.

It was handy for buffalo, too. He'd seen a bull with a lung
shot that should have killed it stand around awhile before it
even lay down, when hit by Shaughnessy's .41. Nope, he
wanted a load that would tumble a running buffalo when
the ball slammed into meat and bone. He liked the balance
of the gun, the way it lay across his thighs on the fork of the
mule's saddle. The short country cousin of the fine
Pennsylvania-made small-bore guns was especially for
western use, for the saddle, for the larger game of the West.

Yes, Gabriel was proud of his Hawken, the costliest
single item he had ever bought in his life. It was a part of
him now, along with the bullet mold that turned out the big
shiny marbles the gun hurled. Gabe was pleased with the
accuracy, too. He had a hunch that on open prairie the
heavy bullet would be less affected by the wind than a
lighter ball, hence more accurate, even with the short
barrel. Usually he shot well enough at least to support his
argument. That had made the loss of the contest at Bent's
even more disheartening.

To make matters even worse, he had consumed enough
whiskey that he fell asleep and missed part of the revelry.
When he did waken, shadows were growing long. He ate
some crisp-broiled hump ribs, which did not set too well on
his stomach, and went to look for the leggy Cheyenne. He
knew where her lodge was located; but instead of the girl,
he encountered her irate father, who threatened him with
a heavy stone war ax and, in sign-talk, told him to be gone.

Ah, well, Cheyennes were funny about their women,
Gabe told himself as he wandered off into the twilight. Not
like some tribes. Mandans, for instance. They'd let you
have a go at a wife or daughter and think nothing of it. Or
that Pawnee he'd had for a little while, in '42. There was a

proper woman. He recalled her warm, yielding softness in the sleeping-robes and thought again of the long-legged Cheyenne.

Maybe he'd better have another drink to settle his stomach. He found his way back to Fremont's camp, where Shaughnessy, Martindale, and a couple of the others sat around the fire. They had a little wooden bucket of trade whiskey, which made clockwise rounds with regularity. Gabe took his place, and a long drag when the pail came past. Somehow, it didn't taste as good as it had earlier; so after a round or two, he got up to go look for a woman again. The conversation wasn't making much sense, anyway.

Eventually, he did find a woman who was willing. He never was sure what her tribe was, but she used sign-talk well, and it didn't matter. It didn't even matter that she was fat and a little ugly. What did matter was that when they wandered off into the dark a little way and she spread her blanket, Gabe was unable to perform. Too much whiskey, he figured. The woman was a little peeved at first, and then decided it was funny. She laughed at him and called him, in sign-talk, "horse-without-stones."

She jumped up, swept the blanket around her shoulders, and strode back toward a group of lodges, loudly talking in her own tongue. Gabe buttoned his pants and followed her, weaving a little as he walked. As he came among the lodges, children began to point and giggle, and adults to chuckle at him. *Damn!* Did the woman have to tell everything she knew? He wheeled and staggered out into the dark a little way to puke, then managed to collapse, not quite in the vomitus, and fell into a drunken slumber.

He was wakened by somebody falling over him in the dark. He rolled over and cursed the intruder, who beat a hasty retreat. Finally, Gabe gathered enough strength to get to his feet and lurch unsteadily back to his blankets, where he collapsed in a stupor that would pass for sleep. He had hardly closed his eyes, it seemed, when Shaughnessy shook him awake.

"Come on, Gabe! It'll be daylight afore long. You know the Captain likes to make twenty mile a day!"

So now, here he was, swaying along on the back of Rabbit, trying to recover his balance and wishing his stomach would settle down. One thing, Rabbit was a dependable mule—a claybank dun color, of unknown parentage. Some of the men laughed at him for his choice of mounts, but he didn't care much. He knew what was needed, and he favored a mule for the job. Let the others spend all they wanted for their hot-blood Arabians and Thoroughbreds. Their horses were pretty, sure. But, compared to a mule, they were stupid, Gabe figured. Give 'em half a chance, the damn things would founder.

And they weren't hardy, like a mule. Take last winter, when they were weathered in and freezing in the mountains. Several horses couldn't take it and died from the exposure. Not one of the mules, though. Tough. Smart. Like a man had to be to survive in the mountains and plains.

Gabe wasn't thinking about all this today, though. He was trying to forget the criticism that some of the horse men always threw at the three or four mule riders: uncomfortable gaits. Hell, what did they know? That depended on what kind of a mother the mule had. The daddy always had to be a jackass, of course. But a mule out of a good, well-gaited mare would have the same kind of comfort to ride. Out of a heavy work mare, of course, it would be a work mule, uncomfortable to ride with a saddle.

Rabbit, whose mother was unknown, had nice gaits. A quick, flowing walk; a smooth trot; and a long stride at a canter that ate up distance. His name came from that first jump when Gabe kicked him into a lope. That little head start had let him win a few races, and a few bets from men who didn't know Rabbit.

This morning, Gabe didn't care. Rabbit's usually smooth running walk seemed to hammer his spine into the base of his skull, and when the captain moved out in a trot for a little while sometimes, it became sheer torture. He went so far as to wonder if he should try to trade for a day and maybe ride Ike Shaughnessy's half-Thoroughbred chub. No, he couldn't do that, he decided. That would settle the mule-horse argument for all time, and the others would never let him forget it.

So, he suffered. Gradually, he began to feel a little better; and after the noon halt, he was able to raise his head and look around a little. Maybe, even, he was going to make it.

They were following a sort of trail, he noticed, that paralleled the Arkansas. Their general direction was east, with the river on their right, its winding course marked by the thin strip of timber along its banks. To their left was open prairie, the bright green of the gently rolling country unbroken by any vegetation except the grass. Both in that direction and to the south, beyond the river, the grass stretched away to the horizons. Ahead, as far as they could see, and behind, too, Gabe knew that the grass reached to the foothills of the mountains. He had never seen the ocean, but he had an idea that it would look like this. Gentle swells, and the ripple of the grasses in the south breeze, looking at a distance a lot like water. He rather liked the feel of the wide sky and far horizons. Out here, a man could lean back in the saddle and really stretch his eyes. He was feeling better.

The trail moved away from the river for a mile or so. Or rather, the river left the trail. There was a long bend or oxbow that would have been a long way around, so the trail just cut across. *This must be an old, old trail*, he figured, *used by the Indians for generations. What was it, one of the traders at Bent's had called it? The Southwest Trail? Go south and west out of Bent's, it was said, you could follow it through the mountains to the Mexican settlements beyond. The Santa Fe Trail. It would be interesting to know what was there. Maybe Fremont would try something like that trip next time. There was a lot of trade.*

These wandering thoughts were interrupted as Captain

Fremont rode up alongside him for a moment. Gabe nodded a greeting and noted a twinkle in the captain's eye.

"Well," Fremont said cheerfully, "feeling better, Horse-Without-Balls?"

Jesus, Gabriel thought, *does* everybody *know?*

≈ 3 ≈

Agreeable to your instructions which required me to complete as far as practicable our examination of the Kansas River, I left at this encampment the Arkansas River, taking a northeasterly direction across the elevated dividing grounds which separate that river from the waters of the Platte.
Fremont's report, 1844

It had been a fairly easy day's travel that first day down the Arkansas. At least, it would have been, if it had not been for recent overindulgence. Still, Gabriel Booth felt progressively better as the afternoon passed. By the time the captain ordered camp, Gabe was enjoying the easy travel, the cooling south breeze of the high prairie, and the distant vistas of waving grass.

True, he had taken a lot of ribald remarks about his manhood, but there were others who had drunk to excess and had made fools of themselves, too. Since these were among the individuals who would have been Gabe's chief tormentors, they were, for the most part, rather quiet. He recalled something about those who lived in glass houses. He'd never seen a glass house, even in St. Louis. Probably there wasn't any such thing, but it was an interesting idea. *How in the hell*, he wondered, *would the womenfolk undress?* He assumed that if anyone had a glass house, it would be white folks. Indian lodges never had any glass windows, no glass at all.

Odd, Indians didn't have all the seriousness about being modest, either, like white women. Most Indian women wouldn't mind a glass house, but white ones would. It was the whites, however, who'd have the glass house—if, of course, there was such a thing. Gabe rather doubted it. Not in this country, for sure. He'd seen a hailstorm or two on previous trips that would have sure leveled a glass house in a hurry. Chunks of ice as big as eggs—that would have made short work of anything glass. One of those could kill a man easy.

Now how in the hell did I get to thinkin' about that? he asked himself. Funny how a mind wanders. Especially on the prairie. A man can see so far and look at the country and think at the same time. *Maybe,* he thought, *maybe there are two parts to a brain, and you think with one part, while you look and smell and hear with the other. Like now.* He'd seen that there was a scattered herd of buffalo, off to the north, grazing along a low ridge, even while he was thinking about the damn glass houses. And he'd watched the band of antelope spook up out of the gully ahead, flashing their white rump patches as they skimmed along over the grass. That had been while he thought about the hailstorm. He wondered if maybe the right half of the brain could think about one thing while the left half . . . Ah, well, he'd never know, he guessed.

Rabbit was moving well, and he was beginning to appreciate the mule's comfortable walk again. He hadn't felt like vomiting since right after the noon halt. Yes, it looked now like he might make it and live to see another day. Damn, he'd be more careful next time.

Still, he was glad when Captain Fremont called the halt to make camp. It was a good campsite, a grassy meadow to furnish graze for the animals, and the quiet murmur of the Arkansas just to the south. There were trees along the river, mostly big cottonwoods and scraggly willows.

Seemed like it should be no trouble to find wood for
campfires, but it proved to be in short supply. One after the
other, wood gatherers came back from the river's timber
strip emptyhanded or with only a handful of small twigs.

Well, they'd encountered the same thing on the Platte,
Gabe recalled. There were campsites along the river trails
in the prairie that had been camping places for generations.
They were favorable because of grass and water and
location. Every party of travelers had to have a campfire,
either to cook on or just for warmth. As fast as the thin strip
of timber grew and limbs died and became useful for fuel,
they were utilized.

It was no problem. Without even commenting, the men
turned from the river and began to forage across the
meadow and up the slope, picking up dried buffalo dung.
Gabriel soon had an armful. Buffalo chips stacked well.
Many were nearly a foot across, an inch thick, and could be
stacked in the crook of an arm like a huge stack of pancakes.
In a short while, fires were going and the place looked like
a regular camp.

There was no cooking to be done, since they carried no
fresh meat. The company sat around chewing strips of
jerky, or some of the pemmican they had acquired at
Bent's. William Bent, whose Cheyenne wife gave him a
good rapport with the Indians, was noted for the quality of
the supplies he traded. Pemmican bought at Bent's would
be of good quality, they had been told, and found it true.

Gabe and Ike Shaughnessy sat with several others around
the smoldering fire of chips. In actuality, the fire would not
have been necessary. The night was warm, and the mos-
quitos not really bad—not numerous enough to warrant a
smoke-fire to repel them, at any rate. No, the campfire was
a ritual. There was something about a fire that was a
declaration to whatever spirits might inhabit the vast
wildness of the prairie. A statement in an attempt, perhaps,
to communicate with those spirits. "Here, we intend to
camp," it was saying, as if asking permission to do so. Of

course, Gabriel Booth and the others did not think these thoughts. It was unnecessary. The ritual, through the centuries, had become so ingrained in the human race that the first thought in establishing any camp was where the lighting of the fire would take place. It was as natural as the dedication of the Indians' first buffalo kill each season.

"We are sorry to kill you, my brother," the medicine man would solemnly intone, "but our life depends on you and your kind."

And life would go on without pause. So it was around the fires in the gathering twilight. Gabriel reached to toss another chip from the pile and encountered one a little fresher than the rest.

"Jesus!" he complained. "Somebody picked one too green!"

Everybody in the little circle chuckled at his complaint.

"Reckon thet's mine, Gabe," Ike Shaughnessy drawled. "I had to foller thet bull nearly three mile afore he dropped it. I caught it just 'fore it hit the ground."

The others laughed.

Gabe hefted the big disk, slightly damp on the under-side, and eyed Shaughnessy speculatively. Ike prepared to defend himself as Gabe rose to his feet.

"Aw, come on, Gabe," he pleaded. "Ain't no harm done. Thet ain't really mine, anyhow. I was jest funnin'!"

Gabriel rose with dignity and took a stance like a discus thrower. "Well, we can't have one this fresh in camp," he said seriously. "I'll put it back to ripen some."

With a mighty heave, he sent the chip spinning across the meadow. The evening breeze caught the leading edge of the spinning chip and lifted it, to soar majestically, on and on. Finally it began to wobble, lose momentum, and slice to the right to tumble to the ground, where it disintegrated. The men around the fire howled with delight.

"Hooray!" Ike Shaughnessy yelled.

"Let's see you beat that throw!" Gabe challenged.

"Lemme see a chip."

Ike snatched up a buffalo chip and gave it a toss. I
wobbled, broke in two, and fell, a very poor showing.

"Ike, you just don't get the hang of it," Gabe sai
seriously. "Here, I'll show you."

He selected another chip, balanced it carefully, and le
fly in the same southerly direction as the first. This time
the drier, and hence lighter, projectile caught the breez
and fluttered a moment, then leveled out in flight, hover
ing, hanging, soaring on toward the river. The group by th
fire cheered it onward.

"Come on, come on!"

"'At's it! A little more!"

"Hooray!"

Ike, a little miffed, watched until the chip crashed t
earth. "Okay!" he conceded. "For distance, anyhow. Bu
what about aim? Kin you hit anything? Gimme a good
balanced chip here."

He dropped to his knees to sort through the pile of dung
pawing the poorer specimens aside, choosing one or tw
uniform chips to lay tentatively in front of him.

The others were laughing, yelling, and cheering Shaugh
nessy on. He finally rose, examining an especially fin
specimen.

"Yep, this'll do. Now, you see thet willow bush ove
there?"

He swung an arm to begin his throw and, as he turned
saw a tall slender figure standing near.

"What the hell is going on?" Captain Fremont asked i
wonderment.

His stern visage indicated that he had been watching and
understood quite well. Ike Shaughnessy straightened and
stood awkwardly, glancing from the captain to the chip i
his hand.

"We was havin' a match, Cap'n, sailin' turds. Want t
try?" He extended the buffalo chip generously.

"No, thank you, Shaughnessy," Fremont answered

tight-lipped. "Another time, maybe. Right now I want to see you and Booth. Follow me."

Without waiting, the captain turned on his heel and strode off into the twilight. Shaughnessy stood staring at the buffalo chip for a moment as if wondering how it had got into his hand. Then he dropped it on the pile, and the two men followed the retreating form.

Gabriel was puzzled. Why would the captain care about a little fun? Sometimes he even joined in. Why would he want to make a big fuss over a harmless little fun? Sometimes the captain was a hard man to understand. His head was likely always busy, with all his highfalutin ideas about opening the West.

Fremont stopped and turned on his heel, to stand waiting as the two approached.

"Well," he began, "now that you've recovered from Independence Day, I wanted to ask you two: Do either of you know the country to the north of here?"

The two looked at each other and back to Fremont.

"No, sir," Gabe began, "not till you get to the Platte."

"Shaughnessy?"

"Nope. I been down the Santa Fee Trail, but just as far as Bent's."

"I see. Apparently, we have only Mr. Bent's general directions, then."

"Cap'n," Shaughnessy inquired, puzzled, "this ain't about buffalo turds?"

"*What?* Of course not!" Fremont said, chuckling.

The others relaxed a little.

"Look, I want one of you to ride point in the morning, a mile or so out, with Mr. Fitzpatrick. We don't know what's out there, exactly. Shouldn't be any trouble, but he'll pick a good way to go, in case there's any rough country."

"What direction, Captain?" Gabe asked. "North?"

"No, about northeast, according to Bent."

"Are there s'posed to be any Indians in the area?"

"Probably not. Pawnees, maybe, but they'd be farther

east, I think. They're on government rations, though. Still
if you see any Indians, you'll come right back to the main
party. So, who wants to go?"

"I will, Captain," Gabe said quickly, before Shaughnessy
could answer.

There was still just enough kid in him to relish the idea
of crossing unexplored country with the great mountain
man Broken Hand Fitzpatrick.

$$\approx \quad 4 \quad \approx$$

Old Fitzpatrick wasn't old, actually. Somehow it just
seemed that way. Part of it was his dignified manner and his
talk. Fitz, it was said, had had a considerable amount of
book learning before he took to the mountains in the fur
trade. Smart, too. He'd come up fast and had been one of
the partners in the Rocky Mountain Fur Company. That
was about gone, too, the fur trade was. Changing demand,
people just weren't buying as many furs. Beaver hats were
going out of style. A couple of places, such as Bent's, were
still trading some furs and expanding to include buffalo
hides for robes as the fur market fell off.

But the day of the real mountain man was about gone,
and the smart ones were doing other things. Beckwourth
was a Crow subchief, with several wives. Jed Smith was
dead, killed by treachery, by a couple of young Comanches,
on the Cimarron Cutoff. Fitzpatrick and Walker were
scouts. Carson, who'd never been part of the fur trade, had
developed a reputation as a scout by guiding wagon trains
on the Santa Fe Trail.

Gabriel Booth had been almost too late to get in on the
fur trade, he figured. He'd spent a couple of poor winters at
it and hardly made enough to go out again. When he'd

heard of Fremont's summer expedition in '42, he'd been at
Westport, sort of wondering whether to have another go at
it or go back home to Illinois and see if he could settle
down.

When he met Captain Fremont and saw his enthusiasm,
he knew he couldn't. He signed on for the trip to Oregon.
Lord, how he loved to travel the country, the mountains
and the prairie, under the big blue bowl of the sky. He
hoped he could keep signing on with Fremont as long as the
captain kept mapping the west.

And now, here he was, riding the plain with none other
than Tom Fitzpatrick.

Gabe hadn't said much. He wanted Fitz to think well of
him, and if he talked much, he was afraid he'd make a fool
of himself. Oh, sure, they'd visited a little from time to time
but not really like this, just the two of them, alone under
the sky.

"Have you been through here before, Fitz?" Gabriel
asked.

"Nope. Not this way, at least."

His voice was deep and dignified and hinted at his
educated background, sort of like the way Captain Fremont
talked, but not so urgentlike.

"Mostly, I've followed the Platte or the Arkansas," Fitz
continued, "but this is in between them. A pretty good
river farther east. About this part, I don't know. You know
how they run underground, here. Like the upper Platte."

Gabriel nodded. It was true, much of the flow of the
rivers through this sandy country was in the form of
moisture in the sand itself. At times, the surface might
appear dry, but water was there. It was possible to dig
down a few inches at any point in the sandy bed and let the
hole fill with usable water. He had done it himself, on the
Platte, many times.

Fitz was silent for a while. Gabriel watched him curiously, trying hard not to seem to do so. He was riding a step
or two behind and could study the side of Fitz's face and

cheek. *Yes*, Gabe thought, *it's true. He's not as old as h*
looks. The cheek, beneath the tan, was not rough and
wrinkled, but smooth, the face of a young man. *But what*
then? Probably the snow-white hair, cascading from unde
his fur cap. Some tribes, he'd heard, called Fitzpatrick
White-Hair, instead of Broken Hand.

There was a story about that, too. One you wouldn't ask
about, any more than about the hand. Years ago, Fitz had
been chased by a war party of Gros Ventres along the
Snake. He sent his horse to go on along the trail while he
hid among the rocks. But the Big Bellies were shrewd
trackers, and they came back and camped nearly on top of
him.

He spent several days hiding in a crevice and finally
sneaked out at night. Without a horse, Fitz had managed to
build a makeshift raft to cross the Snake River. However,
he capsized in the rapids and lost his knife, gun, and
tomahawk. He sighted on a distant mountain and started to
travel, living on roots and berries, until he finally collapsed
from hunger and exhaustion days later. A couple of trappers
had found him and nursed him back to life. They had
widely told that Fitz had been headed for the safety of the
Rendezvous, straight as a compass, until he gave out.

The rest of the story was something that could easily be
seen. From that time on, Fitzpatrick's hair had been snow
white from the ordeal.

It was late in the day when the two scouts reined in at the
edge of a swiftly flowing stream some forty paces across.

"Is this the river we're lookin' for?" Gabe asked, puzzled.

"I don't think so," Fitz pondered. "This is too close, and
look—as far as we can see, it runs southeast. Now, look
across it. There's some higher ground on the north side."

Yes, Gabriel could see it now. No wonder Broken Hand
had maps in his head. He could *feel* the lay of the land.

"Yes," the mountain man continued, more to himself
than anyone, "this runs south with the slope." He turned to
his companion. "See, this would have to run into the

Arkansas, below a ways. Our river will be over that high ground to the north, another sleep or two."

"This is a lot of water," Gabe observed.

"Yes, I expect it's been raining upstream. They come up fast, down fast out here." He picked up the reins. "Let's find a place to cross."

· The streambed could be treacherous. In some spots, the shifting sand would suck a horse down.

"You go upstream, I'll go down," Fitz suggested. "Look for a riffle or a rocky shelf. And don't try to cross without I'm there. It's only a foot deep, but the quicksand's dangerous."

Gabe reined his horse to the left without speaking. *My God*, he thought, *give me credit for knowin'* something.

It was about a half-mile before he found a broad riffle, where the water broke and sparkled in the lowering sun and whispered a soft song against the breeze. A long gravel bar, shallower and wider than the main portions of the stream. He turned back to meet Fitzpatrick, after marking the spot in his mind by a lone cottonwood on the south bank. Fitz was loping to meet him.

"I found a crossing," Broken Hand said. "About a mile below here."

"I've got one, too. Up by that there cottonwood," Gabe said, pointing.

"No. We'll use mine," Fitz stated with finality.

He reined back to the south and started at a fast trot across the prairie. Gabriel followed, disgruntled. That was sort of an insult, he figured. Fitz had made the decision without even pausing to look at the crossing Gabe had found. He rode in silence for a little while, until he could stand it no longer.

"Fitz," he said, "don't you even want to look at mine?"

"Nope," the mountain man answered instantly.

Another uncomfortable silence ensued, finally broken by Fitzpatrick.

"Look, Gabe, it's comin' dark before we get back to the

party. We know we've got places to cross, so we've done what we need."

It began to make sense.

"Main thing, though, we'll use my crossing because it's the direction we're going. With yours, we'd have to back-track a couple miles somewhere."

Now Gabriel felt nothing but stupid. They rode on, while shadows lengthened. They were out a little farther than the mile Fremont had suggested, and Gabe thought he'd feel better when they sighted the main party. It was growing darker in the little gullies and valleys, and the brilliance of the sunset failed to dispel the slight uneasiness that crept across the prairie. Gabriel realized that he'd not paid much attention to direction, relying on the skills of his compan-ion. He cursed himself for a fool. He'd been so intent on impressing the man he admired so much that he'd acted like a complete idiot. This in turn made him insecure.

Damn, he told himself, he shouldn't feel like this. He'd been out alone dozens of times, in the mountains or on the prairie. But this was different. Unknown country, and he'd been careless. Not the way of a survivor, such as Broken Hand Fitzpatrick.

This self-accusation made him more insecure, more fearful, and he began to wonder. Was there something about the country itself? Some of the Indians, he'd heard, believed that every place had its own spirit. Was that why this area was largely unexplored, perhaps? A land with a threatening spirit of its own? What strange thoughts. He shook his head to clear it. He wondered if his companion felt the brooding threat, too.

"Fitz," he said conversationally, his voice only a trifle higher-pitched than usual, "the Captain says we're not likely to see any Indians in this area. Is that right, you think?"

"Well, can't tell," Fitz said reflectively. "The tribes are movin' around a lot. Shouldn't be any in through here, but the Kiowas travel through sometimes. Comanche, Arapahoes, too, maybe. Even Cheyennes."

"The Captain mentioned Pawnees."

"Yep, farther east, usually. You know Pawnees, don't you?"

"Well, yes. Had a Pawnee woman for a while."

"You talk Pawnee?"

"No. She talked some English. That and sign-talk. We did all right."

His thoughts turned again to the soft skin, the slim fine body of She-Cat, and how she used to feel in the sleeping robes. Wonderful, that was all. And what a cook! He wondered what had ever happened to her. Married some Pawnee, likely, a couple of kids by now.

Funny, he hadn't thought of her for a long time, till back at Bent's the other day.

"That was up on the Platte," he told Fitz. "Her band was the Loups, the Wolf Band."

"Yep, I know 'em," said the mountain man.

"Anyhow, none of any tribe around here. No sign, anyway."

"Gabe," Fitz said earnestly, "you and I know that's when you got to watch out, when there's no sign."

"Yep," Gabe said confidently.

He was, more than anything, proud at the way Fitz had said "you and I." To be spoken to as an equal by such a man as Broken Hand Fitzpatrick! His confidence was returning.

Even so, he was glad when he saw ahead of them in the lowering twilight, the pinpoints of light from the campfires of Fremont's party.

≈ 5 ≈

*On the 7th, we crossed a large stream about 40
yards wide and one or two feet deep, flowing with
a lively current on a sandy bed. Beyond this
stream, we traveled over high and level prairies,
halting at small ponds and holes of water.*

Fremont's report, 1844

It appeared that the rain that had caused the stream to be
full had been widespread. They encountered many ponds
and puddles, which were useful for watering the animals
whenever they wished to stop. There was some wonderment that there seemed to be water in plenty in an area
reputed to be arid and somewhat desert. Fitzpatrick was of
the opinion that this was simply an unusually wet season.

"This isn't much different country than the Platte," he
pointed out. "You get a wet season, it would look a good
deal like this, too."

The grass was bright gray-green, although short, barely
four inches tall in most areas, and interspersed with sage
and greasewood occasionally. The tall waxy spikes of white
yucca blossoms dotted the prairie. Preuss was kept busy
collecting botanical specimens for the herbarium and jot-
ting notes about each new find.

Most puzzling to some of the travelers were the round
ponds of water in some perfectly level area of grass. Various
theories were proposed, from meteor strikes to sinkholes
like those in the Yellowstone. All the ponds were twenty or

28

thirty paces across, and a foot or two in depth. The party encountered one in every mile or so of travel.

Finally Fitzpatrick, overhearing the discussion, answered the question with a brief comment. "Buffalo wallows!"

"But how are zey formed?" Preuss asked.

"Well, I don't know how they started," Fitz admitted. "They've probably been there for centuries. The buffalo sort of paw the dust and roll, to dust the fleas and graybacks. Then when it rains, the wallow fills up. They roll in the mud sometimes."

They rode on, Preuss still pausing now and then to pick specimens or take a compass bearing.

"Best use for the wallows," Fitz said some time later, "is to defend. You can lie down in one and shoot over the rim."

"In the water?" asked the astonished Preuss.

"Hell, no! You do it when they're dry."

Again, Fitzpatrick and Gabe went out ahead on a scout. The country was still a "high and level prairie," with considerable roll to it. There seemed to be a sort of elevation between the two watersheds, the stream they had crossed and the one ahead, the Smoky Hill. Some of the men were referring to the one behind them as the Big Sandy.

A half-dozen antelope flushed ahead of them and stopped a quarter-mile away to turn and stare.

"Say, we could use some fresh meat," Fitz suggested.

"They're too far out," Gabe protested, "and too fast to chase."

"Then I guess we'll have to decoy them in."

They dismounted and placed their mounts in the little swale just vacated by the antelope. Fitz quickly led the way on foot to a favorable spot, and they lay down.

Fitz removed his fur cap and tied his red neckerchief around it, arranged so that the ends would be sticking up like ears. Then he drew the ramrod out of his rifle stock and

placed the cap on its top. He crawled forward a little way
and stuck the ramrod upright in the sand.

"There," he said. "Now, get into position, ready to
shoot."

Gabe squirmed forward and thrust the Hawken's muzzle
through a weedy clump of vegetation that furnished scant
cover. The animals were moving around skittishly, staring
in curiosity at the strange object on the rod. The largest
buck pranced and bucked and came closer for a better look,
the others following. They were still several hundred paces
away.

"Won't always work anymore," Fitz whispered. "Wait till
they get close, though."

The little band moved closer, curious but showing alarm
in the flash of white rump patches. Two individuals appeared to be the boldest.

"You take the buck on the left," Fitz whispered. "I'll get
the other one."

Gabe laid the front sight in the notch of the rear and
sighted on the buck's shoulder. He cocked the rear trigger,
readying the hair-fine set trigger.

"Wait till I count three," Fitz said softly.

The pronghorns were coming closer yet, nervous but
drawn like moths to flame. Closer and closer they danced,
now perhaps only fifty or sixty paces out. Gabe's finger
caressed the trigger.

"One," Fitz whispered, "two . . . three!"

The Hawken boomed, along with the mountain man's
weapon, and the air was clouded for a moment with the
cottony white smoke of black gunpowder. The smoke began
to dissipate, and the herd was seen bounding away, leaving
two of their number kicking on the grass.

"Good!" Fitz exclaimed. "Let's dress 'em out."

He retrieved his ramrod, reloaded, and replaced the rod
in the rifle stock and his hat and scarf in their assigned
places. Gabe was reloading, too, and they drew knives to
begin the butchering. The animals would be bled out and

the entrails removed. The skin was not removed, to make transport easier.

Fitz quickly gutted his buck and turned to Gabe. "Your mule will pack, won't he?"

"Sure."

They tied the carcasses behind their saddles and led the nervous animals around to get them used to the feel and scent.

"Are we goin' on, or back to the rest?" Gabe inquired.

Fitz glanced at the sun. "Well," he said, "it's pretty hot, but maybe we can find a campsite up ahead and some shade to hang the meat and cool it out. They'll find us. Not too long till time to camp, anyhow."

Fitz mounted, a little clumsily, as it was necessary to swing his leg over not only the horse and saddle, but the bulk of the antelope carcass. Gabe accomplished the same, with Rabbit rolling his eyes and dancing a little at the smell of blood but tolerating it well.

"I reckon they'll appreciate the fresh meat," Gabe ventured.

"Well, ain't like it was buffalo," Fitz stated, "but we've et a hell of a lot worse, ain't we?"

It was odd how Fitzpatrick would talk with all the formality of his breeding and education and then suddenly chuck it all to talk like everybody else.

"Fitz," Gabe inquired, "how far do you suppose it is to the Smoky Hill?"

"I dunno. Prob'ly from where we crossed thet Big Sandy creek, no more'n two or three days. But, you got to remember, we're lookin' for the headwaters. It won't be very big. Not as big as the one we crossed yesterday. We might even miss it! Wouldn't that be a fly in the ointment?"

He chuckled to himself as he rode.

It was not long until they saw a small streambed ahead, marked by its fringe of scrubby trees. They rode forward and chose an area with a little graze and one tree big enough to hang the kills. Potholes in the sandy streambed would furnish water, though there seemed to be very scant flow.

They chopped a couple of short willow poles to thrust through the hamstring of the hind legs of each antelope. The carcasses were then hoisted off the ground by a rope over a limb.

"Damn, the flies are bad," Fitzpatrick muttered. "Let's not skin 'em yet, till we're ready to cook."

"Mebbe if we'd build a fire," Gabe suggested.

"Yep, good. Then they'll see it."

It was a trifle early to make camp, but the opportunity for fresh meat was not to be ignored. They began to gather firewood and chips.

Not until the fire was beginning to crackle did Gabriel notice something. In the pile of fuel they had accumulated were many more sticks than at previous stops. Now why would this be? He pondered a little while and finally broached the subject to his companion.

"I don't know, Gabe," the other man mused. "This isn't a regular trail, so not so many come this way."

But why not? Gabriel asked himself. They hadn't even seen any Indians since leaving Bent's. He began to have that same eerie feeling he'd felt just before dark a day or two ago. Was there something here, something evil about the spirit of the place, that made people avoid it? He wondered if Fitzpatrick noticed anything or had heard anything of the sort as a reputation of the area. If there was anything, Fitz would surely know.

"Fitz," he began tentatively, "I—"

He was interrupted by a hail from the south. Shaughnessy and Dodson were loping toward them, followed by the rest of the party in the distance.

Ike slid to a stop and dismounted.

"Fresh meat," he said, chortling. "We seen where you gutted 'em out."

Gabriel pointed to the carcasses in the tree.

"Yep," Fitz said apologetically, "ain't buffalo, but maybe it'll help out some. Maybe we can find buffalo later."

Long after dark, Gabe lay in his blankets, stared at the starry dome that reached from horizon to horizon, and listened to the night sounds. In the distance, a coyote called, and another answered. He had come to like the sound—a comforting part of his life under the big sky. He knew some of the men thought the coyote sounds ominous, but he didn't feel that way. It was just part of the night. A night bird called from a little way down the creek.

Funny, how different things were after a good meal and when rolled in a warm blanket. He was glad he hadn't had a chance to ask Fitz about the odd feelings he'd had. They were gone now. There didn't seem to be any threat in the region at all, like he'd wondered about.

Nope, his only problem, seemed like, was that he wished he had a woman to share his blankets this night, clear and cool on the high prairie after a hot day. He thought of She-Cat, the Pawnee girl who had shared his blankets. Soft. Warm. That was some kind of a woman, he figured. He finally fell asleep, still half-dreaming of long supple legs and a warm, yielding body next to his.

≈ 6 ≈

On the morning of the 8th, we encamped in a cottonwood grove on the banks of a sandy stream where there was water in holes sufficient for the camp. Here several hollows or dry creeks with sandy beds met together, forming the head of a stream which afterward proved to be the Smoky Hill fork of the Kansas River.

Fremont's report, 1844

"But which is the main channel?" Preuss persisted.

"Everybody spread out, circle the camp, we'll find it!" Fremont exclaimed excitedly.

The party scattered, searching. The cottonwood grove was an admirable stand of woods, the largest they had seen since they had left the upper Arkansas. The grove had been seen almost as soon as daylight made distant objects visible. At first, someone had reported a distant cloud of smoke on the horizon. As the light became better and the distance closer, however, it was seen to be not smoke, but a cluster of huge cottonwood trees, foresting an area perhaps a half-mile in diameter. A sizable streambed, mostly dry, seemed to emerge from the grove and flow to the east.

Captain Fremont called a halt to camp in the pleasant grove. There was fine comfortable shade, and he wished to more accurately map the upstream portion of this stream-bed, which he believed to be the river they sought.

But there seemed to be no incoming main channel. There were several small shallow gullies, entering the grove from various directions, but no main bed. In the grove itself, the sandy soil seemed eroded and gullied by such a maze of washed watercourses that it was impossible to decipher.

"They all come into the woods here and run out that way," Raffie Proue said, pointing.

"It is as if," Fremont observed sagely, "there is a gathering of the waters here for the purpose of uniting into a great river!"

"Zis makes the trees to grow here," Preuss contributed.

"Yes, of course!"

The captain was in one of his poetic moods, Gabe noted to himself. Almost like the time he got all choked up over that bumblebee up on the snowbank in the high country. Well, that was just the way the captain was.

"Gentlemen," Fremont announced majestically, "today we have discovered the headwaters of the Kansas River system. This is the Smoky Hill fork of the Kansas River."

Gabe felt as if Fremont wanted them to cheer a little or something, but nobody did.

"We'll camp here for the day," Fremont announced, "while we take compass readings and map the area."

This time, Gabe figured, the men probably felt more like cheering but couldn't very well if they hadn't before. Preuss set to work with his compass and maps, and the others lounged around or repaired damaged saddles, tack, and clothing.

Gabriel walked out to the east along the sandy riverbed for a ways. This really was a sizable stream, looked like. Considering the way the rivers behaved here on the plains, come a rain this would be one to reckon with. He followed it with his eyes as far as he could see, the gouged-out channel meandering across the high prairie. On the south bank, some miles away, there appeared to be some hills or bluffs, dark gray-purple in the distance. Distance did that, of course. Those bluffs might be almost any color. Distance and changing light. That was one of the things he loved about the prairie. You could look at it a hundred times and see different shades of color every time, at different seasons and in different lights.

He didn't know what might be down this river, but he had the old thrill of excitement and adventure, strong as ever. He understood the captain's enthusiasm, because he felt sort of the same way. There was just a trifle that was foreboding about the dark smoky-looking bluffs in the far distance, but Gabe shrugged it off. It wasn't the same threat, here on a sunny morning, as the uneasy feeling he'd had late in the day a couple of times. It was probably nothing, he decided. Surely, no evil spirits. What had he been thinking of? My God, he'd almost asked Fitz about it. He turned and made his way back to the camp.

The next few days were uneventful. It became apparent that the river they had encountered was being joined by little creeks and gullies, and its size appeared to increase

rapidly. They were traveling on the south bank. Standing
on high ground, it was possible to follow the river's course,
almost due east, until it was lost in the distance. There was
a feeling of excitement in the party. It appeared that their
trail was open and easy. They had only to follow this stream
until it emptied into the Missouri, some four hundred miles
to the east. Men began to count the days to civilization. At
their present rate of travel, they could expect to be in
Leavenworth in less than three weeks. There was much talk
of intended debauchery—whiskey, gambling, and women.

No one seemed more anxious for the expedition to end
than Charles Preuss, who seemed eager to rejoin his family
after fifteen months of hardships. Again, Gabe wondered
why the German would hire on with Fremont. His attitude
and his complaining were constantly the butt of jokes by the
others. Gabe had worried about the man when they were
starving in the mountains. Preuss had refused to eat mule
meat. That was his choice to decide, of course, but that was
all there was. Gabriel still thought that if Preuss had not
changed his mind and agreed to this necessity of diet, he'd
have starved to death.

"Booth," the captain interrupted the reverie, "I want you
to cross the river and scout that side of the watershed. See
what sort of country, other streams, whatever."

"With Fitz?"

"No. I've sent him ahead to the east. Shaughnessy is with
him. I want you to go north three or four miles, make a
loop, and meet us back at the river. If you see any Indian
sign, come right back."

Gabe nodded and turned his mule toward the river. This
would be a pleasant diversion, he figured. Get to see a little
country on his own. And, of course, it was a bit flattering to
have Fremont pick him for the scouting job.

The stream was hardly ankle deep most of the way across,
and Rabbit clattered up the bank to the grassy slope on the
other side. Gabe waved to the others and nudged the mule
into a trot across the prairie.

He traveled a couple of miles without encountering even a memorable landmark of any kind. There was a sameness in the rolling country that was deceptive. Distances were distorted, and direction also. Once, after rounding a low, sloping hill, he discovered that he had turned almost northwest without noticing. He'd heard of lost travelers walking in a circle until they starved to death or died of thirst. He stopped and took a drink from his canteen. This country could be dangerous. He reoriented himself by the sun, glad that the day wasn't cloudy. Then he might easily have become lost.

Once more he had that odd feeling that he'd had ever since they'd entered this river's watershed. It seemed sometimes that this harsh land lay here in ambush, a brooding presence, just waiting for somebody to make a mistake. On the other hand, he told himself, it was really pretty good country. High, wild, and free. That's what he liked about it. If water was only a little more predictable.

They'd been lucky, he knew. This was a rainy summer. It took little imagination to know that they could have very easily *not* found water while they crossed the upland to the Smoky Hill. Nature had been kind. She could have just as easily destroyed them. Mother Nature could be a bitch and frequently was.

He saw ahead to the north what appeared to be another streambed. He stopped to trace it with his eyes, then headed toward it, noting what landmarks he could. Yes, it seemed to run southeast and would join the one they were following within a few miles.

Gabe followed the sandy stream for a while and then turned south again, back to the main party, where he reported to the captain.

"Not much up there, Cap'n. More of the same. About three or four miles, there's another stream, the size of this one. Looks like they'll join up ahead a few miles."

"Any landmarks?"

"Not really. A couple of mounds on the south bank.

Rounded, sort of, and close together. Looks like a pair of big tits out there on the prairie."

Shaughnessy, riding nearby, grunted with mirth. "Jesus, Cap'n, Gabe's been out here too long. He thinks everything looks like tits. Not that it'd do him any good."

Fremont smiled ever so slightly. "Very well, Booth. When we stop, you show Mr. Preuss where to locate these landmarks on his map."

He turned his horse away and then reined back again.

"Oh, yes, Booth. Would traveling be better on the other side?"

"I don't think so, Cap'n. We'd have to cross back or cross that other fork pretty quick."

"Very well."

He touched heels to his horse and loped forward toward the head of the column.

≈ 7 ≈

We made a detour to the north to get out of the way of some Comanches.

Charles Preuss's diary
July 12, 1844

Gabriel Booth stood beside Fitzpatrick, and both looked to the southeast through cupped palms. Yes, there was no mistake. A thin plume of smoke, several miles away, reached into the blue of the sky, delicate and wavering.

"Indians?" Gabriel inquired.

"Probably," Fitz grunted. "I thought the Pawnees were farther east."

"What tribes would be here?"

"Don't know. We'd do well to find out, though. You go

back and tell the Cap'n to take the party across the river. Then they can follow the north bank a while. You come back across and meet me ahead there."

"Want any more men?"

"No. Fewer the better. We ain't goin' to fight, just see what's up." .

He pointed to the east. "Looks like a stream down there a mile or two. Meet me where that joins the Smoky. And be careful."

The two men swung up and hurried in opposite directions.

Fremont was not quite convinced. If there was to be any action, he wished to be there. With some difficulty, Gabriel convinced him to cross the river.

"Mr. Fitzpatrick was real sure about this, Captain. He wants to avoid them if we can. I think he'll scout them to see for sure who they are, but he thinks the party will be safer on the north bank."

"Very well," the captain agreed reluctantly. "And he asked you to rejoin him?"

"Yes, sir."

"Well, be gone, then."

Gabriel kicked Rabbit into a lope and overtook the scout just as he reached the mouth of the stream they had mentioned. It was a little bigger creek then they had expected, forming quite a canyon that opened into the Smoky.

"That smoke is probably a camp upstream, on this same creek," Fitz said. "Let's follow the canyon a ways."

"Down in it?"

"No. Along this rim. Maybe down in it later."

It would be easier, if necessary, to run on the open ground above than in the uneven rocks, brush, and trees down in the canyon.

They followed the little ravine for several miles without seeing any sign of human presence. Could they have been mistaken? Then, a slight shift of the breeze, some warning so slight it might have gone unnoticed. Fitzpatrick held up a hand to stop, then signaled for silence, as he sniffed the air. Gabe had heard that old Fitz could smell Indians, and he tried it, too. Yes, there it was, a faint acrid odor of wood smoke. Fitz motioned forward, still cautioning silence. They did not dismount. If they ran into trouble, it would never do to be on foot with the horses tied somewhere else. Gabe's palms were sweaty on the Hawken's stock.

The smoke smell lay heavier now. Fitz pointed ahead. A thin fog of smoke hung over the canyon. There Gabriel could see the ruins of an adobe pueblo. There was a small fire in front, tended by an ancient woman so thin it seemed her bones must push through the parchmentlike skin of her cheeks. She was bending to place some small sticks on her little fire. There seemed no evidence that anyone else was around.

This was a woman left behind by her people, the scouts knew. For the nomadic tribes of the prairie, survival was always a problem. In the Moon of Hunger, February, as food supplies became exhausted in a hard winter, there would be some who would not survive. In order for the tribe itself to survive, the young must be protected. Therefore, if it came to a choice, the old would do without. Through the generations, it had come to be that many of the elderly would choose their time and simply stay behind at a place where the tribe had camped. This would be such a case. She had taken refuge in the adobe ruins. But what was her tribe, and where were they going?

Fitz called out, and the woman started to run, then seemed to realize it was useless and stopped, waiting for the two riders. They rode up beside her, and the woman cowered as if she expected a blow. Fitzpatrick shook his head, dismounted, and began to use sign-talk.

"No, no, mother. We mean you no harm."

She did not answer.

"How are you called?" Fitz asked.

"I am Yellow Basket." She looked at Fitz's clawlike hand. "You are Broken Hand!"

Fitz nodded, noncommittally. "What is your tribe, mother?"

The old woman extended her left hand, palm down, and rubbed it lightly with her right fingertips. Then with her right forefinger, a wavy motion pointing forward.

"'Snake People,'" Fitz muttered. "She's Comanche!"

He turned again to the old woman.

"Where are your people?"

She pointed vaguely to the southeast.

"How long have they been gone?" he asked.

She shrugged. "Many sleeps."

"Where were they going?"

Again, she pointed vaguely.

Fitzpatrick turned to Gabe. "I don't think she knows. She's probably a little crazy."

. He turned and reached into his saddlebags to find several pieces of dried buffalo jerky wrapped in a cloth. He took these over and pressed them into the bony hand of the old woman.

"Here, mother. It is all I have."

She nodded eagerly and began to eat. Gabriel fished around in his own saddlebags and found a few more sticks of jerky, which he gave to Yellow Basket.

They rode in silence for a time. There wasn't much to say. Gabe, even though he knew this was the way of the country, was deeply touched. He thought Fitzpatrick had been, too. Old Fitz hadn't said a word since they left the starving woman.

They came to the river, having ridden up the east side of the creek and its canyon on the return trip. This would avoid another crossing. The canyon, Gabriel noted for possible future reference, ran nearly due south from the Smoky, allowing for a little meandering.

It was nearly evening as the animals splashed across, and

they were immediately hailed by Shaughnessy, who had
been posted to watch for them.

"Cap'n's just ahead," he said as they rode up. "What'd
you find?"

Gabriel waited for Fitz to answer.

"Comanches been here," Broken Hand said simply.

Shaughnessy looked around in alarm.

"No, they're gone. Some time ago," Fitz answered the
unasked question.

"What about the smoke?"

"An old Comanche woman, half-starved."

"You shoot her?"

"Hell, no, Shaughnessy. She wasn't doin' no harm."

"Well, you know the only good one . . ."

"Shut up, Ike!" Gabriel almost yelled.

"Okay! I didn't mean nothin'!" Ike seemed mystified at
his friend's reaction.

The three loped after the main party and soon overtook
them.

Fitz reported to the captain, almost formally. "There
have been Comanches in the area, Captain. We have
reconnoitered and have reason to believe they have now
departed."

"Very well. We will camp here, then. It grows late."

For a wonder, Captain Fremont did not press them for
details. Gabe was glad. For some reason, he didn't want to
talk about it.

Word spread through the camp like a prairie fire.
Comanches! The circumstances of their having learned of
this were lost in the excitement of the telling. Men checked
their weapons and stayed close as the sun sank and darkness
deepened. Fremont posted double guards.

Gabriel volunteered for first watch. He needed to get
away by himself to think a little. He watched the stars
wheel and listened to the night sounds, and by the time Ike
came to relieve him, he was feeling a little better. Not
much, but a little.

Shaughnessy sat down beside him. "Anythin' doin'?"

"Nope. Coyote over on the hill yonder."

They sat in silence a little longer.

"Anythin' doin' in camp?" Gabe asked.

"Nope. Some of 'em not sleepin' much. Too much Comanche talk, I reckon. Proue's pretty goosey."

"You slept any?"

"Shore. Used the water clock to get up."

It was an old Indian trick that the frontiersman had adopted. On retiring, Shaughnessy had drunk all the water he could hold. He could count on a full bladder to wake him partway through the night.

Gabriel nodded absently and finally rose and stretched. "Guess I'll go catch a little," he said as he ambled off toward his blankets.

He was still restless, not really sleepy. Still in his mind's eye was the haggard face of the starving old woman. He had seen the frightened look of a cornered animal in her eyes, fully expecting to be killed. Damn, things were in a sorry shape, when somebody like Ike Shaughnessy would even ask about killing old women.

This was all too serious. What he needed, he guessed, was something to relieve his tension. No whiskey. No woman. Something that would get a laugh, maybe. Some prank, just for pure orneriness. Maybe he could circle around and sneak up on Ike, scare him a little.

He started to turn aside, being quiet so as not to wake anyone. Soft snores came from the scattered forms around the camp. He'd just go on through, like he was stepping out to take a pee, and then circle on around to where Ike was sitting. He'd have to spot the other guard, though.

He paused as a blanketed form stirred and mumbled. Raffie Proue was talking in his sleep.

≈ 8 ≈

Proue caused a great commotion last night. He maintained a wolf had taken hold of his blanket. I think he just dreamed. If a wolf had had the audacity to get into camp, he would have found plenty of meat more tasty than a dirty woolen blanket.

Charles Preuss's diary
July 12, 1844

Gabe stood in the dim starlight, his thoughts racing. He had instantly abandoned the joke on Shaughnessy. Here was a better go. Proue was already scared of the Comanches, Ike had said. He was restless, talking in his sleep. It wouldn't take much to really warm him up.

Gabe paused a little longer, figuring the best way to get a rise out of the sleeper. *Let's see, a good Comanche yell in his ear,* he thought. *No, that would wake everyone.* Something that would just scare Raffie. Proue seemed to have an inordinate fear of being scalped, he'd heard. Well, he'd just sneak up and tug on his hair a little. That ought to do it.

He dropped to all fours to be inconspicuous and crawled carefully toward the prostrate form. Proue muttered in his sleep. Gabe couldn't make out any words, but he paused to wait till the sleeper quieted again.

His position was near Proue's feet now, and as he lay quiet a moment, waiting, he had time to think about his joke. He'd tug on Raffie's hair, and then . . .

Jesus, he thought, *what am I doin'?* It would be one thing

44

for Raffie to think-he was being scalped, but quite another when the entire camp came awake to see somebody bending over Proue's blanket. Everyone slept with his rifle in bed with him, and . . . *Jesus! That could get dangerous in a hurry.*

Still, this was an opportunity that just wouldn't happen every day. He had to do *something*, he figured. He lay there a little longer, studying the sleeping form. Maybe he could just steal the blanket off of him. He hated to settle for such a bland trick after what he'd set out to do, but it seemed like his scheme was sort of falling apart. Hell, he'd do it.

He got a light grip on the corner of the blanket and started a gentle pull. The blanket slid a little, and Proue muttered and rolled on his side. Gabe waited until his victim quieted and began to pull again. This time, the blanket slid freely, and Gabe paused to see if Proue would waken. He almost decided to give it up right then, but by now it had become a challenge.

Gently, with infinite patience, he teased the blanket loose. Gabe was totally preoccupied and had the cover down as far as Raffie's waist, when Raffie suddenly sat up, looking straight in his tormentor's face. Gabriel had not thought this far in his modified plans. Proue was staring straight at him, and Gabe felt like he was caught in the cookie jar. He was still trying to figure what to do next when Raffie Proue began to yell.

There are yells and hollers, screams and cries of all sorts, but Gabe had never heard anything like this. You'd have thought the legions of the damned were howling. It raised the hair on Gabriel's neck, even as he tried frantically to figure out what to do. His first impulse was to jump up and run, but his instincts told him no. He'd be a better target for anybody that got trigger-happy if he was standing up.

Raffie kept yelling.

Gabe backed off and retreated on all fours, trying to remove himself from among those coming awake all at once. He scuttled out of the immediate camp area, stood up, and sprinted around the perimeter, fixing to come back in from the other side and act innocent. There was a lot of yelling and somebody's gun went off. He could hear Raffie still hollering, mostly gibberish, it sounded like.

He ran headlong into Shaughnessy, who was headed toward the source of excitement.

"What's the matter?" Gabe hollered innocently.

"Don't know. Come on!"

Ike charged on toward the disturbance, and Gabe followed, greatly concerned. Had Proue recognized him during that moment they had looked each other full in the face? It would be hard to tell. One bearded face might look much like another in the dark. He couldn't figure why Raffie was making such a fuss over it, though. He still had his damn blanket. Maybe he hadn't recognized his tormentor at all and thought a Comanche had him.

Well, Gabe thought, even as he ran, he'd have to be prepared for the fact that Proue might accuse him. If he did, Gabe's best bet would be to try to let on that he, Gabriel Booth, was the one that was sleepwalking. *Yes, that might work.*

Fires were flaring up, and somebody lighted a torch. Gabe charged into the firelight. Might as well take the bull by the horns.

"What's the matter, Raffie?" he yelled.

"A wolf, Gabe! Right there, where you're standin'! He damn near stole this blanket clean off'n me! He run right off thataway, out of camp. Didja see him?"

"No, I didn't see him."

There was loud, spirited discussion. Somehow nobody seemed to bring up the point that wolves don't usually sneak into camp *or* steal blankets. Gabe sure didn't intend to bring it up.

"Really somethin', ain't it," he said to Fitz, "how bold them critters get sometimes."

"Aw, he probably just dreamed it."
"Well, more'n likely, I guess."

When the camp arose, groggy from loss of sleep, it was found that a large herd of buffalo had moved in from the north during the night. The nearest animals were scarcely a half-mile away, and the herd stretched from there to the horizon.

"Seems like all the caterwaulin' in the night would of scared 'em off," Shaughnessy observed.

Yet there they were, grazing quietly along the lush green of the plain.

"Shall we get some meat, Captain?" Fitz asked.

"Yes, by all means, go ahead."

Quickly, a small party was organized. Fitz in charge, Gabriel, Ike Shaughnessy, and Dodson.

"Make it as close as you can," somebody called.

"Mebbe Ike can rope one and lead it in," Fitzpatrick offered.

Ike Shaughnessy had sought instruction with the rope from Kit Carson, before they reached Bent's.

Carson, who had learned the skill from the Mexican vaqueros in California, was skilled enough that the Indians at Bent's had begun to call him Rope-Thrower.

"Shore," Ike said. "Somebody help me, I'll drag in a bull."

There was general laughter. The huge bulls, weighing up to a ton, were notoriously ill-tempered. Most horses were advisedly cautious around them, if not downright afraid.

The four riders approached the nearest group of buffalo, seeking a fat specimen. This appeared to be a band of cows and calves, with a few yearlings from the previous season still following their mothers. They showed no fear whatever.

"Looks like these haven't been hunted," Fitz observed.

More experienced animals, wary from the chase, would

be more likely to bolt and run. The riders moved slowly, almost among them, and the buffalo remained calm.

"How about one of those yearlings?" Ike asked.

"That yearling cow looks good," Fitz said. "Who does the shootin'? 'Bout like fish in a barrel."

"Mebbe Ike *could* rope one," Dodson suggested.

"Want to try, Shaughnessy?" Fitz asked. "If it goes wrong, we'll shoot it."

"Might as well," Ike said. He untied his rawhide lariat from the pommel and shook it out, tied the end firmly to the saddle horn, and built his loop.

"Reckon I won't get but one throw, so be ready to shoot," he cautioned.

He kneed the horse forward, walking slowly into the herd. At the last moment, almost within throwing distance, the young cow snorted and ran, Ike in hot pursuit.

"Give him one throw!" Fitz shouted, kicking his horse after them.

The others came pounding behind. Ike's arm whirled the rope around his head once, twice, three times, all the while gaining on the cow. On the fourth swing, he released his loop, which shot forward to settle over the animal's horns. He reined his horse in, and the rope snapped tight.

When the buffalo felt the pull of the rope, her entire demeanor changed. She stopped, turned, and in a blind rage, charged directly at Ike's horse. The horse, dependable though it might be under most circumstances, was not prepared for this. It turned and ran, straight for the safety of the camp, with the buffalo cow thundering behind. The other riders wheeled to follow, at the same time trying to get a clear shot.

"Cut your rope, Ike," Fitzpatrick called, but Ike was too busy hanging on to think about such a move.

Straight to the camp the terrified horse retreated, and in among the scattered blankets. The grunting, snorting cow was now alternating between trying to reach the horse and trying to escape the rope on its horns. Men on foot were stumbling out of the way as best they could as the deadly tug-of-war whirled around and around.

Fitzpatrick rode his horse to a sliding stop and leaped to the ground. On the next circuit, he managed to plant a rifle ball in the vitals of the cow, and the creature fell to lie kicking. Ike quieted his horse, though it still stood trembling and blowing, rolling white-rimmed eyes.

"Well," Ike Shaughnessy said, "anybody help me try for a bull?"

≈ 9 ≈

We were encamped in a pleasant evening on a high level prairie, the stream being less than a hundred yards broad. During the night, we had a succession of thunderstorms with heavy and continuous rain, and toward morning the water suddenly burst over the banks, flooding the bottom and becoming a large river five or six hundred yards in breadth.

Fremont's report
July 14, 1844

Fortunately, there was higher ground nearby. . . . The herbarium, to be sure, is in a deplorable condition.

Charles Preuss's diary
July 14, 1844

Gabriel drew the sodden blanket over his head and rearranged it again. He had drawn the second watch, beginning about midnight. Ordinarily, he enjoyed night watch—it gave him time to be alone, to think. Under usual circumstances, this was good. He could spend a little time in communication with the spirit of a place, though he did not think of it in exactly that way. It was more like a feel for the country.

This country, this river, he was having a little trouble getting the feel. It was different, changing constantly. He still had the feeling of brooding danger occasionally, but it was less now. Sometimes at twilight he actually felt at peace with this harsh land. The cooling south breezes of the high prairie made a man forget how hot the sun had been a few hours before. The beauty of the stars, the cry of the night creatures, was comforting to him.

He had felt a different emotion in the canyon of the starving woman. Actually, he had decided, there were two separate feelings there. First was the shock of the woman herself, dying slowly by her own choice—that her grandchildren might live through coming times of hunger. That had affected him deeply and reminded him of the fragile thread that all life depends upon. He'd felt the same way when Badeau had been killed. One minute he was alive and strong. Then his rifle had accidentally discharged, and Badeau was transformed instantly to a limp, bloody, lifeless thing in the bottom of the boat, unseeing eyes staring at the sky.

The other thing Gabe had felt at the canyon was the presence of those who had built and lived in the ruined pueblo. Who were they? How long ago? Where had they gone? As never before, he had begun to think of them as people who ate, drank, slept, made love, and laughed at jokes. As soon as he began to wonder about them as people, he felt their kinship with the old Comanche woman, and with himself. The thin thread of life was no longer than to the next heartbeat, for any of them. It could snap as easily as it had with poor Badeau.

Then he had begun to wonder. Did this country lead to such dark thoughts? Was there something here that caused a man to feel how insignificant he was? Well, he decided, that was full circle. He'd met his thoughts coming back.

That was about the time it had started to rain. Physical discomfort had a tendency to drive away any thoughts other than wet, cold, uncomfortable, and a soggy pair of boots. They'd had a few summer storms for the past several days. They had been interesting to watch sometimes. You could see them start to build up in the far distance, in the southwest. A low, dark cloud bank, looking for all the world like a distant mountain range. It would grow and build, coming closer. You could see lightning flickering orange in the belly of the blue-gray storm, even before the mutter of the thunder could be heard in the distance.

They could watch the progress of the storm sometimes twenty or thirty miles away, coming toward them or passing by at a distance. The slanting blue slash of the rain would sometimes be plainly visible, while the travelers remained in bright sunshine.

You could tell how far away the storm was by the lightning. At the flash of the lightning bolt, you'd start to count: "*One*-steam-engine, *two*-steam-engines, *three*-steam-engines . . ." until the boom of the thunder. That number would indicate how many miles to the lightning's strike. Then there were the rainbows. Gabe had never seen such rainbows. With the wide sky to see them in, they were huge and bright, especially in the afternoon as the storm moved on to the east with the sun behind it. One especially vivid show featured the complete arch, from the ground across the sky to the ground on the other side. As if that wasn't enough, just above the rainbow's arch was another, reaching the ground on both sides, but with the colors in reversed order. The Indians would figure that was powerful medicine, he thought, and then wondered at his thought. Why would he think a thing like that?

Tonight, he wasn't thinking about anything except being wet. He'd brought his blanket on watch with him, largely because it did look a little stormy. He wasn't worried much.

He could see the lightning in the distance when he started the watch, and it was interesting to see it move across the plain, its progress marked by the lightning flashes. It wasn't nearly as interesting when the drizzle started, a fine, foglike mist that seemed to soak through everything. He'd made a kind of a shawl out of his blanket and pulled it over his head. It cured the damp for a while, but by the time the rain started coming down harder, the blanket was pretty well soaked through. Water from somewhere, from everywhere, trickled down his neck or dripped from his beard.

He walked back and forth, because walking wasn't quite as bad as standing still. The water in his boots kept squishing when he walked, though. He was trying hard to keep the lock of his rifle dry, with a piece of buckskin wrapped around it. He knew even that was getting pretty soaked up.

The rain fell even harder now, a beating, driving deluge. The storm moved on in, and the time between the lightning flash and the thunder became shorter. By the time he couldn't count even one-steam-engine, Gabe was becoming really worried.

Then, suddenly, the rain stopped, and the lightning and thunder shifted off to the northeast. The sound of falling water ceased. Gabe took off his blanket, wrung the water out of it, and put it back around him. He was shivering cold and, even wet, the blanket helped some.

It was apparently raining yet to the west, because he could hear a low rushing murmur in that direction. Funny, though, no thunder and lightning. Now the sound was growing louder. Something was wrong. He took the blanket down from over his head to see and hear better and peered into the darkness upstream. He had nearly figured it out when there came a flash of lightning from the receding storm, a sort of a last hurrah. For the space of a heartbeat or two, the entire area was dimly lit by the flicker of the lightning. It was all of two-steam-engines before the answering crash of thunder boomed, but Gabriel wasn't counting. He'd had only a glimpse of the rushing wall of water cascading down the streambed, bursting over the banks to fill the waterway to the hills on both sides, and rushing down on the camp.

"Get up!" he yelled at the top of his lungs. "Flood!"

He ripped the cover off his rifle and fired a shot in the air to waken the sleepers. Miraculously, the powder was dry enough to ignite, and the Hawken's boom echoed across the flooding valley.

Men were tumbling out of the tents, yelling and snatching up their possessions. Gabe felt the first wave of the flood wash around his ankles, warmer than the rain had been. Even at the moment, he paused to wonder that it was warm. He dashed toward the picketing area to release the horses, and in two strides the water was at his knees.

"To the high ground!" he yelled as loudly as he could, grabbing the lead ropes of two or three horses, untying the slip knots.

The rest were excited, plunging and pulling. Other men, Gabe couldn't tell who, were working with the horses, too. Another lightning flash illuminated for an instant the rearing plunge of a big dark gelding, jerking its picket pin out of the ground to run frantically into the night. Somebody fell near him, and the current rolled the man forcibly against Gabe's legs. He nearly lost his balance and fell, too, but recovered and helped the other to his feet. There seemed to be no more horses in the area, so they turned back toward the camp.

Another distant flash showed a few stragglers, laden with baggage, saddles, and sodden blankets, struggling toward the high ground. The men began to gather on the shoulder of the nearest low hill, calling one another's names. No one could be identified as missing, so they settled down, wet and miserable, to wait for daylight.

It seemed a long time before the sky began to gray. It was a pleasant surprise when the day dawned clear and warm, with the river already falling. Men began to straggle back to look for missing possessions in the flooded campsite.

"We stay here today," Fremont announced. "We'll dry everything and repair what damage we can. It's too wet to travel, anyway."

"Besides," somebody observed, "it's Sunday."

Blankets and tents were rinsed in the river and spread to dry over the brushy growth on the slope. Men cleaned their rifles, and some fired a cap or two to make sure the nipple was open—or a light powder charge without a bullet, to dry the bore.

Preuss was fussing around with the herbarium, spreading his specimens to dry, and worrying that they would sprout, spoiling their scientific value.

Gabriel helped round up the horses and mules and cared for his own possessions, then walked to the top of the rise behind them. It had been a close call, he knew. He had no desire for another experience of that sort.

He could see for quite a distance both upstream and down. The river was subsiding. Almost as he watched, the pools and lakes decreased in size, and the river was returning to its bed.

What a quick recovery, he marveled. He took off his boots and set them in the sun to finish drying, while he sat down to rest. He was sleepy from the night's activities and dozed dreamily in the sun's warmth. Perhaps it was that dreamlike, half-asleep state that produced a thought that startled him awake. It started him to worrying again about the spirit of the country, and he couldn't shake the foreboding thoughts.

Had the cursed river bushwhacked them? Calmly lulled them into being careless and then descended in an effort to destroy them?

What a crazy idea, he told himself. *I've been out too long.* But he couldn't completely convince himself.

≈ 10 ≈

They traveled a few miles the next day, and then were stopped by a flooded tributary. The main stream was still bank full from the rains that had caused the flood. To proceed, they must cross one or the other; so an impromptu halt was called, and the party went into camp at the fork to wait for the water to subside. As quickly as this sandy land drained, that should not take more than a day.

No one complained about the opportunity to rest another day. Captain Fremont wrote in his report, and Preuss fussed with the herbarium, clucking his tongue sadly over the state of the expedition's scientific material. His major concern seemed to be that the dried plant material would sprout from the moisture. The rest of the men slept, smoked, and told tall tales that everyone had heard repeatedly in the past fifteen months. There was also much speculation as to intended debauchery at the end of the trip. The men were beginning to count down the days. Shouldn't be much more than two weeks, barring another flood or something.

The weather was uncommonly fine after the storm, and it could be seen that drying proceeded rapidly. By dark, the water level was dropping in both the river and the creek that entered it from the north.

After some discussion, it was decided by Captain Fremont to cross the river itself, rather than the creek, and proceed down the south bank. It had become apparent that the greater watershed was to the north. The streams they encountered almost daily now were of considerable size.

Those from the south, since they had passed the canyon of the starving woman, had been relatively insignificant in size.

Fitzpatrick was up before dawn, and when the rest rose, he had already selected the site for crossing. It was a typically wide and shallow gravel bar, and the water was now low enough for the pack mules to cross without again soaking the baggage or the party.

By midday, miles were slipping behind them steadily. At the noon halt, Fitz took the captain aside.

"Captain, I think we're going to come up on some Indians."

Fremont was instantly alert. "Have you found sign?"

"Well, no, not exactly."

"*What*, then?"

"Well, Captain, you notice where we're traveling here, it's almost a road or trail."

He pointed to the route of their travel from the west, winding plainly through the grass of the prairie. Then he pointed ahead. Yes, there was a similar trail, continuing along the river.

"Now, that ain't an animal trail," Fitzpatrick continued. "They'd wander around more. This trail is used by people."

"Comanches?"

"No, I don't expect so. They move around a lot, and I think this leads to a village. See, it's pretty well worn. More as we go along."

"You mean, we're getting closer to the village?"

Fitzpatrick nodded. "Yep. Reckon we'll see it tomorrow."

"Not today?"

"I'd hope not. Wouldn't want to come up to it just before dark with no chance to reconnoiter."

"So you think we should hold back a little?"

"Say, that's a good idea, Captain," Fitz said seriously.

Gabe, who was near, had heard most of the conversation. Sly old fox, that Fitzpatrick. Got what he wanted and made the captain think it was his idea.

"Would you want me and Booth to scout ahead a little?"

"Why yes, Fitz, go ahead."

Fitz and Gabe set out after the noon halt, traveling rapidly but cautiously, scouting the trail ahead from each slight rise in the rolling plain. Gabriel had the feeling that Broken Hand knew more than he was saying.

"Fitz," he finally asked, "what Indians do you s'pose these are?"

"Pawnees, I expect. You know them from the Platte."

"Yes."

"They're s'posed to be on the Kaw, too."

"That's good, then. They're friendly."

They rode in silence a little way, and finally Fitz spoke. "Gabe, there's been a lot of folks killed by 'tame' Indians."

"What are you sayin'?"

"Nothin'. Just, we got to be careful. There's always somebody in any bunch of folks who'll want to make trouble."

Gabriel nodded. He hadn't thought of it just that way. There were some tribes that were considered bad medicine, dangerous under any circumstances. Others, more civilized, under government protection, folks had a tendency to consider "safe." Gabriel hadn't stopped to think about the fact that even civilized tribes might have some men who'd do something crazy sometimes. Come to think of it, there were folks who were troublemakers on both sides. He'd known some whites to do some awfully dumb and dangerous things, too. Maybe this was why Broken Hand was still alive—he'd figured that out early.

About midafternoon, Fitz stopped his horse and stood still, quietly looking and listening. Smelling, too, Gabe had no doubt.

"It's ahead," the scout said softly.

Gabriel was never certain exactly how Fitz could tell, but he didn't argue. He figured maybe Fitz could just *feel* it.

"Wait here a little," Fitzpatrick suggested. "I'll go ahead for a look."

After choosing a spot where he could see well in all directions, Gabe dismounted and let his mule graze. He kept watching primarily to the east, in the direction they believed the village to be. He could convince himself that there was a sort of haze there, a fuzziness distorting the distant skyline. Then the breeze would shift and his eyes would deny what he had seen a moment before. Maybe it was only that he *expected* to see the thin fog of the smoke from cooking fires hovering over the river valley.

He strained his ears to listen. A village such as they expected should produce some characteristic noises—the barking of dogs, shouts of children at play, the nicker of horses—all blended together in a buzz of sound that indicated human habitation. Again, he occasionally thought he heard the life-sound, but with the change of the prairie wind, it would be gone again, replaced by the sounds of the grassland.

A grasshopper with bright black-and-yellow wings flew past the point where Gabe stood, startling him a little. He always marveled how the dry rustling music of a 'hopper's wings in flight could make him think of a rattler's warning buzz. The grasshopper dropped to earth, and the bright wings folded beneath their dust-colored sheaths. Instantly, the creature became invisible, blending into the earth. *That would be a handy trick*, Gabe told himself.

A meadowlark glided in to land on a sumac stem a few steps away. The bird seemed uneasy at Gabe's presence and soon moved on. He wondered if its nest was somewhere near, and he was interfering with its return to the eggs.

He was startled to hear hoofbeats of a walking horse and whirled to see Fitzpatrick approaching on foot, leading the animal. The scout had circled and come in from the prairie side, rather than by the trail. Gabriel was embarrassed to have been caught unawares, but Fitz pretended not to notice.

Fitz swung up, turning his horse on the back trail.

Gabriel followed. They rode a little while, and Fitzpatrick had not said a word.

Finally, Gabriel could no longer contain his question. "Well, what'd you find?"

"I ain't sure, Gabe."

He rode a little longer before he continued.

"They're there, all right. Three, four miles. It's a big village."

"Pawnees?"

"Yep. Regular Pawnee earth-lodges. But somethin' ain't right."

"What do you mean, Fitz?"

"Don't know, exactly. You know them little brush arbors the Pawnees use for livin' outside in good weather?"

"Sure."

"Well, there's an awful lot of 'em. From what I could see, a lot more than there are earth-lodges. The horse herd is too big, too. Somethin's goin' on."

"A council?"

"Yep, I think so. A lot of visitors stayin' at this village for a while. I don't like it."

"But the Pawnees do that. Tribal councils, I mean."

"Yes, I know that. But usually earlier, don't they?"

"I don't know," Gabriel said. "It's only mid-July."

"I don't know, either," Fitzpatrick muttered, as if to himself. "It just don't feel right, somehow."

Gabriel had enough faith in old Broken Hand's instincts to pay attention. This was an odd situation. They'd crossed the Rockies twice in the past year, been in contact with some of the most dangerous tribes on the continent. Fitz had taken it in stride. But here he was, worrying about a bunch of tame town-dwellers. Pawnees. Hell, they'd been on government rations for a generation. Since that young chief—what was his name? Petalesharo, that was it—spent some time in Washington. Pretty famous, for a while, there, he recalled. It was when Gabriel was pretty small, but he remembered folks talking about it. The Great White

Father had figured the Pawnees his children ever since. Why, then, was old Fitz feeling his doubts, talking bad medicine? Was this country, this river, bad medicine as he'd suspected before?

It was growing late when they met the main party. Fremont had already tentatively selected a campsite.

"Found it, Captain!" Fitzpatrick announced as he swung down. "Pawnees."

"Good! Then they'll receive us well!"

Broken Hand, unsaddling his horse, exhaled a deep sigh. "Hope so, Captain."

≈ 11 ≈

> On the 17th, we discovered a large village of
> Indians encamped at the mouth of a handsomely
> wooded stream on the right bank of the river.
> Readily inferring from the nature of the encamp-
> ment that they were Pawnee Indians, and confi-
> dently expecting good treatment from a people
> who received an annuity from the Government,
> we proceeded directly to the village, where we
> found assembled nearly all the Pawnee tribes,
> who were returning from crossing the Arkansas
> where they had met the Kiowa and Comanche
> Indians. We were received by them with un-
> friendly rudeness and characteristic insolence.
> . . . The little that remained of our goods was
> distributed among them but proved entirely in-
> sufficient to satisfy their greedy rapacity. . . .
>   Fremont's report, 1844

The village was larger than Gabriel had expected. Well, not

the village itself, but the coming together of the Pawnees. Though Fitz had told him of the brush arbors, indicating visitors from some distance away, their number astonished him. He made an estimate of the number of shelters compared to the earth-lodges of the permanent inhabitants. There must be at least six or seven bands from other villages. This appeared to be a major council, involving the entire Pawnee nation.

"A celebration in our honor!" Fremont exclaimed.

He led the procession into the village like a conquering hero. Mounted warriors rushed out to meet them in one of the mock charges that were so unnerving to the uninitiated. Gabriel well remembered his anxiety the first time he saw such a ceremony, up on the Platte. He had thought he was doomed, when painted warriors rushed upon him, weapons raised. He could hardly refrain from defensive action, but he had been cautioned not to show any aggressive move. He had gripped his weapon with sweating palms, clenching his teeth and grimly refraining from response. After the first mock charge, it had been apparent that it was a ritual of welcome, a ceremonial show of strength to honor the visitors.

This appeared to be an entirely different situation, somehow. There was an aura of hostility that was difficult to define but came at him with a rush, even ahead of the physical charge of the warriors. Gabriel felt helpless. It would be a breach of protocol to show any sign of defensive action or readiness of weapons; yet this situation could degenerate rapidly, he felt. He glanced at Fitzpatrick. The scout was looking grimly ahead, playing out the hand. Gabriel, knowing Fitz's previous doubts, could sense the resignation on that leathery face. The situation was not good, but Broken Hand was committed to play it out to whatever end came his way.

Captain Fremont seemed not to realize the degree of danger. He rode like a military leader entering a conquered country. Even when warriors struck out at the travelers in

passing, coming dangerously close with their weapons,
Fremont showed nothing beyond irritation. He led the way
to the center of the earth-lodge village and dismounted.

"We will stay here for the day," he announced.

Fitzpatrick looked aghast but recovered quickly. "Keep
your weapons handy, but for God's sake don't start nothin',"
he called. "Stay together."

Fremont glanced at the scout for a moment and seemed
about to speak. Gabriel wondered if he was about to
challenge Broken Hand's authority, but the captain let it
pass.

The warriors were crowding around them, touching the
pack animals or even the persons of the travelers. Gabriel
had the unpleasant feeling that this was a ritual of some
sort. It was much like the counting of coup by some of the
buffalo tribes. To strike an enemy without killing him was
the utmost of bravery. It was possible to count coup several
times on the same enemy prior to his death. That was the
thought that sent a chill slithering up between his shoulder
blades to settle at the back of his neck.

A warrior brushed roughly against him, and Gabriel
wondered as if in a dream whether the man had been
counting coup on him. He saw another strike Captain
Fremont lightly on the upper arm. The situation was
looking almost desperate.

Fremont was now ordering the packs opened from one of
the mules and was distributing some trade goods. This
seemed to distract some of the more aggressive Pawnees, at
least temporarily.

Gabriel felt a tug at his arm and turned to defend himself
if necessary. He found himself looking into the most
beautiful face he had ever seen. The girl's eyes were large
and dark, as deep and liquid as ever. Her full mouth, which
he remembered as warm, moist, and sensuous, looked ripe
and inviting.

"She-Cat!" he gasped.

His eyes roved down over her slim body and the softly

rounded bulges under the buckskin. The feel of that shapeliness in the sleeping-robes came rushing back to memory. He was pleased that the girl had not started to become heavy bodied as had some of the women of her people. He reached to take her in his arms.

"No, Blanket-Man!" she warned, using her pet name for him. "Be still and listen to me. Some want to kill your Soldier-Chief. No, say nothing! You must all leave quickly. I will come to you later. Now, forgive me for this!"

She took a step back and began to shout at him in her own tongue, augmented by sign-talk, so that no one would miss her meaning.

"Son of a mangy dog!" The girl screamed at him. "Your mother is a dung eater. I spit in your face!"

She proceeded to do just that. Gabriel stood dumfounded, spittle trickling down his right cheek, as the girl turned and strode away. The noise had all but stopped as everyone turned to look. There were a few chuckles and then a roar of laughter. He hardly heard, because he was preoccupied with watching her long swinging stride that he admired so much, the familiar provocative sway of her hips. Just now it reflected anger. *How in hell*, he wondered for just a moment, *can a woman show she's mad just by the way she swings her butt?*

"What is it?" Broken Hand had sidled up to him and faced him with concern. Gabe shook himself out of his astonished reverie.

"Your woman? Something up?" Fitz asked.

"I . . . I don't know."

His head began to clear a little, and her words started to come back to him. The words before her tirade.

"Fitz, she says the Captain's in danger," he spoke quickly. "They want to kill him."

"I figgered something was up," Fitz said through clenched teeth.

He turned to work his way through the crowd to the captain's side. Gabriel followed.

"Captain," Fitzpatrick said firmly, "these people are dangerous. We must leave."

"This is what comes of treating them well!" Fremont stormed. "Ungrateful beggars! They draw Government rations!"

"Yes, sir," Fitzpatrick said, "but right now, we'd better go. I'd suggest we give 'em all our supplies and get out while they're arguin' over 'em."

"Shouldn't we teach them a lesson?" Fremont asked.

"Captain, there are twenty-seven of us, and about a thousand Pawnees. That ain't a lesson I'd relish."

"Yes, yes," Fremont said. "Very well, open the packs."

"Give 'em the pack mules, too," Fitz suggested. "We won't need 'em."

The pack mules were quickly sorted out, saving the mules carrying their tents, bedding, and scientific equipment and records. The warriors who had been most aggressive toward the party now became the most interested in the spoils. They tore open the packs, belligerent among themselves over the best of the loot.

"Reckon this is a good time to leave," observed Broken Hand sarcastically.

He mounted, and he and Fremont led the way out of the encampment, the others crowding closely together. No one wanted to see what might happen to a straggler. There were no incidents as they proceeded on their way. A couple of obscene gestures, some threatening shouts, but no overt attacks. As Broken Hand said later, they "was damn lucky."

Gabe looked back over his shoulder just before they moved completely out of sight of the village. It appeared that the Pawnees had killed one of the mules and were preparing to cook it. They'd likely have a feast and dance and carry on all night to celebrate having faced down Soldier-Chief. That would be the reason for the mule roast. Sort of a symbol for the affair. Of course, mule wasn't bad eating, he'd learned on this trip. Lots better than antelope, most thought.

What he'd really looked back for, of course, was to see if he could get a last look at the woman She-Cat. He couldn't find her. Lord, how she'd get his heart pounding. He hadn't realized just how much he'd come to feel for that girl. She was probably the best woman he'd ever known, in a lot of ways. Pretty, smart, a good cook, and hellacious in bed. He'd missed her a lot, and he was just now realizing how much. On top of all that, she'd probably saved his life, and the lives of all of Fremont's party. *Lord, what a woman!*

Fitzpatrick rode up alongside Gabe's mule, jogging along in silence for a little while before he finally spoke.

"Well, we got out, anyhow," he observed. "Can you tell me about what happened back there?"

Gabe shrugged. "I ain't sure, Fitz. That was She-Cat, my woman, but I don't know what she's doin' here. I thought she was up on the Platte. She's Loup, you know."

Fitz nodded. "She say anything to you? Beyond explainin' your parentage to the crowd, so to speak?"

A twinkle of humor appeared for an instant in the scout's eye and was gone.

"Not really," Gabe pondered, choosing to ignore Fitz's jibe. "She just said some wanted to kill Fremont, and we'd better git."

Fitzpatrick nodded but did not answer immediately. When he did speak, finally, it was as if he spoke to himself.

"Onliest thing I cain't figger," he said, lapsing completely into frontier dialect, "is what the hell stopped 'em. By God, they had us dead to rights."

Gabriel had wondered that, too, and a couple of other things. One was, why a desirable woman like She-Cat hadn't married. What was she doing here on the Smoky Hill? And most of all, what had she meant by that one remark—"I'll come to you later?"

≈ **12** ≈

They traveled rapidly, covering fifteen miles before they were overtaken by nightfall. A defensible position was chosen, and three guards assigned to each watch. There had been no sign of pursuit, but everyone was uneasy. There was no complaint about extra guard duty.

Gabriel drew first watch again and was able to observe the brilliant sunset while he familiarized himself with the landmarks of the place. He still saw no indication at all that they had been followed.

The creatures of the day quieted, and their voices were replaced by those of the night. Gabe noted no departure from the usual as one by one he identified the trill of a screech owl, the hollow hunting cry of a horned owl in the tree across the river, and whippoorwill's eerie song on the slope behind. One hunter's call defied identification for a little while, until he realized that it was the soft whicker of a raccoon.

In the main, the importance of all this was that the creatures of the night were apparently undisturbed. It was some indication, no matter how slight, that no hostile warriors were approaching the camp. Once, he heard a horse snort in surprise; but it immediately quieted, and he decided the snort was insignificant.

He caught a flash of motion over the river and watched the noiseless glide of a great owl as it passed over him, blotting out a patch of stars as it floated past. It was at about that time that he heard a soft rustle in the darkness near him. He came instantly alert, crouched as low as possible to the ground, and reached for his knife. He was wishing he had not gambled away his tomahawk back at Bent's.

"Blanket-Man?" a quiet voice called.

"Yes."

He stuck the knife back in his belt.

"It is Cat-Woman."

"Yes. Come on in."

She materialized noiselessly in the darkness at his elbow, and he felt the warmth of her body and smelled the faint woman smell of her.

"I am alone," She-Cat said reassuringly.

Gabriel was so carried away by her very presence that he had not even thought to wonder. Besides, why would she save them only to betray them? He folded her in his arms, his mouth seeking hers. She yielded for a moment, then pushed him gently away.

"No, Blanket-Man, we talk first. Besides, you are watch."

They sat down.

"What . . ." he began.

"No, no, I will tell you."

He relaxed a little, his arm around her.

"All Pawnee tribe is here," she said. "All bands. Big council."

"Why?"

"Council decides, they will kill Soldier-Chief."

The slithering cold fear began at the back of his neck again.

"But why?"

"I do not know, only some hate him. Not Loups! Loups called him 'Pawnee Chief'!" she said proudly.

"Yes," he agreed, "but why did the others not kill us?"

"I am telling you, Blanket-Man! Others want to kill him. Loups say no!"

"To do this, *all* must say so?" he asked.

"Yes! What I tell you! But some man might start fight, you all killed. So I tell you, get out."

"Good. You are a good woman, Cat. Tell me, you have no husband?"

"No. I took a man, after you left with Soldier-Chief. He was killed."

"You have children?"

"No."

He held her again, tight and warm.

"You come, sleep with me?" the girl whispered.

"Where?"

She pointed toward the hilltop behind the camp. "There. It is good. I will come, when the watch is over."

She nodded, kissed him again, and slipped away.

Gabriel felt the watch would never end. It was so exciting, the reunion. Why had he ever left the girl, the one who could stir him like no other? He knew quite well why. He had signed with Fremont and had left to explore and map the Oregon Trail. Women were not permitted. And he had not returned to her—just hadn't gotten around to it. Then this other expedition. He'd signed on, and they'd been out nearly a year and a half now.

But it was about over. Yep, if things went as well as he expected tonight, he'd figure they were meant to stay together. He could speak to Captain Fremont and leave the party a few days early. Shouldn't be a problem. The captain had let those men leave the group at Sutter's with his blessing, to settle down.

Ike finally came to relieve him, and Gabriel figured he'd best tell him what was going on.

"Ike, my woman's up on that hill, there. I'm goin' up."

"You shore, Gabe? You be real careful, now!"

"Yeah, real careful, Ike."

"See anything else?"

"Nope. Cat-Woman says there's no one else."

"You believe her, Gabe?"

"Hell, yes. She saved our ass, you dumb Irishman."

He was more than a little upset with his friend.

"I didn't mean nothin', Gabe, I jest . . ." Ike began, but Gabriel was gone.

She-Cat had spread her blanket in a soft grassy place near the top of the slope. Gabriel saw as he approached that she had chosen a spot that offered visibility in all directions. It would be very difficult for any potential enemy to approach. She was standing by the blanket, smiling demurely at him in the light of the rising moon.

"I have come to you," he said.

She did not answer but spread her arms wide. He laid his weapons aside and enfolded her in an urgent embrace. They sank to the ground, rolling on the blanket in the satisfaction of a long-deferred hunger. *Jesus*, he thought, *how could I have left this woman?*

Some time later, their hunger mutually satisfied for the moment, they lay in each other's arms, staring at the starry black dome above. The night air had a slight chill now, and Gabriel brought his own blanket from where it had dropped. He spread it over them and lay back down with her. They had still said very little to each other.

"I will never leave you again," he whispered.

"Oh, yes," she said, smiling a little sadly. "You have your trail to follow."

He started to protest that they were nearing the end of that trail and to share with her his plan to leave the expedition early. Then he realized she was speaking of the life-trail. His life would travel on a different trail than hers, she was saying.

"No," he protested. "Our trail is the same."

She chuckled softly, the musical little laugh that he remembered and loved. She kissed him warmly.

"No, our trails only cross sometimes," she murmured gently.

"But you have saved my life," he said.

"Yes, you are my Blanket-Man," she giggled.

She blew in his ear and tickled him in one of the little

secret places that only she knew how to use to advantage.

"Stop it, Cat, we must talk. I want us to be together."

"We *are* together," she whispered, tickling him again.

The girl was driving him crazy with her cuddling and tickling, and there seemed only one way to resolve the situation.

"We will talk later," he mumbled, as he gathered her in his arms again.

Their passionate lovemaking completely disheveled the blanket. As they began to quiet down, she rearranged their bed.

"Move over," she whispered, pushing him gently.

Gabriel mumbled sleepily and rolled over while she shook out the blankets and spread them smoothly. The last he remembered before falling asleep was that she had snuggled against him again and spread a blanket over them both. The warmth of her body was a quieting comfort. He slept, deeply and dreamlessly.

When he woke, the eastern sky was graying with the false dawn, and he was cold. He reached for the girl beside him, to discover that he was alone. She-Cat was gone. It was as if she had never been there. Well, not quite. He smiled dreamily for a moment and then became irritated. He sat up to look around.

He was lying on his own blanket, which was folded over him. She had taken her blanket with her but had quietly covered him before her departure. His weapons were within easy reach.

But why? Why in hell, when they had just found each other again, would she leave him? He jumped to his feet, fully intending to go and look for her.

There was activity in the camp below, and he hastily gathered his belongings. He managed to slip into camp unnoticed in the gray predawn light and began to go through the routine chores that went with starting each day. Probably the girl was right, he tried to convince himself. They were from two different worlds. She'd never fit in with white folks. He just couldn't imagine her on a farm back in Illinois. Even less, in town.

On the other hand, he didn't think he could be an Indian, either. Some of the men had done it. Jim Beckwourth, with his Crow wives, was a regular member of that tribe. Somehow, though, Gabe couldn't see himself as a Pawnee squaw man. Not that he had anything against the Pawnees. Or squaw men, either, for that matter. *Damn, what a puzzle*. He didn't know whether he was irritated at himself or at the girl. Yep, she was probably right, he continued to try to convince himself, mostly unsuccessfully. He was building up a dangerously explosive temper. It was Shaughnessy who finally caught the brunt of it.

"Hey, Gabe, where you been?" the Irishman asked with a knowing leer. "I thought somethin' had happened to you."

Gabriel whirled on him furiously. "Goddammit, Ike, just shut up!"

He turned away to saddle Rabbit, wishing he could be alone. One thing that had him so mad was that Ike was probably right. Something *had* happened to him up there on the hill in the moonlight. He just couldn't figure what the hell it was.

≈ 13 ≈

Gabriel Booth poured himself another drink and shoved the bottle across the rough tabletop toward Shaughnessy. Ike drunkenly slopped a couple of fingers of amber liquid into the glass in front of him.

The coal-oil lamp that hung from a beam in the ceiling cast a dull sooty light through its dull and sooty chimney. Its illumination barely penetrated the blue haze of tobacco

smoke that hung in the little tavern. The room was hot and
smelled of stale drinks and sweaty bodies and coal oil and
smoke.

"An' remember," Shaughnessy continued, "how the
Cap'n faced down them goddamn greasers at Sutter's?"

He slapped his knee and roared with laughter. They had
set out with the express purpose of drinking themselves
into oblivion. It wasn't working for Gabriel. As Ike became
drunker, he had also become louder. Everything that was
said was funny, and Shaughnessy laughed until his face
turned red, his eyes squinted shut, and tears of laughter ran
down his face.

At least, Gabriel thought, *he ain't a cryin' drunk. A
laughin' drunk is one thing, a cryin' drunk something
entirely else. Either one*, he guessed, *is better than a mean
drunk, or a sick one*. He smiled ruefully. Lord, how sick
he'd been at Bent's Fort.

He'd been all set to really celebrate tonight, too. End of
the trip, they'd been paid off and headed for the taverns and
whorehouses along the riverfront. There, various and sun-
dry purveyors of worldly pleasures waited to separate the
travelers from their pay. Gabriel and Ike had drifted into
one of the first taverns they had encountered and systematically set about the business of drinking. Lord, he'd been
ready. He'd been sort of depressed ever since She-Cat had
left him sleeping and gone back to her people.

Somehow, though, it hadn't worked out. The liquor
seemed not to have its usual sting. It was apparent that it
had not lost its potency in Ike Shaughnessy's case, however;
so Gabriel figured it must simply be a problem of his. He
did not understand how he could sit there and match Ike,
drink for drink, and feel nothing. Yet, that was the way it
seemed. Hell of a thing, when a man really needed to get
drunk and couldn't.

He had all but stopped talking now. Ike was doing
enough for both, anyway. Gabe was glad to sit back and
quietly sip his whiskey. *Maybe*, he thought, *I'm another*

kind of drunk tonight. A quiet drunk. Yes, there could be such a thing, he figured. A person would never notice a quiet drunk, because he wouldn't be bothering anybody much. It was all right to just sit there and pay no attention to Ike's drunken rambling. Gabe could nod or chuckle occasionally, and Ike wouldn't even notice that the drink wasn't working for him.

His mind, maybe a little fuzzy from the whiskey, began to wander back over the past months. Jesus, they'd seen a lot of country. There were times when it was wonderful, and others when it had become terrible, such as crossing the Sierras in winter. Likely even Captain Fremont would hesitate to try that again. They'd all lost a lot of weight and eaten some things he didn't relish thinking about; but, by God, they'd come through.

He wondered why, though, when he thought of the whole trip, why the most vivid part of it in his memory was this side of Bent's Fort. It wasn't that it was just the most recent, he reckoned. And it wasn't just that he'd run across She-Cat again. Lord, there was a woman! He wondered where she was, what she was doing. No, there'd been something unsettling about it, that portion of the trip. Especially, he recalled, when they began to get into the watershed of that Smoky Hill River. That, he remembered, was where the spirit of the country started to change. He'd had the feeling of evil about it a time or two. Not a fear of Comanches, or even Pawnees on the warpath. Jesus, that had been something. Probably more danger, there, than any time on the whole damn trip. He still wasn't sure that the captain knew how close that had been.

But no, that wasn't the feeling he'd had. It was sort of a threat by the country itself, with a spirit of its own. Like the night they'd been ambushed by the river and nearly drowned in the flood. He shook his head, a little confused. What the hell was he thinking—that the river itself would scheme to kill them all? Jesus, he must be drunker than he thought. But the thought remained—that of a place of evil, of death.

Why, then, had he felt so *good* about it, part of the time? There had been times when he'd watch a sunset and feel that he was part of this land. And the time or two he'd been out on a scout alone, riding under the wide sky with the far horizons. Yep, a man could stretch his eyes some in that country. He found himself thinking of it like he'd relish another look. Maybe it was like loving a woman who was fiery enough to be dangerous. If you were man enough to handle the situation, and willing to take the risks, that could be pretty good.

He *was* drunk. Here his thinking was, all mixed up with thinking about making love and dangerous women and dangerous country, and it seemed all the same, somehow. He thought of the night on the hill in the moonlight, when both the country and the slim Pawnee girl were at their finest. That was good. The best, maybe.

Dimly, through the haze of his fuzzy remembering, he realized that Shaughnessy was asking him a question.

"Huh? What'd you say, Ike?"

"I jest asked . . . are you all right, Gabe?"

"Sure. I was just thinkin'."

Shaughnessy slapped his knee and roared with laughter.

"Hell, I ain't gonna believe *that*, Gabe! Thinkin'!"

He laughed again, long and loud.

Gabriel was a little irritated at his friend. There were times when the jovial Irishman was a joy to be with. This was not one of those times. Gabe was trying to be serious, and . . . hell of a note, come to think of it. Drinkin' and tryin' to be serious. He must be in bad shape.

"Sorry, Ike," he apologized. "I jest wasn't listenin'. What did you ask me?"

Ike quieted. "I said, are you goin' to sign on with the Captain again?"

"Oh, I dunno, Ike."

He surprised himself a little. There was a time, not long

ago, when he'd have said hell yes, he'd sign up for anywhere John Fremont wanted to go. What was happening to him, anyhow? Was he getting soft? No, it wasn't that. He wanted to be out under the big sky. Maybe it was that feeling he'd had that he didn't want the whole damn country mapped, so settlers could come and tromp all over it. No, that wasn't it, either. He knew changes were coming. It was just that the country seemed to have a pull on him, like the attraction of a candle for a moth. The moth might get burned, but it would have a hell of an experience with the dizzying circles that tempted the flame to do its worst. It was like the pull of a former love, left behind but not forgotten. Like his memories of the long legs and warm body—damn, there he was doing it again! How did she keep popping into his thoughts of the prairie country? Now he knew he was drunk.

Shaughnessy was trying to talk to him again. "I said, what are you gonna do, then?"

Gabriel methodically poured himself another drink, spilling only a little.

"I'm gonna kill this bottle," he said solemnly.

Ike laughed appreciatively.

"An' then, maybe I'll go see my brother in Illinois."

Yes, that would be good. Get away from it awhile. Out of sight of the candle, maybe the moth could manage to fly better, with more sense. Yep, get away, put a little distance between him and the Smoky.

"You fixin' to settle down to farmin'?" asked the astonished Shaughnessy.

"'Course not. Just a visit," Gabe snapped indignantly. "I dunno what next, but I'm thinkin' about it."

About the high and level prairie, the way the grass greened up after a summer rain. The sunsets, the moonrises that dusted the hills with silver. The closeness of the stars on a moonless night. The feel of the warm body next to him—there, he was doing it again, making it all part of the same thing again when it wasn't. She-Cat had left him, because it wasn't right for them to be together. Just wouldn't work. She'd likely marry again. Maybe had already. Shouldn't be any shortage of young studs snortin' around a filly as trim as that one. The thought made him a little depressed, and he quickly tossed off his drink.

It didn't help, just made his belly burn. He was probably going to be sick again. He'd never learn, looked like.

Well, he'd go visit his brother and his family, for a little while. Then, he'd figure out what he'd ought to do. Didn't know what yet, or why. Not even *when*, come right down to it. Seemed like he'd ought to take another look at that Smoky Hill valley, though. Maybe he could figure out what it was that kept callin' to him out there in the shortgrass country.

Yep, some time before he died, the moth would have to take another good look at the candle.

"I dunno, Ike," he repeated, "I'm thinkin' about it."

≈ PART II ≈

≈ 14 ≈

It was a warm day, the kind a man hopes for in early spring when there's plowing to be done. Lemuel felt the warmth of the sun through his shirt, especially when he turned the mules at the end of the furrow, his back exposed fully to the sun's rays for a little while. It wasn't uncomfortably cool without it, but there was a nourishing warmth to the sunshine that made him feel good about the world.

The leaf buds were swelling on the willows along the creek, making the trees look yellowish green, almost as if they were ready to bloom in that color. It was a little early for the wild plum thickets to blossom. The fruit trees below the house had a ways to go yet, too, but spring was unquestionably coming.

The texture of the rich black bottom soil was just right for turning. Lem liked to watch the loam curl up over the moldboard like shavings from a plane or a chisel when working with wood. The long straight furrows stretched across the field, making a uniform pattern in the sunshine. He was proud of his straight furrows—that had always been a special pride of his father's, one Lemuel had tried to master to gain approval.

It would be a while before time to plant corn, he knew, but the field would be ready. He'd wait to plant until the leaves on the maples were the size of a squirrel's ear. That would be pretty safe, after the last frosts. The ground had to warm enough to mother the corn seed and nurture it to grow. Already, though, the musty smell of the loam came invitingly to his nostrils, promising warmer weather. It was beginning to *smell* like spring, the sun on fresh-turned earth making a warm steamy scent that Lemuel always loved. Even the smell of the sun on sweaty mules seemed part of the springtime.

He watched a dozen crows from the timber along the river swoop down on that portion of the field he'd already plowed. They were busily hunting and squabbling over insects and worms turned up by the plowshare. Lem always found the birds amusing to watch as they followed the plow. He viewed them with mixed feelings. Their present occupation was beneficial, but he'd not think so kindly in a few weeks when they pulled up his sprouting corn.

Lemuel glanced up, as he made the turn at the far end, to see a man leaning on the rail fence by the road. He was wearing town clothes and had a foot propped on the lower rail, watching. He saw Lem complete the turn to head the mules back along the furrow and straightened to wave.

"Lem! Come over and rest a little."

Lem sighed. His brother, although three years older, had always been a little impractical. Both were young when their father died from pneumonia, and it had fallen on them to run the farm. Sam was always ready to go to town, to hang around the store and visit, even when there was work to be done. Eventually, he had moved to town, working in the store, while Lem continued on the farm. The other children were grown now, and Sam had married and had children of his own.

Lemuel had not yet married. He was just eighteen and courting the Clarke girl down the road. Their mother still lived on the farm, keeping house for Lem—part of his intended bride's reluctance, he suspected.

He sighed again. He should finish plowing this field to have it ready for planting. Any day at this season, a spring storm could hold up field work, and he needed the time. But Sam was excited about something.

A little irritated, Lem stopped the mules and wrapped the lines around the plow handles. He headed over toward the shade tree where he'd left his water jug, and where Sam now waited. Sam probably had some damn fool idea to save work, which would be more work and would lose money. Well, this time he'd just refuse to go along with it. He picked up the water jug and took a long drag. It was good, a man's own well water. Funny, how it could quench your thirst when strange water couldn't—even water from the well on the next farm.

"Lem," his brother was saying excitedly, "looka here!" He unrolled a dog-eared newspaper from his pocket and pointed to the headline: GOLD ON CHERRY CREEK. Below, in smaller type, GOLD SEEKERS HURRY WEST TO STAKE CLAIMS.

Lem was unimpressed. For *this* his brother had interrupted his work?

"Yeah, I heard about it, Sam. It's out in Kansas Territory somewhere, ain't it? Nothin' to do with us."

What was Sam up to? Wanting to buy a gold mine, likely.

"Look, Lem, here's our big chance. You and me can take a year and find enough gold to make us rich."

"Sam, that's the craziest thing I ever heard. I'm goin' back to work."

He started across the field. Damn fool. Didn't want to buy a gold mine, but to go look for one.

"Wait, Lem. Listen a minute. Look at where the trail is to the gold fields. Just read a little of this."

An editorial in a box on the corner of the page was proclaiming the advantages of the Smoky Hill Road. It was a Kansas paper, no doubt with a vested interest in persuading gold seekers to use their trail. There were such phrases as "closer to Denver by 200 miles" and "the safest and fastest way to Pikes Peak."

"Look, Sam, this doesn't have anything to do with us."

"Yes, it does. That's the Smoky Hill they're talkin' about. Our Uncle Gabe helped Fremont lay out that trail."

Lem didn't remember Uncle Gabe very well. Once or
twice, when the boys were small, he'd show up for a few
days and then be gone again. Their mother never said
much, but there was unmistakable disapproval in her
tight-lipped silence. Gabe talked loud and rough, ate with
poor manners, and smelled of rancid grease and the smoke
of a thousand campfires. He had endless tales of exploration
parties, buffalo, winter in the mountains, Indian fights, and
clear blue skies. Sam had been fascinated by the mountain
man's stories. Once, when Sam was seven, he had tried to
follow Uncle Gabe. He'd been dragged home. The last time
they'd seen Uncle Gabe was years ago, before their father
died. He'd been restless and uneasy and stayed only
briefly. One morning, he was gone.

"But, Sam— "

"Don't you see, we know the trail they're taking, because
Uncle Gabe told us about it."

Lem thought that was a pretty flimsy connection. He
didn't remember very much that was specific about Gabe's
stories, except that they were tall tales. Maybe Sam
remembered more about Uncle Gabe's mountain-man stories than he did.

"Sam, I still don't think . . . . my God, man, you have a
family."

"Yes, Lem, it's for them I'm doin' it."

His brother was serious, sincere.

"Lem, I know I've done some dumb things, but this is
our big chance. One season, and we can give 'em everything. Ed Bolliver says so, too."

"Bolliver's goin'?"

That might be another story, thought Lem. Ed Bolliver
was a young man he'd always looked up to. Sam's age, Ed
had taken over his father's harness shop and was considered
one of the most stable young men in the area.

"Sure, Lem, we want you to go, too. Listen, you could
have enough money that Emily'd marry you in a minute!"

Maybe that was what started to change Lem's mind.

Changing the mind of their mother was another matter.

"It is out of the question!" Rachel Booth almost shouted. "I forbid it!"

"She'll come around," Sam whispered confidently.

Lemuel had his doubts. This time, maybe Sam had pushed it too far. He had always seemed to know the exact limits of their mother's patience and could wheedle her into almost anything. What Sam couldn't persuade, he'd do, anyway, and then shamelessly butter her up, expecting forgiveness as a matter of course. It had always bothered Lemuel considerably, the flagrant manner in which his brother managed to push his luck almost to the edge. However, it seemed that Samuel had miscalculated the depth of their mother's resolve in this matter. Lem gave it up as a bad job and turned his attention back to farming.

It was with a great deal of surprise, then, that Lemuel heard his mother broach the subject of the gold fields again. The two of them were at supper, and Lem, hungry from his day's work, was manfully stowing prodigious quantities of fried potatoes. He'd finish, he was thinking, maybe clean up a little, and walk over to the Clarkes' to see Emily.

He noticed his mother's stern glance and slowed his eating a little. She was always at him not to eat so fast. "Your food won't nourish," she'd say, "unless you chew it well." So, he slowed. But that apparently wasn't it. His mother continued to stare at him disapprovingly. Lemuel racked his brain to remember any infraction of which he might be guilty. None came to mind.

"I'll finish plantin' the south field tomorrow," he offered, hoping to establish some sort of conversation. "Reckon we'll try oats in the seven-acre patch again."

Still there was no answer. Lem was about to ask point-blank, when his mother gave a great sigh.

"Lemuel," she began seriously, "if you boys went on that gold strike, how long would you figure to be gone?"

So that was it! Lem had all but forgotten Sam's scheme.

Apparently, Sam hadn't. Likely he'd been working quietly on their mother all along.

"I . . . I don't know, Mother," he stammered, caught completely off guard. "What did Sam say?"

Rachel ignored the fact that she knew more of Sam's plans than his brother did.

"Well," she mused, "the planting's mostly done. I suppose the neighbors can get the crops in, if you ain't back."

He knew he ought to be talking *against* such idiocy, but Sam and Ed Bolliver had painted a mighty attractive picture. Apparently, it had been attractive to Rachel Booth, too, he speculated. He looked at his mother in a new light. She was stolid, unemotional except to chastise, and had always seemed to frown on anything that smacked of fun or enjoyment. Could it be that she too had been caught up in the excitement of gold? Was there a spark of adventure behind the thin-lipped frown and the severely pulled-back hair? He felt sorry for his mother, more than ever before. It must have been difficult for her, raising a family alone, even though the older ones were grown enough to help. Lem had thought of the death of his father primarily in terms of his own loss. Now he saw his mother's bereavement and pitied her.

"Mother, I . . ."

He paused, unsure what it was he wanted to say. He brushed the hair back from his forehead nervously. He wished he knew more about what Sam and Ed Bolliver had talked of, and what Sam had told their mother. Now she had more information than he, Lemuel, did. He felt at a disadvantage to enter this discussion.

"Lemuel," his mother was saying, "I can manage."

She said it severely, disapprovingly, with an accusing sigh of resignation. Even if she *wanted* them to go, he realized, she'd make them feel guilty about it if she could. For the first time, he understood that this was her way of trying to maintain control over her sons. Lem resented it a little, the more so because he'd never understood this before. Sam had figured it out and had left home to escape the never-ending guilt. For a moment, Lem hated them both for using him this way.

But now that he understood how the game worked, he could play, too. Yes, he figured now, she *wants* us to go but is going to make us feel bad if she can. Then if anything good happened, she could share; but if it turned out bad, she could still say "I told you so."

"Mother," he said firmly, "I'm goin'."

Rachel was still haranguing him when he finished his plate, mopped up the grease with a piece of bread, and rose from the table, still chewing. Inwardly, he was smiling. He'd guessed right. So *this* was how Sam handled her. He stopped at the door and looked back a moment.

"I'm goin' over to see Emily," he announced, and turned again into the twilight of evening.

Behind him, the harangue continued, including dire predictions about catching his death if he didn't wear a hat, out in the night air. He smiled grimly to himself. He felt free, unfettered. Yes, by God, he *would* go west.

≈ 15 ≈

Lem didn't know quite what sort of reaction to expect from Emily when he told her about the plan. He visited with her folks for a little while, patted her younger brothers and sisters on their heads, and tried to be polite. He was always a little uncomfortable about this part of the evening. It was better when he and Emily were alone. Not that the Clarkes weren't nice folks and all that. It was just the way they peered at him without saying much, tight-lipped, like maybe they suspected his intentions toward their daughter a little.

Of course, he knew they approved of him in general.
Emily had told him how they spoke of him as one of the
hardest-working young farmers around. They were ready to
accept him as a son-in-law, probably, if Emily would come
around. She just seemed to enjoy things the way they were,
teasing him and flirting with the other boys when occasion
offered.

It seemed a long time before Emily jumped to her feet
and held out a hand to him.

"Come on, Lemuel, let's go for a walk," she exclaimed, as
if she'd just thought of it.

It was sort of a ritual, the conversation that drifted along
uncomfortably until Emily decided it was time. It was
always the same.

He rose and took her hand, and they moved through the
doorway out into the warm spring night. Spring peepers
were trilling out in the meadow, and there were exciting
smells of growing and blooming things. Lem thought he
heard the call of wild geese, moving northward high and
fast, somewhere in the distant sky. Emily snuggled up to
him as they walked, falling in step so that her hip and thigh
moved against his at every stride. He liked the way she
moved, and it was always exciting when she rubbed against
him as she was doing now. They'd never "gone all the way,"
but he figured the time would come. Maybe tonight. He
felt the excitement of the thought. But, he told himself,
they needed to talk first. He needed to tell her all about the
great adventure he was ready to begin.

"Shall we go down by the creek?" she asked suggestively.

There was a little meadow there, hardly more than a
clearing, where the grass grew thick and soft, and they
could listen to the murmur of the water. They had come to
think of it as their special place.

"Sure," he said, his voice tight with emotion. "We need
to talk."

Emily looked at him with surprise but said nothing. They
parted the willows and stepped into the seclusion of their

meadow. The girl led the way to the fallen tree where they liked to sit. She sat down and patted a spot beside her on the big trunk. Lemuel joined her and put his arm around her waist.

She lifted her face to his. "Kiss me!" she demanded.

Lem complied. The kiss was soft and warm and exciting, and he hated for it to end, but he finally pulled away.

"Wait, Emily, I need to tell you something."

They were both breathing hard, and he was afraid that if he didn't get the talking done, he'd forget it in the excitement of the night. The girl sat upright and looked at him curiously in the dim light.

"I'm goin' west," he blurted.

"You're *what?*"

"I'm goin' west, to the gold fields."

"You're joking, Lemuel."

"Nope. Me and Sam and Ed Bolliver. We'll spend a season and find enough gold to make us rich."

Emily laughed, a little nervously, he thought.

"Well, that's nice," she said tentatively. "Does your mother know?"

He might have weakened, up to that point, if the girl had asked him. But now his resolve stiffened.

"I told her tonight," he said firmly.

"And she'll let you go?"

Anger flared in him for a moment. "I'm grown!" he said roughly. "I don't have to answer to anyone."

Emily sighed and shrugged. "Well," she stated coquettishly, "I'm not sure I can wait for you, Lem. Karl Grubb asked to take me to the box supper at the church next week."

He knew she was teasing him, trying to make him jealous. Well, she was succeeding. He knew full well that Emily would never be caught dead in public with Karl Grubb. Well, he didn't think so, anyway. And it wasn't fair for her to rile him this way, when he was trying to have the most serious talk of their lives.

He didn't know what to say, so he pulled her to him and kissed her again, firmly. She responded eagerly, and almost at once his irritation vanished. They slid from the log together onto the soft grass.

"Careful," Emily whispered breathlessly, "let's not get grass stains on my skirt."

In the process of moving from the log to the ground, her skirts had managed to slide above her knees. Lem could see, in the dim starlight, lovely rounded thighs. The girl pressed eagerly toward him, her warm mouth searching for his, her hips thrusting toward him.

"Oh, Lem," she panted, "let's go ahead. I don't think I can wait."

Lemuel paused a moment. Those were the same, the exact same words she had used a few minutes ago, when she was trying to make him jealous of Karl Grubb. Something was wrong with their whole relationship. Not their attraction for each other. The pure animal lust was driving them together. Her efforts to goad him into jealousy had only temporarily slowed his passion. Even the distraction about grass stains was quite temporary, but somehow her words had interrupted his animal drive. This should be the most important thing in the world to her, and she had used the same words. Was she trying to use this to hold him? Did she *want* to get with child, so she'd have a hold on him?

His physical urges told him to go ahead, she wants it. But now suspicion was aroused. He felt a little like he had when he realized that his mother was using guilt to control him. Emily was trying to use her body to do the same thing. At least, he thought so. He was confused now, and with the confusion vanished the last vestige of physical desire for her. He might take her sometime, probably would, but not now. Maybe when he got back from Kansas, if she'd managed to wait for him. He rolled over and sat up, still breathing heavily.

"What's the matter, Lem?" she murmured. "Come back to me!"

"No," he said firmly. "I guess you'll just have to see if you can wait. And put your dress down!"

Furious, she jumped to her feet, her skirt swirling around shapely legs as it fell. She slapped him hard.

"You bastard!" she hissed at him. "I'll tell my father you tried to rape me! He'll shoot you!"

Ordinarily, that would have caused Lemuel a certain amount of anxiety, but not tonight. He was tired of people trying to manipulate him, use him for their own ends. He felt good, that he had seen through Emily's little scheme, though he'd come awfully close. Damn, what if he'd had to marry the conniving wench? His confidence was high, and he felt invincible.

"All right," he snapped, "let's go ask him!"

He didn't really intend it as a bluff. It was just that he was so certain that he was in the right.

Emily's eyes fell, and she began to cry. "I'm sorry, Lem. I wouldn't do that to you. I'll wait for you, as long as it takes."

She dissolved into his arms, still crying. He held her, comforting her, but something had changed between them. Where before, he had worried about whether she'd wait for him, now he didn't care much. He'd almost rather she didn't.

He dropped her off at her door and started home. There was a sense of freedom tonight. He could hardly wait to talk to Sam and Ed, to see when they could start.

How strange, he thought. In trying to hold him, Emily had freed him, removed the last fetter that held him from going.

On an impulse, he passed on by their farmstead. A light burned in the kitchen, and he wondered if his mother was still up. Without pausing in his stride, Lem headed on toward town and the house of his brother Samuel.

≈ 16 ≈

It was raining as the three men moved along the road that was little more than a trail. Not a hard rain, just a steady drizzle that kept them uncomfortable and damp. Their oilskin slickers, designed for rain, left much to be desired on such a waterlogged day. They had considered stopping to camp but rejected the idea. There was no shelter available, unless they stopped in someone's barn, and those who lived along the road were understandably suspicious of strangers.

So they kept moving. Sam Booth and Ed Bolliver were in the lead, followed by Lemuel and the pack mule. It bothered Lem slightly that the others had assumed that the responsibility of the mule would be his. He had to admit, it did make sense, though. He was the most experienced in the use of mules, and he had chosen old Dick, one of his farm team, to fill the function of pack animal. Dick balked a little to begin with, at the unaccustomed burden of a pack saddle, but finally became resigned to the new occupation. Just now, the mule plodded along the muddy road, ears drooping, with tiny droplets of water falling from their sagging tips. Occasionally, the animal inhaled deeply and gave a great sigh. Lemuel felt the same way.

He wondered how their supplies were faring under the canvas tarpaulin. Their bedding could be dried, but it would be difficult to salvage wet flour or beans. The beans, he supposed, would either mold or sprout if they got wet. There was no point in stopping to check the load. Even unfastening the tarp to look would allow more water to enter the packs.

Sam had taken on himself the selection of provisions from the store. He'd done a good job, Lem had to admit. The best of staple goods—bacon, flour, salt, and dry beans. They'd make it to Denver all right, even without the game they hoped to shoot on the way.

Bolliver's main contribution had been the pack saddle, the sawbuck design with some innovations of Ed's own. It had proved quite useful, easy to pack with the extra fittings and hooks to hitch the lash ropes.

They were proud of their outfit, confident, and excited as they started west. If there was anything that was in short supply, it was probably ready cash. But, they reasoned, there would be little to spend for. They were heading into a country famed for its game and probably self-sustaining. Then as soon as they reached Denver, they would have all the gold they needed.

They hadn't shot any game yet but, of course, hadn't really left civilization. They had two guns among them for when the time came. Bolliver carried one of Colt's new .31 caliber pocket revolvers, which he'd taken in trade at the harness shop. It was a marvelous piece of mechanical cleverness and could throw six balls as fast as a man could cock and pull the trigger. The Booth brothers had their father's smoothbore musket, which could be loaded either with a single ball or a scatter of smaller shot. So far, Sam had taken charge of the musket.

The trip had actually gone quite well. They paid out some of their precious dollars to ferry across the Mississippi at St. Louis. After that, the road led almost straight west, roughly paralleling the Missouri. They'd forded the Gasconade River, and the Osage, and moved on. The road was well traveled, and there seemed to be quite a few travelers heading west. They'd overtake a slower party sometimes, only to be passed in turn by somebody on horseback or with a fast team. They'd paused at one rest stop to visit with a grizzled old frontiersman in buckskins, who squatted on his heels over a little fire. He'd brewed a can of tea and was cupping his hands around its warmth as he sipped and watched the travelers pass on the road.

Mangum, he'd said his name was, in answer to their query. He didn't say whether that was his first or last name, and they didn't ask. They'd heard it was impolite to be too inquisitive out here. Had he been to the mountains?

"Shore. Lots o' times. Is thet whar you boys are a-goin'?"

"Yes, sir. Can you tell us about the trail?"

"Wal," Mangum said, pausing to take a long pull at his pipe, "depends whar you're headin' fer."

"The gold fields!" Sam stated proudly.

The old man chuckled. "Figgered so. Hope you know what yer doin'."

Sam looked a little irritated. "Reckon we do. Can you tell us the best trail?"

"Ain't much trail, son," Mangum said sympathetically. "I guess you jest foller the crowd."

Lemuel tried another approach. "What's up ahead, sir? Westport?"

The man in buckskins studied Lem for a moment. "Yep. What you'll see, though, is a new town goin' up around the landin'. City of Kansas, they're callin' it."

"We head west there?"

"You kin. Most cross the Kaw and jump off from Leavenworth or Atchison. You could go by St. Joe, but you'd have to cross the Missouri twicet. Crossin' the Kaw's easier. There's a ferry."

"Are you heading west, too, sir?" Bolliver asked.

The implications in the questions were plain, and the old man backed off. "Mebbe," he said cautiously, "when I get ready."

"How far to Westport?" Lem asked.

"Two sleeps, mebbe, on foot."

They'd noticed a leggy mule grazing, still saddled, behind Mangum's little camp.

"Maybe we'll see you again," Lemuel offered.

The old man took a long time answering. It was clear that he took a dim view of gold seekers.

"Mebbe," he said reluctantly.

That was yesterday. They'd awakened this morning with the drizzle of rain in their faces, and it had continued ever since. They'd encountered no other travelers. Anybody with sense, Lem suspected, would be holed up somewhere out of the rain.

The drizzle let up just before dark, and they made a campfire that helped dry damp clothing and raise their spirits a little. Other travelers were camped in the area, and they took turns standing watch with the old musket.

The old frontiersman had been correct in his description of the activity around the area where the Kansas River entered the Missouri. The sounds of saws and hammers reverberated along the riverfront, and the smell of fresh-sawed wood hung in the air. Barges loaded with lumber were lined along the bank, being unloaded by a small army of stevedores.

They inquired as to a ferry across the Kansas and were pointed to a wharf where a flatboat plied its way back and forth across the river. There was a waiting line of travelers as the boat pulled in on the south shore. People scuttled aboard, shoving and pushing.

"Sorry, boys, I cain't handle no more this trip," the boatman said as they prepared to board. "Get you next trip."

They waited on the dock, fidgeting impatiently, while the ferry moved slowly across, unloaded, and made its way back with only a handful of passengers.

"Now, then," the boatman exclaimed as the last man stepped to shore, "hop on board. Dollar a man, three for the mule."

"Six dollars?" Lem gasped. "Why, in St. Louis—"

"Sonny, you ain't *in* St. Louis," the boatman said, laughing. "Take it or leave it! Who's next?"

"Come *on*, Lem!" Bolliver insisted. "We don't want to wait for the next run."

They pulled and shoved the reluctant Dick on board while Sam paid out a five-dollar gold piece and a silver cartwheel from their dwindling supply. The crossing was uneventful, though the mule rolled white-rimmed eyes in doubt. The larger ferry at St. Louis had seemed much more stable.

On the other shore, they paused to reconnoiter. There was expansion activity going on here, too.

"What now? Which way?" Bolliver asked.

"I dunno," Sam mumbled. "Guess we ask somebody."

They talked it over. It would not be seemly, they agreed, to simply ask the way to the gold fields. They'd inquire about the road to Leavenworth.

The first man they encountered wore a town suit and a derby hat. He looked them over a moment and then smiled. "Headin' for the gold fields, eh?"

"Well, yes," Sam admitted sheepishly.

"Tell you what, boys, you're sure right to start out from Leavenworth. Shortest way, good wood, water, plenty of game. Yep, right way to go."

"Yes, sir, how do we get to Leavenworth?"

"Just follow this road. Can't miss it. But"—his expression became confidential— "what about beyond Leavenworth?"

"Well, we thought we'd ask— "

"Wouldn't do that," the man said with a worried frown. "So few people can be trusted." Suddenly his face lighted. "I've an idea!"

He fumbled in his side coat pocket and came forth with a slender book. "Here," he said, holding it out for their inspection. "You need something like this. This is my personal copy."

"*Guide Book to the Smoky Hill Road,*" Sam read the title aloud. "Where could we get one?"

"Well, I don't know," the man mused. "But look here"— he flipped the book open, pointing quickly to maps and descriptive paragraphs—"see, here's the fork where the Republican and the Smoky Hill join to form the Kansas River. Then the Smoky runs nearly straight west, almost to Denver."

"Then we can just follow the river," Ed observed.

"Sure, but which fork? Look, you take a wrong turn here, get on the Solomon or the Saline by mistake, you wind up in Nebraska in the Badlands. It'd be easy from the *west* end, but you got to know every fork headin' from here! Unless, of course, you've been there," he said.

"No sir," Sam admitted, "we ain't. What we need is such a book."

"Now that's a problem, boys," the man said, frowning. "These are getting pretty scarce. Don't know when I've seen one for sale. Big demand, you know. You can look this one over, though."

"No, we'd ought to have one to carry," Sam pursued. "Maybe we can find one in Leavenworth."

"Don't think so," the man in the derby said, frowning again. "Tell you what. I like you boys. I'll sell you my own copy. You need it more than I do. It cost me five dollars, but you can have it for three, just so I can help you out."

Sam was already reaching for their money pouch.

Before they reached Leavenworth, they had four more opportunities to buy guidebooks, priced at a dollar or two. It did not help their spirits to note that two of the books were identical to the one in Sam's pocket.

≈ 17 ≈

Leavenworth was bustling with activity. There were the
expected ever-present blue uniforms from the fort north of
town. The dirt streets were clogged with freight wagons,
farm wagons, carts, soldiers on foot and on horseback. It
was apparent, however, that a major portion of the hustle
and bustle was provided by the influence of the gold
seekers. Outfitters, liveries, wagon yards, and general-
merchandise stores seethed with activity. A constant stream
of customers trickled in and out of their doors like ants
systematically looting the remains of some discarded food-
stuff.

The three young men easily spotted the way out of town.
The road led west, and every little while, by ones and twos
and small groups, people were setting out. There were
people on foot, on horseback, and in vehicles of all sorts.

"My Lord!" Ed Bolliver exclaimed. "Look at 'em! We
better get started."

The others nodded. They had already checked and
repacked their supplies, and the mule was waiting at the
hitch rail in front of the general store while they took a look
around.

"Yep, we better go," Sam agreed.

They turned to cross the street and had to jump back to
safety to avoid the rush of a buggy. The driver fought his
horse to a standstill and looked over at the three on the
board sidewalk. Even with the amazing assortment of
vehicles that milled through the streets, this rig seemed out
of place. It was a single-seat buggy, new and shiny, bright

paint gleaming in the sun. The horse was well suited to the expensive rig. It was a shiny black high-tailed strutter, head held at a proud angle by a severe checkrein. Even the harness itself was expensive-looking, shiny, with polished brass studs and decorations. Ed Bolliver, the harness-maker, whistled in admiration.

If the rig seemed out of place on the bustling street that was the gate to the frontier, the driver was even more so. He was a soft-looking, portly man of middle age, dressed in a dark business suit, topped with a bowler hat. He shifted his long cigar to the other corner of his mouth. He did not even apologize for the near-accident.

"Which way to the gold fields?" he asked.

The young men were so completely astonished that no one answered for a moment. Finally, Sam raised a hand and pointed, still wordlessly, down the street in the general direction.

"Thanks." The pudgy man nodded, flipped the reins, and clucked to the spirited gelding to rush on down the street and out of sight.

"Is *he* going to the gold fields?" Lem wondered aloud.

"I dunno," Ed said. "Boys, he don't even have any blankets."

"Or supplies," Sam added. "Reckon he'll buy along the way?"

"But can he do that?" Lem questioned. "I thought the Smoky was unsettled."

Still puzzled, they recovered the mule and hurried to join the current of humanity that was flowing steadily west. The road, such as it was, was said to follow the course of the Kaw River. For the first day of travel, however, they did not even see the river. Then it appeared well to the south. The road continued in a fairly straight direction, while the river meandered away to the south for a few miles at times. At other times, their path lay almost along the river's north bank. They passed several little settlements, raw and new-looking against the green of the new land. Corn fields drew the admiration of Lemuel, while the others reacted more toward the businesses and stores.

"This sure is settlin' fast, ain't it?" Sam noted. "Mebbe thet feller in the buggy knew what he was doin'."

From time to time, they walked for a little way with other travelers, exchanging comments on the weather, the gold strike, and the road.

"See that town acrost the river there?" one talkative individual said, pointing. "Them Slave-staters tried to burn it, year or so back."

"Why? What do you mean?" Ed asked.

Their informant looked them over as if they were totally ignorant. "'Cause it's a Free-state town! That's Lawrence, the capital."

Lemuel wondered the capital of what, but hesitated to ask, since their companion had already expressed such disdain.

"Only," the man continued, "they're movin' it."

"The town?"

"Hell, no, the capital. Down the river to Topeka. You'll pass it tomorrow."

They walked a little way, and the other traveler seemed to relent a little. "You boys ain't from around here, are you?"

"Nope. Illinois," Sam volunteered.

"I see." The man nodded. "Well, you'd not know about it, then."

They walked in silence until finally Ed Bolliver could stand it no longer. "What about it?"

"Well, we're tryin' to get in as a state. It'll go free or slave by vote of them livin' here. So both sides are tryin' to run the others out."

He paused and studied them a moment. "Say, you ain't slavers, are you?"

"No," Sam said, "hadn't thought much about it."

"Tell you what, you'd ought to settle here somewheres,

then. The territory's openin' up and could use some good men like yourselves."

"We're just passin' through," Sam told him. "Goin' to Denver."

"I figgered you for gold hunters," the man said. "Well, to each his own."

His tone was obviously disapproving. The silence grew a bit embarrassing.

"You live around here?" Sam finally asked.

"Yep. Over by Topeka—well, I'm goin' to. Lookin' for a place."

Once the man had determined that he had nothing much in common with them, he seemed to lose interest in conversation. When they paused for a rest stop, he continued on down the road. Lem had the odd feeling that the other traveler's main interest in talking to them had been to try to recruit Free-state votes.

Topeka sprawled on the other side of the river, in a rolling flat that stretched toward a prominent flat-topped hill a couple of miles to the south. A fork of the road headed down to the river, where a ferry waited.

"What do you s'pose *he* charges?" Ed asked.

The three chuckled but very quietly. It was not really much of a joke, and they were glad they did not have to pay for the passage.

They moved on westward before stopping to camp for the night a few miles farther down the trail. Sam took out the guidebook, and they studied it by the light of the campfire.

"How far you reckon we've come?" Lem asked.

"Oh, fifty miles, mebbe." Sam's answer was authoritative. "Not bad for four days."

"Well, three and a half," Ed pointed out. "That first day we didn't leave Leavenworth till after noon."

They nodded together, pleased. They figured and refigured their rate of progress. Actually, so far, it had been little different from their travel across Missouri, but it

seemed different, more adventurous, since they left the
military protection of Fort Leavenworth.

"Reckon we're makin' fifteen miles a day," Bolliver said,
and grinned.

"Yep. We'll hit our stride purty quick," Sam said.

Lemuel was a little more reserved in his evaluation.

"How far from Leavenworth to Denver?" he asked.

Sam flipped pages and glanced at maps for a moment.
"Don't say, exactly. I don't reckon anybody knows, Lem.
The whole trip hasn't been staked out, more'n likely. I'd say
six hunnerd miles."

Well, so far it hadn't been too bad, Lem had to agree.
Pretty pleasant travel. If they'd traveled fifty miles so far,
then tomorrow, their fifth day, they'd be a tenth of the way.
Lem figured a little in his head. That would mean maybe
fifty days from Leavenworth to Denver. Say sixty, to allow
plenty of time. Two months. It was now late May, and
they'd be in Denver by the end of July. That would give
them plenty of time to stake a claim and start to gather the
gold. He wondered how to do it. They'd brought a pick and
shovel but didn't have much of an idea beyond that. Maybe
they'd watch somebody doin' it or ask around.

Lem was dozing off to sleep when he was roused by
footsteps. He raised to an elbow to look into the darkness
while he listened. A horse or mule, it sounded like, not
trying to keep quiet or anything. Their own mule, Dick,
snuffled a low greeting to the incoming animal.

"Hallo, the camp," someone called, "I'm comin' in."

Ed Bolliver had thrown sticks on the dying coals of the
fire, and their growing light now pushed back the circling
shadows. A lanky figure strode into the light, leading his
mule.

"Howdy," the newcomer said, "room for another'n?" It
was Mangum, the frontiersman.

"Sure," Sam answered.

"Oh, it's you boys. Made it this far, did ye?"

He was stripping saddle and gear from the mule as he

talked. "Don't like to move in on anybody's camp like this, but this here's where I allus stop. Best water along this stretch." He pointed to the stream. "Usually more folks here than this."

"Are you goin' to Denver, Mr. Mangum?" Ed Bolliver asked.

"Oh, mebbe so. Ain't decided yet."

He spread his blankets and sat cross-legged.

"Well, now, how do you like the travelin' by now?" he asked, chuckling.

"It's all right," Sam said. "We're makin' fifteen miles a day."

"Yep," agreed Mangum. "An' it's good road an' good weather."

"What do you mean?"

"Well, it ain't allus goin' to be, you know. Farther out, there *ain't* no road. There's heat, an' sand, an' water's scarce—an' Injuns, mebbe."

"But," Sam protested, "this guidebook says there's wood and water."

"Oh." Mangum chuckled again. "You got one of them! Look, son, the feller what wrote that prob'ly ain't never *been* there. Some of 'em even start you out this way, an' then route you south t'ward Santa Fee, and back north from Fort Lyon."

He shook his head and chuckled sadly.

"Then where is the Smoky Hill Road?" Bolliver asked.

"Son, there *ain't* any Smoky Hill Road. You got to know what you're doin'—know yer trail."

He suddenly rolled in his blankets and turned his back to the fire. The conversation seemed at an end, but he spoke once more over his shoulder.

"Straight out the Smoky's best. It's the most dangerous, too."

Within seconds, he was snoring.

When they awoke at dawn, Mangum was gone.

≈ 18 ≈

West of Topeka, the country became more open. There were trees only along the watercourses, and most of the landscape consisted of grassy plains. It was not flatland, as the travelers had expected, but low rolling hills, stretching into the distance to the horizon. The distant ridges became more bluish in shade, until the farthest were almost indistinguishable from the blue of the sky beyond.

"Gawd, it's big, ain't it?" Lem gasped in awe as they stopped to stare. "I never seen so much grass."

The vastness of the prairie was a bit overwhelming. Distances became deceptive, as they could see clearly farther than they could travel in a day. There were fewer settlements, too, and a sense of isolation began to bother them. Other travelers apparently felt it, too. It was comforting, now, to encounter others and travel together. It was not so much protection against the hazards of the trail, as mutual support against the unknown dangers of this big empty land.

The stark reality of their endeavor was brought to attention one morning by an object beside the trail a half-mile ahead. At first, they could not identify it; but as they drew nearer, the familiar lines became apparent. A buggy, lying crippled at a crazy angle, a shattered wheel twisted underneath the chassis. Another wheel, still intact, turned slowly, the sun's rays shining on bright new paint. There was no sign of life.

"Say, ain't that . . . ?" Bolliver began.

"The one from Leavenworth," Sam finished.

They walked around the wreck but could make no explanation. It appeared that the vehicle had broken down and had been abandoned by the driver. They could not imagine the pudgy man in the dark suit riding for help on the fiery horse they had seen.

Had even more bad luck befallen him? Had someone stolen the horse and harness and killed him? Were Indians part of the mystery? They cast apprehensive glances around the landscape but were never able to fathom what sort of tragedy had actually occurred. It was a sobering experience.

At Fort Riley, a new military post beyond a settlement called Manhattan City, they joined with several other travelers, making a band of fifteen men with three pack mules. There was a strength, a spirit of camaraderie in this venture that made everyone more cheerful and confident. At the fort, there had been disturbing stories of Indians, deserts, and wild animals. It had been impossible to determine how much had been tall tales on the part of the troopers, but there seemed security in numbers.

Within three days, however, they were quarreling. They had no organization, hence no leadership. Some of the party wished to travel faster, some slower. When they came to a river they believed to be the Saline, the entire situation came to a climax. Camped at the fork of the rivers, they argued far into the night. There were two maps in the party, and they disagreed in some details.

It was plain to see, however, that the Smoky Hill River, if they followed it, would take them straight south. They could discern no turning of its course as far as the eye could see. On the other hand, the river that joined it at this point entered from the northwest. Whatever its name, it seemed questionable that its direction was correct. Sam's guidebook appeared to trace the trail straight west, to arrive at the Smoky Hill River again in a day or two. There was indeed a suggestion of a traveled path that headed west.

One faction of the party, led by a burly German named

Van Zont, advocated staying with the Smoky even if it was farther.

"Ve know vere id goes!" he kept insisting.

"Now look, Dutchie," Smith said, a quarrelsome individual whose background seemed rather vague, "we ain't follerin' the damn river all over the territory on your say-so."

Several of the others nodded agreement.

The other guidebook in the party belonged to a quiet capable-appearing man from St. Louis whose name was Charles Monroe. He had early assumed the role of peacemaker.

"Look," Monroe had said, "we don't *have* to stay together. Anybody who wants can pick his own trail."

That had quieted things for a time. Nobody relished the idea of being on his own.

Monroe's guidebook indicated the trail bending southwest from the river junction where they believed themselves to be camped. It would rejoin the river ahead. There was a further suggestion that though longer, a safer route from that point on might be to drop south to strike the Santa Fe Trail at the Great Bend of the Arkansas. Smith and a few of his followers advocated that course. Furthermore, Smith argued, somebody had to be in charge. They should elect a captain and abide by his decisions.

That seemed a reasonable approach, and the election was held immediately around the fire. Smith was nominated by one of his cronies, and there were no other immediate suggestions.

"Well." Smith grinned. "If there ain't any others, I—"

"I'll nominate Charles Monroe," said Lemuel in desperation.

He had some inkling what a tyrant Smith might become. There were several nods of agreement, but Smith's dark stare of hate fixed on the Booths.

The sullen looks darkened even more when Monroe was elected captain by a vote of nine to six.

"All right," the new captain said modestly, "I didn't ask for it, but I'll do my best. Now, let's get some sleep. In the morning, we'll head across country to strike the river ahead. When we get there, we'll hold another council and vote whether to go on or go south to the Santa Fe Trail."

There was some grumbling from Smith's faction, but all turned in feeling that at least something had been accomplished.

Two days later, Monroe's guidebook was vindicated when they did indeed cross the high ground to strike the river again. They managed to kill a buffalo, and the camp that night was almost one of merrymaking. They were so intent on the success of their decision that they feasted and turned in for sleep without discussing the next step. Smith volunteered to stand watch, in an openhearted gesture to show he was willing to let bygones be bygones. Lem fell asleep with more confidence than he'd had for some time.

A shout roused him just before dawn. Van Zont had awakened and gone outside the camp to urinate and noticed that the mules were gone.

"Ya, undt dot Schmidt and der others!" he was pointing out.

By the increasing light of the coming day, it became apparent that Smith and his followers were all missing, six in all. Also gone were not only the Smith party's mule, but Lemuel's and the one belonging to Monroe. Various other items were missed, and the frustrated party realized that the whole thing had been planned in detail.

"By God, let's go after 'em!" Sam Booth said, sputtering.

"Well, I don't know, boys." Monroe pondered. "I've a hunch those are dangerous men. Did you notice they all carried guns?"

"Hey!" Bolliver yelled. "My Colt! It's gone!"

"How many guns do we have?" Monroe asked.

A quick count indicated only Sam Booth's old musket, a flintlock pistol, and one plains rifle among them.

"An' they've got at least seven," Monroe pointed out. "Maybe we best just shut up and take our lickin'."

It seemed the only reasonable approach, even if they could overcome the head start now enjoyed by Smith. If, of course, that was his name at all. It was assumed that the thieves had headed for the Great Bend, as Smith had argued before. They looked for footprints but without expertise were unable to identify their tracks.

The group agreed with Captain Monroe's suggestion that they pool their remaining supplies and divide them to backpack. Some of the tents and heavier equipment would have to be abandoned. Most of the morning was occupied in this effort. The sack of flour was most troublesome. Without smaller sacks, there was practically no way to divide the bulky, unwieldy load. They were still discussing the problem when a hail sounded, and a rider approached.

"Mangum!" Ed Bolliver exclaimed.

"Who's that?" Monroe inquired. "You know him?"

"Sure. Well, a little," Bolliver said. "He camped with us before."

"He reliable?"

"Yes, we thought so."

The frontiersman rode in, dismounted, and took everything in at a glance.

"Havin' troubles?"

"None we can't handle," Monroe answered, still not quite willing to trust the newcomer.

Mangum nodded and turned to Lemuel. "Lose your mule?"

"Yes, sir. Some of our party robbed us."

"Yep. It happens. You got enough supplies?"

The travelers nodded.

"Looks like that sack of flour's goin' to be a problem," he observed. "Tell you what. I'll pack it on my mule and travel with you a ways. Mebbe I can get a little meat for us from time to time. You're follerin' the river, ain't you?"

"Yes. Is that the best way?" Sam asked. "We think our thieves went south."

"To the Great Bend?"

"Yes," Monroe answered. "Is that a good route?"

"Shore, if you're goin' to Santa Fee. Hell of a way to get to Denver, though. Foller the river, I'd say."

Even with their losses, having someone in the party who had traveled the route before made everyone more confident. They were soon prepared to travel. The bulky flour sack was wrapped in a piece of canvas tarp and lashed behind Mangum's saddle.

"I'll walk a ways, I reckon," he said.

They had seen no signs of settlement since they left the Saline.

"Is there any settlement beyond here, sir?" asked Lemuel politely.

The old frontiersman's eyes twinkled. "Shore," he answered, "or did you mean other'n Injuns?"

Lemuel figured it would be just as well not to answer. He fell in step beside Mangum as they moved out.

"Mr. Mangum," he finally asked, "have you decided yet whether you're goin' to Denver or somewheres else?"

The man in buckskins studied him a little while with amusement. "Well," he said finally, "mebbe so, mebbe not. But we're goin' the same direction right now, anyhow."

≈ **19** ≈

They camped at the fork of the stream. It was not really time to stop and make camp yet, but a serious disagreement had arisen, their first since they were robbed.

"I tell you, this is the main streambed," Sam insisted.

"But, Sam, this fits Mangum's description," Monroe almost pleaded. "He warned us."

The assistance of the old frontiersman had been invaluable during the many days he had traveled with them. He had almost seemed to enjoy the opportunity to teach them the little tricks of survival on the prairie. He taught them how to dig an "Indian well" in the apparently dry bed of a stream to release the underground water for use in emergencies. They were long since adept at fire building with buffalo chips, but Mangum introduced them to the delicacy of buffalo-hump meat cooked directly in the glowing coals of a buffalo-chip fire.

"That lets it flavor its own self," he advised.

They had encountered some Indians, whom Mangum said were Cheyenne. He had conversed with them in sign-talk, and the Indians, though rude and arrogant, had nodded and departed.

"What did you say to them?" Lemuel asked.

"I jest told 'em we're passin' through, not stoppin'. They'd like some presents but kin see we ain't got much. I told 'em you was robbed before I found you. They allowed it was prob'ly whites, an' I told 'em shore, I wouldn't expect Cheyennes to bother somebody who's already got nothin'."

Mangum had become more talkative as he became better acquainted with the group.

"Could you teach me sign-talk?" asked the fascinated Lem.

"Shore. It ain't hard. A lot of it's jest common sense. Like 'eat'"—he pointed a finger in his mouth— "or 'talk,' comin' back out. This is a 'question' sign."

He went on, demonstrating "water," "man," "woman," and the variety of signs for names of different tribes. "White man" was indicated by touching the brow, to indicate a hat brim.

"You might see Comanche, Arapaho, Kiowa, Pawnee, mebbe even Sioux, out here. Most of 'em ain't bad to get along with. Didn't used to be, anyhow. They're sort of uneasy about all the whites comin' out so thick now."

They walked on a while before he spoke again.

"Tell you what, though. There's good ones and bad ones in every tribe, red or white. You got to watch out for the bad ones."

As they reached the shortgrass country of the high plains, Mangum had become restless. There seemed to be something about the land that affected him. When they stopped to camp for the night, he paced like a caged tiger, watching the far distances.

"Is something wrong?" Lem had asked him.

"No, son," the frontiersman had answered, "more like somethin' right, I guess. I'd forgot how I missed it."

Then came the night when he'd announced that he was leaving them. "You don't need me now," he had stated. "You ain't tenderfeet no more. Jest foller the river, take the south fork, an' when it peters out, go northwest acrost the high plain into Denver."

"Where will you go?" Monroe asked.

"Oh, I dunno. Down to Bent's, maybe, see what's goin' on. Fort Lyon, I guess they call it now. I jest got to be loose a while."

He showed them how to use the sleeves of a couple of extra shirts to carry their flour, instead of a single big sack. He tied each cuff with a thong, filled the two sleeves with flour, and tied again at the shoulder. Lem realized that Mangum could have shown them such a trick the first morning if he'd chosen to. Instead, he had traveled with them, assisting them without appearing to do so. He had helped Lemuel become reasonably adept with sign-talk, had helped them immeasurably, and had departed as suddenly as he had arrived, riding south across the open plain.

Now his advice was badly needed, and he was gone. There was no way to tell whether this was actually the fork of the Smoky Hill or not. They knew—from the maps, from

hearsay, and from Mangum's advice—that the Smoky consisted of two streams at its west end, the North and South
forks. Mangum had impressed on them that they must
follow the *South* Fork.

"The other'n don't go nowhere," he had pointed out, "jest
meanders up there and quits. You *might* make it, but
there's no water or game. Nope, you got to be sure you're
on the *South* Fork."

Now, they were unsure. There was a marked difference
of opinion about this spot, and whether this was actually the
fork of the Smoky or not. For the tenth time at least, they
walked the terrain and studied the lay of the land. The left
branch was comparatively dry, not large, and seemed
inconsequential compared to the other.

"Hell, we've passed a hundred gullies like that," Sam
insisted. "It ain't part of the river, it's just a little crick. This
here's our river."

He pointed to the other branch, where there was a fairly
good trickle of water connecting the deeper holes. A person
could make a good argument either way.

"All right," Monroe finally said, "we'll vote and follow
whichever way the vote goes."

There was a bit more discussion, and the captain called
for a show of hands.

"Those for this north branch, let's see 'em!"

Sam's hand shot up, along with Ed Bolliver's, Adams's,
and Simpson's. Four.

While Lemuel was still pondering, Monroe called for
those who favored the south branch. Those voting this time
were Monroe, two of his St. Louis men, and Van Zont. Lem
still sat, thinking.

"Well, Lem," Samuel snapped, "you got to vote one way
or the other."

Lemuel hated for the fate of the entire party to hinge on
his vote, either way. The responsibility was too big. He
wished that Mangum was still with them or that another

party would come along—or anything that would lessen his responsibility in this.

"Come on," his brother urged, "this ain't the fork we're lookin' for, Lem. It's goin' to fork proper on west a ways."

"Let him alone," Monroe insisted. "It's his vote."

Lemuel took a deep breath and pushed the hair back from his forehead.

"Well," he said finally, "I got to go with the captain. I say we go the South Fork."

"What?" Sam yelled at him. "You goddamn fool! Look at it! That ain't no river to follow!"

The party erupted in a storm of argument.

Finally, Monroe yelled for silence. "Look, boys, we've agreed to vote, and we've voted. Now let's get some rest."

He rose to walk over and ready his blanket for sleep.

They posted guards for the night watch, and the camp settled down to an uncomfortable quiet. No one felt right about the way things had gone. The group had been together long enough to have a certain amount of pride. They had had disagreements, but these had been minor. All in all, the travelers had developed a feeling of respect and affection for one another. They were like a large family, with the expected arguments and petty quarrels but ready to fight against any outside threat. This split was different. It had ripped the fabric of the party into two disunited portions. Not only had it divided the larger group, but had alienated the actual blood relationship of the Booth brothers. Everyone felt it as they settled down for the night.

Perhaps Lemuel felt it most of all. Sometimes he had become so depressed over the entire venture that his only wish was to go home. His goal had become not wealth, but merely to get to Denver and spend enough time on Cherry Creek to raise a little money to go home. He thought of Emily's soft embrace, the feel of her body, its urgency as she pressed against him. How had he ever gotten into this mad scheme?

He lay, sleepless, and watched the Big Dipper wheel slowly around the North Star. It might have been a beautiful night, if the circumstances were different, but there was the all-pervading gloom. *Damn this country*, he thought. *It makes a man crazy, while it sucks the life out of him*. At times, he had thought it the most beautiful country he'd ever seen, this spectacular grassland. Now, he was bitter. The land seemed brooding, treacherous. It had lured the travelers out into its endless vistas, only to divide and destroy them.

He stopped with a shocked thought. He had, without realizing it, begun to think of this valley of the Smoky Hill as if it had a spirit of its own. He had just, in his thoughts, accused the country of *intent* to harm them, of plotting to destroy them, almost. It was as if he thought for a moment, there, that the river and its valley were a *person*—an evil, brooding soul bent on their destruction. Could he be going mad? he wondered.

Someone quietly shuffled near where he lay, and Lemuel tensed, then relaxed when he recognized his brother's silhouette against the sky.

"Lem!" Samuel whispered, "are you awake?"

"Yes."

"Lem, we've talked about it. We ain't goin' with Monroe and the others tomorrow. They're goin' the wrong way. We want you with us."

"But Sam, they're right. Mangum said—"

"To hell with Mangum. He left us. I figure he was mostly talk, anyhow."

"Sam, you're wrong about this."

"Like hell. We're goin' to Denver. Are you comin' or not?"

Lem didn't answer for a moment. His mind was whirling in confusion. He was convinced that this was the fork of the river that Mangum had described. But how much loyalty did he owe to his brother? Maybe Sam *was* right. And the old frontiersman had admitted that it was possible to reach the mountains by way of the North Fork of the Smoky.

"Sam," he said finally, "I just don't know. Let me think on it. I'll tell you in the morning."

≈ **20** ≈

The remainder of the night was restless for Lemuel. He tossed and turned in his blankets and fought sleep without knowing he did so. It was as if he was reluctant to let down his guard, so important was the dilemma he faced. When the gray of dawn began to pale the eastern sky, he was still awake, still in the anguish of indecision.

The others began to stir, and Lem rose, shook out his blankets, and rerolled them for travel. He still did not know what to do when the time came to take his stand.

By the time the sun had cleared the horizon, the travelers were lifting their packs and preparing to move. There was not much packing to do, because supplies were growing scarce. So was game, Lem reminded himself. They had seen no animal larger than a jackrabbit for several days, except for a distant coyote the day before. Nothing edible. If they took the wrong route, he realized, it could be pretty risky. Their survival might depend on it.

"Captain," Sam called.

"Yes. What is it?"

"Captain, we ain't goin' with you," Sam stated flatly.

Monroe flushed red above his collar, and a tiny muscle bunched along his jaw.

"And who is 'we'?"

"Me and Lem, Bolliver, Adams, Simpson."

Monroe turned and looked at each in turn.

"Anybody else?"

The others shook their heads.

"Well, you'll have to do as you see fit. We voted, but I can't force you to stay with the group."

"Appears to me *ours* is the group, Monroe. You go your way, we'll follow the river," Sam said arrogantly.

Lemuel, practically trembling with emotion, stood with sweating palms, watching and listening. His brother's arrogant assumption that Lem would follow him began to irritate. Lem's neck hairs started to prickle.

"Well, boys, I wish you all the luck in the world," Monroe said regretfully. "No hard feelings?"

He extended a hand, which Sam ignored. Monroe shrugged and turned away.

"Good luck, anyway."

"Thanks," Bolliver said. "You, too."

The two factions drew apart, disturbed at the turn of events but reluctant to part company. Lem had still said nothing.

"Sam," he finally blurted, "I'm goin' with the others. With Monroe and them."

Sam stared in disbelief. "You goddamn idiot! Why?"

"Because I think this is where Mangum warned us about. The North Fork looks good but ain't."

"Lemuel, I don't care. You can see this is the river. That's a dry wash, over there."

Lem shook his head. "I ain't goin' with you. I'm sorry, Sam."

"Go to hell, then," Sam snapped. "Come on, Ed, let's get started." He turned on his heel and strode away.

"Sam, I—" Lemuel called.

His brother did not turn.

"Ve see you in Denver," Van Zont said as Sam passed him.

"If you're lucky, Dutchie."

"Well, Booth, I hope we're right," Monroe said sympathetically. "It should be possible to get there either way."

Lemuel nodded, numb from the disturbing encounter.

He could not forget how definite had been the warning of Mangum. He watched his brother and the others grow smaller in the distance and wondered when he would see them again.

"Come on, Lem, we'd best be goin', too," Monroe said gently.

Lemuel followed the others, glad to bring up the rear so they would not see the tears that came so easily. By noon, as they paused for a rest stop, he was feeling somewhat better. There was still the empty hollow in the pit of his stomach when he thought of his brother, marching resolutely upstream toward the unknown.

Within three days, the party had begun to think that perhaps those in the other group had been right. They were still headed west, still following the mostly dry streambed, but they seemed to make little progress. The landscape looked exactly the same as it had yesterday and the day before. They might as well have been walking in one place, except that now the country was drier.

Lemuel dreamed that he was walking, walking endlessly, doomed to an eternity of sameness, with the blistering sun burning the back of his neck. He would wake with a start and appreciate the cool of the night, still dreading the dawn of a new day of heat and thirst and sameness. His lips were blistered and cracked, and when he licked them to try to moisten the dry membranes, he tasted the salt of their bleeding.

Lemuel was shuffling tiredly along, not paying much attention, when the calamity struck. He had just noticed that they were stopping to rest more often, and that each stop seemed less satisfactory than the last. At noon, they had halted longer and had dug down into the sandy streambed for a few mouthfuls of seep water. He was preoccupied, wondering how long it might be until they reached the cool of the mountains, and whether they could survive until then. Probably his preoccupation caused the accident.

It was actually quite small, the portion of the stone that

protruded above the sand. Just enough to catch the toe of
an unsuspecting boot. Lem lurched forward, catching his
balance with a clumsy skip step to keep from falling. He was
so near exhaustion that such an effort seemed to sap the last
of his strength. He was tempted to sit down and rest a little
but wanted to keep up with the others. He did not wish to
be accused of slowing the party's progress.

At the next brief rest stop, he sat down to examine the
boot. It had not felt quite right since he stumbled. He
pulled it off and dumped the contents out on the ground,
noting with surprise the large amount of sand. No wonder
he had felt that he had something in his boot. He turned it
to look at the toe and discovered that the sole had been
pulled away from the upper for perhaps an inch at the tip.

"Damn!" he muttered under his breath.

He was thinking of this as a minor nuisance, and its
seriousness had not yet occurred to him. He took off his
sock, brushed the sand out of the toe, turned it inside out,
and repeated the process. When he replaced the sock and
the boot, it felt considerably more comfortable.

Within a mile, however, it was as painful as before. He
could feel the hot sand under his toes, and with each step
new sand being picked up and squeezed through the hole
in his boot. He stopped again to clean it out and saw that
the sole was separating progressively from the upper. The
opening at the toe was larger. He still did not comprehend
how serious this difficulty would be.

He stopped repeatedly to clean out the sand and small
stones that persisted in finding their way into the boot.
With each stop, he could see the change in the size of the
defect. At first, he was afraid that he would hold up the
others' progress. Then, that they would leave him behind.
Gradually, he realized that the others were suffering nearly
as much as he. Van Zont's light complexion was burned
beet red, and there were blisters on his nose and cheek
bones. Monroe was showing his age in slower response.
The man might possibly be fifty, Lemuel figured. It must

be more of a strain for him to keep going than for someone not out of his teens. That thought kept Lemuel going. It must be easier, even with a damaged boot, than it was for the older man.

By nightfall, Lemuel's boot sole was flapping loosely and making him stumble. They stopped to make camp beside the dry streambed and took turns scooping out moist sand to develop their only source of water. To their alarm, it was painfully slow. The hole in the sand was nearly two feet deep, and the seep was so slow that it was obvious it would take hours to obtain enough water to satisfy their thirst.

Dimly, in his suffering pain, Lemuel tried to sort out how long it had taken to dig the hole and how long for the water to seep. There must come a time, his befuddled thought processes realized, when the digging and the waiting would occupy so much of their time that there would be none left to travel. Wherever that occurred would be their last camp, and their final resting place. There had to be something to break the routine into which they had fallen.

The cool of evening helped morale a little, but not much. The travelers took turns lying face down in the Indian well to sip a few swallows of the precious water. Lemuel attempted to repair his boot, tying the sole to the upper with strings cut from his canvas pack. Finally, he cut up the pack itself to use the canvas. He had practically nothing to carry, anyway.

They talked over their predicament that night. Perhaps, they decided, it would be better to travel by night, during the cooler hours, and rest during the heat of the day. They rose with the rising three-quarter moon about midnight and moved on.

This strategy seemed to work well, except that Lemuel could not see as well where to step. His makeshift canvas boot repair was soon chewed to pieces on the abrasive soil, and the leather sole flapped with each step. He developed a swing to his stride that would allow the loose portion to flap forward with each step before he set the foot down.

That worked until he realized that the muscles of his other leg were beginning to knot up in protest to the unnatural gait. It was with great relief that Lemuel welcomed the rising sun and the chance to stop and rest.

"I'll dig first," Monroe said briefly.

The others dropped their blankets and meager packs and sank to the sand, exhausted. Lemuel drifted off to sleep, and when he wakened, Monroe was snoring next to him. Overton was digging, and Van Zont moved restlessly in fitful slumber.

Overton saw that Lem was awake and rose to come over. He sank to the ground, exhausted. "You kin take it a while," he mumbled.

Lemuel struggled to his feet. The thought flitted across his consciousness that Sam and Ed Bolliver had been right. He should have gone with them. They were probably camped now by a sparkling stream, with cool breezes rustling the shade tree overhead.

He fell to his knees and looked down into the sandy hole. Dry sand trickled down the sides. Only in the very bottom of the excavation, there was enough dampness to feel cool to the touch.

Behind Lem, Overton spoke weakly. "While you're diggin', wouldn't hurt none to pray, if you know how."

≈ **21** ≈

It was the next morning, as they stopped for the day, that they saw a glimmer of hope.

"Look!" Overton pointed to the west. Low on the horizon lay a blue-gray mound, stretching north and south for some distance. Lemuel licked his dry lips. A cloud bank holding the hope of rain. He studied it for a little while. Yes, it was wide enough to be a general front, which might provide lifesaving moisture for the travelers. He felt like cheering but did not have the energy.

"How long you reckon till it gets here?" he asked. His own voice startled him with its harsh croak.

"Gets here?" Monroe questioned.

"Yes, the storm." He pointed to the blue cloud bank in the distance.

"Son, that ain't a storm," Monroe said. "That's the Rocky Mountains."

"The mountains? Are you sure?"

"Of course. I grew up seein' mountains, back east."

"How far are they?" Lemuel demanded.

"Hard to tell. Mebbe fifty, mebbe a hundred miles. Even more. Air's thin here and deceivin'."

Lem sat down, dejected, his tongue thick and dry, dried saliva crusty on his lips. He felt like he had a mouthful of cotton batting. For a moment, there had been elation, as he realized their goal was in sight. Then the truth had struck him. Those mountains, so blue and cool-looking on the distant horizon, were as out of reach as ever. At their present rate of travel, a few miles a day, it still might be weeks before they arrived. And their deteriorating physical condition would not allow them that long. They had, at best, a day or two, he figured. He pulled off his boot, or what was left of it. The sole of his boot looked like raw meat where the hot sand had first blistered, then abraded his skin. For the past few stops, he had been wearing a makeshift bandage he had created from the tail of his shirt. He wasn't certain that the foot would last another day—or that *he* could, without water. He settled back on an elbow to stare at the misty blue of the mountains, so deceptively beckoning.

Nearby, Van Zont was digging, muttering to himself. Lemuel saw the man straighten to rest his back and look off to the west at the mountains. Suddenly, he seemed to see something around the bed of the stream.

"*Ach!*" he fairly screamed. "*Mein Gott in Himmel!*" He came stumbling up the bank, pointing and jabbering in German.

"Hold it! Calm down, Van!" Overton insisted. "What is it?"

The others were grabbing weapons and looking upstream. Van Zont pointed, still babbling incoherently.

"Van!" Monroe said forcefully. "You got to talk English! Tell us!"

The German's stare calmed a little, and he turned to Monroe. "Dere vas a dead man!" he said simply.

"A dead man? Come on, Overton," Monroe snapped.

Overton picked up his Hawken and followed Monroe, whose flintlock pistol was at ready. Lemuel, unarmed, got to his feet but could do little else. In a short while, the others returned. Overton was pale and looked as if he would vomit at any moment.

"There's a dead man, all right," Monroe said grimly. "Died tryin' to dig for water, looks like. Coyotes been at the body some."

"Are we goin' to bury him?" Lemuel blurted.

"We'd ought to, I reckon," Monroe said. "But we have to use our strength diggin' for water first."

He walked down to where Van Zont had been digging and picked up the short-handled spade, the only digging tool they had left. He began to dig.

Lem watched him for a few minutes. He was curious about the dead man but hesitated to go and look. Van Zont was seated, mumbling to himself in German; Overton was sitting nearby, still looking sick; and Jackson, who never seemed to react much to anything, was trying to rustle up enough sticks for a campfire.

An idea struck Lemuel. The dead man had undoubtedly been wearing boots. He'd have no use for them now, and for Lemuel Booth, it might make the difference between life and death. Lem wouldn't mind, he told himself, if it was him lying there in the sand. If it would save somebody's life, they'd be welcome to anything he had. He pulled on his damaged footwear and hobbled upstream.

The man lay face down in the sandy creek bed. He was wearing butternut jeans and a linsey shirt of nondescript gray. His hair was reddish in color, and there was some sign that coyotes or other scavengers had started to work on the bloating corpse.

A woven hickory hat lay nearby where it had been dropped. Between the outstretched arms of the body was the shallow Indian well he'd been digging. Ironically, it was damp in the bottom, and a half-dozen tiny yellow butter-flies were grouped there, sucking life-giving moisture.

Only after the shock of viewing the dead had subsided did Lem remember his mission, the boots. With a fresh shock, he realized that the body in the sand wore no boots. The feet were bare. Someone had stolen whatever footwear there had been.

Lemuel's first reaction was a wave of anger, that anyone would stoop to robbing the dead. It took only a moment to realize that he had been ready to do the same, but that someone had beaten him to it. Now a fresh wave of anger, followed by a profound wave of depression. He sat down on the bank near the unfortunate man in the sand and began to cry.

"Why, Lord, *why*?" he asked repeatedly, pounding with his fists on the sandy ground.

He wished he was home walking behind the mules and watching the mealy loam curl up over the plowshare. He thought of Emily and how he'd likely never know, now, how it felt to bed a woman. Hell of a thing. He'd even relish arguing with Sam, if he could back up time a ways. Here he was, about to die of thirst and starvation, and Sam was safe. Maybe the others would even be in Denver by now. Probably Sam would always wonder what had happened to his brother Lemuel on the way to the gold fields. And no one would ever know. In a few days, they'd all be as dead as this poor bastard, and coyotes would scatter their bones on the sand. He cried some more.

"Booth?" somebody called.

"Over here," Lem answered, trying to compose himself and dry his tears.

Overton walked around the bend of the streambed, carrying his Hawken rifle. He avoided looking at the corpse in the sand.

"Lem," he said, "we got a little moisture. Better come."

Lemuel tottered to his feet. He turned for a look at the distant mountains.

"Overton!" he whispered. "Look!"

Some fifty paces away, an antelope stepped daintily down to the streambed, sniffing along as it moved, searching for the spot to paw for water.

"Get him!" Lem urged.

The moisture in the animal's body, even the slime of the paunch, Mangum had told them, could be lifesaving. Such an idea had been nauseating to the travelers at the time. Now their outlook had changed. Lemuel had not the slightest doubt that he could drink the blood of the animal standing before them and relish the life that its fluid would provide.

Overton lifted his rifle and took careful aim. The Hawken boomed, and for an instant Lem was choked by the cloud of white powder smoke. He ducked to the side, his ears ringing from the muzzle blast, and saw the antelope kicking on the ground. The marksman's aim had been true. The others came running.

"What is it?" Monroe shouted.

"Overton got an antelope!" Lem yelled.

"Somebody get a pan!" Monroe called. "We got to be careful and do this right, now."

There was only brief discussion. Most of them had been present or assisted at butchering and understood the proper bleeding of a carcass. They carefully held Jackson's skillet under the throat of the antelope while Monroe skilfully opened a vein.

"There, let it drain a little . . . hold it, now. We better drink some. Pass it around."

Monroe pressed a hand against the gash in the throat while the others passed the frying pan. Lemuel wondered what Emily would think if she could see him now, eagerly gulping warm blood from the skillet before giving it up to the next man. They utilized all possible blood from the animal's body, lifting it by the hind legs to obtain complete drainage.

"Let's use the meat now," Monroe suggested. "This will keep us going. Bring it back to camp."

Lemuel would never have thought that strips of raw or half-cooked meat could be so deliciously satisfying. After his hunger and thirst had been sated somewhat, an idea occurred to him. He crawled over to the carcass of the antelope, and sliced off a piece of the hide.

"What are you doin', Booth?" Monroe asked.

"Not sure, Cap'n. Thought I'd try to fix my boot."

He was thinking how handy it had been to have some strips of rawhide around the farm. He had even fixed a broken ax handle once. It was a temporary job, of course, until he could make another of hickory. The wet, stretchy skin would shrink as it dried, drawing tighter like a vise, and hardening till it was like iron.

He cut and trimmed a strip of the antelope hide and bound it around his damaged boot, the hair-side out. Narrower strips tied the makeshift repair firmly to the boot, and he set it in the sun to dry, hoping devoutly that the scheme would work.

Through the heat of the day, they lounged around the camp area, resting well for the first time in many days. As night fell, they prepared to move on. Lemuel pulled on his repaired boot and tested it for a few steps. It seemed solid and gave him hope.

Not until the first rest stop, however, was he really sure.

Then he removed the boot and examined it, mostly by feel
in the darkness. The rawhide repair seemed secure and had
even shaped to his foot as he walked. He replaced the boot,
smiling as he did so.

"Sam," he murmured, "we're goin' to make it now. I'll
see you in Denver!"

$$\approx \quad 22 \quad \approx$$

Samuel Booth sat staring at their tiny campfire, too weak
from thirst and starvation to think rationally. This was
punishment, he reckoned, for leaving his brother. Lem and
the others had been right. He'd figured that out on the
third day. Or was it the fourth? No matter. All the days
blurred together now in a thirsty hell that held out no hope.

The water in the potholes of the creek bed had quickly
given out—before they realized it, actually. It was evening
of the second day, or the third, he didn't remember, that
they camped and talked about the fact that they'd seen no
water standing all day. There was the thought of going back,
but that would be another day's travel, in the wrong
direction. No, they'd have to go on. They dug for water that
evening and moved on, still optimistic. It was worse each
day after that.

Their supplies dwindled rapidly. They abandoned the
last few pounds of their flour supply. It was useless without
water to mix with it, and dry flour could not be choked
down dry throats. The game they had confidently expected
to shoot had not materialized.

Two days ago, they had come upon the dried and rotting
bodies of two travelers. It appeared that one had been laid
out for burial. The other had apparently been occupied in
digging a grave, which he had never finished. He had lain

down to rest from his labor and failed to rouse again. The shovel still lay beside his lifeless hand.

"Shall we bury them?" Bolliver suggested.

They looked from one to the other, not sure they still possessed the strength. As a compromise, they shoved both bodies into the partly finished grave and shoveled sand over them. Adams mumbled what he could remember of some scripture and asked that the dead men, whoever they were, might find their way to God's care. He didn't mention the devout hope that all of them now began to feel about their own survival. They staggered on.

"Monroe and them was right, Sam," Adams said that evening.

"I know" was all the answer Sam could muster.

It was the next day that they sighted the mountains, cool and blue in the distance. Charlie Simpson, from Virginia, recognized them for what they were and estimated a hundred miles or more to their goal.

"We can't make it that far," Bolliver confided to Sam as they plodded onward that day.

They were making barely four or five miles a day now.

"Maybe we can if we get a shower," Sam said hopefully.

Bolliver looked from the sun in the coppery sky to the blistering sand that stretched endlessly ahead. A few stalks of yucca pointed stems toward the sky. Mostly, there was only scattered sagebrush in gray-green clumps. The shimmer of heat waves made the entire landscape a vast mirage, with the cool blue mountains beyond.

"Sam, be sensible. There ain't goin' to be any shower!"

Sam didn't answer, and they plodded on. They camped early, because Adams was fainting from exhaustion. He may have even had a sunstroke, looked like. They took turns digging but had not found any water yet. Even the sand was barely moist.

It was disconcerting to Samuel, during the rest of the day, to watch a pair of vultures high overhead. The birds soared effortlessly, never moving their wings, scribing perfect circles in the hot afternoon sky. Their flight was pretty to watch, he'd have thought, if he didn't know their purpose. He shuddered a little.

Night brought some relief from the heat but none from the thirst. Someone suggested that they moisten their tongues by sucking small stones from the creek bed. It didn't help much. Sucking mouthfuls of the damp sand from the bottom of the unsuccessful well was even worse. It became necessary eventually to spit it out, and with it, precious moisture.

Adams became worse, and now was out of his head, raging with fever. He babbled constantly, lying on his blanket a little aside from where the others sat. He kept talking about the swimming hole and how cold the water was at the bottom.

"What are we gonna do, Sam?" Ed Bolliver asked. "We can't leave Adams."

"Don't know, Ed. Simpson, could one of us make it to the mountains and bring help?"

"I don't hardly think so. We need a rain or some game, or we ain't goin' to make it," Simpson said gloomily.

"How would game help us if we don't find water?" Bolliver demanded bitterly.

"You remember what that mountain man Mangum told us?" Simpson snapped angrily. "You can drink blood, and the slime from the paunch, if the critter's drunk recently. The raw meat's got water in it, too. Jesus, Ed, don't you remember nothin'?"

"Don't argue," Sam said. "We got to save our strength."

"For what?" Bolliver asked. "To bury the others?"

"Mama!" Adams cried from the darkness. "You brought me buttermilk! I love buttermilk. Kin I have some more?"

"There's one problem," Simpson said grimly. "He ain't goin' to make it, anyhow. Want to leave him and make a run for it? Tonight, while it's cool?"

"Jesus, Simpson! He's your cousin, ain't he? You can't leave him."

"I know," choked Simpson, "I can't, but if you boys want to, go ahead. I'll stay here and bury him. I'll catch up."

"No, we best stay together," Sam stated firmly. "We'll make it, or not, by helpin' each other. Maybe we get a rain or one buffalo—even an antelope would do for us. We'd make it then."

"Antelope's most likely," Simpson said, "but we ain't seen any since before we left Monroe and them others."

"Charlie?" Adams called weakly.

"Comin', Jimmy." Simpson scrambled to his feet and stepped over to where his cousin lay.

"S'pose he's better?" Ed asked.

Ed and Sam hurried to bend over the still form with Simpson.

"Charlie?" Adams asked again.

"Yeah, Jim, I'm right here."

"Oh. Charlie, I need a drink of water."

"I know, Jimmy. We all do, but we ain't got any."

"Oh, yes, I forgot. I knew that. I forgot."

He was quiet for a little while. Simpson felt his forehead. "I think he's cooler. Guess the fever's what put him out of his head."

Adams stirred a little. "Yeah, though I walk through the valley of the shadow . . ." he mumbled.

"What'd he say?" Ed asked.

"Nothin'. He's out of his head again. Quotin' scripture."

Adams's eyes opened wide in the dim starlight. "No, I ain't, Charlie. I ain't out of my head."

"All right. Just rest, then."

"No, you got to listen. I got somethin' to say."

"All right, Jimmy. We're all listenin'."

Adams took a deep breath, and they thought he'd drifted off to sleep, but he stirred again. "Listen, you got to go on. To the mountains."

"No, Jimmy, we ain't goin' to leave you."

"Be still, Charlie. I got to tell you this. I'm dyin'."

"No, you ain't. We—"

"Yes, I *am*, Charlie. Now shut up."

Simpson lapsed into silence, and the sick man resumed his monolog.

"I'm dyin', and you got to go on. I'll be gone come mornin'." He took a deep breath, as if to gain strength. "Here's what you do, Charlie. You need some game, somethin' to eat to furnish moisture. Well, when I'm gone, you got *me*!"

His cousin recoiled in horror. "Oh, my God! No, Jim, don't even talk like that!"

"No, you listen to me, Charlie."

The dying man's hand reached up to grasp at Simpson's shirtfront.

"You listen to me. Think about it. It's the onliest chance you got."

"No, Jim, we ain't—"

"Think about it. Talk it over, afterward. Ain't no sense buryin' what could save you. Charlie, I'll be savin' your life!"

Simpson dissolved into tears and staggered away. Adams started to babble scripture again. Sam felt his forehead. The fever was returning.

"You get some rest now," he told Adams.

"I shall fear no evil. Thy rod and Thy staff, they comfort me."

"What'd he say?" Ed asked.

"Just more scripture."

"Thou preparest a table before me, in the presence of mine enemies . . ."

"My God, Sam, do you think—"

"How in hell do I know, Ed? I was never in a fix like this, neither."

Simpson returned and squatted beside the still form. "How's he doin'?"

"Not good, Charlie. He's out of his head again, spoutin' scripture. Fever's back."

"This is my body, which is given for you," babbled Adams. "Take, eat. . . ."

≈ **23** ≈

The streets of Denver were a veritable madhouse. The scent of fresh-cut pine lumber was all-pervasive wherever a person turned. Bright yellow new buildings blossomed before their eyes, almost; and the ring of hammers pounding nails into beams, studs, and rafters echoed across the basin.

And the tents. Lemuel had never seen so many tents. There were all sizes, shapes, even colors, though most were the white of new canvas, weathering to soft gray in time.

"Vell, vat do ve do now?" Van Zont asked.

"Split up, I guess," Monroe answered. "Lem, what are you goin' to do?"

"Look for my brother, I reckon. Then we'll look for a gold claim."

"You want to come with us, Van?" Monroe asked. "You'd be welcome."

The German scratched his nose, where the blistered skin was peeling. "Vell, vy not?"

They shook hands.

"Lem," Monroe said, "I'd ask about your brother in the saloons and supply stores. Have you got enough money to get you by?"

"Yes, I think so," Lem answered, thinking of the few silver dollars in his jeans. It was, in fact, about *all* he had.

He could certainly use a new pair of boots but knew he could not afford them. The left one, with the strange-

looking antelope-hide repair, was holding up well enough
to get by. He saw people wearing stranger things.

He shook hands with the rest of the party, and they
parted. Monroe and the others headed southwest down
Cherry Creek, where the bulk of the gold strike was
located. Lemuel wandered aimlessly along the street,
looking anxiously at every face, hoping against hope that he
would recognize it. He'd stepped into several stores and
bars, but no one had seen or heard of Samuel Booth.

This was a losing proposition, he realized quickly. No one
would give his name while merely drinking or trading.
There had to be a better way. He found a centrally located
outfitter, The Gold Nugget, and talked with the proprietor,
explaining his situation.

"Maybe I could work for you," Lem suggested. "That
would let me see a lot of miners, so I could ask everyone."

The proprietor looked him over, as if wondering what
was wrong with this proposition.

"You want to work?" he asked incredulously, "instead of
huntin' gold?"

"Yes, sir. I'm likelier to find my brother here than out on
the creek somewhere."

"That's true. I can't pay you much, though. You can sleep
in the back room, and I'll feed you."

"Fair enough. I don't need much."

"You got any money at all?"

"Not much."

"Well, all right. But we got to get you some boots. Jeez,
boy, that'd be bad for business."

He pointed to the antelope-skin repair.

"I can just take 'em out of your pay. Go pick out a pair."

In a short while, Lem was outfitted in a new pair of boots
and was helping wait on customers.

A hundred times a day, it seemed, he asked for Samuel
Booth and received blank unknowing stares or negative
shakes of the head. Should he, he wondered, go down on
Cherry Creek and look? He decided against it. He was

fitting in well with the operation of The Gold Nugget, and Mr. Walsh was increasingly giving him more responsibility. At the end of two weeks, the outfitter had given him a raise and announced that the new boots were paid off.

But Lem was restless. He wondered if there was something else he could do to locate his brother.

"Why don't you go to the claims office and the assayer?" Mr. Walsh suggested. "If he's filed a claim or brought in any ore, they'd have a record of it."

Both possibilities proved fruitless.

"Want to go look for a claim?" Walsh asked. "I'd like to have you stay here, but you came for gold. I can keep askin' for your brother."

Lemuel declined. It had quickly become apparent to him that those supplying the miners were the ones accumulating the gold. Saloons, stores, bawdy houses, all were constantly buzzing with activity, independent of who found gold.

"No, I'll stay here," he told his employer. "At least, till I find Sam."

"All right. But Lem, you got to think about it. What if you *don't* find him?"

Lemuel wasn't ready to face that possibility—not yet, anyhow.

"Haven't got that far yet," he mused. "I've got to go home sometime."

He dreaded crossing the plains again, but there had to be a way. The growing sack of silver dollars Mr. Walsh was keeping for him would be a help. There was even a rumor of a stage line from Leavenworth to Denver.

Then came the day, in answer to the ten-thousandth time he'd asked the question. "Booth? Sure, I know him. Lives out west of town a ways. Jest foller the road west. A tent, up-side the ridge, 'bout a mile."

"How'll I find it?"

"Hell, ask somebody. Look, are you goin' to get me my goods or not?"

Lemuel hastily filled the order and explained to Walsh.
"Sure, go ahead, son. And good luck. You'll be back?"
"Of course. I'll be back, no matter what I find."

He thought it important enough that he stopped by the
livery and rented a saddle horse, to make better time, and
hurried out the west road. It was a good horse, probably the
best Lem had ever ridden. Of course, he had ridden only
work animals, as a rule. He moved along the west road at a
trot, looking ahead toward the first low ridge. There were
a number of tents scattered along the slope. He overtook
two men on foot and paused.

"Could you fellers tell me where Samuel Booth's tent is?"
"Shore. Thet's it, yonder, facin' this way. Don't seem like
that name's right, though."
"You mean Booth?"
"No, the other."
"Samuel? They call him Sam. He's my brother."
"I dunno. Mebbe so. He a squaw man?"
"Squaw man?"
"Yep. Got an Indian wife. She's somethin' of a looker."

Lemuel was confused. Could Sam have taken up with an
Indian woman? It was possible, he had to admit. It had
been several weeks since they parted.

"You're sure that's Booth's tent?"
"Gospel certain. Sounds like you don't know your
brother too good."
"Mebbe not. I haven't seen him for a spell."
The man chuckled. "It happens," he said.
Lem reined aside and rode up to the tent.
"Hello," he called. "Sam? Are you there? Sam Booth?"
The tent flap lifted, and a woman peered out. She was an
Indian woman, nearing middle age, but still strikingly
beautiful. She dropped the flap, and he heard a low buzz of
conversation inside. The flap lifted once more, and a tall
man in beaded buckskins stepped through and straightened
to look the visitor over. The clear blue eyes seemed to
Lemuel to look right through him. Long dark hair and full
beard completed the picture.

"I'm Booth," said the mountain man. "What do you want?"

Lemuel was confused even more now.

"No," he stammered, "I'm afraid I have the wrong man. Sam Booth. We were separated on the trail, and I reckon he got here first."

"Nope, don't know him," said the bearded one. "My name's Gabe. Gabriel Booth. But say, my brother had a boy, Sam. He was a little tyke, last I seen him. What'd you say yore name is?"

Lem was sitting on the horse, his mouth open in astonishment. "Uncle Gabe?"

"By Jesus! Be you Jim's boy? Git down, boy, come on in." He turned and called into the tent. "Cat! We got a visitor. This here's my brother's boy. What's yer name, boy? Lem—that's it, Lemuel. Well, by God, who'd of thought it? Come on in. How's yer mama? I ain't been back in years."

They entered the tent and sat down to talk.

"Tell me all about it, son."

"Well, I guess you knew Papa's dead."

"Yes, I knowed that. I would of come back to help out, but yer mama never did cotton to me much. The other youngsters well?"

"Well, the girls are married. Sam, too. All but me. Sam and me come out to look for gold."

Gabe shook his head disapprovingly. "But you said you was lookin' fer him."

"Yes, we got separated out on the Smoky Hill. Him and some others went one way, and the ones I was with went another'n. I ain't seen him since."

"Oh, Jesus, boy, that's bad. There's some bad forks to that trail. Where was this?"

"Don't know, exactly. We'd been warned about the North Fork, but— "

"He took the North Fork?"

"Well, I ain't sure. There was a fork—the south branch

dry and sandy, the other'n had a little water in it. We damn near died follerin' the south one."

Gabriel shook his head again. "But that's the way it is out there, Lem. That North Fork's worse. It'll be lucky if we ever see Sam again. Howsomever, we'll try. Where are you stayin'?"

"At The Gold Nugget. I'm workin' there."

"Good. You kin stay with us if you want. We're shootin' meat for the miners and all. We go out ever' couple of days, get an elk or mebbe a buffalo, sell the meat. It's a livin'."

The woman, who had been outside, entered with some broiled meat on a couple of wooden trays and sat to join them.

"Reckon I didn't introduce proper," Gabriel apologized. "This here's my wife, Cat. She-Cat or Cat-Woman, in her people's tongue. She's Pawnee."

"Howdy." Lem nodded, ill at ease.

"It is good to have you in our lodge," Cat said, smiling.

They finished the meal, and Gabriel wiped the grease from his hands on his buckskins.

"Now, let's see," he said. "We can put the word out to look for Sam. He's with three others, right?"

Lem nodded. "Last I saw him."

"Now that's Arapaho country out there. Cat, we know some Arapahoes, don't we? Can we have them ask around?"

He turned back to Lemuel. "You see, nothin' much goes on the tribes don't know about. We'll ask. And I'll look hereabouts while I hunt. Best you keep your job and come out oncet a while to see us. Or you can stay with us. You'd be welcome."

"No, I'll stay in town, Uncle Gabe. But I'll come out."

As he rode back to the livery, Lem was astonished at how much better he felt. Somehow the weight of the world had been lifted from his shoulders. He might be no closer to finding Sam—might never find him, it appeared—but just the same, he felt better. There was someone now to share his troubles. Someone who was *family*.

≈ 24 ≈

The season moved on into late summer. Days became shorter, though they added together to lengthen into weeks. Lemuel felt more confidence now that he had help in his search for his brother. Gabriel asked among the Indians and took short trips into the plains, but it was as if the prairie had opened to swallow Sam Booth and the little party of travelers.

Several times, Lemuel attempted to write his mother and, as often, tore up the letter in frustration. What could he tell her—that Sam had disappeared without a trace, that they had not even tried to look for gold, and that he could not afford the supplies to come home? No, he'd wait until he had something more solid to recount.

Every day or two, Lem made his way to the tent on the ridge. Cat-Woman, with no children of her own, seemed to take great joy in feeding her husband's young nephew and in visiting with him. Lemuel had never been around Indians and was uneasy at first, ill at ease with unfamiliarity. This disappeared rapidly as he began to realize that his aunt was an intelligent, interesting person with a quick sense of humor. He found himself laughing at her jokes, the first time he had laughed in months. When she discovered that he had begun to learn sign-talk, she helped in the development of this skill.

"No, not like that. This way," she corrected.

"But Mangum said—"

"You know Mangum?"

"Yes, we met him on the trail."

"*Aiee!* He and my man trapped together one winter. Where is he now?"

"I don't know. He was going down to Bent's."

"That no-good! He never settled down. He should have stayed with you and your brother!"

What a strange statement, Lem thought, *from an Indian, noted for lack of responsibility.*

"But we meant nothing to him," he protested in Mangum's defense.

"Yes, I know. I only meant that . . . your brother—"

"You think he's dead, don't you, Cat?"

"Who knows? What will be, will be. But the country is cruel out there."

Lemuel was startled. This remark seemed to echo the strange feeling he'd had, that the valley of the Smoky Hill had a spirit of its own—a dark, evil spirit that lay in wait, plotting the destruction of the unwary.

Cat smiled. "I am sorry, Lem. If it is his time, he is dead. But we will keep asking. The Arapahoes are asking for us, too."

"I know. I am grateful. But Cat, you said the country is cruel. What does that mean?"

She glanced at him, a quick sidelong glance, with a slight question in her eyes. "You have felt its spirit?" she asked simply.

Lemuel was caught off balance, confused. Could Cat possibly understand what he felt?

"Well . . . I . . . what do you mean?"

The woman looked him full in the face, her large dark eyes deep and wise. She smiled gently. "Yes," she said quietly. "You have felt it. Your spirit tells me so."

"I . . . I don't understand," Lem stammered.

Cat-Woman chuckled, the musical, throaty little sound that came so easily to her. "It is harder for your people to understand than for mine," she admitted. "It is a thing of the spirits, and the whites do not believe."

"Spirits?"

"Yes, of course. Every place has a spirit. This one is a powerful spirit, strong medicine."

"What do you mean, 'this one'?"

"The river valley, the one the whites call Smoky Hill. Its spirit."

Yes, Lemuel thought, *I was right. The cursed river* does *have an evil spirit*. "It is a place of evil, then?"

"No, no. Cruel, dangerous. There can be things of good there, too."

"Other spirits?"

"No. See, you do not understand." She turned away.

"But I am *trying*, Cat."

"Yes," she agreed. "That is true." She turned back to him again. "The spirit of a place is not all good or all bad. It is like a man or a woman—some good and some bad in each one."

She paused and chuckled again.

"Like your uncle, my man," she continued, almost tenderly. "Some see only the hard, strong part of his spirit. They do not understand. There is a soft, gentle part, too, that is for me."

Lemuel nodded. He had seen the unspoken devotion of this couple.

"But what of the river's spirit?"

"It is the same. Some see its cruel, hard side. Those who understand its medicine see something else."

Lemuel almost blurted the question "What?" but paused to think a moment. Slowly, he began to understand. It was a difficult metamorphosis. He thought of brilliant sunsets, when he had stood in awe of their beauty. There were places where he had paused to gaze at the grassland with a warm, comfortable feeling that this was home. He remembered soft nights when the full moon silvered the rolling hills, and he hesitated to sleep, for fear of missing some major event of spiritual importance.

Maybe, he thought, it was like his relationship with his mother. He had never questioned his love for her, even when he was annoyed and upset over her attempts to manipulate him. Or his quarrels with Sam—it was still his brother.

Cat-Woman had suggested that a place has a spirit. Could he be sometimes in tune with that spirit, and at others, at odds with it? It was much like the mixed feelings for his mother or for Sam, he decided. Or, for Emily. He was beginning to understand. There might be either good feelings or bad toward someone, or some place, almost at the same time.

The valley of the Smoky Hill was neither "good" nor "bad." It could be either. Either way, as Cat-Woman suggested, its medicine was powerful. Those who attempted to understand the medicine of the river and to move *with* it were those who would benefit from its strength. Those who tried to defy it would be destroyed.

Lem shivered a little. Back in Illinois, he could never have considered such thoughts. He was learning much, and he felt that the medicine of the grassland they had crossed was influencing his thinking. He turned to look into the dark eyes of Cat-Woman.

"I . . . I think I see this now," he murmured.

Her smile was calm, serene. "Yes," she said softly. "I am made to think you do."

She rose.

"I will start to cook," she said. "Gabriel will be home soon."

"He is hunting?" Lem asked.

The comings and goings of his uncle were so unpredictable that Lemuel hardly bothered to try to follow them. Sometimes both Gabriel and Cat-Woman would be gone for a day or two and would return with pack animals laden with elk or buffalo. At other times, Gabriel hunted near Denver, while Cat stayed at the tent. Lem had assumed this to be one of his days of hunting near at hand.

"No, he went to meet some Arapahoes," Cat-Woman said.

"Do they know something?" Lem asked eagerly.

"I do not know," she said, shaking her head. "We heard someone had been found out on the Starvation Trail."

"Why didn't you tell me?"

She spread her hands in a gesture of helplessness. "There was nothing to tell. It might not be your brother, and we do not even know if this one is alive or dead."

"How many? Just one? There should be *four*."

"So, we do not know. But sit down. My man will be here soon."

Lemuel sat, fidgety and frustrated. This was another thing that had puzzled him. Both Cat-Woman and his uncle seemed to know by some instinct when to expect the other. The woman moved gracefully around the fire, placing firewood and cooking pots.

It was no surprise to see Gabriel top the rise to the west and lope easily toward the tent. He seemed to be in a hurry, and Lem jumped to his feet in anticipation. His uncle waved but said nothing until after he dismounted. Then he turned seriously to the eager Lemuel.

"Lem, they found your brother," he announced.

"Is he alive? Is he all right?"

"Well, now, he's in bad shape. Half-starved, an' all. They're bringin' him in on a travois."

"And the others? Bolliver and them?"

"Lem, there wasn't any others."

Lemuel's head reeled with the enormity of the discovery. "But Sam's alive? Who's bringin' him? Where are they?"

"Some friends of our'n. I rode on ahead to tell you, but they'll be along. Lem, you got to understand, he's awful sick. They been some time jest gettin' him well enough to travel. He's still awful weak. He's outa his head some, part of the time, so you mustn't expect too much."

Even with Gabriel's warning, Lemuel was not prepared for his brother's condition. Samuel couldn't have weighed a hundred pounds. He lay there on the platform of the pole-drag behind the roan pony, staring up at his brother with hollow, burning eyes.

"Lem!" the sick man said, choking. "Lem! You're alive!"

Tears were running down Lemuel's cheeks. He tried to speak but choked on the words. He knelt beside the travois and took the emaciated hand that his brother reached up toward him.

"Come on, let's get him in the tent," Gabriel interrupted.

Gabe bodily lifted Sam like a baby and carried him inside. Close beside him, a young Indian woman hovered in concern over the invalid. Cat-Woman nodded and smiled to the girl, and the two of them quickly prepared a pallet of robes and blankets for the ailing Sam. Gabe laid him gently on the bed, and the Indian girl dropped to her knees to try to make him comfortable.

"This here's Blue Rain," Gabe explained. "Her daddy, Last Antelope, the man outside, found Sam almost dead. He drug him in, and Rain seems to have took over raisin' him. They say he's come a long way."

"Lem!" Samuel babbled again, "You're alive! Chrissake, Lem, I'm sorry, boy. You were right."

"Easy, Sam, it don't matter none. Where are the others?"

Instantly, Lem wished he hadn't asked. Sam gave a scream of anguish and burst into tears. Blue Rain looked up at Lemuel with a dark frown of hate.

"Don't!" she snapped.

Sam continued to yell. "The others! Gone!" he screamed. "Adams first. Then Bolliver. My God, Ed, I'm sorry!" He paused to vent a series of long, shaking sobs. "I'm sorry. Then Simpson." He pounded a fist on the ground. "Chrissake, Charlie, why did we do it? I'd rather of died."

He broke down into a series of sobs again, while Blue Rain attempted to comfort him.

"You rest, now. I bring meat."

She rose and went outside. Sam lay moaning and mumbling, until she returned with a cup of Cat-Woman's stew from the kettle.

"Here. You eat now."

The girl attempted to raise Sam's shoulders, and Lem hastened to help her. He held an arm behind Sam's back while Blue Rain fed him with a horn spoon. Sam's sobbing decreased, and he ate all of the cup's contents. They lowered him back to the bed.

"It is good. You sleep now."

She stroked Sam's brow, smoothing the frown away until he dozed off, exhausted. Then she rose and faced Lem.

"Thank you," she said.

"No. Thank *you*," Lem said, smiling. "My uncle says you saved my brother's life."

Blue Rain dropped her eyes, embarrassed. "I did nothing," she protested. "He needed someone."

"But you were there and helped him when you did not need to. I thank you for his life."

Lem was thinking that he had never seen so beautiful a girl. She was perhaps a year or two younger than he, slender and willowy, the soft graceful curves of her young womanhood apparent under her buckskin dress. Her facial features were even and well-proportioned, her high cheekbones exquisitely chiseled. Most alluring were her eyes, like deep pools, rich golden brown in color, a shade lighter than those of Cat-Woman.

What had attracted her to the starving Sam Booth? he

wondered. Sam seemed almost oblivious to his surroundings, even to this beautiful girl who waited on him. *Ah,
well*, Lemuel supposed, *some women seem to feel called to
feed people, to mother them, to take in strays*. He envied
Sam the attention he had received from this girl.

They moved outside the tent, where Cat-Woman was
ladling stew for the others of the party. There were Last
Antelope, a woman who must be his wife, and a boy
somewhat younger than Blue Rain. Probably her brother,
Lem decided. He accepted a bowl of stew from Cat-Woman
and went to sit beside the boy. The bowl was hot, and he set
it down to cool. With both hands free for the moment, he
turned to the youngster.

"How are you called?" he asked in sign-talk.

The boy stared for a moment, startled.

"I am Yellow Pine," he signed, speaking aloud meanwhile. "Do you speak my tongue?"

"No. You are Arapaho?" Lem asked with the chest-thump
sign for that tribe.

The boy nodded.

"Do you speak mine?" Lem asked.

"No. Only a little. How are you called?"

"Lemuel."

The boy rolled the unfamiliar syllables over his tongue.
"No," he said in signs, "you are Brother-of-Starving."

Lemuel was shocked, depressed. He was aware of the
custom of bestowing meaningful names, but this seemed a
cruel and excessive thing.

"No," he protested. "I—"

"Go ahead, wear it," Gabriel advised. "It don't matter
none. You kin change it later."

Lemuel was surprised at how quickly the Arapaho family
accepted him. Then he realized that it was because of their
friendship with Gabriel and Cat-Woman. In fact, Cat-
Woman's quick acceptance had been because of Gabe, he
now realized. If he had met any of these people under other
circumstances, he would have encountered the reserved,

taciturn coldness that his people had come to expect from Indians. Here, under these circumstances, the group chatted comfortably while they ate—talking of the weather, the hunting, and of Sam's recovery. Most of the talk was a mixture of English, sign-talk, and some native tongue, probably Arapaho, he figured. He could follow most of the talk by the signs and the broken English. He was concerned, however, when Last Antelope, with an obvious reference to Sam, shook his head with a doubtful expression. Then Antelope touched a finger to his own temple and shook his head again.

"What did he say?" Lemuel asked, alarmed.

Gabe paused a moment before answering but finally turned to Lem. "He says your brother's been real sick, Lem. Out of his head, like."

"But he'll be all right?"

"That's what he's talkin' about. Sam's spirit's been wounded, he says. They've been tryin' to heal it."

"What does that mean, Gabe?"

"Well, it's hard to tell you about, I reckon, unless you know about their 'medicine' and all. They figger Sam's still a little out of his head, on account of all that's happened to him. They've tried to help him. It's more or less like prayin' for him, I reckon. Or usin' their spirits to give him strength . . . aw, hell, I don't know."

Gabe became frustrated at his attempt to explain and abandoned the effort. "Anyhow, Blue Rain seems to be the best at it. Quietin' him, that is."

Last Antelope and his family camped nearby for two more days before leaving to rejoin their own band.

"We meet them at Bent's," Antelope explained. "Winter someplace south. Come back to hunt next season, maybe so."

At Gabriel's suggestion, Lem brought small gifts for the people who had helped his brother. Tobacco and knives for

Antelope and Yellow Pine, and mirrors and needles for
Blue Rain and her mother.

"How did you come to know them, Gabe?" Lem had
asked.

"Oh, we run acrost them, four, five years back, out on the
Smoky Hill. Me and Cat were camped, and these Arapahoes moved in, gettin' ready for a big buffalo hunt. We
offered to hunt with 'em. They can always use another gun
or bow in the hunt, y'know. Well, we hit it off purty good,
and Antelope jest sort of figgered we're brothers, seems
like."

It was somewhat more than that, Cat-Woman had confided later. During the hunt, Gabriel had been unhorsed,
and Last Antelope had risked his own safety to lope in and
allow the man on foot to swing up. Later, Gabriel, having
recovered his mount, was able to stop a charging bull with
the heavy Hawken, returning the favor. The two men had
been as brothers since.

When word had spread that Gabe's nephew was missing,
Last Antelope had taken a small party out on the upper
Smoky Hill to search for him. This was a dangerous venture
at that time of year, but fortunately they had been successful. At least, partially so.

Lemuel was sorry to see them move on. He was impressed with the influence that Rain had over the mood of
his brother and wondered if Sam was really ready to
recover on his own. There were times when Sam seemed to
be doing well, but other times were quite doubtful. He
would stare into space for long periods of time, sometimes
crying silently. Then he would suddenly call out the names
of the others.

"Ed! Oh, Christ, Ed, I'm sorry! Jimmy, too! Gone! Oh,
for Christ's sake!"

When he was in these flights of memory, there was no
way he could be consoled, especially after Blue Rain's
departure. Cat-Woman attempted to comfort him, but
usually Samuel cried himself to sleep.

It had been decided that Sam would remain at the tent, at least for the present, where Cat-Woman could look after him. Lemuel continued to live and work at the store, spending as much time as possible with his brother. At least, Lem could see, Sam was growing stronger. There was a little meat on his bones. Before long, he thought, they'd be able to plan the trip home.

Again, Lem found reasons to postpone writing their mother. Now he had an extra reason. How was he going to break the awful news of the death of Ed Bolliver? Maybe, before long, Sam would be able to write Ed's wife. He'd be the logical one. Sure. Best wait until Sam could do it.

≈ **26** ≈

Mr. Walsh was more than cooperative with Lemuel's need to be with his recovering brother.

"Hell of a thing," he noted. "Yer brother's lucky to of pulled through at all. Damn lucky. You just go ahead—do what you need to. Just let me know how it's goin'."

Lem resolved not to take advantage of his employer's tolerance and worked even harder to make certain he pulled his weight. He regularly reported on Sam's progress, which was distressingly slow. Physically, Sam seemed to gain weight and strength fairly well but still seemed listless, morose, and depressed. He would not talk about his experiences on the Smoky Hill, except when the depression overcame him and he broke into one of his crying fits. At those times, he seemed completely out of contact with reality and could not be consoled. Again and again, he called out to his dead comrades.

Cat-Woman, too, related that Sam often wakened screaming in the night.

Lemuel tried to explain. "He figures the whole thing was his fault, I reckon. He talked me and Bolliver into comin' west to begin with. Then he talked them others into takin' that North Fork."

Still, he had the uneasy feeling that he didn't have the whole story. Somewhere a piece was missing. Even with Sam's obvious physical improvement, this prevented Lemuel from beginning to plan their trip home.

Mr. Walsh brought up the subject in the store one day. "I s'pose you'll be leavin' soon."

"Well, we hadn't decided."

"Better think on it some. I don't want to run off my help, but winter's comin'. That's no time to be travelin'. Sam still gettin' better?"

"Yes, sir, I think so."

"How you plannin' to go, when time comes?"

"Hadn't really talked about it, much. I've got saved about enough for a couple of horses, ain't I?"

"Sure. Ride the back trail, then?"

"I guess so. Foller the river."

"Think Sam's able to ride?"

"What are you gettin' at, Mr. Walsh? Something wrong?"

"No, no, of course not. I thought maybe you'd try the stage."

"Stage? Wouldn't that cost a lot?"

He had seen the big Concord stages of the Leavenworth & Pikes Peak Express Company come and go since he'd arrived in Denver. It hadn't occurred to him that it was something he'd ever do, ride the stage with the rich folks.

"Ain't sure," Walsh admitted, "but it's only a ten-day trip. Save somethin' on food."

"I ain't sure," Lem protested.

"Well, go find out. It's slow today. Go on."

Lem took off his apron and made his way down the street to the L.&P.P. office. A long-faced man with pockmarked cheeks answered his query.

"Sure, we got regular service, son. Was you wantin' to send freight or ride?"

"Neither, maybe. Just need to find out about rates."

"Oh. Well, freight's twenty-two cents a pound, takes about a month, by ox team. More if the weather's bad. The stage, hunnerd and twenty-five dollars a passenger. You can carry twenty pounds of baggage. Get you to Leavenworth in ten days. New Concords."

Two hundred and fifty dollars. Might as well ask for the moon, Lem thought. There couldn't be more than fifty dollars in his pouch at Walsh's. He thanked the man and turned away. He'd almost reached the door when an inner office door opened.

"Hold on, son," a man called. "Be with you in a minute. Have a seat, there. You drive mules?"

Confused, Lemuel sat down in one of the wooden chairs in the front office.

"Yes, sir, I can," he said, wondering what was happening.

"No, sir," the clerk said, "he's just— "

"If he says he can drive, I'll talk to him, Abner," the man in the doorway snapped.

Lemuel looked him over. Short, a little pudgy. Gray business suit. *Must be hiring drivers*, Lem figured. He'd just play out the hand here. The pudgy man picked up some papers from the desk and ducked back into the office. Lem could hear voices, and in a few moments the pudgy man returned to the doorway, still shaking the hand of a tough-looking man in heavy boots and rough clothing.

"Glad to have you with L. and P.P.," the man in the suit was saying. "We can use a man of your experience."

"Yes, sir," the teamster said, grinning, "I'll drive them oxen to hell and back for you."

The other man's face fell. Slowly, he took the contract in his hand and tore it in half, then tore it again.

"I'm sorry, sir," he said stiffly, "L. and P.P. employees are not permitted to use profanity."

"Well, then I won't," the teamster protested. "Makes no difference to me."

"Sir, you already have," the other said, coldly. "Your services have been terminated."

"But you jest hired me!"

"A mistake, obviously. One I have just rectified."

"You mean, I'm *fired?* For *that?*"

"I'm afraid so. The terms of your employment were quite plain." He pointed to the torn contract.

The teamster was reddening above his collar. "To hell with you, then! I wouldn't work for this goddamn outfit, anyhow!"

He started for the door and noticed Lemuel sitting there. "Better come on, son," he advised. "You don't need these bastards!"

Lem said nothing, and the big man stalked on out the door, still swearing to himself. Lem reminded himself to avoid any suggestion of impious language, as the pudgy man ushered him into the inner office.

"Ah, yes, so unfortunate," the man was saying. "He was quite well qualified, too. Now, what is your name, young man?"

"Lemuel Booth, sir."

"And you drive mules?"

"Yes, sir, I can."

"Very well. I'll speak frankly. We're losing some drivers since we changed routes."

"You don't follow the Smoky Hill?"

"No. Yes, I know it's closer that way, but we have a mail contract from St. Joe to Salt Lake City. We're using that route now, along the Platte."

Of course, thought Lemuel. *It would be two or three days longer. If they're paying drivers by the trip, they've got some unrest. Probably some quitting.* Well, whatever the reason, it was none of his business, he figured.

They talked a little while, and the man asked when he

could start. The wages he'd mentioned seemed like all the money in the world.

"Sir," said Lem apologetically, "I have a brother here who is sick. I need to get him back to Illinois, but I don't know when he'll be able to travel. I really didn't come in to apply for a job, and I'd much prefer to wait until he's better before I leave him."

The man looked at him for a moment, displeased.

"Well," he said finally, "I admire honesty. When your brother's better, come back."

They shook hands, and Lemuel left, feeling better about the world than he had for some time. He stopped by The Gold Nugget, where Mr. Walsh was closing, to tell him the good news, and then hiked out to Gabriel's tent. What a piece of luck, he was thinking. Maybe he could make a trip or two, build up a nest egg, and then head on home from Leavenworth at that end of the run. If worst came to worst, he figured, he could cuss a little at the Leavenworth end and get fired. He smiled to himself. Things were finally going to work out.

Shadows were lengthening as he walked. He saw the sun sink behind the front range, bringing the odd prolonged mountain twilight. It was still quite light, however, when he reached the tent. Gabriel had just returned, and Lem told the three his news of a job that would enable them to go home as soon as Sam was able to travel. Much to his surprise no one seemed very excited about it.

"Ain't that good, Sam?" Lemuel asked.

His brother burst into tears and dropped to his pallet.

"I can't never go home, Lem," he wailed. "Ain't no way I can face Ed's family. Or mine. Oh, Christ, Lem, I'm so sorry." He started to sob again.

"Come on, Sam, you'll feel better when we get home," Lemuel pleaded.

"Lem, come outside—we got to talk," Gabriel whispered.

He led the way outside, and Cat-Woman followed them. She had lighted a coal-oil lantern and set it on the dirt floor. It was growing darker, and the lantern's light gave a yellow-orange glow to the wall of the tent.

"What's the matter, Gabe?" Lem asked. "He's got no call to act like this. That whole thing wasn't his fault, that them fellers died."

"Lem," Gabriel said gently, "I reckon there's something you ain't figured out yet. You know them that died? Well, what he . . ."

A gasp from Cat-Woman interrupted him. She pointed to the tent. There, silhouetted against the lantern's glow, Sam had risen from his pallet and had picked up Gabe's rifle. He cocked the hammer and pulled the rear, or set, trigger, readying it to fire. Now he carefully placed the weapon's butt on the floor and his head on the muzzle.

"Jesus!" Gabriel cried. "The Hawken! No, Sam, *no*!"

All three ran toward the tent as Sam's hand touched the hair trigger. The gun boomed, shockingly loud in the dim light, and the shadow on the tent wall was hurled backward to crumple on the floor. Gabe reached the tent first and threw back the flap. A distant echo resounded from the foothills, and still another.

"Aw, no," Gabriel said softly.

Sam lay on his back, eyes open. A half-inch hole with blackened edges loomed inappropriately in the center of his forehead. The back of his head was missing, and dark flecks spattered the canvas wall behind him. But his features were peaceful.

"Aw, no," Gabriel said again.

"Gabe," Lem pleaded. "What is it all about? What was the matter with him?"

"He jest couldn't forget, I reckon, son. About the others."

"*What* about the others? Why wouldn't he talk about it, Gabe? What happened to the others?"

Gabriel took a deep breath. "Ain't you figgered it out yet, boy?" he asked quietly. "He *et* 'em!"

Outside, Cat-Woman's voice rose in the plaintive, wailing cadences of the Pawnee song of mourning.

≈ 27 ≈

Lem pulled the big Concord to a stop and paused to let the team breathe for a few minutes. The mules were blowing hard after the heavy pull up the hill. From here, it should be easier—at least, from the description he had been given. A straight shot east, following the course of the Platte.

The coach rocked gently on its leather springs as the passengers shifted restlessly. Lem debated whether to let them dismount. He hadn't been given much in the way of instructions, but he knew his bladder was full, and he supposed everybody else had the same problem. There was hardly a rock or a tree to go behind, but some things had to happen anyway.

"We'll stop a few minutes," he called as he set the brakes, wrapped the lines around the lever, and climbed down.

The six passengers came stiffly out of the coach, brushing the dust of travel from their clothing. Lemuel hadn't paid much attention to them originally, except that there were six. The trip had been rather sudden—so abrupt, in fact, that his head still swam. The Saturday run, which was always indefinite, had been canceled. L.&P.P. had a stated policy that the stage would not leave Denver unless there were six passengers, and only four had appeared. Lemuel was assigned to the Saturday run and was allowed to practice a little to become familiar with the Concord and the six-mule hitch.

Then at the last minute, a middle-aged couple had

appeared at the stage office. There was a flurry of activity. The regularly assigned driver had gone off somewhere to hunt, prospect, or just drink. He was nowhere to be found.

"Booth," someone had asked, "can you make this run?"

"You mean now?"

"Yep. 'Bout an hour."

"Well, I . . . sure! I'll be ready."

It had taken all of three seconds to decide. Lemuel could not wait to shake the dust of Denver from his boots.

Following Sam's death, the heartbreak, disappointment, and tragedy had come crashing in on him. With the help of Gabriel and Cat-Woman, he had managed to give his brother a decent burial. He spent part of his savings for a good suit for Sam to be laid out in, because he knew that would be important to their mother. He managed to write home—that Sam and Ed Bolliver were dead, and that he'd be home but didn't know when.

The pudgy man at the Leavenworth & Pikes Peak was glad to see him again and immediately hired him as a stage driver. He was given a short lecture on the L.&P.P. The line was new, obviously, and still struggling. Their original route had followed the upland between the Smoky Hill and the Platte rivers, wandering a bit for ease and safety. Lem followed the route on the map that hung on the office wall. The changed route, after only a few months' operation, had been brought about by the U.S. Mail contract. There was some grumbling by drivers, and by passengers, who objected to the extra day; but the road up the Platte was well traveled and, for safety and practicality, seemed to be working.

Lem parted with his job at The Gold Nugget, with a kind word from Mr. Walsh.

"If you ever decide to come back, come see me."

Parting with Gabriel and Cat-Woman would be more difficult, and he postponed it until the last possible moment. He had moved out to the tent with his few belongings when he left the store. Now with the sudden departure, he hurriedly rode out on a borrowed horse. Gabriel was out hunting, and Cat-Woman gave him a quick hug.

"You will come back?" she pleaded.

"Maybe," he said, and smiled.

He hated to admit how reluctant he was to leave these people. They had become closer than family to him. He almost wanted to assure her that of course he would be back but was not certain he could. It was another world to which he was returning, and he might not be able to escape again. Immediately, that thought struck him as odd. He should be thinking of escape from this cruel and violent western land.

"It is good," Cat-Woman stated. "If it is meant to be, we will see you again."

His new employer had showed him the route on the map, with a stock station where he could change teams at midday. He and the passengers would be served a meal while the fresh team was harnessed. The night stop offered beds for those who desired, but the other teamsters advised him to take his own blankets.

"Never know what's livin' in them cribs," a grizzled veteran advised.

This was fortunate, Lemuel thought. He could take his blanket roll without question and be ready to quit his job in Leavenworth to head on home.

The trip so far hadn't been bad. The route was well traveled, and the stage stops well spaced. Now, five days out, he was beginning to gain confidence. At Julesburg, he'd picked up the eastbound mail pouch from Salt Lake. They'd met one L.&P.P. coach, a ways east of there, going west, hell-bent.

He hadn't even had occasion to wonder about the effectiveness of the shotgun in the leather scabbard beside him. He'd checked to see that it was loaded and thought no more of it. He knew, however, that in an emergency, there'd be only two shots, one from each barrel. Even with the scatter of buckshot, that wouldn't stop more than two or

three attackers. He made a mental note that if he were to
stay with this job, he'd have a Colt revolver with its five or
six ready shots.

The passengers sorted themselves out now, men on one
side of the coach and women on the other. Lem joined the
other men, where they grouped together a few paces away,
and faced the open prairie to urinate. The location was
important, he'd quickly learned. Only an absolute green-
horn would try to piss into the wind. Therefore, the men
were, by unwritten law, always grouped on the downwind
side of the coach, facing away. They discreetly refrained
from watching how the women handled the situation. It
was impossible not to notice, however, that one woman,
spreading her long full skirt, might effectively screen
another from any chance glances. There were two women
in this party, and Lemuel wondered how a lone woman
would manage.

He walked up and down, stretching cramped muscles,
and the other men did likewise. His stomach still seemed to
feel the rolling sway of the Concord. There was even a little
sway to his walk, he noticed.

"How far to noon stop?" asked a well-dressed man with
an expensive flowered vest.

Lemuel had figured him for a gambler or a drummer. His
luggage didn't seem to include a sample case, so a gambler
was probably likeliest.

"Not real sure," Lem said. "We'll get there about noon."

He hated to admit that this was his first run. The
gambler, whose livelihood depended on judging people,
probably knew it anyway. However, his livelihood also
depended on knowing when *not* to ask questions. He
nodded and drifted away.

The couple who had filled the quota sauntered over. Lem
couldn't quite figure them out. They seemed just like an
average town couple back home. Fairly well dressed, but
not fancy. What had they been doing in Denver?

"Will there likely be any Indians, Mr. Booth?" the woman asked, a little fearfully.

"Hard to say, ma'am. They're not likely to give trouble. There'd be mostly Pawnees along here, and they're pretty friendly."

The woman seemed reassured. They're not westerners, he decided, but he'd never know their reason for being here. Everybody out here had his own story, and no one asked unless invited.

How much he himself had changed, Lem realized. So much had happened, most of it bad. But there was good, too. He understood the problems of the passengers on his coach. He'd been able to speak realistically of the possible Indian danger. If they did meet the Pawnees, or others, he'd be able to communicate with sign-talk, thanks to Mangum and Cat-Woman. The thought gave him great confidence. He found himself thinking of the frightened townswoman with a certain degree of pity, though he wasn't far from that status himself.

What was it? he thought. What was he feeling? There was a tendency to think of himself as a man of the plains, a Westerner. This was a new feeling. For a long time, he'd wished only to get out, to return to the routine of the farm and his predictable life with Emily. Now this feeling of confidence was good, but it was unnerving, too. There was a certain pride about his having made his way in the West, but it bothered him a little. Did he *want* this secure feeling? He thought of the difficult parting when he left Cat-Woman. He hadn't even been able to say goodbye to Gabe.

His passengers were becoming restless.

"Load up!" he called, climbing back to the driver's seat of the Concord.

He hoped he could remember where the stage station was located. It would certainly be embarrassing to have to stop and ask directions. He vaguely remembered seeing the sign when they came through in the spring: Leavenworth & Pikes Peak Express Co. He'd not thought of it at the time, but the name was a bit misleading. The stage line didn't come within sixty miles of Pikes Peak. It was purely a line to the gold fields near Denver. No matter, he guessed. Folks back home didn't know the difference. Likely a lot here in Leavenworth didn't, either. "Pikes Peak" just had a nice ring to it, and Lem reckoned it was a pretty good name.

He moved on toward the main part of the town. Another big red Concord came toward him, and the driver pulled his mules to a stop.

"Howdy!" he greeted. "Any trouble on the road?"

"Nope. Good trip," Lem answered.

"Good. You're new, ain't you?"

"Yeah. Name's Booth. Lemuel Booth."

It wasn't convenient to shake hands, so the other merely waved.

"I'm Riley. Pat Riley. See you on the swing trip, mebbe."

Riley picked up the lines and flapped them on the mules' rumps. The coach lurched forward.

All right, Lemuel thought. *They came from up that way. The yard must be there.* He clucked to the team and moved ahead.

Yes, sure enough. Up ahead in the next block, the green sign with gilt letters proclaimed Leavenworth & Pikes Peak Express Company.

He'd done it.

≈ **28** ≈

Lem pulled the coach to a stop in the L. & P. P. yard, and the passengers began to dismount. An old man limped forward to help with the luggage from the rear boot.

"Howdy," he greeted. "I'm Zeke. You the new driver?"

"Lem Booth." Lemuel extended a hand, which the old-timer gripped.

"Have a good trip?"

"Can't complain. We got here."

Zeke nodded, chuckling, as he lifted each piece of baggage and handed it to the waiting passengers.

"Glad to hev you. Best get on up to the office and check in." He pointed to a doorway in the building adjacent to the lot. "The hostlers will unharness."

Lemuel nodded, took his blanket roll from under the driver's seat, and walked into the building. A clerk sat at a desk in an office off the hallway. Lem took off his hat and stepped to the desk.

"I'm Lemuel Booth, new driver from Denver," he began. "This where I turn in my papers and the mail?"

"Yes. Just a minute."

The clerk turned and stepped toward an inner office. Lemuel had the feeling he'd been through this before.

"Mr. Russell," the clerk called, "the Denver Stage is here, with the new driver."

A tall, dignified man stepped out and walked over to extend a hand.

"I'm William Russell," he said. "Come in. Tell me about the route."

Lemuel was nervous in the presence of one of the line's owners.

"Well, sir, I'm not sure I can. This was my first run. We got along."

He laid the mail pouch on the desk.

"Quite so. What is your opinion, then? Are facilities adequate?"

"Yes, sir, I think so. For the frontier, good enough."

"I see. And you had no trouble?"

"No, sir."

He was a little mystified over this questioning.

"Very well," Russell said shortly. "Just asking. Like to get the impressions of a new man. You made good time."

"Yes, sir. The stations are well spaced."

"Yes. Well, go get some rest. When can you start back?"

"Back? Well, I—"

This would be the time to say he was going home, to collect his pay and move on. He looked through the window to where the hostlers were unharnessing the team. The trip had been a real satisfaction to him, and he hated to end it. He'd had a good team, especially the big mealy-nosed lead pair. Good to drive—a real sense of power in those six leather lines between his fingers.

"That's all right, son," Russell said generously. "Go get you a bath, a meal, and think about it. We've got a full load of passengers ready to start tomorrow, if you are."

"But I met a stage, coming into town."

"Yes. We always have one starting out Tuesday, full or not. Other than that, just when we have a full passenger list. Like now."

"I see."

Lem thought a moment. *Yes, still more folks going out than coming back*, he figured. Well, it would give him a chance to save up a little more money—and to see Gabe and Cat again. He'd be back here again in three weeks. It seemed like a good idea.

"Well, all right," he said. "Tomorrow?"

"Good!" Russell said, beaming. "Do you need some pay now?"

"Yes, sir, that would help," Lem admitted.

Russell turned to the clerk. "Advance Mr. Booth some pay," he said as he turned back to his office.

Weeks passed, and it was difficult to think of anything but the stage. Most of the time he spent en route, one way or the other. At the Denver end, he stayed over with Gabriel and Cat, and while in Leavenworth, in a small hotel down the street from the L.&P.P. yard. He had few expenses and found that he really enjoyed the work. Sometimes he met Riley's stage on the road or at the overnight stop at one of the "home" stations. Once he met a party of Indians and was able to converse with them in sign-talk. This impressed his passengers greatly, and their stories increased his prestige with L.&P.P.

Through the winter months, passenger traffic slowed to a standstill. There was often only one stage leaving for Denver and, sometimes, not even that. *Now*, he thought, *now is the time to go home.* But still he stayed on, for just one more run, again and again. It was nearly spring when he realized the truth. He just didn't *want* to go home. He bought a revolver, one of Colt's .36 caliber six-shot weapons, and wore it when he drove—but never had to use it.

Gabriel and Cat moved into a cabin for the winter.

Spring was opening up before he knew it. There had been a few weeks in midwinter when the line shut down— too hazardous to challenge the wrath of potential storms on the plains. Later, Lem realized he had not even considered utilizing that break in the schedule to travel home. He thought less and less about the farm in Illinois. If he wasn't home in time, his mother would get somebody to farm it.

He thought less and less about Emily, too. There were times when he woke in the night, hungry for the warmth of her body. The thought of merely being with her, however, was not nearly so exciting. He remembered now that during the time they had spent together, they had never really talked seriously about anything. Most of their conversations had been based around her teasing him, pouting over some pretended insult, or pretending anger just to see him react. There must be more to it than that, he now realized. By contrast, a woman like his uncle's wife was enjoyable to be around. Cat-Woman could talk, seriously or in fun, just as one person to another, without all the silliness or pouting that seemed to be usual for Emily.

Lem did try to write Emily once. He realized after a slow and painful page or two that he was merely repeating what he had already written his mother. Emily would already know that. For some reason, he felt guilty about repeatedly coming halfway home from Denver and returning without going on home. Therefore, he didn't tell her about his present job. With nothing to say, he crumpled the page and discarded it. He was not able to recognize the fact that his real problem was his inability to express affection for the girl he left behind. After that, however, he thought of Emily less and less. Even in his erotic dreams, the girl in his arms was not identifiable as Emily.

Now, with spring opening the roads, regular stage travel had resumed. Lem usually had a full load of passengers, eager to head west to the gold fields. On the return trip east, many times the coach was almost empty. He enjoyed the fine weather, the smell of the greening prairie, and the sight and sound of the long lines of geese honking their way northward. He was restless but did not understand what it was that made him so. Sometimes he wondered where the geese would settle down to nest, what the country there to the north would look like. Mostly, though, his restlessness seemed to be simply the call of the prairie. Another run with the stage always helped some. He wondered, from time to time, what the Smoky Hill valley looked like at this time of year. He had almost decided that he'd like to go and see. He'd ask Cat-Woman about it. She would understand.

He pulled into Leavenworth late one afternoon, delayed by a loose shoe on the near wheeler. He was tired, dusty, and glad to turn in the mail pouch, papers of lading, and passenger list. He walked to the hotel, intent on a bath, a good meal, and his bed. As he stepped into the hotel lobby, a man who was sitting there in a chair rose to approach him.

"Mr. Booth?"

"Yes," Lemuel said cautiously.

"My name is Green Russell," the man began. "The clerk told me you'd be in."

"Are you kin to William Russell?"

"No, no, just coincidence. You work for him, don't you?"

"Yes, sir."

"But I understand, Mr. Booth, that you have traveled the Smoky Hill to Denver."

The memories came rushing back—the heat, starvation, heartbreak, and tragedy. Lem's resentment rose with his exhaustion.

"That's right," he snapped, unwilling to discuss it further.

"Can we talk about this?" Russell asked. "I want to survey the road to Denver, along the river."

"Mister, there *ain't* any road!"

He shifted the blanket roll on his shoulder and started for the stairs.

"Wait!" Green Russell called. "I know that. Booth, I need you. Listen, I know about your brother."

Lemuel whirled in a rage. "Know *what* about him?"

"No offense, son," the other protested. "I mean, about your bad luck. Look, I want to lay out a road, so that won't happen to others."

He was talking rapidly, to get his ideas across before Lemuel's temper exploded.

"Who's backin' it?" Lem asked suspiciously.

"The town of Leavenworth," Russell said. "I'll pay well. I'm puttin' a party together to make the trip and want you because you've been there that way. But look, you're tired, We can talk later."

"No, wait," Lemuel said.

The idea was growing on him now. A well-equipped, well-mounted party tracing the same route he and the others had taken last season—marking and laying out a safe trail so travelers could make the trip without fear. This might satisfy his restlessness and make him feel he was accomplishing something. Maybe, even, it could help the gnawing feeling of guilt that chewed at his gut ever since Sam's death.

"Tell you what, Mr. Russell," Lem finally said, smiling,

"I'd like to hear the rest. Let me get a bath and a change, and we'll go talk about it over supper, if you're willing."

Green Russell's face broke into a broad grin. He stuck out his hand. "You're on!"

≈ **29** ≈

It was considerably different to retrace the Smoky Hill with a well-mounted, well-armed party with plenty to eat and at a relatively pleasant time of the year. Lemuel relived some of his pain and anguish at their previous campgrounds, but all in all the trip was pleasant. Lemuel found he could point out features of the terrain new to the exploring party, which he had dismissed from mind but now recalled.

Again and again, he thought of Cat-Woman and her serious talk of the spirit of this valley. At this time, in the pleasant warm sunshine and cool nights of springtime, he felt only friendliness of spirit. Maybe it was as Cat had suggested—his spirit was more attuned and, in this receptiveness, felt the strength of the place. Its medicine, Cat would have said.

They saw few people on the journey. After they passed Ogden, near Fort Riley and the junction of the Smoky Hill with the Republican River, there was practically no one at all. People were afraid of the trail, Green Russell stated. There had been a number of deaths, no one knew how many. One story, unverified, related the finding of seventeen bodies, apparently dead from thirst and starvation. There were whispers of cannibalism other than the case involving Samuel Booth. Lem tried not to think about it and to concentrate on staying in tune with the spirit of the Smoky Hill. Without much difficulty, he could see that the efforts of this party could make the journey to the moun-

tains shorter and easier. Russell estimated that the Smoky
Hill Road, as the party had begun to call it, would shorten
the distance from Leavenworth to Denver by nearly 200
miles, compared to the northern route.

Russell had meticulously kept notes and records of the
journey; and a few days out of Denver, he took Lemuel
aside.

"Booth, I want to get this information back to Leavenworth as soon as possible. Can you take it back for me?"

"Ain't you going back?"

"Well, yes, but I have some other business. If I can send
a letter, it would save time for them if they decide to build
a road."

"Build? You mean, a regular *road?*"

"Yes, that's what I'd hope for. They'll want to do some
grading, fill gullies, level rough places. Probably bring
teams and heavy equipment. Survey and build as they go.
This summer, maybe."

Lem pushed back his hat and let the information soak in
a moment.

"You want your report back to Leavenworth as soon as
possible then?"

"Of course. Any way you can get there."

"Then I'd suggest the L.&P.P. stage. Ten days, maybe
quicker."

"Good! That will get the report back by mid-May! I can
count on you then?"

He extended a hand, and Lemuel grasped it in agreement.

When they reached Denver, Russell paid off his men,
and they scattered.

"Booth, is there something you can do while I finish the
report?"

"Sure. I'll go see when I can catch a stage heading back."

He reined his horse around and trotted down the street
to the stage station. A hostler hailed him.

"Hey, there, boy, glad to hev you back. How'd you come in?"

"Howdy, Bert. Come up the Smoky Hill. When's the next stage?"

"Dunno. Ain't you the driver?"

Lemuel laughed. "No, just a passenger. I quit L. and P.P. at Leavenworth for another job."

"Chrissake, boy, they've got a driver sick and nobody to take the run. I figgered that's why you was back."

"Well, I could, I reckon. I need to get back to Leavenworth."

"Better ask in the office then."

The manager in the stage station was only too eager to accept Lem's offer to drive the run to Leavenworth.

"When can you start? Tomorrow?"

"Don't see why not. I'll be here."

He rode out to see Gabe and Cat-Woman for a few minutes, to explain the situation.

"I'll come back tonight," he said, tossing down his bedroll. "Appears I could go back to drivin' if I want to."

He hadn't had time to take that idea in yet and wasn't certain he wanted to resume the routine. He wondered if somebody, maybe the Leavenworth & Pikes Peak, might not start a routine stage run on the new road. That would be a thing to his liking, though he could not have explained why. He made his way back to the livery stable, where he turned in his horse by previous arrangement and then walked over to the hotel.

"All right, here's the report. It's to go to the man whose name's on the envelope. He's a lawyer there in Leavenworth, part of the committee pushin' the road. Have you got a stage ticket?"

"No," Lemuel said, grinning, "but I'm drivin' it. They're a bit short on drivers."

Russell laughed. "Can't beat that. Here's the cost of your ticket, anyway. Least I can do. I appreciate your help."

He counted out 125 dollars in gold and silver. Lemuel

took the coins and dropped them into his pocket. He'd transfer to his money belt later.

"Tell you what, Booth," Russell continued, "they'll likely be wantin' somebody to guide the work party. You might consider it. You'd handle it with no trouble."

"A guide? I don't know anything about—"

"Listen, son—you've been up that trail twice. That's prob'ly twice more than anybody who'll be with the work crew. If you run into any Indians, well, I've seen you use sign-talk. You think about it. Might as well ask, anyhow."

"Well, I'll think on it. I dunno."

"Fair enough. Have a good trip, and thanks again."

The stage run began like a dozen others he had driven. The teams were good, and he had no inkling of trouble. He made good time and had passed the mouth of Lodgepole Creek, headed for Julesburg. There he'd pick up the mail pouch from Salt Lake and hit the better-traveled part of the run. He had only two passengers. One was a frightened-looking man in a new suit, who said very little. He was obviously a working man, with cracked, calloused hands. A miner, probably, who had found a little dust and was frightened for his safety. Lemuel wondered if the man was actually carrying his pile.

The other passenger was a man in a dark suit, with soft hands, an expensive hat and tie, and a gold watch chain across his flowered vest. There was something familiar about the man.

"Have we met before?" Lemuel had asked as they placed luggage in the rear boot.

The gambler smiled. "I rode with you once. Your first run, most likely."

"Oh, yes."

Both laughed. There was something likable about the gambling man. Lem had remembered Cat-Woman's observation that there is both good and bad in everyone.

Now the team labored up a slight rise, almost in sight of Julesburg. A flash of motion caught Lem's eye in the road ahead. A young Indian woman was running up the road toward them, with several white men on foot in hot pursuit. Another man could be seen farther on, holding a number of horses, presumably those of the other men.

Lemuel pulled the team to a stop, set the brake, and wrapped the lines around the lever. He didn't know what was going on, but he didn't like it. The girl was within a few paces of the coach when one of the men caught her by the arm and spun her around, pinning both arms at her sides. Lemuel caught a glimpse of the man's face and saw that it was bleeding from several long parallel scratches.

He took the shotgun out of the scabbard and thumbed back the hammers. Even as he did so, he realized that for the first time, he had not checked to see that the weapon was loaded. Well, it was too late now.

"Hold it, there!" he called.

The man fixed him with a dark stare. "You go on, boy. Get that stage outa here. This ain't no concern of yours!"

"Let her go!"

"Go on, now. We're jest havin' a little fun here. Sort of a picnic."

Three other men came up and planted themselves on either side of the struggling couple.

"Let her go!" Lemuel insisted again.

The girl stared at him in startled recognition.

"Is that you, Brother-of-Starving?" she cried incredulously.

"Blue Rain!"

Where before, Lem had been merely concerned, now cold rage washed over him. He could not fire for fear of hitting the girl. He stood up, allowing his coat to fall open to show his revolver. The men on the ground, all armed, began to move slowly, placing distance between them. He pointed the shotgun toward the man on the left, who stopped in his tracks. The others kept moving. In a few moments, they would be able to rush him from three directions; and he had a chance of only one shot, two at most. He could not draw the Colt in time.

"Stand still," he demanded. "One more step, I blow out the man on my left."

The others paused.

"Now look, boy," the man who held Blue Rain said, "you don't want to get yourself killed over a goddamn squaw."

"That ain't likely," Lemuel challenged. "But you fellers don't, either. Let her go!"

"Easy, now. Jest put the scatter gun back in the boot, and we let you live."

"You got till I count three," Lem yelled. "Then I start shootin'."

"Hold it! You get off one shot at ole Edward, there, an' then the others get you. No sense in that."

The man who had been holding horses now ran up to join the confrontation. Lemuel had decided that the next few moments would be his last and was willing to settle for taking as many of Blue Rain's assailants with him as possible.

"No! Hold on!" said the white-faced man under the muzzle of the shotgun, holding a hand in front of him. "Don't shoot!"

Lem's resolve wavered. He wasn't sure he could shoot this man down in cold blood. He started to shift his shotgun to one of the others who presented more of a threat.

The Concord rocked on its leathers, and Lemuel felt someone dismount below. The eyes of the assailants turned to the newcomer, who now stepped around to stand by the off wheeler.

"You take the ones on your side, Mr. Booth. I have these under control."

The gambler stood casually, an ugly little revolver held quite carelessly in his hand.

"Back off, mister. This ain't your game," snarled the man with the scratched face.

"I am dealing myself a hand," the gambler said calmly.

"Any aces up your sleeve? How many want to die over this?"

Without pausing, he continued. "I shall count three, Mr. Booth, and let the cards fall. One—"

"Wait! Let's talk about this," one of the other men interrupted. "No use a bunch of us gettin' killed, us and you, over this squaw. She ain't no count."

"Then let her go," the gambler snapped.

"Let her go, Zeph."

"No, I'm keepin' her."

"Zeph, if you don't let her go, a lot are goin' to be killed."

"Two . . ." shouted the gambler.

Blue Rain twisted free and ran to the coach.

"Up here, Rain," Lem called.

The girl quickly mounted the step and was on the driver's seat beside him. Their attackers slowly withdrew, under the watchful muzzles of Lem's shotgun and the gambler's pistol. The gambler now remounted the coach.

"Let's go!" he called.

≈ 30 ≈

For a moment, it looked as if the hard cases would try to stop the coach as it moved forward. Lem handed the shotgun to the girl. Even as he did so, he wondered if she would use the opportunity to wreak vengeance on her attackers. Apparently they wondered, too, and hastily retreated out of her line of fire. He shouted at the team and the Concord lurched ahead.

As the men retreated from the rush of the coach, he could hear Blue Rain shouting at them. She used a mixture of English, Arapaho, and a sign or two that could have been interpreted as obscenities even by the uninitiated. He gathered that she was casting aspersions on their parentage, dietary habits, and morals in general.

"Your mother eats dung!" she screamed in parting.

As they passed the point where the horses of their assailants had been left, Lemuel heard the crack of the gambler's gun. He yelled at the ground-tied horses, trying to further startle them. With the shooting, the yelling, and the rumble and roar of the stage, the saddled horses began to run wild, racing alongside or following the stage. He glanced back to see their would-be attackers running in futile pursuit of the horses.

He pulled into the stage yard in Julesburg, still trembling with anger and emotion. For the first time since the incident, he could release his grip on the lines and think of things other than driving. He wrapped the lines around the brake and took the shotgun from the girl. She looked up at him, eyes full of wonder.

"It is good!" She smiled. "You are not more Brother-of-Starving. You are Bear-Who-Fights-Wolves!"

"Rain! How did you get in a fix like that? No, tell me later."

Before he did anything else, even check in at the office, he had one thing to do. He drew the ramrod from under the shotgun's barrels and checked the load. Both tubes were empty, and a chilled feeling raised the hair on his neck. It had been a narrow escape.

"You stay close to me," he told the girl as he dismounted.

The two passengers climbed out of the coach, the frightened miner looking as if he'd like to bolt for cover. The gambler stepped down gracefully and brushed his sleeve with his hand to remove road dust.

"Sir," Lemuel said, "I'd like to thank you. Reckon you saved my hide back there."

"Think nothing of it. I only tried to even the odds somewhat," the gambler said, smiling. "You had already explained the house rules."

"I don't b'lieve I know your name."

"I don't believe I gave it to you. However, we've bucked the tiger together, so I owe you that. Bannister—John Bannister. I'm called Jack by my friends, as you're welcome to do."

Lem grinned. "Jack it is, if you say so. Reckon you know mine."

"Yes. I like to know who's driving. Tell me, Mr. Booth— "

"Lem, to my friends."

"Quite so. Tell me, Lem, you appear to know this young woman who was the object of contention?"

"Yes. She and her family saved my brother from starvin' last year. I hadn't seen her since."

The girl had moved close to his side as he talked.

"Rain, this here's Jack Bannister, the feller that helped us. Jack, Blue Rain."

Bannister bowed politely as Rain nodded acknowledgment.

"Well, I better check in," Lem said. "See you a little later, I reckon. You goin' to Leavenworth?"

"Quite possibly, unless I decide to stop off first. Not much action here, it appears—of the sort I desire, that is."

Both chuckled.

Lemuel walked to the office and handed in his mail pouch, papers, and the shotgun.

"This here'd ought to be kept loaded," he advised. "It ain't much good this way."

He could tell from the attitude of the clerk that he wasn't making much of an impression. Unwilling to make an example of the incident on the road, he decided to let the matter drop. Besides, the clerk seemed a bit hostile at the presence of the Indian girl in the office.

"Come on," Lem said tersely.

He led the way to the hotel, a small establishment that catered to the somewhat meager needs of stage travelers from Denver, Salt Lake, or Leavenworth.

"Howdy, Booth. You back on the Denver run?" the clerk inquired.

"Yeah. For now, anyhow. How about a room?"

The clerk looked the girl up and down, a slight leer on his face. "Sure," he said, "but we can't take that Injun."

"Listen, Mac, it ain't like you think. She's a friend of the family."

"I never said nothin', Booth," the man protested. "You can sleep with whoever you want. She just can't stay here. We got standards."

Lem was already on the way to the door, seething with anger. If he'd walked in with some trashy slut, they'd have been given a room without question, but because of her skin. . . .

"It is all right," Rain said. "I will go. You stay here."

"And let those varmints come back to bother you? Not likely. Come on."

He led the way to the stable at the stage yard and up the ladder into the hayloft.

"Charlie," he called to a stableman, "we'll be stayin' here tonight."

In the dim of the stable's poor light, he saw the same leer that had been in evidence at the hotel. Now he realized that he was to encounter a similar problem wherever he turned. Blue Rain would not be served a meal at the restaurant where the stage passengers ate.

He solved that problem by walking down the street to the general store to buy some hardtack, cheese, and jerky on which they could make a meal. They returned to the stage yard and found a quiet spot to sit and eat, leaning against the outside of the barn. He opened the wrapped parcels of food.

"Now tell me, Rain, how's it been with you? How'd you get in that fix?"

For a moment, he saw the tragedy in her eyes and thought she would cry. Then her story poured forth, in her broken English, with some sign-talk when words came hard. It was short. Her family had been camped on the upper Arkansas when smallpox struck. It may have been contracted from some Kiowas camped nearby, but it did not matter. Rain's mother had died first; but by the time the mourning had been completed, Last Antelope was dying, too.

Rain and her brother had started north to try to join relatives they believed to be on the Poudre River, but Yellow Pine had fallen ill en route. He lasted only a short while.

"But how did you escape the pox?"

"I did not escape it. I had it with my father, but only a few sores. He died, I lived."

She lifted her hair to show a pock mark on her temple and another on her neck.

"I was looking for my people when they caught me. Then you came."

Blue Rain lifted her face and smiled at him, a happy, adoring smile. No one had ever looked at him like that. Embarrassed, he turned to slice another chunk of the cheese and share it with the girl. Both were silent for a little while.

"I heard about your brother," she said softly. "My heart is heavy for you. His was a troubled spirit."

Lem nodded, unable to answer.

They were finishing their meal when John Bannister appeared, looking as cool and sophisticated as if he had not traveled for days on the dusty coach. He carried a bottle in his right hand.

"May I join you?"

"Sure. Want somethin' to eat?"

"No, thank you. I have eaten."

Bannister meticulously inspected the spot he selected, brushed at the ground ceremoniously, and sank to a sitting position beside the others, leaning back against the barn. He took a drink from his bottle and handed it to Lemuel. Not wishing to appear unappreciative, Lem took a sip. The fiery whiskey burned his throat. He had no qualms about drinking whiskey, though his mother would probably not have approved. It was simply that his drinking experience was somewhat limited. He returned the bottle to Bannister, who took another drag. Then, as if he had forgotten his manners, the gambler leaned forward to reach across Lemuel and offer the bottle to the girl. She shook her head, and Bannister took yet another sip and officiously corked the bottle. He slipped it into an inside pocket of his well-tailored coat, and the flat bulge became almost invisible instantly.

"Well," he said conversationally, "it seems we have created for ourselves something of a problem."

"What do you mean?" Lem blurted, a little defensively.

"Well, for one thing, here we sit. I suppose you are not welcome at the hotel or the restaurant? Where will you stay?"

Lemuel smiled. The gambler had seen and understood their dilemma.

"We got a place upstairs." He pointed to the loft.

Bannister nodded matter-of-factly.

"And what are your plans, beyond tonight?"

The man was crowding him a little, and Lemuel felt resentment rise. What right did he have to question, even though he had saved their lives? Well, maybe that *was* right enough. The gambler had "dealt himself a hand" and was merely playing it out. He had a right to know who held the cards, in case of a showdown.

"Really don't have any plans," Lem admitted. "I can't leave Rain here, so I'll take her along tomorrow. She was looking for her people. Her folks are dead, she tells me."

"My condolences, ma'am," Bannister mumbled.

"I do not wish to be trouble," Rain injected. "I will leave."

"No, no," Lem insisted. "No trouble. We are only talking."

"Yes," Bannister agreed. "I took the liberty to ask about our assailants."

Lemuel, a trifle embarrassed, realized that he would not have thought of that. It was quite possible that the episode was not over.

"They are merely local ruffians," the gambler continued. "Opportunists. Not likely to follow through on anything. Except, of course, by chance encounter."

"Well, thank you," Lem said. "And thanks again for the help today."

Bannister dismissed the remark with a wave of his hand. "Forget it. Do try to keep an eye out for the unexpected until we leave in the morning, however. I will be at the hotel if I'm needed."

Bannister rose, brushed off the seat of his trousers, and settled his coat on his shoulders. Lem scrambled to his feet and shook the gambler's hand. He marveled at the feel of the handshake, soft in texture but firm in hidden strength. This man could be dangerous, Lemuel felt, and he was glad to have him as an ally.

The gambler turned to the girl, tipped his hat, and made a slight bow. "Good evening, Miss Rain," he said formally.

The gesture could have been interpreted as sarcastic tomfoolery, but Lemuel knew it was not. The man was being quite sincere, acting according to his own code of respectability, and caring little what anyone thought. Bannister turned and walked toward the street, proudly, almost majestically.

It was growing dark. Lem and Rain talked at some length and finally climbed the ladder to the loft. The night was becoming chilly, and it felt good to snuggle in the warmth of the blankets, sharing each other's body warmth.

"Do you want me?" Rain asked simply.

Lem was confused, embarrassed. "Not now," he blurted, "not that way."

Even as he said it, he knew he lied. He had never wanted any woman so much. Even worse, he sensed that the girl was hurt and offended at the rejection. He held her close, wondering whether he could change his answer, hoping for her to understand.

"You have a woman?" she asked.

"No. I . . ."

He did not understand how he knew, but he was aware that the moment had passed. They snuggled for warmth, but the opportunity was lost for anything more. He cursed his inexperience.

He lay there a long time, thinking of all that had happened in the past year. He had left home, the calm routine he had actually found satisfactory to his needs. He'd had to be prodded to do so. The exciting dream of the gold strike had not materialized; but he'd been relatively successful, anyway. Only now, there was little desire to go back to Illinois. He was afraid—even aside from the difficulty of explaining about Sam—afraid that his mother, his brother's family, and Emily would not understand.

How could he possibly explain the man he had become? It baffled his own understanding. Only today, he had participated in a showdown with armed ruffians and won. Look at his few friends, people to whom he felt closer than anyone in the world—a renegade uncle and his Pawnee wife, a hard-drinking gambler, a beautiful Arapaho girl with whom he now shared his bed. His mother would never understand that, and Emily sure as hell wouldn't.

≈ **31** ≈

The station manager stood on the ground beside the coach, glaring up at Lemuel.

"Booth, that ain't company policy."

"And you ain't drivin' this coach."

"You may not be, either, when they find out you're carryin' Injuns."

Blue Rain sat primly beside him, embarrassed, uncomfortable.

"That may be," Lem shot back at him, "but until then, I carry who I want. I'm payin' her way."

He unwound the lines, kicked the brake off, and clucked to the mules. The coach moved ahead, out of the yard, and into the street, turning east toward the road.

He heard a slight intake of breath from the girl and turned to look. There on the boardwalk in front of a nondescript building that appeared to be a saloon stood three men. They lounged casually against the wall and followed the coach with their eyes as it passed. Lem recognized them from the day before. The dark-visaged one in the middle had been the ringleader, the one who held Rain. Lem thought he had never seen such a look of hate on any face. He must speak to John Bannister again about these men. He was not yet ready to accept the idea that they were harmless. The Concord swung briskly down the street, leaving the town behind.

"I have brought trouble to you," the girl said apologetically.

"No, no. I told you, it is nothing. It is good to be with you. My heart is good."

She leaned against him, a trifle closer. "Then my heart is good, too."

At the noon stop, Lem prepared to seek out the gambler. This was a rest stop, with no team change and no arrangements for a meal. However, the station agent carried a few supplies and groceries. The passengers could buy provisions if they wished.

Lem finished checking the teams and seeing that they received a little grain and turned toward the building that served as stage office, store, and home for the agent's family. Bannister and the girl were coming toward him, carrying some small packages of the usual crackers and cheese. Blue Rain was smiling, and a pang of jealousy struck Lemuel.

It was a little unexpected. He had not completely thought out his feelings for the girl. Actually, he had not even thought about what he was going to do with her. Obviously, he could not leave her at Julesburg, where she would be in further danger from her assailants. He must take her along. This, however, led to several problems. He was taking her farther and farther from her people. Already, it was proving difficult to provide her and himself with food and shelter. This would continue and probably become worse. Then, at the eastern end of the run, he would need to provide for the girl and for her return to her own tribe. In addition, he would probably be without a job for allowing her to ride the stage. Perhaps he could buy a couple of horses and some supplies, and they could follow the river back home. *Home.* How strange, he thought, that he had just thought of the Smoky Hill valley as home. Not Illinois, the place of his birth, the place of the family farm and its rich loamy soil.

Bannister and the girl approached him.

"Will you join us for dinner, sir?" the gambler asked formally.

Blue Rain chuckled. Lem had rarely seen her laugh, and it bothered him again that it was not he, but Bannister, who brought the pleasure to her face.

"Sure," he mumbled clumsily.

Bannister led the way to the shade of the little barn by the corral, and the three sat down once more.

"We're in luck," the gambler stated. "He had some dried figs and a barrel of pickles." He triumphantly displayed the items.

"I have never seen figs," Rain said. "What is it?"

"A sort of fruit, mademoiselle," Bannister informed her. "Here, try some."

The meal proceeded on this level, with the girl enjoying

the scene and Lem somewhat uncomfortable and, yes, jealous.

"John," he asked, "do you know anything else about those men we tangled with yesterday? What's the name of that one?"

"The ringleader? Stallard, I believe they called him. You saw them as we pulled out?"

"Yes, that's why I asked."

Rain finished her food and rose to attend to her private needs.

"Maybe you'd better watch for that one," Bannister said quietly. "I did not fancy his looks."

Lem nodded.

"You seem to have gathered some problems unto yourself," the gambler continued. "What are you going to do about the girl?"

"What do you mean?" Lem spoke defensively.

"Oh, come now, my friend. Your hand is face up. You're already in trouble for bed and board, and possibly for employment."

"Well, I . . ." Lem mumbled uncertainly.

"There's one easy way out," the gambler said, smiling.

"I won't leave her!"

"Of course not. But you need only to marry her."

"*What?*"

"Marry her. Look, I can see how you look at each other. If she's your wife, no one will dare to say that she can't be with you. She could probably even ride the coach free or at half-fare as your wife, right?"

"Well, I guess so."

"All right, then. If memory serves me, the station agent down the line a day or two is a preacher of sorts."

"But will she have me?"

"Ask her. You're holding all the aces."

They were married at one of the home stations on the L.&P.P. by a somewhat dubious agent and part-time preacher. The best man was John Bannister—and the witnesses, the frightened miner from Denver and the stage agent's plain little wife. Their wedding night was spent under the stars on the hillside behind the stage stop. Lemuel thought of Emily, but only for a moment, to realize that with her, it could never have been like this.

This solved some problems but did not help with others. Now he could boldly introduce the girl as his wife, secretly enjoying a little the startled or even disapproving looks. However, he was faced with even more responsibility, the responsibilities of a married man.

They discussed the possibilities at length, including that of joining the Arapahoes on the upper Smoky Hill. Lemuel decided he wasn't quite ready for that. What he really needed was a chance to talk to Gabe and Cat-Woman and make a few solid decisions about where his life was going. Maybe he could continue to work for the stage line, at least for the present. If they'd let him, he could take his wife back to Denver, leave her with Gabe and Cat, and continue to drive while he replanned his future.

Blue Rain approved. "It is good, Bear-Who-Fights," she agreed.

John Bannister approved, also. "Yes, that's good. I'll be back to Denver in a few months. I'll look you up. Have you any plans for long-range?"

"Not really. Always thought I'd farm, but I seem to be gettin' farther from it."

"Well, when the right choice comes, you'll know it. For now, play the cards you have."

They arrived in Leavenworth May 15, 1860, and Lemuel found that he did have a job with the L.&P.P. if he wanted it. He and Rain parted with Bannister, who bowed gallantly to the embarrassed girl and shook Lem's hand.

"May our paths cross again," the gambler said grandly.

Lem choked up with emotion. "Thank you, John," he murmured.

"Thank you, my friend, for a most interesting trip!"

"Where are you going?"

"St. Louis, for now. But I'll be back."

They watched him down the street, tall and confident, with his flowered carpetbag swinging in his left hand.

"His heart is good," Rain said simply.

Their next step was to deliver Russell's letter. Without much trouble, they located the office of Henry Green, attorney-at-law. Lawyer Green was ecstatic over the report.

"Wonderful!" he chortled. "Booth, are you presently employed?"

"Well, yes, sir. Why?"

"I'll be heading the work force to build the road. I need someone to guide the way."

Yes, Lem thought, Russell had suggested something of the sort. But that was before he'd had the responsibility of a wife. He was about to refuse, when an idea struck him.

"Sir," he began, "I might be interested, for reasonable pay, of course—if I could take my wife along."

"Your *wife*? My God, man!"

"No, sir, you don't understand. My wife, who is waiting outside, grew up on the Smoky Hill and would be very valuable to your project. She knows the entire country."

"Grew up there?" Green was astonished.

"Yes, sir. Her people were Arapaho."

"An *Indian*?"

Lem flushed uncomfortably and was about to turn away. *Hell with you*, he thought to himself, *I don't need this*.

"Wait, Booth," Green said, "this may be just what we need. Please bring your wife inside."

≈ 32 ≈

Despite the fact that Henry Green had no apparent experience on the frontier, he seemed to be a good leader for the road-building party. From the day Russell's report reached his hand, Green had been rushing around—organizing, hiring crews, soliciting financial support, and publicizing the project. On the basis that the Smoky Hill Road would bring massive amounts of trade to the area, towns along the route were solicited for donations. Green was so convincing that the town of Topeka offered five yoke of oxen, and a promise of a $500 cash donation later. Junction City offered $500 in bonds; and nearby Ogden, a yoke of oxen. Auburn and Vermillion offered more ox teams and a work mare. Manhattan promised $500; while Lawrence, unwilling to speculate, raised $155 in cash through a hurried fund drive. Leavenworth, instigator of the project, had voted $2,000 plus $3,000 in bonds to allow work to begin.

Furthermore, Green seemed to have the knack of true leadership, the ability to delegate authority. He hired capable people for the special jobs. The survey officer was a young lieutenant assigned by the Signal Corps. Green hired the heavy-equipment operators, the wagon drivers, and livestock handlers. The work crews totaled over forty men, with 150 horses, mules, and oxen. Lem heard that the road-building project might cost as much as $7,500.

With this much organization and strength, the road moved ahead rapidly. There was little to do except survey at first, though the earth-moving teams did do a bit of

improvement and filling of low spots as they went.
Lawrence, Topeka, Wamego, and Manhattan fell behind,
with the local population turning out to cheer them on.
Junction City marked the point where the river could
properly be termed the Smoky Hill, above its union with
the Republican. Past the mouth of the Solomon and the
Saline, the work party moved ahead.

There, at the town of Salina, the road builders paused
long enough to take part in a celebration. It was a double
celebration, honoring the road builders and the anniversary
of Independence Day on July 4. This first 120-odd miles
had taken only sixteen days; but, of course, they were just
coming to the more unsettled part of the Smoky Hill. The
road so far was already usable.

It was here that Lemuel began to feel the excitement of
the country. Here there was the mystical feel of the spirit of
the place, much stronger than farther east. He tried to
remember where the feeling began. Near Manhattan,
probably, with the transition to grassland, and the rounded
bluffs on the south side of the river, which followed the
stream for miles. He wondered if the cavalry soldiers at
Fort Riley felt it as they rode out on patrol in the rolling
hills.

This was his third trip up the Smoky Hill, and the uneasy
excitement was still there. Along with it, this time, was a
new feel of success. This road would make travel safe for
travelers. In addition, it would be shorter by many days.
Sadly, he thought of Sam and Ed Bolliver and the others.
This road, if it had been in existence then, would have
saved their lives. Even so, it gave Lem a good feeling to
think that he might be helping to save someone else, some
future traveler. In a small way, this seemed to help his
feelings of remorse for having been unable to help Sam.

After Independence Day, the road builders moved on
westward. It was elected to take a direction across country
due west, to shorten the distance. They would meet the

river again in a day or two, after it had circled to the south and back, a loop of some sixty miles.

Despite the advice of local people that "you can't miss it," Green was dubious. It was at this point that they evolved the idea of marking the trail, where no natural landmarks existed. Teams and earth slips were used to grade up large mounds of earth every mile or two. This would assure that no traveler could become lost, because one of the mounds would always be within sight.

Large stones were sometimes moved to clear the road-bed. Gullies were graded and sloped to allow easier passage of the wagons, and smaller ruts filled. It had been intended to build bridges; but except for a small span or two, it was found easier to find a place to ford the streams. These crossings were duly marked with earth mounds.

With plenty of teams and equipment, it was possible to leave a crew working on a mound, ravine, or gully, while the rest of the party leapfrogged ahead to begin the next construction, and the surveyor's crew worked ahead still farther.

Blue Rain was astounded by all of this activity. Lemuel feared she did not entirely approve. Still, she did admit that it would make travel much easier.

"But the land might not like it," she cautioned.

Lemuel was startled. He recalled some of his conversations with Cat and being in tune with the spirit of the land. Perhaps this was why the feeling was becoming stronger as they moved westward. He remembered his occasional feelings that the land was a dark, brooding thing, waiting quietly for the chance to destroy.

Most of the time, though, this journey up the Smoky Hill was pleasant. The weather was uncommonly fine, with warm days and cool nights in which to revel in the shared warmth of his new bride. They watched the magnificent prairie sunsets together or rode ahead of the work parties, even ahead of the surveyors, to select the best route. On these occasions, there was the sense of being alone, the first man and woman in all creation. It was as if they were one with the ancient spirits of the prairie, very real and very close.

They watched silver minnows in the still shaded pools of the river; the red-tailed hawk as it circled overhead on fixed wings, hunting a rabbit or some smaller creature. They laughed at the antics of two young coyotes, ostensibly hunting but more intent on playing and wrestling.

Occasionally, Lem shot a buffalo for meat for the camp. He had provided himself with a practical weapon, a heavy-caliber plains rifle, short barreled for carrying on horseback. With the first animal that fell to his rifle, Lem learned the custom of his wife's people over a buffalo kill. Rain propped up the head as they prepared to begin the butchering and addressed it ceremonially in her own tongue.

"What did you say, Rain?"

"I only told him that we are sorry to kill him but our life depends on his flesh, as he lives on the grass."

"Do your people always do this?"

"No, not every time. But the season's first kill—other important kills."

The road builders moved on. Lem was able to show Rain some places where they had camped the previous year. It seemed a lifetime ago. They shared enjoyment of some of the spectacular chalk bluffs and other rock formations along the route that were to become landmarks on the trail. Some, at a distance, resembled castles, monuments, or chimneys. Lem had not been able to examine these closely before; but now, as part of their scouting responsibilities, they could ride to the formations for a closer look. He was fascinated by fossilized remains of fish and other marine life in the chalk beds. One fishlike skeleton was several paces long.

"Do your people know about this, Rain?"

"Only a little. It is a place of water spirits."

They remounted and moved on. A few days farther west,

Rain pointed to the mouth of a stream that entered the river from the south. "I know this place. That is the home of the Old Ones."

"Old Ones?"

"Yes, long-ago people. I will show you."

It was only a few miles. They sat on their horses at the canyon's rim, and Lemuel stared in astonishment.

"See? There are their lodges."

She pointed to the pueblo ruins below. He could clearly see the crumbling walls of several buildings, and one stood nearly intact. They spent a little while wandering among the ruins. He could almost feel the presence of the Old Ones, who had lived, loved, laughed, and mourned here.

"What is this place called?" he asked.

"We call it the place of the Old Ones. Sometimes your people call it Starving Woman Creek. I do not know why."

Lemuel longed to know more but could not pursue it further at this time. The brief incident affected him deeply, however. Somehow, with each such experience, he was increasingly understanding that there had been others, through the generations, who had felt as he did about this strange country—a mixture of excitement, fascination, awe, a little fear, and even dread, perhaps. But with all this, his strongest emotion was probably fascination. He could not satisfy his curiosity about the giant skeletons in the chalk, about the dwellings of the Old Ones, and, above all, the overwhelming spirit of the Smoky Hill.

This came to the surface when they reached the Forks campground, where an argument ensued. Henry Green was difficult to convince that the South Fork was the correct one.

"But Booth, are you sure? This North Fork carries more water."

Lemuel felt his heart beat faster, and his palms began to sweat. He very nearly blurted out that this was a trick by the river to destroy those who were unwary. Then he realized that it would sound a little crazy.

"Mr. Green," he said slowly, trying to control the catch in his voice, "this is where I lost some friends and a brother. I *know*."

"I'll side with Booth, Henry," Lieutenant Fitch, the surveyor, said. "I've heard of this. They're calling the North Fork the Starvation Trail."

"You agree, Mrs. Booth?" Green asked.

"Yes, that is true. Bad medicine the north way."

They took the South Fork, with Lemuel and Blue Rain scouting well ahead for campsites and water.

The following day, Lieutenant Fitch pointed out a matter of interest. "Right about here," he said, "will be the state line."

"I don't understand," Lem questioned. "What state line?"

"There's a bill now in Washington to bring Kansas in," Fitch explained.

"But don't Kansas run clear to the Divide in the mountains?"

"Does now. The Territory does. But they'll make the western line about here if it becomes a state. The west part will be part of a territory called Colorado."

Lem didn't see that it would make much difference. Fitch went on about how important it all was whether the new state would be Free or Slave, and the possibility of war. Lem remembered the man near Lawrence the previous year, and how worked up he'd been about it. Oh, well, he decided, it was of no concern to him. He rose to join his wife in the blankets.

≈ 33 ≈

Gabriel and Cat-Woman welcomed the bride of their nephew with open arms.

"Our lodge is yours!" Cat said, beaming.

There followed long discussions about the plans of the newlyweds. Gabriel wanted Lemuel to join him in the hunting trade that was part of supplying the growing population of the Denver area. It suited Gabe ideally. He could work, or not, on his own schedule, as the spirit moved him.

Lemuel, on the other hand, was firmly imbued with the work ethic of the farm. He did take a hunting trip or two with his uncle, between stage runs. He enjoyed the excitement, the thrill of the hunt, and riding in the open in the clear thin air of the foothills. But there was something missing, and he did not quite understand what it was.

He did know that he enjoyed the long leg of the stage run across the open prairie. There he could "stretch his eyes," as Gabriel had once said. There was something about the broad sweep of the sky and the grass stretching from horizon to horizon. He wondered how the road on the Smoky Hill was working out. He knew there was some travel, because there was talk in town about the much shorter and easier route. This made his heart strong, as Rain would have said—but it would have been even stronger on the Smoky.

Lem tried without success to convince his employers that it would be practical to resume a stage schedule down the Smoky Hill Road. They did not have enough Concords, they said; the traffic would not support it; winter was coming; and the final argument: the U.S. Mail contract required that they meet the run from Salt Lake City at Julesburg.

So he continued to drive the northern route. He and Rain bought a tent, which they pitched near that of Gabriel and Cat. Lemuel's preoccupation with the Smoky Hill led him to inquire from travelers occasionally, but there were fewer now with fall approaching.

To everyone's surprise, Mangum turned up one crisp fall day, just passing through. He had been on the Smoky Hill Road and reported it "a sight easier to follow."

"The buffalers is pawin' down them piles of dirt, though. Won't be able to find 'em next year, time the wind blows the sand around a bit."

"The prairie takes back its own," Blue Rain said to no one in particular.

"Well, I best be movin'," Mangum stated, after a day and a night of visiting and eating and drinking. "I reckon I'll winter down by Bent's or somewhar."

They watched him ride on.

"That one will never stop wandering," Cat observed. "He is half-buffalo."

The major problem faced by Lemuel through these weeks was that of separation from his wife. The round trip to Leavenworth took three weeks, even if there was no waiting for the return trip. He took her along on one trip but decided that was not good. Rain was embarrassed by the stares and sidelong glances of disapproval.

What he really needed, Lem decided, was to settle down somewhere and take to farming again. Maybe somewhere along the Smoky Hill—far enough east to take advantage of the better rainfall for crops. Too far west, the rainfall was scant and water a constant problem. There were areas of lush grass along the valley—if grass could grow, surely wheat could, too, as lush and thick as the native grasses. Far enough west, however, to feel the spirit of the valley.

He did not understand that feeling, probably never would, but it was there. Possibly, even, that was what he had been searching for, ever since he left Illinois—a way to use the strength of the Smoky Hill's medicine.

Lem came to this conclusion on one of the last trips before winter, on the eastward run. The long stretch along the Platte gave him much opportunity to think, and by the time he set the brake in Leavenworth, his mind was made up. He would talk to Rain, and if she was agreeable, they would select an area and settle there, as soon as spring began to open up. He felt good about it, as he climbed down and headed for the stage office.

On the way to the hotel, someone called his name.

"Hey, Booth! Lemuel Booth!"

Lem turned to see John Bannister swinging down the street toward him.

"Will you join me for a drink and dinner?" Bannister inquired as they shook hands.

"Of course! Let me get rid of some road dust and change. You're staying at the hotel?"

"Yes. Waiting for the stage to Denver. You driving?"

"Guess so. Good to see you, Jack."

"Likewise. And how is Mrs. Booth? Well, I trust?"

"Yes, she's fine. Listen, I'll tell you all about it. Meet you in the lobby in an hour?"

"I shall be there."

It was pleasant to share a drink, dinner, and a cigar with John Bannister and exchange information on what had happened since they last met.

"Have you seen any more of the ruffians at Julesburg?" the gambler asked.

"No. Well, I don't think so."

"Don't *think* so? Christ's sake, man, you have or you haven't!"

"Well, this one time, near there, I heard a shot. Couldn't see anybody, but it was pretty close. I wondered about it."

"Lem, you're not taking that seriously enough. When was it?"

"Last week, on this trip."

"Yes. Just the sort of stunt that varmint would pull. Shoot from ambush. Bad."

"You think that's it?"

"Lemuel, I'd bet on it."

"Then what . . .?"

"Well, I don't know, but we'll think about it. We've got a few days."

"Well, if it's meant to be . . . but tell me about you. How was St. Louis?"

"Still there. I'll tell you, though, Lemuel, there's a lot of war talk. Oh, you knew that new party got their candidate elected president?"

"No. Who's that?"

"They call themselves Republicans. You know, they ran John Fremont last time. He was beaten because of being a bastard, I'd suppose. This time, a man named Lincoln from Illinois. You haven't followed this?"

"No. Afraid I'm not up on politics. Why the war talk?"

"Well, nobody's sure what he'll do. He's a lot more sympathetic to the antislavery people than Buchanan. And you know about the Kansas statehood push."

"Yes," Lem answered truthfully.

"Well, both sides are bringing in all the settlers they can to swing the vote, free or slave. I figure there'll be war."

"You *do*?"

"I can't see it any other way, Lem. It's on a collision course. That's why I'm going back to Denver. I think it will be less affected by the war. What will you do?"

"Hadn't thought much about it, I reckon."

He had, actually, ever since Lieutenant Fitch's talk about statehood. He'd have to hold with the North, he figured, since he couldn't go along with the slave situation. But he wasn't sure that was what it was all about, anyhow. He didn't want to say too much about it, though, because he had an idea Bannister was a southerner, from his manners and his soft, gentlemanly drawl.

"What will you do?" Lem asked cautiously.

"Stay out of it, if I can. Denver seems remote enough, but I don't know. Times are troubled, my friend. Let's have another drink."

Next morning, when the stage rolled out, Bannister sat on the seat beside Lem, at the latter's invitation.

"You're right, it is pleasant," the gambler observed a few miles down the road. "Not nearly so dusty."

They talked of many things, of Lem's desire to stop the forced separation from his wife, and of his desire to settle down to a more stable existence. Bannister looked a little wistful over this.

"Where did you grow up, Jack?" Lemuel asked.

He felt that they knew each other well enough to handle such questions now.

The gambler answered dreamily. "New Orleans. I killed a man, over a girl, and left to save my family embarrassment."

Lemuel regretted having brought the matter up.

"Reckon he needed killin' then," he said.

"If anyone does," Bannister said softly.

The subject never came up again.

They talked about the possibility of trouble near Julesburg, and how to deal with it. It seemed possible that with winter coming, Stallard, the ruffian, might see this as a last chance for revenge.

"Perhaps it would be advisable," the gambler suggested, "that on the day we approach Julesburg, I ride inside the coach and take your shotgun with me. This would act as an ace up your sleeve, so to speak."

Both men chuckled, and the coach rolled westward as they discussed the details of the plan.

≈ 34 ≈

Even with the best-laid plans, trouble comes with a degree of surprise, and this was no exception. For the last day's run, John Bannister carefully charged and capped the twin tubes of the scattergun and took his place in the coach, facing forward.

"I'll be on the right side," he told Lemuel. "You can shoot better to your left."

Lem had already checked his revolver and holstered it, fully loaded, with the hammer resting between chambers for safety.

There were only two other passengers on this run, a pair of well-worn ladies of the evening ready to mine the gold of Denver's saloons.

An hour or so out of Julesburg, the road dipped to cross a shallow creek bed and, as it took the rise on the other side, made a sharp turn. This was a tricky crossing, because the wheelers were just settling into the harness for the pull up the slope, while the leaders must begin the turn. It required all the attention of the driver. Therefore, it was disconcerting to see a man step into the road ahead of the lead team, waving his hands to stop. Lem started to comply before he thought.

"Full speed ahead!" Bannister called. "This is it!"

Almost at the same moment, someone yelled from concealment. "Yeah, it's him! Let's take him!"

The man in the road drew a pistol and threw a shot at Lem, who had his hands full with the lines. Lem felt something pluck at the crown of his hat, and then a volley of firing broke out. Several men were emerging from cover to enter the road, shooting as they came. Bannister's shotgun boomed, and the first man, in the middle of the road, was blown backward by the force of the charge. The gun spoke again, and another man fell.

The mules were plunging and fighting in terror now. There was another burst of sporadic firing, and Lem heard the popping of Bannister's small revolver. The off mule of the lead team reared high in the air and fell, kicking and struggling in a tangle of harness. The other leader shied to the left, pulling the rest of the team along, off the road. The front wheels were forced into a cramped turn, locking to the left and throwing the front of the coach off balance. At the same time, the left rear wheel began to sink into soft sand at the road's edge. The coach began to topple, like a falling tree, ponderously, but gaining momentum in its fall. The heavy oak beam that formed the tongue of the coach caught at an impossible angle, shattered just in front of the kingbolt, and the coach crashed to the ground beside the road.

Lemuel jumped and rolled clear. For a moment he still held the lines, but the mules were now fighting in terror. They were no longer held back by the weight of the shattered coach, and the lines burned through his fingers. He released his grip and pulled the Colt from its holster, crawling toward the road, firing back at the cottony puffs of smoke that seemed to come from everywhere. He saw Bannister climbing up out of one of the windows of the coach, firing as he came.

Then Lemuel was knocked flat by a numbing blow to his right arm. He tried to pick up his revolver, but his hand refused to work. He looked down to see a spreading stain on his sleeve midway between shoulder and elbow. His head was spinning, and he seemed to see the entire scene through a fuzzy haze.

Bannister slid to the ground beside him, dropped his

empty gun, and grabbed Lemuel's Colt to continue firing as he ran.

Suddenly, all was quiet. Dimly, Lem heard the sound of hoofbeats as the surviving attackers retreated. He lost consciousness for a moment and roused to find one of the women attempting to stop the bleeding from his arm with strips torn from her petticoat.

"It went clean through," she assured him. "Tore up the meat a little but missed the bone. You'll be fine."

She patted him affectionately on the rump.

"I've patched up a lot of gunshots," she continued, "and yours ain't bad."

He was a bit surprised that there was very little pain, only numbness and inability to use his hand. He rose and walked over to lean against the coach.

"Where's Bannister?" he asked the woman.

"Don't know. Oh, here he comes."

The gambler walked across the road and stood looking at Lemuel. He looked tired, dog tired, and the usual spring was missing from his walk.

"Are you all right?" he asked Lemuel.

Lem nodded weakly and then noticed the ashen gray of the gambler's face. "Jack! You're hit?"

Bannister pulled back his coat to reveal a spreading stain just above the waist on the left side. Lem had the momentary thought that Bannister would abhor the damage to his immaculate embroidered vest.

"I think it went clear through," Bannister said. "I thought at first I had merely bumped myself in emerging from the coach."

He sat down, tired, oblivious of the dirt that would have been unacceptable to him under usual circumstances.

"You need not be concerned about Stallard," he added.

"Here, let's get your clothes off, honey," the woman said. "We'll see how bad it is."

She quickly assisted Bannister in stripping to the waist.

"Yes, here's where it came out. All right, we'll wrap you up and get you taken care of."

"We have to get help," Lem said. "Do either of you women ride?"

"Their horses are gone. They took them," Bannister stated. "You'll have to use one of the mules."

The other woman, who had avoided contact with the wounded men, stepped forward.

"I'll go," she said firmly. "I was ridin' work mules before I could walk."

She started after the crippled team and soon returned leading a tall red mule. Her full skirts were cumbersome, and she finally abandoned trying to hold them up to mount the animal.

"Hell with it." She loosened the garment at the waist, ripped it off and threw it aside. Unencumbered, she leaped astride in one long motion.

"Where to?"

"On into Julesburg, I reckon," Lem said. "Go to the stage station. But be careful."

She waved and was gone.

Through the afternoon, they waited. The woman who remained with the wounded men puttered and fussed over them, brought water from the creek, and found a bottle of whiskey in the overturned coach. At one point, she drew Lemuel aside to talk of Bannister.

"He ain't bleeding much," she noted, "but he might be, inside. He don't look too good."

Lem was increasingly concerned over his friend's appearance. In addition, he was feeling the remorse of having been responsible for the incident. His own wound had begun to throb, and he welcomed the slight relief that the whiskey offered. The three of them shared the bottle.

At dusk, they built a fire against the chill of the night. Bannister appeared worse and talked fitfully in his restless sleep. By full dark, when the wagon arrived from Jules-

burg, he was gone. Lemuel sat, holding his friend's head in
his lap and crying unashamedly.

He hated the irony of the situation. John Bannister, a
gentle and cultured man, hating violence, had been pursued by it. He had left his home because of a violent act.
They had met because of another. At the last, Bannister had
left civilization to avoid the violence of the war clouds that
were gathering. To what purpose? He had met with a
violent end on the frontier, dying with his boots on. At
least, Lemuel hoped, the strange, lonely man died knowing
that he was with a friend at the last.

As for himself, he felt that he'd just lost the best friend he
had ever had.

Lem spent three days in Julesburg, arranging for the
burial. There was a well-worn, stained letter in the gambler's carpetbag, with an address in New Orleans. Lem
wrote a letter, not knowing whether it would reach anyone
who cared but feeling that he had to try. He described the
circumstances of Bannister's death and the stone he had
ordered to mark the grave.

John Bannister
18— 1860
He died
for
a friend

Lemuel arrived back in Denver as a passenger, not a
driver, with his wounded arm in a sling. His first act was to
walk to the office and resign. Even if he fully recovered the
use of his arm, he did not think he could climb up on the
driver's seat of a Concord again. He only wanted to get
away from the memories, far away.

He was too weak to walk and wasn't sure he could ride a
horse, so he asked one of the stablemen at L.&P.P. to take

him home. Rain was over at Gabriel's cabin and flew into his arms as he entered.

"What happened? We heard there was trouble."

Lem sat down, dead tired, and quickly told the story.

"*Aiee!* My heart is heavy for John," Rain said sadly. "Did you mourn for him?"

Did he mourn? Not with the songs of mourning, Lem told the girl gently, but in a private way that John Bannister would have understood.

"Yes, Rain, I mourned for him."

"It is good."

They talked around the fire, and Lem told of quitting the stage line.

"What will you do?" Gabriel asked. "Hunt, with me?"

Lem held up his injured arm. "I couldn't right now. Maybe later. I have some thinkin' to do, Uncle Gabe."

Gabriel nodded. He could relate to this dilemma.

Later, snuggled warmly in the blankets, Lem and Blue Rain held a whispered conversation.

"I am glad to have you back," she said in his ear.

"It is good to be here, Rain."

"You are already thinking of something," she observed.

The girl had always been able to tell when something was troubling him. He started to deny but then decided she could help. After all, she would be a major part in his decision. What he needed now was a clean break with the past, to explore some of the questions that had bothered him of late. He wasn't ready to settle down and farm yet.

"Rain," he whispered, "do you have people on the Smoky Hill?"

"Yes, why?"

"Could we stay with them a while?"

Maybe, he thought, *maybe I can get some of their feel for the land, understand its spirit. Rain can help me.*

The girl snuggled closer against him. "Of course, my husband," she whispered. "They will be proud to welcome the Bear-Who-Fights."

≈ **PART III** ≈

≈ 35 ≈

Lemuel Booth clucked to the team and kept them moving. It was a long haul from the farm to the mill at Salina. In fact, they'd stay over, sleeping under the wagon, and return next day, after their wheat was milled into flour and part of it exchanged for corn meal and rolled oats. Sometimes he wished they'd settled just a bit closer to town, but only for a little while, on a day such as this. Mostly, he loved the area they'd chosen along the Smoky Hill.

Fourteen years it had been since they left the Arapahoes to settle down. The two seasons with his wife's people had done him a world of good, had helped him put his life in order and stop fighting the scheme of things—to learn to move with the current instead of against it. He could now look back with few regrets. The loss of his brother, his friends, his family, these things had assumed proper places in his past as he and Blue Rain planned together for their future.

"I'll drop you and the children off at the store while we unload," he told her. "Then I'll pick you up."

"It is good," she said simply.

There had been a time when he would have hesitated to leave her among whites, his own people. Even now, an occasional sidelong glance told of resentment, of Indian troubles in other areas. Among those who knew the Booth family, however, there was little thought of the fact that

Rain Booth's dark beauty was because of her Indian heritage.

Their two sons, John and Samuel, could have been of any ancestry, as the mixture of immigrants poured into the plains. The third child, a little girl-child with huge eyes and her mother's beauty, was called Joy and had earned her right to the name.

Lem pulled the mules to a stop in front of the store and set the brake while Rain and the children climbed down.

"Stay with your mother," he called. "I'll be back directly."

Rain waved at him and stepped on inside to begin her shopping, and he drove on.

There was another wagon unloading at the mill dock, and he stepped down to walk around and work the stiffness out of his joints. He watched the traffic on the street—farmers, townspeople, an occasional Negro, still wondering what to do with his newly acquired freedom.

It scarcely seemed like twelve years since the war ended, or that the Union would be a hundred years old this summer. Likely there'd be a big celebration for Independence Day next month. Maybe they should bring the youngsters in to watch the fireworks and all. The boys would get a lot out of it, though Joy was pretty small. He'd talk to Rain about it.

It was then that he saw the platoon of cavalry moving down the street. From the look of the unit, with full baggage and field equipment, they were just passing through, heading west on the road. The road he'd helped build, Lem thought with pride. It was heavily traveled now. The Butterfield Overland Stage had kept a regular schedule, until the Union Pacific replaced it a few years ago. The army still patrolled the Smoky Hill Road, all the way to Denver. He could hardly believe the changes since he'd first followed the Smoky Hill.

This particular unit, he figured as he watched the troopers, consisted of replacements for one of the forts out west. Likely, these were new troops just out of training at the cavalry center at Fort Riley. They'd have an experienced sergeant, a corporal or two, possibly a green lieutenant just out of West Point, heading for his first duty post.

The detachment clopped down the street toward him, and, without a better means to pass the time, Lem began to notice individual soldiers. Some were raw recruits, bouncing amateurishly in their saddles, their neck scarves still bright new yellow, matching the stripes down the sides of their blue uniform trousers. The sergeant was a grizzled old veteran, who probably had seen service in combat during the war.

It was the corporal who caught Lem's eye—a young man with sandy hair and an open midwestern face burned brown by the sun. Beneath the brim of his campaign hat, clear blue-green eyes swept the street ahead from side to side. His lanky frame seemed to fit the McClellan saddle as if they were part of the same structure.

When the corporal's horse was only a few steps away, the sweep of the blue-green eyes met Lemuel's gaze and stopped short. Lem almost spoke, thinking that he knew the man, and stopped himself. He had the odd impression that the corporal had almost spoken in recognition also. There was a space of a few heartbeats, the men nodded to each other, and their two pairs of eyes swung away. It was a strange feeling, Lemuel thought, and he turned to watch the young man ride on past. The soldier was perhaps fifty feet on down the street when he seemed to feel the other man's eyes upon him. He turned in the saddle, right hand on the cantle, to look back, and their eyes met again for a moment.

"Booth! You ready to unload?" someone called.

"What? Oh, yes. Sorry! I thought that boy was somebody I knew."

He quickly mounted the wagon and pulled up to the dock, still puzzled over the affinity he had felt for the young man, the sense of familiarity. He finished unloading, pocketed the mill slip, and stepped to the wagon again.

Rain had finished her shopping, and they loaded the parcels of coffee, tea, salt, yard goods, and such necessities into the wagon. Lem spent a few minutes admiring a new Winchester rifle, a repeater that would load itself with a single throw of a lever underneath. It was an improvement on the earlier Henry rifle, the storekeeper said, with more stable ammunition. Lem had never seen a Henry, either.

"Want to try it out?" the man asked.

"No, thanks, Abe. 'Fraid I couldn't afford it."

It was growing late, and they drove out of town to camp for the night, Rain quickly kindling the mandatory campfire. Whether it was needed for warmth or not, the fire was an announcement, a declaration of intent, Lemuel had learned. The first decision at any new campsite was where to locate the fire. He had talked with Rain about it long ago. It was a statement to whatever spirits might inhabit a place, she said—in a way, asking permission to camp there. "This is my campfire, here I will be tonight." It had finally occurred to him that this was similar to a housewarming, with the symbolic lighting of the fire in a new dwelling.

This fire pushed back the gathering shadows, as the family prepared for the night. The children were quieting down in their blankets under the wagon, while Lemuel and Rain sat for a little while, enjoying the summer night, its smells and its sounds. A great hunting owl sounded its hollow call from the trees along the river. Somewhere, its mate answered. The smaller night sounds of frogs, crickets, and the call of a night bird brought memories of their first years together. Rain's people were far away now, living in assigned areas to the south, remnants of a proud people. They sat close together for a while, not talking. Lem was thinking about the soldiers.

"Rain," he said finally, "an odd thing happened today."

"Yes?"

"Did you see the soldiers?"

"Not really. There were horse soldiers in town, but I did not watch them. Why?"

"Oh, I don't know. One of them looked at me, and I thought I knew him."

"Maybe you did."

"No. He was young, a corporal, probably just passing through. How could I know him?"

"Could he look like somebody you knew?"

"Well, maybe. Only, he seemed to know me, too."

"Oh, yes. A thing of the spirit," Rain observed, as if that answered the entire mystery.

He was frustrated when she did that.

"I should have asked him," he said, half to himself.

"He probably did not know, either."

"I don't know, Rain. He did look something like my brother, Sam. You remember. Well, he didn't look like him—it was more like he *moved* like Sam, or the way he held himself."

"Of course. I know." Rain nodded.

Lemuel knew that she did.

A few miles to the west, Corporal Jesse Booth sat staring into the fire, listening to the quiet sounds of the horses on the picket line. He wondered what his new assignment would be like. Fort Wallace. He'd been past there once, before he'd enlisted, but couldn't remember much about it. One of the forts on the Smoky Hill, established to protect travelers.

It was a little amazing to him, when he thought about it. He'd come west out of curiosity, to try to lay to rest the mystery of his childhood years. He had to see the country that had swallowed up his father and his uncle without a trace. He'd been very small when his grandmother received the letter stating simply that Samuel was dead. For a long time, the family had expected the return of Jesse's uncle Lemuel, but he never came. The wild country had swallowed both of Rachel Booth's sons, and she became embittered. Jesse's mother had remarried, and the family gradually came to avoid the subject of the brothers who had started to the gold fields and had vanished.

Jesse himself had become somewhat bitter. He didn't know exactly why he had felt driven to go and look at the land that had rendered him fatherless. He had expected to hate it. Somehow, he had become attracted to the strange call of the Smoky Hill and had come to love it. He loved its excesses, the blazing glory of its sunsets, the burning heat of its summers, even the howl of its winter storms, if one could be warm and dry while the storm raged outside. By contrast, there were the soft greens of springtime in the rolling grassland, the subtle smells that changed with the seasons, the myriad wild flowers, and the teeming life of the prairie.

He felt its call so strongly that he had enlisted in order to stay and to travel the prairie that he was coming to love. He'd written home to tell of his decision. He could imagine his grandmother, shaking her head sadly and clucking her tongue disapprovingly over the loss of yet another family member to the call of the West.

He hadn't thought of these things for some time now. He'd been busy, pushed by the demands and restrictions of the military. But he had done a good job. He'd risen to corporal and now was being transferred to the area that had really intrigued him, the upper valley of the Smoky Hill. Nearly as far west as the Colorado line, Fort Wallace must be.

He was rather enjoying the trip out, seeing some country in the best of weather, passing through the growing towns along the river. Salina, today. Named, he supposed, for the place where the Saline River joined the Smoky Hill. It appeared pleasant enough.

That had been odd, the way he'd encountered that farmer in the street. The man had almost spoken, it seemed, and had turned away. Jesse wondered if it was somebody he'd met before. Probably not, he decided. The farmer had undoubtedly taken him for someone else and then been embarrassed by the mistake. It was understandable—men in uniform look much alike.

Jesse rose and sought his blankets. It was no matter, he reckoned, who the farmer was. He'd never see him again, anyhow.

≈ **36** ≈

Fort Wallace was much better than a dozen other frontier posts he'd seen, Corporal Booth decided. Facilities were more extensive, the buildings comfortable. The area was relatively flat, treeless except for the thin strip of timber along the streams, and covered with grass from one horizon to the other. It was primarily shortgrass country, as opposed to the tallgrass hills farther east. The old feeling of excitement was strong in him as he rode on patrol up and down the Smoky Hill Road.

Sometimes the troop swung across the river and patrolled the south side as far east as Starving Woman Creek. There were a few settlers moving into the area now, with the Indian troubles over and the tribes settled down in the Nations. The patrols stopped at some of the ranches and farms sometimes, for water or just to check on the newcomers.

Jesse had been interested in the story of this post, too. Its troopers had participated in more Indian battles since the war than those of any other post on the frontier. Some of the well-known names of the opening of the West had been associated with Fort Wallace, such as the famous scout Bill Comstock. Comstock had been assigned to the fort during most of his career, although on detached service with George Custer for a time, while the general was in command of the Smoky Hill region and the posts from Hays to Denver. Custer, frequently mentioned as a presidential candidate, was currently engaged in a campaign in Montana Territory to bring the Sioux into submission.

Some of the older troopers at the post had engaged in a number of battles and did not hesitate to share their stories, especially with the raw recruits.

Booth knew that though these events were comparatively recent, they were not likely to recur. He was amused at the bug-eyed troopers' fascination with stories of Custer.

"Yep," Sergeant Rigdon related, "the Cheyennes called him Star, when we was with him. On account of his general's stars, you know."

He pointed to his shoulder.

"Now when the General found out about it, he sort of figgered that was big medicine. 'Fore long, them newspaper fellers somehow got the idea it was Morning Star. But that ain't what the troops called him. He was one tough son of a bitch to foller. Jesus, he could stay in the saddle all day and night. Hard-Ass, that's what the troops called him. Not to his face, of course."

The sergeant slapped his leg and roared with amusement, while the recruits laughed appreciatively.

"Sergeant, how long you reckon it'll take the General to corral them Injuns? Any chance we'll get to go up and help?"

"Reckon not, son. Way he goes at it, won't take him all summer."

It was only a few days later that the telegraph chattered its news. George Custer and his entire command had been killed on the Little Big Horn by a combined force of Sioux and Cheyennes. Speculation was rampant, and rumors flew. One story told of a widespread Indian uprising sweeping across the West to drive out all the whites. Some of the troopers hoped fervently they would be ordered north to avenge the massacre, while others feared they would.

"Hell," snorted Sergeant Rigdon, "we ain't goin' nowhere. If there is trouble, we'll stay guardin' our own area."

The sergeant's prediction proved true. Routine patrols continued through the summer, as far west as the state line and beyond, with no sign of trouble. In August, the western part of their region gained statehood, as Colorado entered the Union.

All of this was of little actual importance to troopers at Fort Wallace in that summer of 1876. Corporal Booth slipped easily into the routine, enjoying the relaxation that off-duty time gave. He also enjoyed the patrols, however. Sometimes the weather was hot, dusty, and uncomfortable; but always, evening brought cooling south breezes across the upland. Time spent in bivouac on the open prairie was enjoyable to him, with the expanse of stars on a black velvet sky reaching from one horizon to the other. The sights, smells, and sounds of a prairie night never failed to strike a responsive note somewhere in his being. Jesse Booth did not understand it, he only knew it was there.

He saw the settlers and wondered if they felt this same affinity for the land. Why would someone like Charles Hartman, for instance, be striving to establish a ranch out in the vastness of the prairie halfway to Starving Woman Creek? Or, in the other direction, the Polk family on Rose Creek almost to the Colorado line?

These people fought heat, dust, blizzards, grasshoppers, and, until recently, Indians as a matter of daily life. They *must* feel some of the kinship that he felt with the prairie. Especially, he had to concede, this particular area, the Smoky Hill valley, drew him like a magnet.

He once overheard Hartman talking to Lieutenant Murkha.

"The way I see it, Lieutenant, this valley wasn't meant to farm. Its crop is grass. If it fattens buffalo, it will fatten cattle. With more settlers comin' in, there'll be a demand for beef. We got the railroad now to ship 'em. Yep, when I get built up, get my cow herd like I want it . . . but come here, let me show you—I've got some new brood mares."

The two men walked away, Hartman still talking enthu-siastically. He did have some excellent horses, Jesse knew. One of the major interests that the army had in seeing Hartman succeed was that here was an excellent source of remounts.

Yes, Jesse could see, a man could live with this land in that sort of setup. Start with a few good brood mares; bring in fine, blooded stallions; and raise remounts. Possibly, even, introduce a Spanish jack or two and produce mules from the mare band, if there got to be enough settlers to support a market for work mules.

It might even be practical to catch a few wild mares to get started. Wild horses were plentiful, and it would certainly be inexpensive. Maybe he could talk to Hartman about it some time.

Jesse was also interested in the rancher's ideas about cattle. Many of the settlers saw nothing in this country except the opportunity to "break the sod" and plant crops. It was already becoming apparent that the land, especially to the west, was marginal for this purpose. There was not enough rainfall to support corn—and for wheat, barely sufficient. A man could probably raise enough oats for his workhorses, he figured, but he'd want to talk to Hartman about that, too.

The rancher's basic ideas that rather than bust the sod, he should use it as it had always been used, appealed to Jesse. There would be little difference—harvesting the beef from a cattle operation would be quite similar to the Indians' harvest of the buffalo.

The buffalo were about gone now. Jesse had seen none of the large herds he was told migrated through the area only a few years past. Only stragglers turned up occasionally. The prairie was now dotted with wild horses, occasional antelope, and, in the locality of Hartman's ranch, cattle. As a boy in Illinois, Jesse was familiar with cattle. Mostly, however, they had been family milk cows. These were cattle for a different purpose: beef. When the railroad had been built through the prairie a few years earlier, men had been hired to furnish beef for the track crews by shooting buffalo along the right-of-way.

There were even more people to feed now, but the buffalo were gone. The last of the big Texas cattle drives to the railheads along the Smoky Hill were over. The gunman-marshals—Wild Bill Hickok, Wes Hardin, and the Earps—had moved on to new frontiers, and the country was settling down. It seemed that Hartman's idea of raising beef here, on the grassland that had been grazed for thousands of years, was a valid one. The prairie, all along the Smoky Hill for several miles, supported fat cattle with Hartman's brand on the left hip. It was a heart-shaped brand with a slash across it, like a Cupid's arrow on some Valentine card. Hartman called it the Heart Ranch. The cowboys called the brand the "slash-heart" or the "Cupid's-heart."

Jesse was doing some powerful thinking ahead. His enlistment would be up in two years, and maybe he could scratch together enough savings to get a start. With the remounts, a few cows—yes, it could be made to work. He could even catch and brand maverick cattle with no brands. They were considered fair game to anyone with a rope. Quite a number of escapees from the Texican herds had established themselves in the gullies and ravines of the prairie from the Arkansas to the Smoky Hill.

Booth went so far as try out some ideas for a cattle brand of his own, scratching lines in the dirt. Maybe, he thought, a square, open at the bottom, to represent a booth, for the name tie-in. He considered a letter *B* and a closed square, to be read "B square" to denote honest dealings. Maybe that was a little too sweetly sentimental, though. He abandoned that thought and concentrated on the letter and open box in various combinations and positions. The exact solution continued to elude him.

It was on one of his patrols past Hartman's that Jesse saw the girl. They had stopped in the barnyard to rest their mounts for a few minutes and to drink—the well at

Hartman's was a favorite. Hand dug, lined with stone, it
was one of the best wells in the region, with water sweet,
cold, and clear. A small creek beyond the barn furnished
water for the horses, but the troopers gravitated to the
yard, where the well rope and pulley were kept busy
drawing water to wash dusty tongues and throats. Jesse had
walked over to lean on the corral fence while he waited for
some of the others to slake their thirst. There would still be
water pretty soon. He stood admiring the horses in the
enclosure. One uncommonly fine roan mare appealed to
him.

"Some water, Corporal?" said a soft musical voice beside
him.

He had seen the girl before. The Hartmans' daughter,
oldest of three or four youngsters, maybe eighteen years.
He had marveled at the blue of her eyes, the silky sheen of
her yellow hair, and the way her long body moved. This
was the closest he had been to her, as she held out a tin
dipper dripping cold water. Her smile was like a ray of
sunshine—just a trifle shy, but friendly like. He longed to
say something brilliant that would stay in her memory, but
his brain wouldn't function.

"Thank you, ma'am," he blurted.

"Suzannah!" a woman's voice called from the house.

She flashed the beautiful smile again, took the dipper,
and ran toward the house. Jesse Booth thought this must be
the most beautiful girl he had ever seen.

≈ 37 ≈

The three chiefs sat in the lodge of Stone Bull and smoked and talked until far into the night. There had been much sickness in the tribe since they had been forced to move south to the Nations. It was not good, no way for the People to live. This southern country might be all right for some, even for the southern clans of the People, but not for those from the north.

The white man did not understand. The spirit of the country was not the same. There was an absence of the crisp clean air of the high prairie, the moving of the tribe when the time seemed right to follow the buffalo. Of course, there were few herds now. The killing had been widespread. The whites did not understand the way of the buffalo, either. They would take only the skins, maybe only the *tongue*, and leave the meat to rot on the prairie. There was no respect.

Somehow, it seemed that things would be better in their own country. If they could only break away, move back to join the Lakotas, who had been allowed to stay there. It was a long way, but it seemed possible. As Yellow Calf said, it might be the only way to survive.

"But the soldiers will not let us leave," Crane's Feather protested. "They have told us we must stay here, near Fort Reno."

"Then we will not tell them," Yellow Calf said. "We will leave our lodges standing and move out in the night."

"It might do," Stone Bull said, nodding, "but everyone would have to do exactly as we say."

213

"No," insisted Crane's Feather. "They will discover we are gone, some time. Then they will be angry. They will come and kill our women and children in the lodges, as they did to Black Kettle's."

"They may do that, anyway!" Yellow Calf snapped angrily. "This way, at least we go down fighting."

"Stop, my friends!" Stone Bull held up a hand in protest. "We must not quarrel among ourselves. If we must fight, let it not be with one another."

The door flap lifted and another man entered, moving with the lithe grace of a hunting cat. He was not a big man, but his sinewy frame marked him as a fighter.

"Sit down, Red Horse," Stone Bull invited. "Here, we have tobacco." He offered the pouch. "We are talking of a plan."

While the newcomer shaved tobacco from the hard-twisted skein and packed it into his pipe, Stone Bull outlined the plan. Red Horse replaced the tobacco in the pouch and handed it back, then ignited his pipe with a burning stick from the fire. He blew a soft column of bluish smoke upward toward the smoke-hole.

"Yes," he agreed when Stone Bull paused. "I have thought of such a thing, too. We would move rapidly and be halfway to the Lakotas before they know."

"But they will kill us," Crane's Feather protested.

"Are you afraid to die?" Red Horse demanded.

"My friend," Crane's Feather spoke sadly, "we have fought together, and you know my courage better than to ask that. I am afraid, yes, for my wife and children. For them alone, I cannot do this thing."

"Let it be so," Stone Bull said diplomatically. "Then if we go, Crane's Feather, you and your family will stay behind?"

"Yes, my chief. I cannot go."

"Perhaps this is good," Yellow Calf said. "Feather's people can move about, going from lodge to lodge, keeping fires burning, making it look as if we are still there."

"Yes, that is good," Stone Bull said. "We will ask

everyone. If they wish to go, it is good; but those who stay behind can be of great help."

The planning continued.

"What of the big village of Long-Knives on the Arkansas?" Yellow Calf asked.

"We will go around them to the east," Stone Bull said.

"Yes," Red Horse said, "and kill everyone we see, so they cannot tell."

"No!" Stone Bull decreed firmly. "We must kill no one, Horse. That would certainly tell them that we must be stopped. If we appear harmless, they may let us go."

Red Horse nodded in assent, but it could be plainly seen that he was not convinced.

In the ensuing days, the four chiefs talked individually with every family in the band. Some of the People were old and unable to consider such a trip. Others were discouraged, tired of the constantly deteriorating fortunes of the People as their civilization collapsed before their eyes. These elected to stay behind, no longer possessing the will to continue. There were still others who took the same view as Crane's Feather—the advantages of being in their former homeland were apparent, but they feared for their families' safety. They, too, would stay behind.

To the last lodge, however, everyone agreed to help the plan. There were, in all, 117 men, women, and children who would participate in the break. Perhaps an equal number would stay behind to move among the lodges, keep fires going, sit and smoke in the sun, and try in every way to make it appear that the village was engaged in normal activity.

A night was chosen carefully for the departure, one with no moon to reveal their activity. The country to the north had been carefully scouted, and an area selected for their first stop.

"May your medicine be strong, my friends," Crane's Feather wished for them as they prepared to depart.

"And yours." Stone Bull grasped the wrist of the other in the traditional salute. "May our trails cross again."

They took only a few horses, the best of the buffalo-runners, for the scouts to use. It would be too difficult to hide a large band of horses during their stops. Besides, many of the travelers would be on foot, and the speed of travel would be determined by the slowest of the column.

Even so, they had covered twenty miles by the time the sun rose. The refugees bedded down for the day in a previously selected growth of scrub oak, tired out but excited. If they could have but a few more days before their departure was discovered, they would be well on their way.

Their leaders were becoming optimistic about the possibility of success, when after five nights' travel they had seen no one. It was that day, however, that the incident occurred that was the first of their worsening luck. At mid-morning, the People were resting or sleeping in the concealment of the trees along a stream, when a rider suddenly appeared. He was alone, and it required only a moment to determine that he was one of those whose duty was to herd the spotted buffalo.

The sentries cautioned the others, and everyone maintained a hushed silence while they watched. With luck, the man might ride on. He seemed to wander this way and that, probably looking for the spotted buffalo, Red Horse decided. It was sheer coincidence, apparently, that drew him straight toward the creek where the People lay hidden.

He was practically among them when his eyes widened suddenly. In terror, he reined his horse around, attempting to escape. The turn was barely complete, however, when Red Horse's arrow struck him between the shoulder blades.

"No!" Stone Bull called, as the man tumbled from his horse. "We agreed, no killing!"

"I could not let him go," Red Horse protested. "He would tell."

A council hastily assembled.

"Now, where are we?" Stone Bull asked.

"Near the Arkansas, maybe."

"We must hide this man and move on."

"What about his horse?"

"Let it go. It will go home, and they will search for him."

"No, we should take it. Then they will think he just rode away."

"But if we are caught with the horse, they will know we killed him."

It was finally decided that they would take the horse for a day or two and then release it, still saddled. Meanwhile, busy hands were burying the body of the unfortunate cowboy.

Before full dark, the People moved on.

When Slim did not return from checking the heifers at the west end of the ranch, the owner became concerned. It was nearly dark, so after a cursory search, plans were initiated to begin next morning.

Even so, it was noon the next day when the searchers returned to the ranch headquarters with disturbing news. They had found no trace of the missing hand but had stumbled on a place where at least a hundred people had spent the night.

"Soldiers?" the puzzled rancher asked.

"No, sir, reckon not. There was tracks of a few horses, but mostly moccasins. These was Injuns."

"My Lord! We have to let the army know."

"Yessir."

"Curly, you want to go?"

"Sure. Can I use the bay?"

The rancher hesitated. He had not envisioned this use for the racing stallion from Missouri, his pride and joy. But this was important, and lives might depend on it.

"All right, go ahead. But pace him a little. Remember, if he breaks down, you're on foot."

* * *

It was only an hour or so short of daylight when the
sentry at Fort Dodge challenged an incoming rider on an
exhausted bay horse. He was questioned briefly by the
officer of the day, who quickly sent for the commandant.
Before daylight, the telegraph keys were clicking frantically
to other frontier posts.

Fort Reno, in the Oklahoma Territory, discovered that a
hundred or more of their reservation Indians had departed
some days before. On the assumption that the party on the
Arkansas had been the same renegades, a general pattern
emerged.

"They're trying to go home, sir," a scout told his superior,
pointing to the wall map. "See, they've skirted Fort Dodge,
and they'll cross the Smoky Hill about here. They'll get
about this far today."

"Get Fort Wallace on the wire," the captain snapped.
"With luck, they can head them off before they reach the
Smoky Hill. Damn that Stone Bull! We'll teach him a
lesson."

He finished scribbling his message and flung it at the
signalman. The telegraph began to chatter.

≈ **38** ≈

Corporal Booth sat on his bunk, uneasy and anxious. After
a winter of forced inactivity, the prospect of some action
was welcome. The other troopers were cleaning weapons
and joking and laughing about how many redskins they
planned to kill.

Jesse himself had seen no combat action since his
enlistment. There had been very little combat in recent
years, and never in an area where he happened to be.
Usually, a few renegade Indians off the reservation, doing a

little burning and killing, and the army coming along to bury the dead. The culprits would be back on the reservation practically before their predations were discovered.

There was the unfortunate massacre of that family of travelers a year or so before. A couple of the children were carried off and ransomed later, he recalled. And the attempt to burn the railroad roundhouse at Brookville. Nobody was hurt in that one, and the story was told and retold. The townspeople had taken refuge in the roundhouse, not realizing that it was the target of the raid, the "stable of the iron horse." When the attempts to burn the structure began, the townspeople fired up the boiler on one of the engines and drove it out through the closed doors, whistle blowing to raise the dead. The people huddled in the tender car to escape the expected hail of arrows and bullets as they emerged. The sight of the roaring iron horse had apparently been too much for the attackers, however. They had fled the area and did not return.

Jesse Booth wasn't certain but somehow felt that this situation was going to be different. He was still remembering the Custer massacre on the Little Big Horn last year. People who could accomplish that must be taken seriously. Little was known about the present situation, but the commanding officer was being kept informed by the telegraph. Word filtered out to the troops via the company clerk, but it was incomplete and sketchy.

A sizable force of Indians, it was said, had left the reservation in the Nations and were heading north. Apparently, their leadership was capable and well-informed, or very lucky—they had traveled several days before their absence was discovered. By this time, they had crossed the border into Kansas, skirted around Fort Dodge on the Arkansas River, and were moving toward the Smoky Hill. There had been some killings, rumors said, and isolated ranches were burned and pillaged, according to whispered tales.

Rumors estimated the renegade force at anywhere from

a hundred to a thousand warriors. Jesse noticed that each time he heard the story, the number of "hostiles" increased. Their motive, according to the military grapevine, was to attack Fort Wallace. This would remove the army's protection from the Smoky Hill Road and stop traffic to the west.

Jesse was inclined to doubt this theory. As far as he knew, there had never been an instance of an all-out Indian attack on a military fort. It was not the style of the renegades. They would strike and run, attack isolated areas as opportunity offered, burn a railroad trestle or a stage station. They would be gone like the night fog when the rising sun burns it away.

No, he expected no direct attack on the fort. Their part in this would be different. The troops had already been placed on full alert, and each man had been issued fifty rounds of ammunition. This, of course, implied expected trouble. Twenty rounds was the more usual amount issued for routine patrols. The order of the day also called for full field equipment.

Sergeant Rigdon had ceased telling his stories and sat quietly, methodically cleaning his carbine again and again. Some of the men were writing letters home, possibly last letters.

Booth shook his head to clear it. What was he thinking? This would likely be a minor incident, at worst. Allowing for the exaggeration of the military rumor mill, this was probably only a handful of poorly equipped Indians out on a buffalo hunt. Likely, they'd turn back before they came this far north.

Behind this reasoning, though, was the disconcerting memory of something Sergeant Rigdon had once said. The barracks talk had centered around a frontier incident in which there had been few casualties. One of the troopers had referred to it as a "little skirmish."

"Son," Rigdon had said firmly, "there ain't no 'little' gunfights. You're jest as dead if it's a big battle or a three-shot bushwhack, and don't never forget it."

The interminable waiting dragged out for the entire day, and darkness had fallen when a message came down to the barracks: all noncoms of B Troop to report to headquarters. Sergeant Rigdon gave a deep sigh and rose from his bunk.

"Reckon this is it. Come on, Booth."

The little handful of noncommissioned officers gathered in the office at headquarters. The room was bright with coal-oil lamps, and a table was littered with maps. The captain rapped on the table for attention, and the room quieted.

"This is the situation, gentlemen," he began. "A force of hostiles, perhaps as many as a hundred warriors, has left the reservation near Fort Reno. They have women and children with them, so it appears that they may be trying to return to the Dakotas, their former range."

He paused to point to a dotted line that had been sketched on the map.

"This, we believe, is their approximate route. They skirted Fort Dodge two days ago."

"Where were they last seen?" a young lieutenant asked.

The captain turned a cold stare on him. "They have *not* been seen, Lieutenant. They camped near the Arkansas, about here, two nights ago. We estimate they will be about here." He paused to point. "Now, our mission—B Troop will move out at dawn, the other troops remain here. We will try to intercept the renegades before they reach the river."

"We are to engage?" a lieutenant asked.

"Our orders are to capture and return this band to the reservation. However, it will depend entirely on their willingness. If they want a fight, so be it."

There was a murmur of assent.

The troopers walked back to B Troop's barracks. There would be little sleep tonight. Immediately, the excitement spread.

"The only good Indian is a dead one," someone joked. "Reckon we can make some of 'em good ones."

Sergeant Rigdon was very quiet.

"Something the matter, Sergeant?" Jesse Booth inquired discreetly.

The old soldier looked at him quizzically. "No, reckon not. These boys, they don't know what it's like. Hell, I guess I'm jest gettin' too old for this. I figgered it was about over."

"Maybe it won't amount to much, Sergeant."

"Corporal, it always amounts to somethin'. If it's your name that comes up, it's much."

The barracks was stirring long before daylight; and when the bugle sounded reveille, everyone was more than ready. The sun was barely showing its blood-red rim when the troop moved out. Their direction was almost directly southeast. The intention was to head off the moving column of Indians well south of the river. Lieutenant Murkha rode in silence, ramrod straight, and said nothing. Booth would have liked to ask a number of questions, but such a thing was inappropriate.

Toward noon, having seen nothing out of the ordinary, the troop halted briefly to rest men and horses. Sweaty troopers loosened their cinches and stretched out in whatever thin shade the willows along the creek might furnish. Sergeant Rigdon, with the security of seniority, asked the question that had been uppermost in Jesse's mind.

"Lieutenant, do we have any new information as to their strength and position?"

Murkha shook his head. "Rigdon, to tell the truth, we know less than we did. Reason we're out here is to try to find out. The telegraph went dead last night."

"Cut, sir?"

"Who knows? It's always goin' out. Wind, lightning, buffalo knock the poles down."

"But, Lieutenant, there ain't been any storms, and buffler are pretty scarce any more."

Murkha fixed the sergeant with a stony stare. "Exactly, Sergeant."

≈ 39 ≈

Stone Bull, Yellow Calf, and Red Horse stood looking up at the thin wire. It ran from pole to pole, stretching to earth's rim in both directions. The breeze made the thing hum like a swarm of bees heard faintly at a little distance. Their scouts had discovered it this afternoon.

"What does it do?" Stone Bull asked.

"It is a medicine of the Long-Knives," Yellow Calf explained. "They can use this to talk."

"To *talk*?"

"Yes, it is a sign-talk, I have heard. Someone at that end puts signs into the talking wire, to be heard by someone at the other end."

"*Aiee*, this is bad," Stone Bull said, shaking his head. "They can tell the Long-Knives ahead that we are coming?"

"Maybe so."

"My friends, I have not given enough thought to this talking wire at Fort Reno. We must cut it to destroy its medicine."

"Would this be dangerous?" Yellow Calf asked. "It hums like many bees."

"I think not, Calf," Red Horse said. "Look, a bird sits on it and is not hurt. I will cut it."

He reined his horse over to the nearest pole and stood in the saddle seat, holding on to the pole. One swing of his belt-ax, and a length of copper wire fell to the ground.

"Maybe its medicine will make *me* strong!"

He jumped to the ground and chopped off a length of wire to wind around his right wrist. The others followed his example and turned back toward their main party. Red Horse was rubbing the wire on his legging, burnishing away green corrosion to expose the brightness of copper.

The others had begun to rouse from the day's hiding and rest, and were preparing to start. It would be dark enough before long.

"Stone Bull, do you think we are discovered yet?" Yellow Calf asked.

"Maybe. It troubles me that we have seen no one except the one. They may have missed him when he did not return and come looking for him. Did we turn his horse loose?"

"Yes, Red Horse released it last night before we traveled."

"Good."

At dawn the next day, they entered a brushy strip of trees along a creek to find a place of rest. The scouts were startled to hear a large animal crashing through the brush and moved cautiously forward. The creature burst into the open and turned to stare stupidly at the intruders.

"A spotted buffalo!"

"Shoot it! We need meat!"

It was quickly decided. One of the warriors with a bow would down the animal to avoid the noise of a shot. He drew the arrow to its head and let fly. The cow flinched and fidgeted, ran a few steps, and stumbled to fall kicking in the grass. People ran forward to begin the butchering. The band would eat well today.

"What is this sign on the hip?" someone asked.

"A medicine-sign," another said, "like the sign on a lodge to tell who lives there."

Stone Bull was inclined to take the matter more seriously. This mark of ownership meant that somewhere a white man would be upset at the loss of his spotted buffalo. Even worse, his lodge would probably be nearby. Stone Bull sent the scouts to circle widely, but they reported nothing.

"Keep the fires small," the word filtered through the camp. "As little smoke as possible."

"Eat well," Stone Bull told his people. "We may not have another kill for a while."

He was beginning to tire. He was not as young as once. Now, in the harsh reality of this journey, it seemed sometimes like a crazy dream, an impossible effort. Still, he felt they were right to try.

One of his concerns was the changing attitude of some of the warriors. There was a certain faction, largely followers of Red Horse, who seemed to be eager for a fight. It had begun after the killing of the cowboy. When that incident made no change in the day-to-day sameness, the young men began to feel a confidence that seemed unjustified. Stone Bull was certain they had not heard the last of that killing. He dreaded the time when they would contact some more whites, as surely they would. He felt unable to control the excesses of the young men. Yellow Calf would try to approach the situation conservatively, but he was unsure of Red Horse and the young men who saw him as their ideal. He took Red Horse aside to talk of these fears.

"Of course," Red Horse agreed. "We must avoid trouble. But if it comes, our young men must defend themselves. We cannot ask otherwise."

This conversation only made Stone Bull more uneasy. It appeared that Red Horse himself was eager for a fight. Stone Bull's heart was heavy. He wished they had not cut the talking wire, because Red Horse had not been the same since.

That afternoon, while most of the People were sleeping, came the incident that seemed to make their medicine go bad. Every effort had been made to keep the smoke from cooking fires at a minimum, but it was not possible. In the clear prairie air, even a slight blur on the horizon a day's travel away could be seen. Still, they had to eat. They were not carrying enough supplies for the entire trip.

It appeared later that the man may have seen their smoke and had come to investigate. At any rate, one of the scouts, well north of the camp, had encountered a rider unexpect-

edly. The man had wheeled his horse to escape, firing with
a revolver as he ran. The noise of firing alerted several
young warriors, who leaped on horses to join the fight.

In the running fight that followed, a shot struck the white
man's horse. He quickly took shelter behind the dead
animal, firing at his attackers as they charged. Red Arrow,
the scout who had first encountered the white man, was
killed instantly. The other attackers circled, firing, while
the lone defender expended the last of his ammunition. He
succeeded in wounding two more warriors before he was
overrun.

Now two more riders appeared, attracted by the firing.
The scent of blood and battle was fresh in the nostrils of the
young warriors of the People. They charged as the two
white men whirled to run for their lives.

By the time the main force of warriors approached the
scene of the first skirmish, the situation was entirely out of
hand. Blood had been shed by both sides. There was no
holding the young men back now. Stone Bull realized it was
over and he had lost.

The two who had escaped had taken refuge in a large
stone lodge such as the whites use. There were other
structures nearby, as the scouts evaluated the farmstead in
the fading daylight. A number of good horses stood in an
enclosure, horses that would enable faster travel. They
must not be harmed.

Probably there were not more than two or three fighting
men here, maybe a boy or two. It should be easy to set fire
to the wooden roof of their lodge. That would bring them
out into the open. They would wait until morning, of
course. This must not be rushed. Let the entire band come
up to participate, to share in the glory.

Meanwhile, they killed a few more of the spotted buffalo
with the medicine-signs on their left hips. Fires were
lighted, and the People settled down to wait for morning.

As darkness fell, war talk began. In vain, Stone Bull and
Yellow Calf urged that they move on as quickly as possible.

The young men refused to consider it before avenging their losses.

Red Horse was of no help. "We must defend ourselves," he insisted. "Anyway, these are not soldiers. There are only a few of them. We will kill these and then move on."

With the way the young men were acting, it was useless to protest. Stone Bull's heart was very heavy, and the meat of the spotted buffalo, which his wife cooked and brought to him, was like ashes in his mouth.

≈ 40 ≈

Charles Hartman gripped his rifle and peered out through the heavy shutters. The strange yellow-gray light of the impending dawn was beginning to show in the eastern sky. He could scarcely believe this sudden turn of events. They had heard shooting, and he and one of the hired hands had ridden out to see what was happening.

They had been too late to help poor Reb, who was already hacked to pieces when they arrived. They'd been lucky to escape with their own lives. Lord, he'd never seen so many Indians. That was something of a surprise; but even more, that they had attacked. What few Indians were usually around, he'd gotten along with pretty well. He'd given them a yearling steer a time or two and even counted a couple of them as friends.

These were different. Outsiders from somewhere. Didn't seem to want anything, except to attack. He'd seen them killing cattle, just before dark. Some of his best stock, the crossbred whitefaces he'd saved for breeding. Damn, he hated that. Then he realized this was a bit ridiculous. He was worrying about his cows, when the real question was whether any of his family could survive. There must be fifty

armed warriors out there in the dark. From the number of
fires that ringed the farmstead, it looked like that many
more. He couldn't figure that. Could there be women and
children on this war party? He was sure he'd seen some
butchering his cows, just before dark.

He'd sent Sarah and the children to the cave along
toward morning. He and Curly, the remaining hired man,
would keep watch. The attack likely wouldn't come until
dawn, anyway.

The cave was roomy and dry, only a few steps from the
house, laid up tight with stone and with a good solid door
to close. Most folks had one for storage and to get into in
case of a twister. Cyclone cellars, some called them.

He used to tease Sarah about it, about how she'd dreaded
the windstorms when they came west and insisted on the
well-built cellar. The "'fraidy-hole," he'd called it. Since
they settled here, though, they'd never seen one of the
dreaded funnel clouds. The 'fraidy-hole was used for storage.

Until now. He knew that if worst came to worst, it would
be no defense; but it was some consolation to know they
would be safe from stray bullets.

Now Sarah came up beside him. She'd refused to stay in
the cellar.

"I can shoot as well as you," she said, "and Suzannah can
look after the other children."

He put an arm around her shoulders.

"It looks pretty bad, don't it?" she asked.

"Yes," he admitted. "I'm sorry, Sarah."

"It's all right. We've had some good years. I'm sorry for
the children, though."

"Maybe the army will come," he said, not believing it.

"Yes, maybe so."

He could tell she didn't believe it, either.

A long, arching brand of fire reached out of the thinning
darkness near one of the campfires, and he heard some-

thing thud softly on the roof. Then another burning arrow followed the first.

"Jesus," he whispered, "they're settin' fire to the house."

"Charles," Sarah said, "don't take the Lord's name in vain."

"Let's pray, then," he murmured, though he figured that was in vain, too.

It seemed only a few moments later that smoke began to filter down the narrow stairs. He ran to look. There was no way to fight the smoldering fire in the wooden shingles overhead. He ran back down.

A shadowy figure flitted toward the house and took cover behind the well curb. In the growing light, Hartman could see the outline of an elbow or knee protruding from behind the stone.

"By God, I'll let 'em know they've been here," he muttered.

He took careful aim and squeezed off the shot. A yell of pain told him it had been true. But now there were more shadowy figures running. From the rear of the house, he heard the boom of Curly's rifle. The smoke was growing thicker now, and he coughed from the irritation.

Over by the side window, Sarah knelt praying. Pretty quick, they'd have to decide whether it would be better to die in the open or suffocate in the smoke of their burning home. He looked at Sarah. He'd heard of men killing their families to keep them from falling into the hands of the Indians. He knew he couldn't do it. While there was still life, there was hope.

But not much, he reflected grimly, searching for another target in the yard.

Some miles away, the civilian scout of B Troop returned to report.

"Lieutenant, there's a trail about a mile ahead."

"A trail?"

"Yes, sir. About a hundred people, mostly on foot. A handful of horses. Some women and children, headin' north."

"Jesus, Harrison, you can't know all that from the tracks."

The scout pushed his hat back on his forehead and spat across his mule's withers, on the side away from the officer. "No, sir, I can't. But my Ute tracker can, and I'll stake my life on it."

"Old Broken Knife? He knows all that?"

"Lieutenant," Sergeant Rigdon interjected, "he can track a moccasin acrost solid rock, damn near, and tell you how tall was the man wearin' it."

"Very well," Murkha said impatiently. "This means, then, that we have failed to intercept the renegades?"

"Yes, sir."

"Then we must pursue them."

He struck spurs to his horse and headed in a northeasterly direction, followed by the troop. When they struck the trail of the fugitives, Lieutenant Murkha turned to follow it, slowing to an uncomfortable but ground-eating trot. Each hour or so, he called a brief rest stop, but the pace was exhausting.

It was during one of the rest stops that the scout, Harrison, came loping back. He pulled his mule to a sliding stop so sudden that the long fringes on his buckskins swung to and fro for a moment.

"They've killed a cow up ahead, Lieutenant. It's been butchered out, and a lot of cookin' fires where they spent the day yesterday."

"So, we are one day behind them?"

"Yes, sir, I'd say so. Broken Knife went on ahead a ways. He thinks this beef kill ain't all that's goin' on, but I don't know what else."

"Mount up!" called the lieutenant.

They examined scattered pieces of skin, the skull, and occasional bones near the still-warm ashes of campfires.

The troopers were still poking around the abandoned campsite when Broken Knife rejoined them.

"Dead man ahead," he said, pointing.

A mile away lay a dead horse wearing an ordinary stock saddle, with a lariat still in place on the cantle. That was the only way that the nearby corpse could have been identified as a cowboy. The man had been stripped and scalped, probably alive, it seemed. He was staked out on the ground, spread-eagle. Parts of his anatomy had been slashed off and stuffed into his mouth. As a last, terminal torture, his tormentors had built a fire directly on his exposed abdomen and left it to burn.

"Jesus God!" one of the troopers said softly.

Another moved a short distance away and dropped to his knees to vomit.

Lieutenant Murkha appeared very pale but maintained his composure well.

"All right, let's have a burial detail," he snapped. "Jones, O'Hara, Cameron. The rest, mount up."

They had barely topped the next rise when someone pointed to a gray column of smoke in the distance. In the warm still air it rose straight upward, high into the sky, before spreading like a thin, ethereal mushroom against the blue.

"That is bad," Sergeant Rigdon muttered.

The direction in which the smoke could be seen lay precisely on the course of the track they were following. They sat for a moment, studying this new development.

"Is that where they're camped?" one of the new recruits asked.

"No, son," Rigdon said gently. "It ain't. It's where somebody used to live."

Slowly, the realization began to dawn on Corporal Booth, clutching at the pit of his stomach with an icy claw. He wanted to deny it, could not accept it, much less speak of it. It fell upon Lieutenant Murkha to verbalize what some of them were beginning to suspect.

"Sergeant," Murkha said, "we usually come in from the other direction but wouldn't that be about where the Hartman place is located?"

≈ **41** ≈

The formerly well-kept farmstead was a shambles as they rode in. The stone walls of the house still stood, but the roof had collapsed into the interior, and smoke still drifted up from the pyre inside. Furniture, bedding, and housewares were strewn around the yard.

The bodies of Charles and Sarah Hartman lay within arm's reach of each other, just outside their doorway. Both had been scalped but not mutilated.

"Must of left in a hurry," Harrison speculated.

"Scatter out," Lieutenant Murkha called. "See if you can find anybody alive. Then we'll go after them."

The corral was empty of Hartman's fine, blooded horses. Here and there lay dead or dying cattle. For some odd reason, the barn and the smokehouse remained standing.

Jesse Booth looked frantically for a trace of the girl Suzannah. He told himself he would have the same concern for anyone, but he knew he lied. He could not remember the other members of the family or what they looked like. No, it was Suzannah Hartman who occupied his thoughts, the most beautiful girl in the world, who, in addition, had smiled at him. His throat tightened at the thought of what might have happened to her, and he thought with a sickly feeling of the corpse out on the prairie. None of the other searchers could know the dread with which he searched around the barn and along the creek.

Some of the troopers were turning up bits and pieces of information as they moved like ants around the farmstead.

There was a burned corpse in the smoldering remains of the gutted house. It appeared to be the body of a man, still clutching a Spencer rifle. All other weapons had been carried off by the attackers. The fire had apparently been too hot for them to salvage this one. The stock was burned away now.

"That's the hired hand, likely," Lieutenant Murkha said.

"Looks like his Spencer," Rigdon added.

"Sir, there's two children in the cave," a trooper reported.

"Alive?"

"No, sir. Scalped. A boy and a little girl."

Revolting though the idea was, Jesse Booth received this news with hope. As long as they had not found the bodies of the two older girls, they might be alive.

"Lieutenant," he said to Murkha, "both of the older girls seem to be missing."

"Anybody see anything of the two oldest girls?" Murkha called.

There was only silence.

"I'd say they took 'em, alive," Harrison stated.

"Then we'd best get after them. Water your horses and fill canteens. Which way did they go, Harrison?"

"Looks like due east."

"*East?* What in hell . . ."

"There's a canyon over that way, 'bout a day's ride. Runs north, right to the Smoky Hill."

"Starving Woman Creek?"

"Yes, sir. If some of them happen to know this country— well, that's where I'd go."

"Jesus Christ!" a trooper yelled from over at the well, retching and spitting. "Lieutenant, them bastards shit in the well."

"Then use the goddamn creek!"

Everyone was becoming testy. It seemed to Jesse like the ultimate insult. It was not uncommon for a war party to foul the water supply of the enemy, but this . . . He seethed with anger. They had no right. This well was not only the sweetest water in the area, but she had drawn him a dipper of it with her own hands. *Damn* them!

"Wait!" Murkha called. "Is there anything else down the well?"

"Like what, sir?"

"Like bodies, damn it! Let's lower somebody down to see."

"I'll go down, sir," Booth volunteered.

If her body was down there, maybe stripped and mutilated, he didn't want anyone else finding it.

"Very well, Booth. Have we a rope?"

"The well rope looks good. We can use the pulley," Rigdon said.

Jesse stood with a foot in the bucket, and they lowered away, until he struck the water and called for them to stop. He poked around with a pitchfork carried down for the purpose. There was nothing. No trace of a body, only the cool damp of the well, and the slippery stones that lined its walls.

"Pull me up!" he yelled.

As he came blinking back into the sunlight and handed the pitchfork to someone, the burial detail rode up.

"Oh, yes, we need to bury these," the lieutenant said. "But, a new detail."

"Thank you, sir," O'Hara said weakly.

Murkha ticked off the names of the new burial detail.

"Bring the youngsters up from the cave," he continued. "Why don't you put them all on that slope behind the house. A nice straight row, and mark them well, now."

"Yes, sir."

"Now, the rest, mount up!"

In a few minutes, the troop was moving east.

"Harrison, if we travel all night, we should catch up to the renegades at the canyon, right?"

"Yes, sir," Harrison said glumly, "but I ain't sure we want to. They outnumber us some."

"Don't tell me my job, mister," Murkha snapped. "You and your goddamn Ute are supposed to find the enemy and tell us his strength and position. Now, it seems to me you're doing a poor job of that. We don't even know how many of these hundred you talk of are women and children. Now, by God, we *are* going to catch them, and by that time you'll have me some better information!"

Corporal Booth was astonished at this outburst. The lieutenant was ordinarily well respected, but under the stress of this mission he was becoming downright unreasonable. Booth half expected Harrison to tell the lieutenant to go to hell. The scout, after all, was a civilian employee, not serving an enlistment. He could walk away if he wanted to, with nothing worse than the loss of his pay.

Harrison was silent for a few moments, riding alongside the officer, looking straight ahead.

"Lieutenant," he said finally, "I reckon I'll just act like you never said that."

He nudged heels to his mule and cantered away on the broad track left by the retreating hostiles. Broken Knife was already out of sight ahead.

It was scarcely an hour later when Harrison was back.

"They killed one of 'em, Lieutenant. One of them girls. Broken Knife found her in a gully. Tomahawked and scalped."

"Which one?" gulped Jesse Booth.

Both the scout and the officer turned to look at him in surprise.

"Why, I don't know, Corporal. I don't know the names of 'em. Does it make a difference?"

"Yes, Corporal, does it? One's just as dead as the other."

"No, sir, I reckon not. Only I just knew the one a little better, is all."

"Well," Harrison said, "I never knew 'em apart. 'Course, they could *both* be dead, and we ain't found the other'n. Well, I'll be gettin' on."

"Lieutenant," Jesse suggested, "I could ride on ahead

with Harrison and take care of this body. That wouldn't hold up the troop any."

"Good suggestion, Booth. Yes, go ahead."

He wrapped the dead girl in the blanket from his saddle roll, thanking the good Lord all the while that it was not Suzannah. He felt grief for her sister, but it was in no way the same. He tied the blanket and was just wondering what his next move would be, when the troop arrived.

"Did you find which one it is?" Murkha asked.

"Yes, sir, the younger one. Katy, I think she was called."

"Very well. One still missing, eh?"

"Yes, sir."

For a moment, he hated the lieutenant, all cool and businesslike, just wanting the numbers to come out right when he made his report. However, the officer showed that he had, at least, done some thinking since his confrontation with the scout.

"We'll camp here," he announced. "It'll be dark soon."

"Shall we bury the girl here, sir?" Jesse asked.

"We have to, I guess. Can't leave her here or take her along. You tend to it, Corporal."

Jesse was grateful, in a way, to have the diversion, so he wouldn't need to think too much. He picked another trooper, and the two began to dig while the others went about the routine of establishing the picket line. Shadows were lengthening, and the grave was nearly filled, when Harrison returned. Jesse left the shoveling to go over and hear the scout's report.

"They're still ahead of us, Lieutenant. Broken Knife says they're headin' for Starving Woman Creek."

"Ah, we'll catch them tomorrow, then?"

"Yes, sir. Probably not before they reach the creek, though."

"Can we head northeast and get ahead of them?"

"Mebbe so."

"Good. You inform your Ute. We'll rest a few hours and

then move out. Forced march. We'll surprise them in the canyon."

"One other thing, sir. Broken Knife says there's a storm comin' tomorrow."

"Nonsense. I can see it's a clear evening. We've had good weather for a week."

"I dunno, Lieutenant. They have ways of tellin' things like that. I'd count on some weather, if I was you."

≈ **42** ≈

Suzannah huddled under the dirty scrap of blanket and shivered a little, no more from the chill of the prairie night than from the terror of the day. The routine of the ranch had suddenly been destroyed. In fact, her whole world had come crashing down in shambles, like the crash of the roof into the interior of the stone house that had been her home. She had watched that through a crack in the door of the 'fraidy-hole. The sparks had risen in a spectacle like the fireworks she'd seen last year at Independence Day, when the nation was a hundred years old.

That seemed unimportant now. She tried to move her hands a little, but the rawhide cords cut into her flesh, making the pain worse; and she tried to relax again.

She attempted to account for the rest of the family, turning the horrible memories over again in her mind. The terror had started a day ago, before dark, when her father and Curly, the taciturn old hired hand, had come pounding into the yard on lathered horses, pursued by a dozen Indians. They had related that Reb, the other hand, had been killed. There had followed a sleepless night of terror as more and more Indians gathered, and their campfires ringed the farmstead. It was an impossible thing, she told herself. The hostilities had been over for several years. But it was happening.

When their mother took the children to the cave just before morning and then left to join their father, Suzannah had realized that it was all over. She continued to reassure the little ones; but in her own mind, she had given them all up for dead, including herself. She had been watching through the crack when the first fire arrows struck the roof of the house. She did not do or say anything. She had been cautioned and made to promise before her mother left them, that she would remain hidden and try to protect the little ones.

When the roof had fallen in with its crash of fire and sparks, she was not sure what had happened to old Curly. She had seen him in the back window not long before. Her parents were apparently in the front of the house. She had heard shots there from time to time. There was a lot of yelling and a flurry of shots just before the roof fell, and she was afraid to think of what she knew it meant. Her parents must have been driven out by the smoke and flames, and . . .   She lapsed into tears, trying not to make any sound. Earlier, one of the women had beaten her severely for crying aloud.

There had been Indians running everywhere, then, after the house fell. She saw one yelling warrior dash past on horseback, wearing a scarf of her mother's around his head. They were throwing and dragging small items of furniture, clothing, and dishes, pots, and pans that had been spared by the flames. It seemed especially amusing to them to break the china that had been a source of pride for her mother. A white-and-brown tea-leaf pattern, the dishes had been packed with care in a big barrel and hauled all the way from New England in the wagon when they came west. Suzannah saw one man tossing plates in the air while others shot at the spinning targets.

Then came the horror of discovery. A warrior paused, looked for a moment, and pointed to the cave door with a yell to the others. In the space of a few heartbeats, the door crashed open and the warriors rushed inside, dragging the fugitives into the open. The younger ones were struck down before her eyes, and there followed what seemed to be an argument over Suzannah and her sister Katy. Various men pinched, poked, and felt their arms, legs, breasts, and buttocks. Finally, their hands were tied and they were prodded up the slope and turned over to a group of women.

Suzannah had expected that the women might prove more compassionate, but the opposite was true. Their treatment worsened. They were beaten, shoved, and yelled at. Of course, they understood not one word of their captors' tirade and understood nothing of what was expected of them.

When the raiders tired of looting and pillaging, they took the horses from the corral, killed any remaining cattle in the area; and the band moved on, dragging the two captives.

Suzannah was concerned about Katy, who was behaving very badly. The younger girl sobbed constantly and screamed hysterically sometimes when someone touched her. This brought yells and blows, which drove Katy into further hysterical sobbing. Suzannah, while still terrified, was able to observe the effect of all this on their captors.

"Katy," she whispered, "you have to pull yourself together. You're making them angry. Keep your head, now—be dignified."

For this attempt at communication, Suzannah received a cut across the shoulders with a quirt; and they moved on. It was near noon when Katy seemed to become completely irrational. Her eyes took on a glazed, faraway look, and she babbled incessantly. Several times someone yelled at the girl, but she ignored all attempts to quiet her. Arguments broke out between a sinewy warrior, who appeared to claim Katy, and one who seemed to be a leader of the group. Katy continued to shriek and cry.

Finally, the leader shrugged and walked off, as if he was

tired of argument. The other man jerked Katy out of the line of march and shoved her ahead of him, toward a shallow ravine. Suzannah started to protest, but the woman with the quirt shook her head firmly and motioned ahead. Fearful for her own safety, Suzannah stumbled on. It was a short time later that Katy's captor rejoined the column, alone. Suzannah was startled, then horrified as she realized the implication of the hank of long blond hair hanging from the man's waist. Involuntarily, she gave a little cry. The quirt descended on her back, and she whirled on the woman in anger. An icy stare stopped her. The woman had drawn a knife, and the implied threat was plain. Suzannah tried to appear calm as she backed down, but it was useless. She turned away, tears streaming down her cheeks. They moved on.

She could not understand a word of her captors' talk. If any of them spoke English, they were avoiding it. There was no hint of where they might be going or for what purpose. She only knew that her home had been burned and that all of her family had been killed. They seemed to be traveling east, and also appeared to be concerned about pursuit.

Suzannah decided she would do her best to please her captors. They showed so little regard for life that any small displeasure might prove fatal. She was certain that poor Katy had been killed merely because she was loud and annoying, though the beauty of her long blond hair may have been a factor. Suzannah shuddered, and for the first time in her life regretted the carefully brushed sheen of her own tresses.

A woman paused beside the trail and squatted to empty her bladder. Suzannah, who was becoming uncomfortable herself, saw an opportunity. She paused, turned to the woman with the quirt, and pointed, first to the squatting woman, then to her own abdomen. The quirt-woman nodded and motioned to go ahead. Suzannah held up her bound wrists questioningly. The woman seemed to consider for a moment, then shrugged and released her with a cautioning motion toward her knife hilt. Suzannah nodded earnestly and ran to squat near the other woman. Quirt-woman took the pack from her shoulders and set it beside the trail, resting while opportunity offered.

When Suzannah returned, on a whim she motioned to the pack and to herself, with a questioning glance at her captor. The woman nodded, and Suzannah picked up the burden and swung it to her shoulder. It was heavy but well balanced, and she soon had it settled for travel. This move accomplished what she had hoped. Her hands were not tied as they moved on.

The entire band, which Suzannah estimated at near a hundred, paused late in the day to rest a short while and eat a little. Her captor, who appeared to be the wife of one of the leaders, tossed her a greasy chunk of poorly cooked meat. It was unappetizing, but no worse than what the others were eating. Suzannah knew that to survive, she must keep up her strength; so she ate.

The quirt-woman and her husband watched their captive and carried on a discussion, which the girl found very disconcerting. She tried to ignore it. If she was to be killed, she reasoned, they would not waste food on her. Finally, the man nodded, rose, and rejoined some of the other men.

The group moved on quickly, and some time after dark reached a wooded creek that appeared to flow northward. Here they turned to follow the stream. Suzannah wondered how she could leave a trail for anyone attempting to follow or rescue her. In the back of her mind, she had never given up the idea that the army would come. Though she had no reason to think they knew about her plight, it was comforting to contemplate. Even as she tried to contrive a way to leave a sign, she knew it was unnecessary. If they were followed, it would be easy to track the movement of a hundred people. Such a trail could not be missed. If they were not followed, it would not matter anyway.

She wondered if they would travel all night. She was

exhausted, stumbling in the dark, and the rawhide carrying
straps of the pack were digging into her shoulders. When
the leaders finally called a halt, she sank to the ground,
exhausted.

The woman who was her captor retied her wrists tightly
and threw a piece of dirty blanket over her. Suzannah did
not think she could rest, but exhaustion took its toll. In a
short while she slept.

Stone Bull glanced over at the still form when he
rejoined his wife.

"The girl sleeps?"

"Yes. She is tough, that one. She will survive."

"Yes. *Aiee*, Blackbird, I had no thought it would come to
this. Red Horse, the young men. They have tasted blood.
They will kill again, until it ends. Then we all will suffer."

Blackbird sighed and reached to draw the scrap of
blanket over the shoulder of the sleeping girl.

"How many have we lost?"

"Three. Two more wounded. There will be more," Stone
Bull answered sadly.

≈ **43** ≈

Someone kicked her in the ribs to awaken her. It was night,
and people were moving around, dimly seen as shapes in
the darkness. It took her a moment to remember where she
was.

Then all the horror, the terror, and despair came rushing
back to her, aided by the realization that her hands were
still bound. Suzannah scrambled to her feet, trying to choke
back tears of grief and misery. A woman spoke to her,
removed the thongs that bound her wrists, and handed her

the heavy pack she had carried before. The girl lifted it to her shoulders. Then the woman pressed something into Suzannah's hand. It felt like a short stick or piece of wood, and she was confused.

"Eat!" the woman grunted.

Suzannah was startled. Perhaps the woman knew more English than had been apparent. That would bear further watching. Suzannah sniffed the object she had been handed. It smelled faintly, an animal smell, like drying rawhide, or . . . meat! Of course—Dried meat. Jerky, she had heard it called. Well, it must be edible, though she was sure her mother would have questioned its cleanliness. She mustered courage to take a bite. The substance was tough and chewy but broke off crisply as she bit. Someone shoved her, and she moved in the indicated direction, chewing as she walked. Her captors were moving on, northward down the creek.

It must be toward dawn, she estimated. Yes, there was a pale glow in the eastern sky, a mere softening of the darkness at the horizon. It was becoming easier to make out the dim forms of the others as they moved quietly along the trail.

She quickly realized that she had taken too large a bite of the jerky. From the moment she began to chew, the thing seemed to grow in her mouth, becoming rapidly bigger. It was much like the fascinating way dried apples would grow as they soaked in water, while her mother mixed flour and lard together to create the pie crust. Tears came to her eyes again. Such memories were going to be difficult if, of course, she lived long enough to have any memories.

No, she *would* live, she vowed. Whatever it took to survive, she could do. Other women had done so. She would unhesitatingly do whatever they wished. Yes, even that, she told herself with a shudder. She must survive and keep herself in the best possible condition, so she would be able to escape. Yes, that was it. She could not really count on the army—it might be days before they learned of the massacre. No, she must be on her own, keep her wits about her, and be ready when opportunity offered. She must somehow acquire a weapon. Yes, a knife, maybe. She would watch her chance.

She fumbled the cud of jerky around in her mouth and spit out about half of it into her hand, gnawing it loose from the rest. The remainder of the still-dry stick she had slipped into the pocket of her dress for future use. Maybe she could accumulate a little store of food this way. She chewed with more success at the meat in her mouth now, extracting the juices. She wondered what sort of meat it might be but hesitated to think too much about that. She had heard that some of the Indians were fond of dog meat, and there were many tales of horses and mules butchered and eaten by the tribes. This did not prevent her from enjoying the bite of jerky. She swallowed it and immediately popped the partly chewed wad from her hand into her mouth.

She must watch, now. Some time, maybe today, her chance to escape would come.

They continued to travel northward along the creek, which meandered in that general direction. At times the stream was broad and shallow, more so now from the recent dry weather. At other places the gully or ravine would narrow, and the walls were steeper and of greater height. There was brushy growth in the floor of the ravine, and in some places it became quite rocky.

The travelers kept to the cover of the thin timber that scattered along the creek, or the concealment of the canyon walls when opportunity offered. At all times, however, there appeared to be a scout or two on each side, riding well out from the main party. She assumed that there must also be scouts in front, ahead of the main group.

There was little pause for rest. Her captors appeared to be pushing hard, trying to put distance behind them. She wondered if they were followed, perhaps by the army. Maybe these people knew, and this was the reason for the hurry. No, probably not, she told herself. If they knew such a thing, their assault on the Hartman ranch would not have been so leisurely. No, they only *feared* the pursuit that would come eventually. Her thoughts sank into disappointment. She could not expect the dashing troopers of the Fort Wallace cavalry unit to come charging to her rescue, though it was a nice fantasy. Anyway, she rationalized, they weren't all that dashing. Most were either inexperienced boys or hard-bitten old veterans who smelled bad and talked worse. Her mother had been very much against the girls' slightest contact with the soldiers.

It was doubly sad, now, to think that the soldiers had not been the danger to the Hartman daughters. The soldiers were, in fact, Suzannah's only slim hope for help, if they discovered that the renegade party was out on the plains. She wondered how they might discover that. Sooner or later, somebody would find the burned ranch and report the attack. Then a patrol from Fort Wallace would come.

A distressing thought struck her. What if they did not even realize that she was missing? The army probably paid little attention to how many children each family possessed. No, she decided, she must assume that she was entirely on her own. She shifted the pack and wondered if her strength would enable her to do the things she knew she must.

It was late afternoon when a scout rode in from the west to talk with some of the chiefs at the head of the column. The rest of the people halted, appearing glad for the opportunity to stop the grueling pace.

There was much conversation with gesturing and pointing off to the west. Suzannah stepped to a rock to enable her to see better and stretched to look into the distance. She did not know what she expected to see—a column of blue-clad troops, perhaps, with their pennant flying at the head—but there was nothing. Only the gentle rolling grassland.

Then she lifted her eyes slightly. Yes, there in the far distance, a thin blue line lay along the horizon. It was not a line of troopers, however, but of storm clouds. They lay

heavily, ready to roll forward across the rim of the earth, a
dirty-looking mass. Even as she watched, she could see the
flicker of orange lightning playing among the blue-black
clouds.

The quirt slashed across her legs, and Suzannah half
jumped, half fell from her rock. She leaped aside to avoid
the next blow and sank cowering to the ground. The woman
with the whip stood yelling at her for a moment, then
turned and stalked away.

Suzannah sat, resting, and thought about the current
state of her captivity. She had not understood the tirade
that followed her attempt to see what was going on, but the
general idea was plain. She would be more careful hereaf-
ter.

Her main line of thought, however, was concerned with
the cloud bank. That storm would come sweeping in from
the west, with wind and lightning and thunder, probably
with driving rain. That would cause confusion and possibly
offer her chance at escape. Her captors were aware of the
coming storm, of course—that was the reason for the halt
and the discussion among the leaders. They would be
making some sort of plans to camp and seek shelter. She
tried to guess what they would do. They would attempt to
find a heavily timbered area, possibly. A big lone tree
would be dangerous in a storm because of lightning, but a
thick scrubby growth, such as the ravine offered at inter-
vals, would provide a certain amount of protection. Yes,
they would certainly hurry ahead, then stop at a favorable
spot to set up camp before dark. It had appeared that the
storm front was a few hours away. Probably it would arrive
at the creek they were following somewhere near nightfall.

Her spirits rose, due partly to the fact that she was proud
of her ability to reason and guess the plans of her captors.
The other thing was, the darkness and storm might easily
provide her opportunity to escape.

As the march resumed, hurried along by the warriors,
Suzannah could hear the low mutter of distant thunder to

the west. She risked a glance when opportunity offered and was startled at how much nearer the dirty blue cloud bank appeared. The air was still and heavy, but she knew that before long the breeze would whip up ahead of the storm, stirring and chilling the air. She estimated now that the storm would arrive slightly before dark. Her captors hurried on.

It was as she guessed, a timbered area slightly above the creek bed, but still avoiding the high ground, when the leaders called the halt. People began to improvise make-shift shelters from robes and blankets stretched and tied from tree to tree and across the scrubby bushes. Suzannah quickly tried to familiarize herself with the surroundings before it became too dark to see. If her chance came, she decided, she would attempt to run upstream, following their back trail and hoping that she would encounter the rescue party, if any, that might be advancing.

A scout rode in, and she saw the leaders gather for another of their conferences. This time there was a greater excitement in their gesturing. It appeared to her that something more than the approaching storm was under consideration. Men began to check their weapons.

There was a flurry of activity in the camp, some shouting, and people began to take down their makeshift shelters. Women and children hurried downstream in disorganized flight. Suzannah lifted her pack and moved on with the others, fighting exhaustion. There seemed to be only one explanation. The scouts had sighted a rescue party of some sort.

Now a new worry came to her. There must be fifty or more warriors in this party. They would certainly outnumber the usual squad of troopers who patrolled along the valley and stopped occasionally at the ranch. She began to fear for their safety. Such a patrol could easily be wiped out in an ambush.

The air was stirring now, a chill breeze that brushed her

cheek and stirred the willows along the stream. She noticed
that the sun, lowering in the west, had met the rising bank
of storm clouds. It was dropping behind the storm front,
leaving the entire plain bathed in an odd gray-green light.
The very air seemed charged with an expectant, supernat-
ural effect. She noticed that the birds were quiet. Even the
insects that would normally have been chirping made no
sound in the path of the advancing storm. Suzannah noticed
that the tiny hairs on her forearms seemed to bristle and
tingle. The woman with the quirt pushed her to move
faster, and there was a tiny blue spark of static at the point
of touch.

Men with weapons ready were moving back upstream
now, past the hurrying women and children. She saw them
searching the canyon walls, looking for places of cover and
concealment. An ambush of the troopers was surely in the
making.

Stone Bull moved back to walk beside his wife for a
moment.

"You know the fight is coming." It was not a question, but
a statement.

"Yes."

"There is no other way now."

"Yes, I know. May it go well with you, my husband."

"And with you. You will see to the girl?"

He pointed to the plodding Suzannah ahead of them, her
blue gingham dress torn and dirty.

"Yes, I will do it."

The old chief nodded, touched his wife's shoulder for a
moment, and turned to join the other warriors in preparing
the ambush.

≈ 44 ≈

Stone Bull's heart was heavy as he moved into position. He knew there was no other way. Since the young men had begun to kill, all chance at an honorable peace had vanished. Although he was the primary chief of this band of the People, the responsibility for a battle plan was not his. By tradition, leadership in war or the hunt belonged to the younger chiefs, while his own area of influence was in politics.

Once he had been a respected war chief. He had led raids against enemies in the northern plains that were still told in story and song. But a man slows with age. He was still revered for his wisdom in the council, but his muscles were stiffening, and his bones ached on cold mornings. The leadership of the young warriors had been handed down.

Red Horse had assumed the position of war chief for this foray. Stone Bull would have preferred Yellow Calf, or even Crane's Feather. All were equally capable, but Red Horse was more aggressive. Ah, well, no matter. Perhaps that would be needed here. There was no question of the bravery or the skill of Red Horse—he was a brilliant and daring planner. The hunts he had led had always been successful. Until, of course, the buffalo disappeared. That had been the beginning of the end.

But, he pondered, there had been no leader in recent years who could inspire the young men to follow him as did Red Horse. The warriors of this party would follow him to the death. Stone Bull only wished they had not begun the killing and mutilation. Once that started, there was always some blood-crazed warrior ready to show that he could think of a more cruel and bizarre way to send a spirit to the Other Side. It had once served a purpose, to arouse men to battle; but now he had come to see it as a bad thing. It served only to infuriate the whites and bring terrible vengeance. He thought of the fate of his friend Black Kettle, whose people were destroyed. Kettle had always preached peace with the Bluecoats and had flown the striped flag of the White Father, but it had not mattered to the vengeful whites. They had hacked his children to pieces, carried off arms and legs, and taken scalps from the private places of young women.

There was evil on both sides, he thought sadly. There had been no purpose in the killing of those children in the cave two sleeps ago. They could have been left behind or taken as hostages. Even less purpose had been evident in Red Horse's killing of the girl during the march yesterday. It had been only because she was noisy and irritated her captor, Stone Bull believed.

Of all the whites they had contacted since they left the Nations, only one was still alive. Probably some of the young warriors would decide sooner or later to make a clean sweep. The girl was not really of much value to them and was another mouth to feed. She could be a bargaining point if they ever entered negotiations with the whites, which seemed unlikely. Her yellow hair was long and beautiful, like that of the other one. That was too bad. Some young admirer of Red Horse might wish to possess a trophy like the scalp that Red Horse now wore at his belt. Stone Bull had considered cutting the girl's hair to remove the temptation but knew it might provoke a killing merely for spite.

His wife, who had taken quite a liking to the girl, was watching her closely. All of their own children were dead, now, the last one from the typhoid last summer. Somehow, Blackbird had felt a resurgence of mothering instinct over this young captive. He had been amused over her use of the whip, and a little puzzled. That was unlike his gentle wife, the mother of his children. He soon realized, however, that if Blackbird struck and abused the girl frequently, others would leave her alone. Blackbird was establishing ownership, to be in a position to protect the girl if necessary.

They had discussed this, last evening after dark, and had agreed on what must be done when the battle came. Especially, if it was going badly.

Stone Bull moved into position behind a rocky outcrop halfway up the wall of the ravine. He reluctantly readied his Henry rifle, the envy of every warrior in the band. It would shoot sixteen times without reloading. The gun-that-shoots-all-day had been a present from one of the officers he had known back in the northern plains in happier times.

It was growing darker now, both from the lateness of the day, and from the rapidly approaching storm. He hoped it would not be necessary to fight after dark. He had never really believed, as some tribes do, that a spirit released in darkness must wander forever, unable to find the way to the Other Side. Well, not *really* believed—but why take chances?

Quiet signals from upstream, now passed along, told that the soldiers were coming. He could see other warriors scattered along both sides of the canyon for some distance, ready to fire down into the column of soldiers when they came along. Red Horse had explained in detail for the benefit of those who had not yet seen battle. The first few soldiers must be allowed to pass, to let the main body enter the ambush. The Bluecoats would always have one or two out in front.

The lightning and thunder were nearer now. The wind was whipping dust along the floor of the canyon. Stone Bull squinted against the flying debris and wiped his eyes to see better the sights on the Henry. Up the canyon, he now saw a blue-coated soldier, leaning in the saddle against the wind. The man was alert, a good soldier, Stone Bull saw. Despite the wind and dust, he was attempting to look ahead, watching the canyon walls.

Stone Bull's position was one of those farthest north. It appeared that when the main body of soldiers was fairly in the trap, this scout would be well past him. For practice, he raised the Henry and laid the sights on the man's chest, following him along as he rode. It would be so easy. Only a gentle squeeze on the trigger. The shot would start the battle. Of course, Red Horse would be furious. His shot was supposed to be the signal. If someone fired prematurely, before the soldiers were fairly in the trap. . . .

The corporal was exactly opposite. Stone Bull could have hit him with a throwing stick. He could see the main body of soldiers now, entering the ambush. His mind worked frantically. There was no time. A flash of lightning lit the darkening sky, and the boom of the thunder followed close on its heels. The storm was almost upon them. Droplets of rain were spattering in the dust. In moments, the deluge would make accurate shooting impossible. Stone Bull's finger tightened on the trigger.

Then, on an impulse, he shifted his aim. The Henry cracked, and the flat-nosed slug ripped into the cantle of the army saddle. The horse, startled by the impact and frantic from the sting of the shattered saddle tree on its spine, began to run wildly, bucking every few jumps. Stone Bull saw the soldier lose his right stirrup and nearly fall from the horse as it raced down the canyon.

A volley of shots rattled from the sides of the ravine. There were yells, a scatter of shots from the soldiers, and a horse screamed and went down. In the space of a heartbeat, the canyon was a confused melee, men dying or wounded and screaming in pain on the ground. Wounded horses floundered through the brush, and several riderless mounts raced past him, following the frightened horse of the scout.

A short distance downstream, Suzannah lay uncomfortably, her hands and feet tied. She had protested, but it was no use. She knew the battle was coming, and of course her captors would want to avoid her escape. The quirt-woman had thrown her roughly to the ground, tied her, and cautioned silence. There was no mistaking the sign of the finger on closed lips, but the woman made certain there was no mistake by drawing her knife and making a motion across the throat. This left little to the imagination, and Suzannah shook her head sincerely.

The men had all disappeared now, she supposed to prepare for the battle. The storm was quite close, and it seemed unlikely to her that they would fight just as the storm started. As if to reassure this, a bright flash of lightning struck nearby, followed by the boom of thunder.

No sooner had the echo quieted, however, than she heard the flat crack of a rifle, followed by a volley of firing. Then ragged gunfire rattled along the rocks. There were yells and screams, mixed with chilling war cries. Suzannah began to sob uncontrollably.

A horse, running wildly, dashed past. In the gathering darkness, wind, and dust, the rider was seen clinging frantically. She thought it was a soldier but could not be sure. Two more horses blundered past, riderless. There was more firing.

Someone moved close to her, and she turned, startled. The quirt-woman was leaning over her and was in the process of drawing the knife at her waist.

"No, no," Suzannah pleaded.

She opened her mouth for what she was certain would be her last scream. The woman clapped a rough hand over it and knelt.

"Be still, girl," she growled.

Deftly, she cut the thongs tying hands and feet.

"Run!" she muttered. "That way!"

She pointed downstream, away from the battle.

No more urging was necessary. Suzannah was on her feet, running as fast as she could. Then the storm struck with all its fury, lashing the canyon with blinding rain. She stumbled on more slowly, her progress illuminated by an occasional flash of lightning.

She nearly fell over the body of a dying horse, struggling weakly in the mud as its life poured out through a wound in the creature's throat. A lightning flash revealed that it had worn an army McClellan saddle. In the boot at the left stirrup was a carbine. The unfortunate soldier had never even gotten his weapon out of the scabbard.

Suzannah pulled it free and moved on, trying to get away from the shots and screams behind her.

≈ **45** ≈

Corporal Jesse Booth rode into the canyon with grave misgivings. The troop had completed the forced march, northeast from where they buried the girl. Just before they reached the creek that was their objective, Harrison and the Ute had rejoined the column to report that the maneuver had failed.

"They're movin' fast, Lieutenant," Harrison reported. "They're still ahead of us."

"How far?" Murkha demanded.

"Not far, Broken Knife says. They'll stop for the storm."

He pointed to the heavy cloud bank that had been rising behind them all afternoon.

"That'll get here by dark."

"Then we'll have to hurry," Lieutenant Murkha announced, nudging his horse forward.

"But, Lieutenant," Sergeant Rigdon protested, "we'd ought to stop when we get to the creek and look for cover."

"Exactly, Sergeant. That's what they'll expect us to do. We have the element of surprise."

"I don't reckon you're goin' to surprise 'em, Lieutenant," the guide drawled. "Likely they've known where you was all day."

"Nevertheless," Murkha snapped, "we move in. This will keep them off balance, not give them time to organize."

"But, sir," Rigdon started to say.

"Sergeant, are you questioning my orders?"

"No, sir," Rigdon said stiffly, "I only—"

"Then move on!"

At the rim of the little canyon, they paused long enough for the lieutenant to order everyone to be alert, which they already were. It was no secret that the renegades were not far ahead. They could not see up and down the stream very well, because of its tortuous course and the intermittent scatter of trees. The growing darkness, the wind, and the approaching thunder and lightning all added to the uneasiness of the troopers.

The old Ute led the way toward an easier slope to the bottom of the canyon. Here he paused and conferred with Harrison, who approached Murkha again.

"Lieutenant," he began, "Broken Knife says only a fool would go into a canyon where he knows the enemy is waitin', when it's gettin' dark. He ain't goin'."

The officer turned dark with rage. "Why, the goddamn coward! He won't be paid!"

Harrison nodded. "Figgered not. I guess he reckons a dead man don't spend much pay. I'll have to agree with him."

"You're deserting, too?"

"Lieutenant, I ain't desertin'; I'm quittin' a job. We hired on to find them renegades for you. Well, they're right in there." He pointed to the darkening canyon ahead. "Now you can do whatever you want to with 'em."

He reined his horse aside but then turned back.

"One other thing, Lieutenant. Broken Knife might be a lot of things, but a coward ain't one of 'em."

The two riders topped the slope and disappeared.

"All right, let's go," Murkha called. "Booth, take the point."

Jesse had never come so close to disobeying an order. He

actually considered it for a moment but was afraid to. With the mood the lieutenant was in, he might easily shoot a man for refusing an order. Probably the canyon was a safer risk at the time. He nodded and rode ahead.

He tried his best to tell himself that the Indians would never shoot the first man to approach. It was little comfort to remember why, that it was easy to kill that man later, after the first burst of firing.

Even though he tried to watch every possible hiding place, he knew it was useless. The wind was gusting down the draw, flinging sand in his eyes. He was fervently wishing he was somewhere else when something whacked into the cantle of his saddle, stinging his buttocks and sending the horse into a frantic, pitching run. He lost a stirrup and clutched wildly at the pommel of his shattered saddle.

There was a blast of sound behind him, and he risked a quick look. Horses were falling, men screaming, and chilling war cries echoed down the ravine. He saw troopers falling from their horses, others struck down while trying to retreat. He did not have a chance to observe further. He was too busy trying to stay on his plunging horse. The frantic animal was running wild, through the slash of overhanging branches. They galloped through what appeared to be a camp of some sort, dimly seen through the dust and the rain that was beginning to turn it to mud. He had left it behind before he realized he must have passed directly through the renegades' night camp. A moment later, he could see nothing at all, as the darkness of the storm dropped like a blanket, with driving rain pelting him in the face. His campaign hat was gone, knocked off by a low branch or blown away by the wind. A lightning flash illuminated the rocky canyon for a moment, just long enough to allow him to see the rocks ahead. Then the horse stumbled and fell, and Jesse found himself flying through the air. He struck head first, hard, and was barely aware of the blow before he lost consciousness.

He was roused by the patter of cold rain in his face. It was quiet except for the occasional boom of thunder, which seemed more distant now. He started to get up, groping in the rocky streambed, and found something encircling his neck and shoulders. It took a moment to recognize the leather sling to which his carbine was attached. Regulations called for the sling to be fastened into the ring of the carbine, so an unhorsed trooper would still be fastened to his weapon. Most men ignored the regulation when they could, but . . . well, it had proven effective in this case. Jesse staggered to his feet, unsnapping the carbine from the shoulder sling. In the darkness, he could not tell if the weapon was intact or not.

He was not thinking clearly, and a wave of dizziness passed over him as he stumbled around in the shallow water. He forced himself to stop and think. There was danger. Yes, Indians. He'd have to find a place to hide for the night, and to weather out the storm. Maybe some rest would help to stop the throbbing in his head. Then he'd have to rejoin the troop.

The troop! My God, he thought. *There was a fight! How* . . . yes, he was remembering more now. Troopers falling, horses running riderless, his own horse had run away. Let's see, now, he thought, he'd been traveling downstream when it happened. The battle was behind him. The safe thing would be to move downstream away from the action and find a place to hide for the night. A distant lightning flash occasionally gave a glimpse of the terrain, and there was no trace of his horse, so it would be on foot. He moved forward, dizzy and staggering a little.

He kept tasting something salty in his mouth, and it took a little while to realize that he was bleeding. The fluid he kept wiping out of his eyes wasn't rain, it was blood. *Jesus,* he thought, *I've been scalped.* He stopped and examined his head in the dark and decided not. There was a large bump near the hairline, and he could feel the ragged edges

of the cut. It would be all right. Scalp wounds stopped
bleeding on their own, or so he'd been told.

There was a story of a track hand on the Kansas Pacific
who'd been struck down, scalped, and left for dead. He'd
recovered consciousness as the Indian was leaving, shot
him, recovered the scalp, and carried it four miles into
town, where the local doctor sewed it back on. At the
moment, Jesse knew he couldn't have walked the four
miles, even with his scalp intact.

He stumbled on downstream, looking for a place to hole
up by the light of each lightning flash. He was still
confused, and in his half-dreamy state he thought he saw
buildings ahead. A town? A ranch? Patiently he waited for
the next flash, which seemed to take forever. Finally, the
brief illumination came.

Yes, now he remembered. There were said to be Indian
ruins on Starving Woman Creek. Remains of a pueblo
town. The ruined walls might provide shelter. He staggered in that direction. By the next flash, he selected one
of the structures that seemed nearly intact. Most were
crumbling walls, merely piles of debris, but he had clearly
seen a doorway. If he could get inside, sit down out of the
rain and rest, maybe get some sleep.

He stooped slightly to enter the doorway and paused
before entering. There was a suggestion of an animal smell,
and he heard movement. These things had no time to form
thoughts of significance in his foggy brain, before the world
exploded in his face. The interior of the structure was lit for
one brilliant second of fire. Before the brilliance disappeared and blackness returned, he caught a quick glimpse
of a figure crouching inside, pointing something at him.
Then the searing heat of the muzzle blast struck his face,
and he was thrown backward to land on his back in the
mud.

"Oh, Jesus, I'm shot!" he heard himself saying, as if at a
distance.

Then things were confusing for a minute or two. The

Indian came scrambling out the door, he thought to attack again. Instead, he realized that his assailant was crying and talking to him in English, and that it wasn't an Indian at all, but a woman. Jesse was back in his dreamy confusion again. His ears rang from the blast, he couldn't see in the darkness, and his head was throbbing powerfully.

"Who—who are you?" he stammered.

"I'm sorry, so sorry," the woman moaned over and over. "I nearly killed you."

Then she seemed to calm somewhat.

"I'm Suzannah Hartman. My family—" She started to cry again.

"Yes, I know," Jesse said simply.

"They're all dead, aren't they?"

"Yes. I'm sorry."

"Are you hurt?"

The sound of her voice was reassuring, bringing him back to reality. If this girl could bear all that she had been through, he certainly should be able to.

"I don't think so. My head's hurt, where I fell off my horse."

"I mean, are you shot?"

"No. I'm not sure I can see. The muzzle flash—"

"Oh, I'm so sorry. I thought you were an Indian."

"It's all right."

"Let's get inside. It's raining again."

They crawled into the shelter, the girl guiding him. A lightning flash showed him that he did have at least some vision left, for which he was grateful.

"Over here," the girl said, tugging gently at his sleeve.

They sat down, leaning against the inside wall. Jesse was bone tired. He had never felt so bad, so weak, so many pains, so chilled from the cold rain and from the wind that still whipped around the corner of the door opening and out through the half-collapsed roof at the other side. His teeth were chattering with the cold.

He felt the girl shivering beside him. *My God*, he

thought. *I'm feeling sorry for myself, and here is this poor girl, with only a wet cotton dress. She'll likely catch her death of pneumonia.* They dare not build a fire.

"Ma'am," he blurted through chattering teeth, "I'm awful sorry, and I hope you won't think me forward, but . . ." He paused, embarrassed. "Ma'am, if you don't mind sort of snugglin' up to me, we can keep each other warm. I wouldn't do nothin'. . . ."

Before he had finished speaking, she had crept close to him, and he could feel the life-giving warmth of their shared body heat. He put his arm around her and held her close against him

≈ **46** ≈

It was a restless night. Jesse would doze fitfully and then wake with a sudden jump, confused and unsure where he was. During the time when he was fully awake, he was quite aware of the girl's soft body pressed against him for warmth. Under other circumstances he would have been excited by her closeness and the stimulation of the shapely young form—now he had little thought of that. It seemed as if the most important thing in the world was for the two of them to be warm.

His teeth had stopped chattering. He was far from comfortable, but it was better now. Suzannah, in the deep sleep of total exhaustion, still stirred restlessly from time to time. She whimpered softly as she cuddled more closely against him, but she did not waken. Jesse was pleased to be able to hold and comfort her, proud to be the one to rescue her from her captors.

It was much like some of the fantasies he had dreamed about Suzannah Hartman. She would be abducted and carried off by hostiles—or outlaws, or somebody—and he would go to her rescue. Relentlessly, he would track her abductors to their lair, defeat them all against impossible odds, and rescue the golden-haired Suzannah. She would fling herself gratefully into her rescuer's arms, and he would enfold and protect her.

Except, it wasn't like that. He had, in all his fantasies, been not only invincible, but clean, comfortable, and supremely confident. In this reality, he was injured, cold, hungry, and grimy with sweat and trail dust. The romance of the rescue was virtually nonexistent, far from his mind, and surely from Suzannah's. Jesse was concerned at the way his thoughts kept slipping away, replaced by the throbbing in his head. At times the pounding of his heartbeat at his temples and in his ears seemed to make him seasick.

Jesse was scared. He did not know much about head injuries, except that they could be very serious. He kept thinking about Wilhelm Oberfeldt, a neighbor boy back home. Wilhelm was about his own age and fell from the hay mow one morning, landing on his head. The boy had been unconscious for nearly a week and finally wakened. Everyone had rejoiced that the Oberfeldts' son had been restored to them, but Wilhelm was never quite the same after that. He laughed or became angry at the wrong times and walked oddly, dragging his left foot.

Repeatedly, Jesse tried to reassure himself that this was different, that his injury was different from Wilhelm's; but he wasn't sure. After all, he didn't know what sort of injury he had suffered, or how long he might have been unconscious. He hadn't even known, at first, that he was bleeding, until blood kept running into his eyes.

His eyes. When it came down to it, that was probably his greatest fear. Without his sight, he would be helpless as a kitten. The explosion of the girl's weapon had been a terrifying thing, the hot flash of fire from the muzzle searing across his face and eyes. He had cried out in terror, but it was a few moments before the burning, stinging sensation of injury washed over his tightly covered eyeballs. He had been alarmed that he might lose his sight but had some reassurance in that he could perceive the lightning's flash.

He had been distracted by the encounter with the girl, but as they settled down, he became increasingly aware of the burning. He tried not to rub his eyes, but it was difficult. He would become drowsy and find himself reaching a hand toward the source of discomfort without thinking.

The storm had moved on now, the mutter of thunder distant to his ears. There was a slight ringing buzz in his right ear, the one nearest the muzzle blast, but he knew that would be temporary. The rain had stopped, but the world outside their shelter was sodden and damp. He listened to the drip, drip of water from the scrubby trees outside. The girl whimpered again and snuggled closer to him. He shifted his arm around her shoulders and touched his face with his other hand. He was alarmed to find that the soft skin of his eyelids was swelling rapidly. His right eye was nearly swollen shut.

Damn! The night was still as black as coal, and he had not been aware of this progressive interference with his sight. He opened his eyes as wide as he could, helping with his fingers. It was useless. He could not be sure, in the blackness of the night, whether his sight was impaired or not. He would have to wait until morning.

This brought back the old fear. What if he could not see, even temporarily, through swollen lids? He could not protect himself, much less look after the girl and escort her back to civilization. His imagination began to play tricks. The drip of water from rain-soaked trees became stealthy footsteps, stalking the fugitive couple as they huddled helplessly in the ruins. From that point on, he slept none at all.

It was an eternity before the black night began to pale to gray. Jesse was grateful, not only that the night was over and they were still alive, but that he could *see* the change to the watery light of predawn. He was discouraged again very quickly, however, to discover that he could see only dimly, and only with his left eye. The right was tightly shut, puffy and rubbery to touch.

He tried hard to focus his left eye on the doorway as the light became stronger. At best, the door post was a vague, vertical shape that could have been a tree, a rock, or a person standing there. Even worse, the increasing light did not help but made things more difficult, causing real pain when he opened the lids.

Suzannah stirred, was still for a moment, and then rolled quickly away from him. Jesse knew it had taken a moment to realize where she was, and her reaction to awakening in the arms of a stranger was an understandable one. Still, he was not prepared for her gasp of horror. Without his vision, for a moment the thought crossed his mind that they were being attacked; but her next words told him her concern.

"Your face!" she blurted.

"What?"

He had not considered how he must look to her in her first waking moments. His cheek must be burned and blackened by the powder, his eye now swollen completely shut, and the other squinting painfully against the light. In addition, he now remembered, there would be matted blood in his hair and in his three-day growth of whiskers.

"You said you weren't hurt!" she protested. "Let me help you, Corporal . . . ?"

"Booth. Jesse Booth, ma'am."

Only now did he realize how exhausted the girl must have been, desperate and ready to fight like a cornered animal for survival. This was a plucky young woman.

"Booth," she said. "Do I know you?"

"Probably not, ma'am. You gave me a drink of water once."

"Of course. At our well!"

She paused, and Jesse knew she was thinking about the well, and the ranch, and . . .

"My family," she said softly. "We talked about them last night, didn't we?"

"Jest a little, ma'am. I'm awful sorry."

He thought she wiped tears away, but she spoke in a moment, her voice only a trifle husky. "But you . . . I nearly shot you."

"Yes, but you didn't. Not quite, anyway. Only thing, I can't see."

"Even with the other eye?"

She knelt beside him.

"Not much. It's just a blur. The light hurts it."

"Then you'd best keep it shut."

"But we have to move. There may still be Indians in the area."

"Then we'd be as safe here as anywhere, wouldn't we? I'll go look around."

"Wait!" he said urgently. "Let's see what we have, first. Supplies and weapons. What kind of gun did you have, the one you shot at me?"

"A trooper's gun."

"Hand it here."

Jesse took the carbine and ran his fingers over the lock and breech. He lifted the thumb latch, opened the breech, and extracted the empty cartridge case.

"You have any more cartridges?"

"No. I just picked up the gun."

He fumbled in the leather cartridge box at his belt, counting the remaining rounds. Five.

"These will do," he announced, more confidently than he felt.

He slipped one of the shiny brass cylinders into the breech and snapped it shut before he handed the gun back to the girl. He had discarded his own weapon when he discovered it was broken through the lock plate.

"Can you shoot?" he asked.

Instantly, he was embarrassed. It was a stupid question.

Of course, a woman on the frontier would know the use of weapons.

"Yes," Suzannah answered, as if she noticed nothing unusual about his question.

"All right. Be real careful, now. Take a long look around before you go outside."

There was a few moments' pause before she spoke from near the doorway. "I don't see anything."

She came back to him.

"Don't worry, I'll be careful. And I'll come right back. Do you have a pocket knife I can use?"

"What for?"

"If I can find the right plants, for your eyes."

Jesse fished in his pocket and handed her his little bone-handled clasp knife.

"Afraid I'm not much use," he complained.

"It's all right. We're goin' to make it now. Don't fret."

It made him feel good, the reassurance of this confident young woman. He did fret, but somewhat less than he might have.

It was beginning to seem that she had been gone a long time when he heard soft footsteps approaching.

"It's me, Corporal. Suzannah," she called.

Jesse had become tense, ready to fight if necessary, but now he relaxed. The doorway darkened for a moment as she stepped through into the room.

"I think the Indians are gone," she said. "I don't see or hear anything."

She squatted beside him and placed a handful of twigs in his palm.

"Here. Chew them."

"*Chew* them? What is it?"

"Slippery elm. At least, it's elm. I'm not real sure it's the right kind, but it's all I can find, so maybe it will work."

"But how do I use it?"

Slippery elm was an unknown remedy to Jesse.

"Chew up the bark. It gets sort of slimy, and you make a poultice for your eyes. Go ahead, now."

He stripped the bark from a couple of twigs and began to chew while he peeled some more. There was practically no taste to the sticky slime, which seemed to increase in volume as he chewed.

"I'd help you," she offered, "but it's s'posed to work better if the one it's to be used on does the chewin'."

He heard a ripping sound and guessed she was tearing a strip from the bottom of her petticoat to bandage his eyes.

"Now," she said, "spit out the slime and put it on your eyes. Then I'll bandage them."

"But then I can't see at all," Jesse protested.

"How much can you see now?" the girl demanded. "Not much, I'll allow. I can see how the light hurts you. We need to get your eyes healed as fast as we can."

She made sense, Jesse had to agree. He let her help apply the jellylike poultices and wrap her bandages to hold them in place. He had to admit there was a soothing sensation about it.

"There!" Suzannah said, tying the last knot. "Now, would you like some jerky?"

"Jerky? You have some supplies?"

"Not really. A woman gave me some jerky yesterday, and I saved part of it in my pocket."

"Maybe we better save it till we really need it," Jesse suggested.

"All right. Now, Corporal, you tell me about where we need to go. I can be your eyes until you're better."

Unspoken between them was the thought that their situation was quite desperate. They were on foot, poorly armed; they must try to return to the fort and had no idea of the location of either the renegades or the troopers.

Jesse had thought about this at length. The troop must have turned back, or there would be some sign of them by now. Likewise, the Indians, who had been traveling north, must have continued in that direction. They would be following this little canyon until it met the Smoky Hill. There they would cross and move on toward their former home in the Dakotas. At least, that seemed logical. And since the Indians were ahead of them, moving rapidly, there was very little danger of an encounter. Their major problem would be food as they traveled. It would be painfully slow at best, with the girl having to show him every step of the way.

"All right," he said, trying to sound more cheerful than he really felt.

The girl had suffered so much more than he and was able to appear confident and assured, he could do no less.

"We'll talk about some plans," he suggested, "but first, will you help me down to the stream? I need to wash some of this grime off my face."

$$\approx \ 47 \ \approx$$

Jesse felt better after a splash bath and a brisk scrub of his whiskers with his cupped hands. He devoutly wished that he could shave. It was a good sign, he supposed, that he felt enough better to be concerned about how his appearance might impress Suzannah Hartman. He reminded himself again that this whole encounter was not one of appearances, but of survival. He must be astute enough to get this survivor safely back to civilization.

"Miss Hartman," he called, after he had replaced his shirt and bandages.

The girl had withdrawn to a discreet distance while he bathed, and now returned to help him back to the shelter.

"Since we're likely to be together a while," she said, "why don't you call me by my name—Suzannah? It will be easier."

Jesse wasn't quite certain that it would be appropriate. He was a noncommissioned officer of the U.S. Army, entrusted by fate with the welfare of a female civilian. He should be cautious not to appear too forward.

"Well, I—"

He was interrupted by a delightful, throaty chuckle from the girl. She was amused at his stiff propriety.

"Well, all right," he found himself saying, "and you might call me Jesse if you like, ma'am, instead of Corporal."

The sun was warm, the sky clearing as they sat down in the doorway of the pueblo to make a plan. It was a never-ceasing wonder to him that in this country a person could suffer from cold at night and be warm in a few hours. It would have been a tough night for both without their shared warmth.

"Now," he began, "I reckon we're on what they call Starving Woman Creek. You think that's right?"

"I don't know," the girl said. "I've heard of it. We came east after I was caught, until we came to this creek."

"Well, this is probably it. If that's right, it should empty into the Smoky Hill a few miles north of here. Then, when we find the river, we follow it west—upstream to Fort Wallace."

"How far?"

"I'm not sure. Only a couple of days for the patrol. But we're on foot. And I'm goin' to be awful slow, I'm afraid."

"Don't worry about it . . . Jesse . . ." she said tentatively. "We'll get there."

She took his hand and led him down toward the stream.

"We'd better cross here, if we want to be on the west side," she suggested. "Watch your step, now. It's a gravel bar, rocky but not deep. I see a game trail on the other side."

They followed the trail along the creek for some time. It meandered through the brush and rocks and was slow going, difficult for the girl to lead him. She mentioned this when they paused to rest.

"Do you think it would be easier up along the rim outside the canyon? It's level and grassy."

"Maybe so. It sure would be on a horse. We need a couple of horses. Haven't seen any?"

Both chuckled at the small joke that was not really a joke at all. They moved on. Suzannah devised an easier way of traveling. She cut a willow stick some four feet long and as thick as her thumb. She walked ahead, holding one end, while Jesse walked behind, guided by holding the other end. Occasionally, she would pause and say "Step up" or "Careful, here." Their progress was much more rapid now.

It was about midday when they found the horse. It was a bay cavalry horse, lying still in death, its muzzle stretched forward on the grass as if asleep.

"Tell me," Jesse urged the girl, "what do you see about it?"

"There's an arrow in the flank," she observed. "It's been dead for some time. Since last night, I guess."

"Why? Why do you think so?"

"Coyotes have been eating on it. Lots of bluebottle flies. I guess we shouldn't eat any of the meat?"

Jesse was a bit surprised that her mind would be working along such practical lines as eating horse meat, but he was pleased.

"Prob'ly not. It's pretty hot weather. Is there any equipment we can use?"

"The blanket roll—that will be handy."

She unbuckled the straps and removed the roll.

"Is his carbine in the boot?" Jesse asked.

"No. Just the roll. There's blood on the saddle."

Jesse wondered which of his companions had been struck from the horse. He could reconstruct the scene in his mind. The first volley from ambush, likely. The trooper injured or dying, clinging a moment while the mortally wounded horse ran crazily to escape the terror in the woods along the creek. It had gotten this far before lying down to die of internal bleeding. They moved on.

"I see the river ahead!" Suzannah exclaimed late in the afternoon. "Jesse, could we cut across the prairie? It would save a mile or so, and we'd hit the river west of the fork."

"I guess so. You don't see any Indians or troopers?"

"No, nothing but grass, and the trees along the river."

"All right. But we need to find a place to camp before dark."

"We'll be there in time," Suzannah answered confidently.

Jesse shifted the blanket roll on his shoulder and followed the girl's long strides. She was carrying the carbine, and they had contrived a sling for the blanket roll from the reins of the dead horse. They had covered several miles by this time, he estimated.

Suzannah selected a campsite near the river but sheltered by a screen of willows from anyone passing on the prairie. They decided against a fire. The memory of last night's terror was too fresh.

The girl selected a spot and spread their salvaged blankets.

"Come here. Sit down. Let's rebandage your eyes," she suggested. "Here, chew some more bark, while I unwrap."

She handed him the twigs, apparently from her pocket, and he began to chew. When the last turn of the cloth strip came away, he could tell there was improvement. He could see light between the swollen lids of his right eye.

"Oh, the swelling is better," Suzannah exclaimed, delighted. "Can you see any better with the left eye?"

"I don't think so, but it doesn't burn as much."

"Good. Let's wrap it up for the night and see how it is in the morning."

Jesse might have preferred to try it without the bandage, but the girl's primitive frontier medicine had proved good so far. He allowed her to replace the bandage.

"There!" she said. "Now, are you ready for some jerky?"

She handed him a stick of the dried meat, and he bit off a small chunk to chew.

"They gave you this?" he asked, hoping to lead to other questions that were troubling him.

"Yes, this old woman. Wife of one of their chiefs, I think."

"Suzannah, were you abused?" he asked.

She leaned over and touched his arm gently for a moment.

"No, not like you mean. I don't know . . . maybe there wasn't time," she pondered.

Jesse was amazed at her frankness, and a little embarrassed.

"I was beaten," she went on, "but it wasn't really vicious."

"Beaten? Who did it?"

"The same woman. She acted like she owned me. Maybe . . . I don't know, Jesse, I think she liked me, somehow."

"*Liked* you?"

"Yes. Did I tell you, she cut me loose when the fight started?"

"No! That's how you got away?"

"Yes. Isn't that odd, Jesse? It was like she tried to save me."

They talked at length, while the sun slipped behind the distant horizon. The sounds of the day quieted and were replaced by the mysterious voices of the night. A coyote called to his mate from a distant ridge. Warm as the day had been, there was a chill in the night air. Suzannah pulled the blanket around their shoulders, and they sat awhile longer, talking quietly as the sky darkened and stars began to appear. Jesse wondered how to approach the subject of sleeping arrangements. It had been easy last night, with both suffering from rain and exposure. But tonight, it was a little different.

Suzannah solved his problem. "Stand up a minute," she suggested. "I'll shake out the blanket before we turn in."

She did just that and then showed him where to lie down.

"Take your boots off."

He felt the other fold of the blanket flutter over him, warming his tired body. Before he could ask the next question that arose in his mind, it was answered for him. He felt the soft warmth of Suzannah's body as she slipped under the blanket with him and snuggled close. Actually, he told himself, there was very little alternative. Their need was not as urgent as on the previous night, perhaps, but just as real. Again they fell asleep in each other's arms.

When Jesse awoke next morning, it was because he was cold. He reached for the warm body beside him, but the blanket was empty. Panicky, he pulled the bandage from his eyes. It was light and already growing warmer. His vision was still blurred, but he could tell that the swelling was continuing to recede. He could make out the outlines of the trees along the river. Suzannah was coming toward him, stepping quickly but quietly.

"Jesse!" she whispered excitedly, "there are antelope out there! Do we dare shoot one?"

"I don't know," he said. "I'm just not sure. What do you think? Seen anything?"

"No. Shall I try it?"

It was a terribly difficult decision. If the Indians had kept moving, as they had after the fight, they would be far away.

On the other hand, they would undoubtedly have scouts watching for pursuit. If they saw none, they might pause to lick their wounds, care for their wounded, and bury their dead by whatever means their customs dictated. In this case, they could be relatively close. Certainly, within hearing distance of a Springfield's boom.

"I don't know, Suzannah. Could you get by for another day without food?"

"Of course. Can you?"

"Sure. It might be better. Maybe we'll see some game tomorrow."

"All right."

He knew that the hunger pangs in her stomach must be like his own. Neither had eaten for two days, except for the slender stick of jerky the night before. But, he reminded himself, they were alive. He started to explain his feeling about firing the shot but decided against it. She was an intelligent young woman. She would understand the situation.

"I guess we'd best be moving," he said.

It was only a short time later that Suzannah suddenly stopped short.

"Get down!" she whispered.

Both dropped flat in the tall grass.

"What is it?" whispered the frustrated Jesse.

"Ssh! I saw someone!"

"Do you still—"

"No, no," she said impatiently. "It was across the river. I saw a flash of movement, and when I looked around, I saw someone slip into a clump of brush and trees."

"An Indian?"

"Yes, I think so. I don't see him now."

Jesse yanked the bandage from his eyes. The light still hurt, but he was seeing a little better. Unfortunately, not enough better. He could see the brushy growth as a darker clump against the light green of prairie grass but could make out no details.

"You'll have to watch for him," Jesse told the girl. "I can't see that well. Don't take your eyes off that brush."

It was possible that the Indian had already seen them. Still, they must be certain. If this man was one of the rearguard scouts, he might bring others.

"Could you shoot him when he comes out?" Jesse asked.

"I think so. Why?"

"Well, I can't see to shoot yet. If this scout gets away, he may figure how helpless we are. Better shoot him so he can't tell the others. Have you got the stomach for it?"

"If I keep reminding myself about my folks, I can do it." There was a little tremor in her voice.

"Good," he said. "Now, why don't you get in a good position and sight the rifle where you saw him last. Then we just wait him out. Shoot when you see him."

It was a long wait, it seemed. The two lay there in the grass—Suzannah staring across the river, and Jesse unable to stare anywhere. They talked a little, though not much, afraid they would alert the hidden watcher. The hours dragged on. Jesse was dozing in the warmth of the afternoon sun when there was a surprised gasp from Suzannah. He came awake quickly.

"What is it?"

The girl was laughing now.

"A doe with a fawn. I'm sorry, Jesse. I didn't get a good look, I guess."

She rose to her feet. It would be safe now. The presence of the undisturbed deer was a good indication that there were none of the Indians still around.

Jesse rose.

"It's all right, Suzannah. I'd a lot rather you'd be too cautious than not enough. Shall we go on now?"

He picked up the blanket roll, and they moved on.

"I guess I should have shot the deer," Suzannah said over her shoulder a little later. "I was just so glad to see her, I wasn't thinking."

"Just as well," Jesse said. "It was on the wrong side of the river, anyway. We'll see something else, on this side."

≈ 48 ≈

Corporal Booth walked across the parade ground toward headquarters, a little fearful about why he'd been summoned. It was nearly three weeks since he and the girl, Suzannah, had staggered back to Fort Wallace, lame, sore, and half-starved. It had been no problem finding the way, it was just the sheer physical effort of getting there.

They had seen no more game, after passing up two chances because of fear. Hunger had dogged their steps and weakened their bodies. They had staggered on. At night they had continued to share the warmth of the blanket salvaged from the trooper's dead horse.

Suzannah had risked a shot and killed a jack rabbit on the third day; and they had decided to stop and build a fire to cook the rabbit before moving on. The meat was tough and stringy, but the hungry couple had wolfed down the meat and then gnawed and sucked the bones.

Jesse found that he was something of a hero at the fort. The Indians had moved on after the fight. It was with a strange chilling feeling that he realized the Indians must have passed in the night the ruined pueblo where he and Suzannah Hartman had huddled together in exhaustion.

Lieutenant Murkha had been one of the first killed, along with several others, he learned. Sergeant Rigdon took charge, organized remnants of the troop, and led them back to Fort Wallace, taking the bodies of the dead with them. They had returned by the route they came, hence not making contact with Corporal Booth and the civilian girl.

Jesse had hardly seen Suzannah Hartman since they

arrived. One of the officers' wives had taken the girl into
her home, while Jesse had returned to the barracks after a
checkup at the infirmary. His eyes, a primary concern at
first, had completely recovered before they reached Fort
Wallace. His only permanent injury, it appeared, would be
an indelible tattoo of gunpowder on the right cheek and
forehead. The tiny scattered scabs were peeling off now,
and it was as the surgeon had said, a pepper of blue
pinpoints. It would be his memento of the night in the
pueblo.

He did not really need a memento. He had the memories
of that night and of the arduous journey on foot, back to the
fort, and of the nights they slept together in the blanket of
the dead trooper. She had asked him about the disposition
of the bodies of her family and seemed pleased at the
location of the graves. He had told her about Katy, and how
he cared for the body himself. They had become very close,
or so he thought, in the shared ordeal on the prairie.

And then, as suddenly as it began, it had ended.
Suzannah had been quickly separated from him. He had
resented the abruptness of it a little. It seemed that the
command at Fort Wallace somehow thought it inappropriate for him to see her. Or maybe, Jesse thought, Suzannah
did not want to see him.

He did not even think about his own vulnerability until
the troopers in the barracks began to tease him after a day
or two.

"That purty good stuff, that blond girl of Hartman's,
Booth?" someone asked.

The others snickered while they waited for him to
answer.

"What do you mean?" Jesse snapped.

"Why, you slept with her four nights, didn't you?" the
trooper sneered. "Don't try to tell us you never got none of
that!"

Everyone laughed, and Jesse was furious. He could not
make too big an issue of it, because it would only attract

more attention. And because . . . well, they had neither
of them intended for anything like that to happen. It really
wasn't like that. It was good, and fine, and . . . well, it
was *right*. Or so it had seemed, under the stars in the cool
prairie night, with the night sounds around them. They had
both apologized and laughed, embarrassed, and it had not
happened again. They had been content with the closeness
and warmth they shared.

Now, with the ribald remarks and jokes in the barracks,
Jesse had become quite concerned. It had taken a while to
realize the enormity of his misbehavior. He, as a noncommissioned officer of the U.S. Army, had betrayed the trust
of a civilian in his care. He could be court-martialed. The
thought even occurred to him that Suzannah Hartman
might be pregnant. She must hate him, and that was why
she was avoiding him. All of these thoughts did nothing to
make him wish to contact her. My God, she could charge
him with rape. He didn't know what the penalty might be
for the rape of a civilian in his protective care. He assumed
it would be quite severe, but there was no way he could
ask.

Now, he'd been summoned to headquarters. The trooper
who brought the word had no idea what it was about.

"Mebbe they jest want you back to duty."

"Maybe so," Jesse said, but he thought it was more than
that. They wouldn't summon him to the office just for that.
His apprehension increased.

He mounted the steps and reported to the clerk, who
motioned him on into the adjutant's office. Suzannah
Hartman sat in a chair near the desk.

Jesse stepped forward and saluted the officer. "Corporal
Booth reporting as ordered, sir."

"Ah, yes, at ease, Corporal."

The adjutant tossed him a perfunctory salute and pointed
to a chair.

"Sit down."

Jesse sat, his heart pounding and palms sweating.

"Miss Hartman has been telling me of her ordeal," the officer said crisply.

Jesse risked a glance at the girl, who sat primly, hands folded. He could not interpret the expression on her face. She sat quietly, her eyes not meeting his. She was beautiful, he thought, in a bright new dress, the healthy color returning to her cheeks.

"Sir, I—" Jesse began, but the officer waved him to silence.

"Corporal, you are to be commended for your management of a delicate situation. Miss Hartman tells me that her protection was your first concern at all times."

Jesse's head swam. It wasn't to be a court-martial, but a commendation. He began to relax.

"There is, however, one other thing. Miss Hartman will return to St. Louis to be with relatives but wishes first to visit the graves of her family. She asks that you take her there. Are you sufficiently recovered to drive?"

"Yes, sir," Jesse said, gulping.

"Very well. You may take a team and vehicle from the wagon yard. I might suggest a buggy and a light team. The sergeant there will assist you. If you start at daylight, the roundtrip can be done in a day."

"Yes, sir, but the Indians?"

"Oh, that's over, Corporal. They were engaged up in Nebraska. The old chief, Stone Bull, is being sent to prison. A man called Red Horse, apparently their war chief, refused surrender and was killed with some dozen others."

"What happened to the rest?" Suzannah asked.

"A few escaped to join the Sioux, I'm told. It's not worthwhile to go after them. The others are being sent back to the Nations. Now, you wish to make your trip tomorrow, ma'am?"

They sat in the buggy for a moment, the girl looking over the remains of the farmstead. Jesse said nothing, not wishing to intrude on her thoughts.

"My folks put a lifetime of work into this place," she said quietly. "I guess it's right that they stay here."

"I'll show you where," he offered.

He helped her down from the buggy and led the way up the slope to the row of graves marked with boards stuck in the ground at the head of each.

"They're in order," he told her. "Your folks there, and in age, on down."

He stooped to pull a few weeds from one of the mounds of dirt.

"I'd like to have better markers," Suzannah said huskily. "What will you do with the place?"

"I don't know. I suppose I'll have to sell it. Maybe I thought coming out here would help me decide."

She walked slowly to an outcrop of rocks and sat down. "I used to come up here to think. I could see the whole place, the house and barns, the garden. Now, it's gone."

"But somebody can fix it up," Jesse said, trying to comfort her. "It's a good place. Look, the barn's in fine shape, and the corrals. I think most of the walls of the house are sound. A new roof, some windows—it's usable."

She sighed. "Can somebody ever love it like they did—my folks?"

"I don't know, Suzannah. Surely they can. Look, the tree's leafing out again."

The big old cottonwood that shaded the door yard had been scorched by the fire; but even on the side next to the house, new leaf buds were indicating an attempt at resurrection.

"Shall we look around?" he suggested.

They walked around the house, absently picking up assorted items that lay scattered. A heavy iron skillet, a single plate that had escaped destruction. Jesse picked up an ax with a broken handle.

"A new handle would fix this like new," he said.

They paused at the well.

"They fouled the well," he told her, "but it's a fine well. It can be cleaned."

They walked to the barn, where tools stood or hung in orderly array. Branding irons with the slash-heart brand stood ready for the season. The horse stalls, empty and lonely, held memories of better days. As if in answer to his thoughts, one of the buggy horses nickered, and Jesse looked out the door. A horse wandered into the barnyard, a good thoroughbred mare. He stepped to the tack room for a halter.

"We'll take her back," he told the girl. "She'll be worth something to you."

When the mare was safely tied at the hitch rail, munching on some oats from the feed bin, Jesse felt obliged to urge that they start back. The girl seemed reluctant to leave, but it would be nearly dark before they reached the fort.

They drove down to the creek and sat in the buggy while the team sucked water thirstily. Suddenly, the near horse threw up its head in alarm.

Out of the willows on the opposite bank walked a cow, making her way to the water. She was multicolored, like the longhorns from the Texas drives of a few years past, but her prominent white face was a distinguishing mark. The left hip plainly showed the slash-heart brand.

Then, behind the cow, a tiny calf struggled out of the willows. It was coal black, with the whitest face Jesse had ever seen.

"Well, you own some cattle!" he said, chuckling.

"Oh, look!" Suzannah was excited. "That's one of Dad's new calves. See, he took Texas cows and used whiteface bulls. Then last year he bought two Black Angus bulls. That's one of the first crop of calves. I wonder how many are left?"

Jesse realized that it would be quite a job to round up the loose stock and even find out what the girl owned. A sale of the ranch, as is, would surely be a mistake. Apparently, she was thinking along the same lines.

"Jesse, could I get someone to check the stock, sort of put things back together before I sell?"

"Well, maybe so."

He was thinking rapidly. In a few months, his enlistment would be up. Maybe, in his time off, he could ride out and begin to make some sort of order out of all this. He didn't suppose he could buy it, but he could help her sell it. In a way, he hated to see it go. The place had meant so much to her father.

"I'd really like to keep it," Suzannah echoed his thoughts, "but I'd need a man around."

It took a while for the open suggestion to permeate his brain.

"Suzannah," he blurted, "will you marry me?"

She snuggled close to him on the buggy seat.

"Of course."

If you enjoyed Win Blevins's epic tale THE POW-
DER RIVER, be sure to look for the next installment
of the RIVERS WEST saga at your local bookstore.
Each new volume sweeps you along on a voyage of
exploration along one of the great rivers of North
America with the courageous pioneers who chal-
leneged the unknown.

*Here's an exciting preview of the next
book in Bantam's unique new historical series*

RIVERS WEST: BOOK 5
THE RUSSIAN RIVER
By Gary McCarthy
Author of THE COLORADO

*On sale February 1991
wherever Bantam Domain Books are sold.*

PROLOGUE

Anton Rostov wiped the stinging salt spray from his eyes. He stared out across the choppy and frigid Gulf of Alaska and felt the hardening westerly wind cut at his sealskin parka. It was almost sunset and the light was dying, barely sufficient to penetrate the gray Alaskan fog. All of his attention was fixed on the Aleuts and their two-man skin kayaks called baidarkas.

There were only five boats remaining in the water but they had been hunting since daybreak and had managed to harpoon only twelve sea otters, not enough yet to be allowed to return to the big two-masted Russian schooner, not even in the face of the weather front that was sweeping in from the storm-tossed Pacific.

Anton glanced to the foredeck where his captain, Vasilii Tarakanov, stood as rooted as the mast. Tarakanov was in his early fifties, stout, double-chinned and single-minded. His heavy beard was flattened against his face by the wind and his gloved hands clenched the oaken wheel. His expression revealed a hardness born of the many years he had sailed these treacherous, stormy waters for the Russian American Company out of Sitka, Alaska. Years before, when the otter had been plentiful off the Aleutian Islands to the north, he had been shipwrecked one winter and survived six months of bone-numbing darkness. His hair had turned white and his teeth had fallen out but he had survived, and the company had rewarded him with a Russian medal and a ship of his own to command.

He will not call the Aleuts in, Anton told himself, not

even when the sleet comes and the ocean spray freezes their faces and blinds them. Not even when they are like little bobbing blocks of ice. No, not even then will he call them in.

One of the harpoon wielding hunters suddenly motioned toward the south and the Aleuts churned their double-bladed paddles silently across the dark, roiling waters.

"Captain," Anton shouted, "I see otter to the south!"

Tarakanov purposely, stubbornly, chose to ignore him and the Aleut who were flying across the water toward their quarry. Anton felt his frozen cheeks warm with embarrassment and anger. He forced himself to pivot toward the rail and grip it with his gloved hands. Of course the captain would not recognize him! The ignorant old fool was too proud to acknowledge that a man half his age might have better eyes.

A full two minutes ticked by and the Aleuts almost disappeared into the heaving sea that was threatening to swallow them whole. Anton seethed. He and Tarakanov had disliked each other from the first moment. It was a matter of class distinction—Tarakanov lacked it from birth, Anton possessed it from birth. Their mutual dislike was that simple and that insurmountable.

Just when the Aleuts were disappearing into the face of the storm, Tarakanov turned the wheel and the sloop sluggishly rolled about to port. Its sails caught the wind and the vessel yawed hugely then drove its bow deep into the water and began to race after the Aleuts until the baidarkas were finally sighted about a mile ahead.

Anton moved to the bow as the Aleuts fought to bring themselves into the killing formation just downwind of what appeared to be a large group of sea otter. It was all the Aleuts could do to keep from capsizing. They were clothed in the waterproof skin of the sea lion and each one had lashed his jacket to a ring around the small opening in which he sat so that not a single drop of water could enter his baidarka. It had never ceased to amaze Anton how these said that you saved them from a sure death. But their loyalties are of no interest in the case. You defied Captain Tarakanov's orders to go below deck. You went overboard without permission and you risked your life—a Russian officer's life—for that of Indians."

Anton did not fail to notice that the governor was watching him with great interest. "Sir, as you have said, my father was a military hero. A man of honor. I came here to do him honor and I would never disgrace my family name."

Baranov nodded and steepled his short, chubby fingers. "Anton, you have in your veins the blood of fighting soldiers—not sailors. There is a difference. Did you know that I was raised the son of a shopkeeper in a village near Finland? And that before I was sent here, I was a glass-maker and then a fur trader?"

"No sir."

"I come from very humble beginnings." Baranov blinked. He had a large, protruding forehead and a long, hooked nose that made him look somehow scholarly. "Yes," he mused aloud, "very humble. Unlike yourself. But unlike Captain Tarakanov, I do not envy or fear those born higher than myself. And unlike the captain, I appreciate men of action and courage."

Anton hoped he was receiving a compliment but was not sure so he did not even dare to relax.

"You were," Baranov continued, "both mutinous and foolish with your life, but you are the kind of man that is not easily found. I have, if you are interested, a way out of the unfortunate situation in which you now find yourself."

"I would like to know of it," Anton said with a gulp. "I would rather die than disgrace my family or country."

"I know that," Baranov told him, leaning his chin on his steepled fingers and looking very pensive. "And it seems obvious to Ivan and me that the Aleut hunters are now ready to die for you. Have you not found many small gifts from them each morning beside your hospital bed?"

"Yes," Anton admitted. "But the gifts . . . well, they

that ran unbroken from the wild Aleutian Islands all the way south to Yerba Buena and the great harbor of San Francisco.

Anton had seen Baranov the empire builder before, but never in his castle that overlooked Sitka and the bay. The governor was in his early sixties and, because he was physically unimposing, it was difficult to believe all the legends that were associated with his name. But they were legends built on facts and results. Anton did not doubt for a single instant that Baranov was still indomitable even in his old age.

Anton nervously shifted his weight. His broken leg still ached but he took comfort in knowing that his lieutenant's uniform was neatly pressed and his black boots polished to a lustrous sheen. His dark, heavy beard made his face appear older than his twenty-one years.

"My dear, young man," Alexander Baranov began, dipping his bald head ever so slightly so that the Russian medallion that signified his lofty position bobbed against his chest, "I am sure you know Captain Ivan Kuskov?"

"I do." Anton bowed with respect toward a peg legged man twenty years his senior. "We met when I arrived last year."

"Yes," Baranov said, "then you must be aware of the immense regard I hold for Ivan. He is my most trusted lieutenant. A man bold, courageous and . . . of course . . . loyal to me . . . and Mother Russia."

"As I will prove to be," Anton said, gazing at both men.

"Sit down," Baranov said. "Ivan, would you be kind enough to pour us refreshments."

Despite his wooden leg, Kuskov moved with surprising agility and grace toward the small wooden cabinet from which he produced crystal glasses and vodka. He poured generously and when he, Anton and the governor had their drinks in their hands, their glasses were raised in toast. "To California," Baranov said.

"To California," Anton repeated even as he wondered at the strange toast.

Glasses were refilled and Anton swallowed feeling the

instant before they sank. The other pair drove their baidarka's straight for the hull and threw themselves at the lifeboat. Anton, with his leg still twisted peculiarly beneath the seat, blindly caught one of the Aleuts just as another wave struck. His fingernails bit into the Aleut's parka as the bones of his leg splintered.

While he lay drowning in pain and water, the Aleuts, men born to the sea, somehow found and tied new ropes to the lifeboat fore and aft so that its broken remains could be drawn up to the rail, then swung onto the deck.

Anton was upended and dropped unceremoniously to the deck as another wave struck and sent him skidding into a deck stanchion. He hung onto it until his fingers were pried away and he was dragged to a hatch, then shoved downward into the galley below where he lay in two inches of sloshing water and heard the ship inwardly moaning and groaning like an old man forced into hard labor.

He tried to get to his feet but the ship rolled so violently that a barrel broke free of its lashing and was hurled through the darkness to pin him against a bulkhead. Anton felt the weight of the barrel crushing his chest. He struggled then slipped into unconsciousness as the barrel rolled away and then spun crazily to the motion of the ship and the sea.

Anton awoke in Sitka and he lay in the hospital for two days while the doctors argued about cutting off his right leg. As soon as he understood the discussion, he asked the patient next to him for a knife and when the doctors returned to cut off the leg, he told them that, if they tried, he would cut off their balls.

Six weeks later, he had carved his own crutches and stood before Governor Alexander Baranov, the crusty old Lord of the Pacific, who almost single-handedly had won Alaska and made the Russian American Company the most successful fur-hunting enterprise in the North Pacific. Baranov had himself been shipwrecked and had fought savagely to claim this land. He dreamed of wresting Northern California from the weak Spaniards who had not the Russian heart or determination to win the vast wealth in fur and timber stunned for an instant. The Aleuts that were still afloat had stopped pelting their kill and were now paddling for their lives.

"Lower the life boats!" Anton shouted, struggling forward across the watery deck and directing the sailors who moved with skill and grim determination. Four Aleut hunters gone in just minutes! More had been lost during the entire winter! There would be hell to pay in Sitka and, if the remaining six were also drowned, every man on this ship would be held accountable.

Anton twisted in the wind and shouted, "Closer! Bring the ship around into the wind!"

But in answer, Tarakanov raised his gloved fist and shook it as one of the sails was ripped free and began to snap like shot in the wind and the schooner seemed to stagger and tremble with each crashing wave.

There were two lifeboats, one on the port and one on the starboard side. They were solid and seaworthy and, normally, the light skin baidarkas would be loaded into these lifeboats and then hauled up on deck. But now Anton knew the baidarkas were lost. All that mattered was to try to get the six Aleuts topside so that the captain could make toward the nearest sheltered harbor.

"Slow the ropes!" Anton shouted, noting how recklessly the lifeboats were being lowered.

In their panic and because the deck was rolling so badly, the ropes were in danger of becoming hopelessly tangled as the heavy portside lifeboat began to slam against the ship's hull.

Anton knew the lifeboat could not possibly survive more than three or four minutes of such brutal pounding. It hung about eight feet below the deck and, even as he watched, the bow and stern ropes tangled.

The sailors he commanded stood in fixed horror and the Aleuts below stared upward with the look of dead men. Anton tore off his gloves, grabbed the bow line and leapt over the railing to slide down a rope that felt like an icicle. He struck the lifeboat, swung out over the angry water and embarrass me. You see, Governor, the Aleuts would have saved my life had the circumstances been different."

"No," Kuskov said, sitting up erect, "not before the storm when you went overboard to save them. But now they would. And I am told you speak their language and Spanish very well."

"I studied Spanish, also Aleut and other languages, but. . . ."

"Then," Baranov said with a beatific smile, "we have a proposition for you."

Anton pushed himself to his feet where he stood straight and balanced as he waited, listening to his heart beat as loudly and frighteningly as the drums of the hostile Tlingits Indians who lived nearby. "Command me to do whatever you will."

"Of course," Baranov said, himself standing. "But I ask, never command. And now I ask that you be placed in charge of the Aleut hunters that Captain Kuskov will be taking south with him into Alta California where he will establish a fort, a foothold in Spanish America which will be held against all enemies of Russia." Baranov's voice shook with the passion of his conviction. "A foothold that will prove to be our anchor in America and which will not only feed Sitka and Kodiak but also yield the greatest kill of sea otter that the Russian American Company has ever harvested."

"My leg," Anton stammered. "I am afraid that I might be found wanting."

Kuskov shook his head. "You will heal soon. You are the man that I want to assist me."

Anton felt his cheeks warm with pride. "You will not regret the trust you place in me. Either of you."

Baranov chuckled and signaled for more vodka to be poured. "Of course we will not. It is the ability to judge the mettle of men that determines who will succeed in authority and who will fail. I judge you have the steel of your father. You have won the undying loyalty of the Aleut. Without them, there could be no harvest of otter. You will command heat of the white liquor warm his extremities and nibble away the pain in his mending leg.

"My dear lieutenant," Baranov began, "are you aware that Captain Tarakanov has filed charges of insubordination and attempted mutiny against you?"

Anton almost dropped his glass. "No, sir," he managed to say. "I have not been apprised of that fact. I was discharged from the hospital just this morning."

"On my orders," Baranov said with a beneficent smile. "You see, young man, I have a special interest in you because of your father. He was one of our great heroes, was he not?"

"He was," Anton said quickly. "But. . . ."

"And he was also a friend of a very close friend." Baranov drained his vodka and Kuskov was quick to keep his glass full. The governor's assistant was himself a respected man and, even though he was acting as a subordinate, Anton was sharply aware that the man somehow retained an immense dignity.

"I want," Baranov was saying, "to help you out of this unfortunate misunderstanding you have had with Captain Tarakanov. I am sure I can do this if you wish."

Anton found himself nodding rapidly. "Of course, Governor. But I beg you to understand that I was not mutinous. I was only attempting to save the Aleut hunters. You see. . . ."

"The governor has heard all about it," Kuskov interrupted, cutting Anton into silence. "The sailors have been interrogated. Testimony has been taken."

There was a long silence.

"And?" Anton whispered when he could no longer be still.

"And," Kuskov said, "if the governor wished, you could be shot this very day."

Anton's glass slipped and almost spilled to the floor. He blinked and wondered if he had heard correctly. "The sailors," he stammered, "they spoke against me?"

"No," Kuskov said. "Quite the contrary. And the hunters

pushed farther from the Aleuts who were still reeling in their kills. The storm intensified with demented fury until the Aleut were in deadly peril. Three of the baidarka paddlers were attempting to chase the ship but two were still reeling in their catch, in spite of the fact that they were being driven farther out to sea.

"He has to move in closer to them!" Anton shouted. Forgetting himself, he stumbled across the sea-washed deck to the captian and shouted. "You're to far from them!"

In answer, Tarakanov cursed his name and ordered him to lower the two lifeboats. Anton shook his head. They were still too far away for that. In these heavy seas, the lifeboats would be smashed against the hull and crack like broken eggs against a skillet before they could be used to bring the Aleuts back on board with their baidarkas.

"Damn you, more sail!" Anton shouted. "We have to have more sail!"

In answer, Tarakanov's gloved fist lashed out and struck Anton across the face. "Rostov, go below!" he commanded.

"No! We must move closer!"

Anton fought his way back to the rail. Three baidarkas had somehow closed the distance, though getting them on board was going to be almost impossible because the Russian sloop was crashing in and out of the sea and sending up huge geysers of water.

But the other two baidarkas were disappearing into the ocean. They still had not gotten their kills reeled in, kills which were acting like a sea anchor.

Anton saw one of those baidarkas suddenly flip and, though he had seen that happen many times before, this was different. The power of the sea tore the Aleut's parkas from the rings of their craft and water flooded into the little vessel which disappeared like a knife dropped in water.

"They're gone!" he shouted in despair and, before he could turn toward the captain, the second baidarka also was breeched by an immense wave and it never reappeared.

Even in the face of the raging storm, everyone was

men could sit motionlessly for ten to fifteen hours, waiting for a kill.

But nothing was motionless now. The howling wind grew louder and stronger by the minute until it was blowing the baidarkas around like leaves on a pond. Despite their best efforts, the rear paddlers were having an impossible time attempting to bring their little skin boats close to the otter so that the harpoon men could strike with their long bone spears. The otter had dived but they would soon be forced to the surface.

"Look at the spear throwers!" a sailor shouted into the wind. "See how they hover like a dog at the first scent of game."

Anton said nothing. He stared, fascinated by the drama, even though he knew the inevitable outcome. The hunters, raised from small children to survive and kill on the water, almost never missed their throws. And now they forged into position, spears held motionless until, suddenly, the otter popped to the surface, just their heads and shoulders pushing above the water.

Anton did not hear the Aleut imitate the distressed cry of a baby sea otter but he did see the adult animals turn with alarm. In that instant, the spears were hurled from their throwing sticks and Anton almost felt the pain of the otter as the bone spears sank deep into their bodies. Two of the otters died instantly but the other three dove again, pulling the thin harpoon cord behind them so that a skin air bladder traced their futile efforts to escape as they swam in dying confusion. The Aleut paddlers followed the skin bags across the stormy ocean as the hunters pulled their kills back to the baidarkas where the otter would be pelted in minutes and their stripped corpses thrown back into the sea.

"Sir," the sailor asked Anton, "will the captain pull for Sitka?"

"He'd better," Anton shouted. "And we'd better get those hunters off the water in a hurry!"

"Going to be a bad one before nightfall," the sailor yelled as the vessel wallowed in the heavy sea. They were being nearly tumbled into the sea before a foaming mountain of water spun him back against the hull of the ship, then raked him along the barnacle-crusted side. Gagging, he was torn back out to sea, then found himself suddenly bobbing in the water as another monstrous wave gathered off the ocean floor.

Anton was amazed to see the lifeboat, filled with sea water and missing its oars, still dangling just below his feet. He dimly heard the cries of the Aleuts as he dropped into the boat, drew his knife and slashed at the tangled stern and bow ropes. When they severed, the lifeboat dropped into the ocean and the Aleuts paddled furiously toward him while the sailors up on deck hurled clear lines downward. They knew as well as Anton that, if the lifeboat was not linked to the ship, it would be swept out to sea and swamped.

Another wall of water sent Anton and his lifeboat soaring upward. The lifeboat spun crazily, nearly tipped over and then balanced delicately on the crest of the swell before it was dropped with such speed that Anton felt his stomach flop. He saw one of the baidarkas splinter against the ship and spill Aleuts into the water.

Anton twisted around to see the other two baidarkas spinning in a maelstrom of white foam and then he felt the sea again gather itself to strike. He shoved his legs under the bench of the lifeboat, took a deep breath and held on for his life as the wall of water flung the lifeboat back against the hull. The boat shook itself like a wet dog and struggled to stay afloat. Anton felt the mighty pull of sea all around him and his right leg seemed to snap below the knee. He roared in pain, his words were torn from his lips by the wind and when he opened his eyes, he was amazed to see two Aleuts floundering in the boat beside him, calling for their companions to abandon their baidarkas and jump for the lifeboat.

Anton shouted, "Come on!"

Two of the four jumped but missed and were swept out to sea. In their heavy parkas, they were visible for only an them, reward them . . . and yes, punish those who slack from their work."

Anton nodded. "When will we sail?"

"In one week."

Anton swayed. "And how long will I be in California?"

"Until," the governor said in a flat, uncompromising voice, "your life or the need for your services ends."

"Yes sir!"

The governor and the captain relaxed and both smiled, satisfied that they had made the right choice.

Baranov's pale blue eyes seemed to glitter as he pushed back from his desk, raised another glass of vodka and said fervently, "To the conquest of Northern America for Russia!"

Anton repeated the toast and threw the vodka down his gullet to discover that the anticipation of what lay ahead was even more heady than Russian vodka.

THE EXCITING NEW FRONTIER SERIES
BY THE CREATORS OF
WAGONS WEST

STAGECOACH
by Hank Mitchum

"The STAGECOACH series is great frontier entertainment. Hank Mitchum really makes the West come alive in each story."

—*Dana Fuller Ross, author of Wagons West*

☐ STATION 48: BUFFALO STATION

                   (28586 * $2.95)

☐ STATION 49: GILA BEND   (28604 * $3.50)

☐ STATION 50: BUCKSKIN PASS (28799 * $3.50)

☐ STATION 51: WILD WEST   (28826 * $3.50)

★ WAGONS WEST ★

This continuing, magnificent saga recounts the adventures of a brave band of settlers, all of different backgrounds, all sharing one dream— to find a new and better life.

☐	26822	INDEPENDENCE! #1	$4.95
☐	26162	NEBRASKA! #2	$4.50
☐	26242	WYOMING! #3	$4.50
☐	26072	OREGON! #4	$4.50
☐	26070	TEXAS! #5	$4.50
☐	26377	CALIFORNIA! #6	$4.50
☐	26546	COLORADO! #7	$4.95
☐	26069	NEVADA! #8	$4.50
☐	26163	WASHINGTON! #9	$4.50
☐	26073	MONTANA! #10	$4.50
☐	26184	DAKOTA! #11	$4.50
☐	26521	UTAH! #12	$4.50
☐	26071	IDAHO! #13	$4.50
☐	26367	MISSOURI! #14	$4.50
☐	27141	MISSISSIPPI! #15	$4.95
☐	25247	LOUISIANA! #16	$4.50
☐	25622	TENNESSEE! #17	$4.50
☐	26022	ILLINOIS! #18	$4.95
☐	26533	WISCONSIN! #19	$4.95
☐	26849	KENTUCKY! #20	$4.95
☐	27065	ARIZONA! #21	$4.50
☐	27458	NEW MEXICO! #22	$4.95
☐	27703	OKLAHOMA! #23	$4.95
☐	28180	CELEBRATION! #24	$4.50

Bantam Books, Dept. LE, 414 East Golf Road, Des Plaines, IL 60016

Please send me the items I have checked above. I am enclosing $_____
(please add $2.50 to cover postage and handling). Send check or money order, no cash or C.O.D.s please.

Mr/Ms _____

Address _____

City/State _____ Zip _____

Please allow four to six weeks for delivery.
Prices and availability subject to change without notice.   LE-3/91

"FROM THE PRODUCER OF WAGONS WEST COMES YET ANOTHER EXPLOSIVE SAGA OF LEGENDARY COURAGE AND UNFORGETTABLE LOVE"

CHILDREN OF THE LION

☐	26912	Children of the Lion #1	$4.50
☐	26971	The Shepherd Kings #2	$4.50
☐	26769	Vengeance of the Lion #3	$4.95
☐	26594	The Lion in Egypt #4	$4.95
☐	26885	The Golden Pharaoh #5	$4.95
☐	27187	Lord of the Nile #6	$4.50
☐	26325	The Prophecy #7	$4.50
☐	26800	Sword of Glory #8	$4.95
☐	27459	The Deliverer #9	$4.95
☐	27999	The Exodus #10	$4.50
☐	28300	The Sea Peoples #11	$4.95
☐	28588	The Promised Land #12	$4.95

Buy them at your local bookstore or use this handy page for ordering:

Bantam Books, Dept. LE5, 414 East Golf Road, Des Plaines, IL 60016

Please send me the items I have checked above. I am enclosing $_____
(please add $2.50 to cover postage and handling). Send check or money
order, no cash or C.O.D.s please.

Mr/Ms _____

Address _____

City/State_____ Zip_____

LE5-5/91

Please allow four to six weeks for delivery.
Prices and availability subject to change without notice.